Praise for *Fairchild's Passage*

"A fast-paced Western novel with extraordinary characters.... As the book reaches its climax, Barton and Williams weave the loose ends together into a tapestry of adventure, love, and coming of age."
—*The Sunday News-Globe* (Amarillo, TX)

"*Fairchild's Passage* blends action, passion, danger, spectacle—are you listening, Hollywood?—and yes, most of the good guys do manage to survive. But it's close."
—*The Dallas Morning News*

"Entertaining."   —*Publishers Weekly*

"The award-winning writing team of Wayne Barton and the late Stan Williams have created a seventh novel filled with love, courage, violence, and coming of age.... As the book heads for a climax, the authors cleverly weave all the loose ends together leaving the reader exhausted but satisfied."
—*Tulsa World*

Praise for *Lockhart's Nightmare*

"Fast-paced."   —*Publishers Weekly*

"Entertaining."   —*Booklist*

"This is a lighthearted novel, fun to read.... Combining historical setting and gritty characters with rip-roaring adventure, the authors have given us a novel both entertaining and suspenseful."   —*Tulsa World*

"[*Lockhart's Nightmare* has] a character every bit as relentless as Tommy Lee Jones.... As enjoyable as the vivid narrative is, the humor is even better."
—*Amarillo News Globe*

"*Lockhart's Nightmare* is an interesting mixing of a Western with a twist .... F___ of the Western who-done-it will enjo_____e."
—___zon.com

"For people wh_____ysteries, *Lockhart's Nig_____s a good feel for the lif_____ has fast action and danger at every turn......_____ead."
—*Lincoln Journal Star*

Forge Books by Wayne Barton and Stan Williams

Fairchild's Passage
Lockhart's Nightmare

FAIRCHILD'S PASSAGE

WAYNE BARTON
AND
STAN WILLIAMS

FORGE®

A TOM DOHERTY ASSOCIATES BOOK
NEW YORK

This is a work of fiction. All the characters and events portrayed in this book are either products of the author's imagination or are used fictitiously.

FAIRCHILD'S PASSAGE

Copyright © 1997 by Wayne Barton and Stan Williams

All rights reserved, including the right to reproduce this book, or portions thereof, in any form.

A Forge Book
Published by Tom Doherty Associates, LLC
175 Fifth Avenue
New York, NY 10010

www.tor.com

Forge® is a registered trademark of Tom Doherty Associates, LLC.

ISBN: 0-812-54422-6
Library of Congress Catalog Card Number: 96-54798

First edition: June 1997
First mass market edition: November 2000

Printed in the United States of America

0 9 8 7 6 5 4 3 2 1

This book is for all our faithful readers.

1

Thoman Silverhorn lay in the shadow of the single stunted juniper clinging to the crest of a sharp, knobby butte. Indian blood told in his hard, cracked-leather face. Long white hair hung to his shoulders. Standing, he would have been a tall man, big in the shoulders and thick through the middle. Now, he stretched silent and invisible as a serpent on the rocky ground. Below him, innocent as Eve before the serpent, eighteen wagons bumped along in a ragged line, following the broad, rutted trace that stretched as far as a man could see in either direction.

Eighteen wagons, each with six good oxen, with goats and milk cows and even one deep-chested bull herded along before them, with money and provisions and soft-skinned settler women.

Silverhorn released his breath through clenched teeth. He was mightily tempted. The train would be a rich prize, if only for its livestock. The afternoon sun was behind him. Its light slanted over his shoulder toward the train, right in the eyes of every driver and team. Every wheel and every hoof cast its pall of pale dust. Every man and every animal would be tired, thirsty, ready to make camp. The time was good.

Behind him, he heard Grace shift impatiently and inch a little closer to the crest. "Any chance, Thoman?" she whispered.

Silverhorn didn't turn. "Shut up," he muttered and drew the brass-tubed telescope from his possible bag. The telescope had served him well. As he opened it, he allowed himself a thin smile, remembering the young surveyor he'd taken it from. Then, wholly serious, he trained it on the wagons.

Eighteen wagons, each with at least one man. Plus a guide and a wagonmaster. Plus no telling how many half-growed kids, plus probably even a woman or two who could shoot a rifle or load one. Eighteen wagons. Thirty guns at the least, Silverhorn estimated. Maybe forty.

"Hell," he said and lowered the telescope. He wanted to have a go at the train. He was tempted, but forty guns were too many. He didn't have enough men, and the ones he had were close to worthless.

Careful to stay under cover, Silverhorn crabbed around to look down the backslope of the butte. Plum and the three Whitley boys squatted in the shade of their horses playing poker. The Kid was holding the horses, smoking, staring back in the direction of the last whorehouse he could remember. Blue Eye and Kills Running, the two Pawnee, were out of sight, as were Middleton and his woman. Worthless.

Of them all, only Grace was alert. She crouched with her back to the others, the hem of her skirt hiked halfway up her thighs, a rifle across her lap, her eyes on Silverhorn. When he looked at her, she opened her knees to him and grinned.

"Whore," Silverhorn muttered. *Even so*, he thought, *she's the best man I've got.* He watched the wagons as they turned, one after the other, and crawled past the butte, past the place for an attack. "Hell," he said again.

"How is it, Thoman?" she whispered, slipping into the tiny patch of concealment beside him. "You seem awful interested."

"Too many wagons. Too many guns."

"You seem awful interested, all the same. Some nice little emigrant gals down there, are there?"

He grunted and passed her the telescope. "Last wagon. See for yourself."

He'd studied the driver of that wagon carefully. She was young, fair, frail. Her sunbonnet shaded a thin face with high cheekbones and wide eyes. Silverhorn could picture those eyes grown wider with fear, could imagine the pale, slender body that lay beneath her brown dress. Another temptation. He wouldn't mind having her himself, at least for a night or two.

"I don't know, Thoman," Grace murmured. She licked her full lips. "You'd use up her kind pretty fast."

"The flankers," Silverhorn said. "Look at the flankers."

The train's forward scouts were already out of sight. Two rear flankers rode abreast with the last wagon, one skirting the thickets along the Platte and the other struggling through the gullies at the foot of Silverhorn's butte. Each seemed to have his attention on that last wagon rather than on his business.

"Young love," Grace said. Laughing silently, she pressed herself against Silverhorn. "Ain't that sweet!"

"Shut up." Silverhorn took the telescope away from her and focused on the flaxen-haired young woman. He understood the flankers' interest in her, but he doubted it had to do with love.

When he looked again to find the flankers, he saw that the nearer of the two had reined away from the bluffs, back into the shadow of the last wagon. The outrider matched his pace to the wagon, speaking earnestly to the woman. She answered him without turning her head.

Then the other flanker appeared in Silverhorn's scope, riding hard, his black hair shining in the sun. He fell in on the off side of the wagon, slapped his hat on his thigh, and shouted at the first rider. Silverhorn was interested. The young woman had allowed her own team to fall a hundred yards or more behind the train.

"You, Grace," Silverhorn said. "Pull that dress down to cover yourself. Then get those worthless coyotes rounded up—Middleton and the Pawnees, too. Get them ready to ride."

Her eyes shining, Grace slid backward. "Sure, Thoman. I'll get them."

Silverhorn's mind was already back with the wagon.

Above and before it, high white clouds were joining to make a wall. A late afternoon thunderstorm was coming at them pretty fast. In half an hour, it would cover the sun and drop a quick ocean of hail and rain. Half an hour. The other wagons had already passed into the shadow of the wall·of clouds. That last lone wagon was still in the sunlight.

"Sometimes you work for it," Silverhorn said quietly aloud. "Sometimes, it just comes to you."

Below him, the young woman whipped up her team, hastening to catch up with the others. Lagging behind, the near rider wheeled his horse suddenly toward the rear. As if he already owned the stock, Silverhorn wanted to kill the man for mistreating his horse. The other flanker had fallen back also. They met, and the dark-haired one swung his hat and struck the other rider across the face. Neither reached for a gun. "Farmers," Silverhorn said in disgust.

The one who'd been struck raised an arm, pointing up a narrow ravine that ran dead toward Silverhorn's hiding place. The other rider spurred past him in that direction. They headed almost directly away from the last wagon, driving their horses as if they had a bet on.

"There's no way to outguess a fool." Silverhorn laughed and snapped the spyglass closed. "Let alone two fools." He didn't have men enough to take the train, but he had men enough to pick off two fools and take their horses and guns.

He slid back down a shallow ravine, stood, and walked toward Grace. She was ready, the gang ranked sullenly behind her, angry at taking orders from a woman. Silverhorn spat in the dust and looked at Grace's legs. She grinned back at him.

"Get mounted." His voice was a blade on a dry whetstone. "We got us a open season on fools."

Ethan Fairchild had been riding flank ever since the noon halt, letting his long-legged sorrel match its pace to the plodding wagons. In ten miles, he had skimmed the edges of a dozen rocky buttes, but he was not vigilant as an outrider. Instead, he kept his eyes and his mind on Jessica Thorne, who was driving the last wagon.

Jess sat with her head bent, perhaps to shade her eyes from the low afternoon sun. Her sunbonnet shadowed her face and hid her golden hair. He had ridden near several times, but she would not look at him. Instead, she kept her face forward and her eyes downcast, as if enrapt in the rumps of her plodding team of oxen.

Fairchild closed his eyes. At twenty, he knew he hadn't much claim to understanding women, but he couldn't imagine why Jess was putting him off. In his mind, he saw her as he had seen her that night a week before—*alone on the bank of the river, her bosom bare in the moonlight, her long hair cascading around her white shoulders, her smile meant only for him. They hadn't planned to meet. Jessica had slipped away from the train after supper to wash herself clean of the clinging trail dust. He had missed her, worried, gone to find her, found her. "Jess." She whirled, frightened, at the sound of his step, bringing her arms up protectively across her chest. "Oh! Ethan. I'm not dressed." He moved toward her, as cautiously as he would've stalked a deer. For a moment, her eyes went wide and frightened as a deer's. Then, slowly, she lowered her arms, her eyes still wide but no longer frightened. Finally she smiled and reached out to him and everything might as well have been planned from the start. He reached her, inclining his face to hers, leaning into her now, tempting her to lie back in the soft grass and the darkness*—when his horse missed a step, and that cool, quiet moonlight gave way to the hot dusty air and the impending storm.

Now wagons rattled. Milk cows bawled plaintively from the herd up ahead, and oxen switched their tails and snorted in the fine, thin, eye-watering pall of dust. The community of the wagon train was sweltering toward the evening's camp, all praying for rain from the oncoming clouds.

Driving Fairchild's wagon, Jessica Thorne rode in stiff, silent remorse. She had avoided him since that night, had moved away whenever he'd tried to talk with her. Today, Jess had chosen to drive Fairchild's rear wagon as if she were outcast from the others.

Fairchild swung away from the knobby butte with its single stunted juniper on top. He stared across at her again, but Jess held her face straight ahead. On the northern flank, patrolling the cedar breaks along the bank of the Platte, David Stuart reined up and glared at him.

Sighing, Fairchild turned back to the narrow gullies that laced the flank of the butte. Stuart behaved as if he knew what they had done. He couldn't, Fairchild was sure. Jessica would never have told him. And Stuart hadn't seen them making love; else he would have spoken up before this.

No, Stuart didn't know, not for sure. But he sensed something, and it was a burr under his blanket. Fairchild understood that because he had been just as jealous of Stuart, until Jessica had chosen him in the oldest manner there was.

Abruptly, Fairchild reined his mount back toward the crawling wagon. Jess made no sign when he fell in beside it.

"Listen," he said.

"Oh!" She started, stared at him. Then her cheeks colored and she turned quickly away.

"Jess, what's the matter? I thought you and I—"

"I know what you thought, what you think," she snapped at him. "Get away from me."

"The thing is—don't you see?—you chose me. We chose each other. We're engaged."

"Engaged!" She made a sound that might have been meant for a laugh. Her wagon began to lag behind the group.

"We're more like married, really. Before God and the stars, we *are* married."

"Before God, we're the worst kind of sinners!" She turned to look at him with wide reddened eyes. He leaned over the front wheel trying to take her arm. She drew away. "Ethan, no."

He heard a horse coming hard and fast. David Stuart was bearing down toward them, pushing his stocky black gelding as if the wagon were on fire.

"What we'll do is get married right away," Fairchild said quickly. "At the next settlement. That'll fix everything."

From the way she looked at him, he knew he'd said something terribly wrong, though he couldn't imagine what it was. Jess didn't answer. She slid across to the far reaches of the seat. Before Fairchild could speak again, Stuart reined his horse up just short of the off front wheel and glared. He was a year older than Fairchild, shorter but heavier through the chest and shoulders.

"Leave her alone!" he shouted. "Jessica, what is it? What's he done to you?"

"I'm all right," Jessica said. There were tears in her voice and her eyes. "He hasn't done anything to me!"

"Well, he's sure as hell offended me!" Stuart swept his hat off and pulled a gloved hand through his curly black hair. He slammed the hat down on his thigh hard enough to lift a cloud of dust. "You, Ethan, you're away from your post."

Fairchild bristled. "No more than you," he told Stuart. "Get back out where you belong. This isn't your business."

"Jess's my business as much as she is yours."

"I'm not anybody's *business!*" Jessica cried. She lashed at her oxen. "Go away, both of you. Just go away!"

Fairchild pulled up short, watching in helpless fury as the wagon rolled along a little faster, starting to catch up to the others. Stuart had stopped also. When the wagon passed, the two faced each other across the ruts of the trail.

"What have you done to upset her like this?" Stuart demanded.

"What makes it your business?"

"I intend to marry her," Stuart said.

"There'll be a lot of us at the altar, then. So do I!"

With no warning Fairchild could see, Stuart drove his horse across and into Fairchild's sorrel. Fairchild fought the reins as the sorrel reared, saw a blow coming, threw up his arm too late. Stuart lashed out blindly, the stiff brim of his hat raking across Fairchild's nose.

"That's enough of that kind of talk. From now on, you'll stay away from Jess, or—"

"*Or* what, town boy?" Fairchild said. He wiped blood off his face.

"Or fight me, farmer."

Fairchild laughed. "Now a good enough time?" he said. "Choose the place."

Without answering, Stuart whipped his horse away from the train and into the shadow of the rocky butte. Fairchild hesitated a second, remembering he was flank guard, remembering that Manasseh Thorne had warned them to be alert along this stretch of trail and river.

"There's Cheyenne along here still hostile from two years ago, and the Lakotas is always restless. So says the Army, anyway. You flankers keep your eyes peeled, understand?"

Then Stuart looked back and gave a mocking laugh. "Coming, plowboy?" he called. "Or are you remembering the last time we fought?"

"I remember," Fairchild breathed and dug spurs into the sorrel's side, racing along behind the other man. He'd fought Stuart a dozen times, in play and in earnest, since they were children. He'd never beaten him. But this time would be different. This time, he had something worth fighting for.

Stuart drove on for half a mile and more around the

base of the butte, Fairchild riding hard behind him. At first, their trail climbed. Then they crossed a low hogback and Fairchild lost sight of the river, lost his sense of direction in the tangle of gullies and brush and thick knots of buffalo grass that studded the backside of the slope. The clouds were closing down fast, turning the sky almost black. Stuart was going a long way from the trail, Fairchild thought uneasily. He spent a thought wondering how and when they'd be able to catch up with the train again, but he wasn't about to let Stuart think he was afraid.

Finally the black horse cut sharply west into a grassy swale bounded by the steep slopes of the butte. It would have reminded Fairchild of an arena if he had been thinking of such things. He reined in and stepped out of the saddle, but Stuart rode hard to the center of the clearing. Then he wheeled his horse and came back at the gallop. Putting his weight on his left stirrup, he dived off at Fairchild.

"Have to do better than that, Stu," Fairchild taunted and stepped out of his way. Stuart flailed for him, missed, and tumbled in a heap a couple of yards beyond.

Fairchild might have ended the fight by kicking Stuart or taking other advantage while the bigger man was on the ground, but that would have violated the unspoken rules they'd followed for years. This one time, Fairchild felt the temptation to finish it quickly, but he checked himself and waited for the Stuart man to get up.

The dive had taken some of the enthusiasm out of Stuart, but he was still full of fight, still wide and solid, still twenty pounds the heavier. He rolled to his feet, took one step, and knocked Fairchild down with a wild roundhouse right.

Fairchild landed on his hip and came up quickly. His jaw hurt, and for an instant his vision was blurry, but he knew he had to go after Stuart. He ducked the next wild blow and landed a hard flurry of punches to his opponent's ribs. A dozen years of friendly fights had taught them both a few things. Stuart had the power and endurance. Fairchild's long suits were speed and deception. Faster and sharper than the heavy man, Fairchild got in a jab to Stuart's jaw.

Stuart's head snapped sideways and his eyes went glassy, but he was too angry to quit. He covered up and tried to move away, but Fairchild was on him like a terrier on a bear. He snapped fast, stinging punches in, most of them landing on Stuart's arms and hunched shoulders. Fairchild felt a few go home, though, and a fierce exultation filled him. This would be his time! He drew back a second, setting himself to bore in and finish it.

But the bigger man fell back suddenly, shuffling out of reach, dropping his guard. As Fairchild started to close again, Stuart's hand went to his belt, to the butt of the Navy revolver he always wore.

Astonishment froze Fairchild for the time Stuart needed to get the pistol out and thumb back the hammer.

"Stu!" Fairchild shouted, unbelieving, but Stuart's revolver came up and level. Sick dread followed disbelief in Fairchild's mind. He had no sidearm himself, and his rifle was still in its boot on the sorrel's saddle. Knowing he'd waited too late, he drove toward Stuart, trying to shove in under the Navy's muzzle, tensing his stomach muscles involuntarily against the expected bullet.

"No!" Stuart's voice came out thick and strangled. Instead of firing, he swept out a big left arm and swatted Fairchild aside, then pointed off toward the western rim of the depression. "There!" He spat out a mouthful of blood and shouted, "Get to the horses, Ethan! Indians!"

Fairchild heard the air whine in agony past his ear. Immediately a rifle boomed somewhere off in the direction Stuart had pointed. Fairchild didn't look; he leaped for the nearest horse, which happened to be Stuart's black. Stuart's revolver barked once and then again while Fairchild wrestled the black under control. More rifles answered, their reports almost lost in a long rumble of thunder. Fairchild caught up the reins of his sorrel before the horse could spook.

"Come on!" he yelled. "We can't fight them all!"

Stuart fired once more. His shot seemed to bring down the rain in a cold, heavy torrent that instantly hid the pursuing riders from view. Stuart shoved the revolver into his belt and turned to grab for the black.

"Hey! My horse!"

"No time!" Fairchild thrust the sorrel's reins at him. "Hurry, while they can't see us! Ride for the train!"

Bullets droned around them, none so close as those first few. Fairchild was sure that the Indians couldn't see their targets, but they hadn't quit shooting. He groped for Stuart's rifle in the saddle boot, then thought better of it; he couldn't see to shoot, either. Their best chance was to run. Bending low on the black's neck, he dug his heels into the big horse's flanks and hung on.

He had come out of the depression three lengths ahead of Stuart, but the sorrel was the faster horse. Within a few rods, Stuart was riding boot to boot with him.

"How many?" Fairchild yelled over the noise of the horses and the storm.

"Couldn't tell." Stuart had lost his hat. He shook his head and water flew from his thick black hair. "Just saw a few of them, but there's surely more. Must be a war party." He pointed off to the right. "Not back to the train! We can't let them follow us in. Cut back east!"

Fairchild wasn't sure of the logic in that, but the bigger man was already pulling away on the sorrel, leaving him behind. Fairchild didn't take that personally. He intended to ride Stuart's black into the ground if that was what it took.

He'd no sooner had that thought than something struck the big horse with an ugly, meaty splat. Hot blood sprayed back into Fairchild's face and splattered the front of his shirt. The black let out a grunt, stumbled, gave way in the withers, started to go over in a kicking headfirst roll.

To Fairchild, it seemed he had all the time in the world. He thought to kick his boots free of the stirrups, realized the sound he'd heard was gunfire and not thunder, saw a

quick, clear vision of Jess gazing up at him with heavy
eyes and parted lips, started a prayer that he'd get back
to her. Before he could finish, the rocky ground slammed
the breath out of him.

He hit as loosely as he could, feeling the grinding, tumbling blow to his head and shoulder. Fire shot through his
left arm. For what seemed a long time, he rolled and jolted
across the uneven ground, and then suddenly the ground
was gone. Before he had time to realize he was falling,
he smashed hard into the bottom of a narrow gully and
lay still.

"Goddamn it, Grace, shoot the men! We need the
horses!"

The shout had come from somewhere a long way off.
The answer came in a high, clear voice directly overhead:
"I got the man, too!" Fairchild opened his eyes, saw a
horse soar across the field of his vision, land on the far
side of the gully and shake the ground with its hooves. A
leaden sky flung cold rain into his face, big drops that
hurt when they hit.

Other horses thundered past to leave him in a vast
swirling silence. He lay there, thinking he would get up
in a minute, trying to remember why he'd picked this spot
to rest when the ground was so cold and wet. The sky
faded into a red haze that graded slowly into black. *Stu*,
he thought in his last conscious second. *They must've got
you, too. Else . . .*

He couldn't think how to finish. He was still trying
when the silence closed over him and he lost all sense of
self in its embrace.

2

David Stuart drove the sorrel up the rise leading out of the arena. It was only when he reached the crest that he realized Ethan was no longer with him. He reined up the nervous horse and looked back, shading his eyes from the rain as if from bright sunlight. At the foot of the slope, the black horse lay in a tangled heap, doubled over itself, its neck obviously broken by its fall.

"Ethan! Ethan, where are you?"

Even as Stuart shouted, he saw where Ethan was. The smaller man sprawled in the bottom of a shallow cut, one arm flung out over the rim as if reaching toward Stuart for help. But Stuart knew at once that couldn't be. Even from this distance, he couldn't mistake the blood that covered Ethan's head and chest.

Raising himself in the saddle a little, he stared back through the rain. With so much blood, Ethan must surely be dead, but Stuart couldn't help searching for some sign of movement, of life.

"Ethan!"

His shout brought no answer, but that didn't matter. He had to go back. Ethan would do no less for him.

Stuart leaned into the sorrel, ready to spur down toward Ethan's body. Just then, a rider burst through the curtain of rain, long black hair flying in the cold wind. With a shrill cry, the newcomer jumped the horse over the gully where Ethan lay and started up the slope.

Others loomed out of the storm on either flank, the nearest close enough to see plainly. Stuart had begun to have his doubts about the raiders, but this one was clearly an Indian. In that first moment, Stuart's mind registered hard black eyes, the look of surprise on the coppery face, the ragged white man's homespun clothing, the stubby muzzle-loading carbine.

The Indian snapped off a hasty shot, the report curiously flat and muffled in the storm. The bullet moaned off into the distance. The raider shoved the useless weapon into its boot and drew out from someplace a long-handled war hatchet. Screaming a battle cry, he spurred straight toward Stuart.

Stuart held his ground. Clawing out the Navy revolver, he leveled it on the Indian's chest. The hammer fell, exploding the percussion cap with a sodden pop. The gun didn't fire.

For a panicked instant, Stuart froze. Then he tried again, but this time got only a soggy click. He couldn't remember how many shots he'd fired when the Indians first came down, but apparently the driving rain had wet the powder in the remaining chambers. The raiders might be equally unable to shoot, but there might be dozens of them, and those on the outside of the line were already converging to cut off his escape.

He cast a last look toward Ethan's body, but there was nothing he could do. With the tomahawk-wielding Indian less than twenty yards away, Stuart reined the sorrel desperately around and spurred into the teeth of the rain.

The sorrel broke away over the uneven ground as if it too were fleeing for life. At first, Stuart only clung in the saddle. Soaked in a sweat colder than the rain, he waited with tensed muscles for the smash of a bullet or a cleaving stroke from the tomahawk. When finally he could manage a look back without slowing the horse, he saw his nearest pursuer was forty yards behind and steadily losing ground. He was the one with the tomahawk, and his face showed a baffled rage that he'd not gotten close enough to use it. The others were no more than gray shapes in the rain. Stuart couldn't see more than half a dozen, but he had no way to know how many were hidden by the mists.

"Bless you, Ethan," he muttered, remembering the times he'd ragged Fairchild for choosing the speedy sorrel over the black's strength and endurance.

The memory of Fairchild, bloody and alone in the gully, was almost enough to make him turn back. But he couldn't fight them all, especially not with a useless pistol. He reached for the rifle in the saddle boot, then took his hand away. With his own Colt's rifle, he might dare to turn and take his chances, but it was lost along with the black horse and Ethan. Trying to fight with Ethan's muzzle-loading Hawken would be throwing his life away.

All right. It was too bad about Ethan, but there was nothing Stuart could do. His duty now was to lead the Indians away from the train. Conscious of the sorrel's ragged breathing, he slowed his pace a little and began turning gradually back to the east.

He was still in the broken country south of the trail. Low, table-topped buttes and bluffs marked the transition from high plains to the broad valley of the Platte. Narrow lipless gullies laced the ground like scars, all winding north toward the river. Stuart saw he would have to pick his way carefully. Many of the slopes were too steep for a man on horseback. The Indians probably knew the country better than he, would be watching their chance to flank him and cut him off. He had to keep a clear path ahead if he hoped to lose them.

Before he'd gone another mile, he realized that wasn't going to work. The sorrel was tiring. It still struggled gamely, but its sweat-streaked neck and heaving sides warned it couldn't take much more. The rain squall had moved on, though high-banked clouds to the west promised more and harder rain later. Rising in the stirrups, Stuart peered back along his trail. At once, he picked up a rider crossing the bright path of a stray sunbeam, far behind but still coming.

"Ethan, damn it," he muttered. But Ethan was dead, and now Stuart was pretty certain he would be joining him soon. All that was left was to pick his own place, before that choice too was taken from him.

Barely trotting now, the sorrel was skirting the foot of a low butte no different from any of the others Stuart had seen that day—or would have seen, had he not been more interested in Jessica Thorne. *Jess!* The word rose in his mind, a single despairing cry, but he shoved it down again. No time. No time to think about Jessica, not now nor ever again.

Anger went through him like a prairie wind, and he clenched his teeth. They would have to fight to get him. They would pay for him, and for what they'd done to Ethan. He yanked the reins around, spurring the tired sorrel brutally to get a last burst of speed. In the temporary shelter of the butte, he flung himself off the sorrel, pulling the rifle from its boot and fumbling with desperate haste to get the saddlebags loose. There was no place to tie the horse. Stuart dropped the reins, thinking as he scrabbled up the muddy slope that he probably wouldn't be needing the animal again anyway.

He reached the top and knelt there, looking back. Two riders in sight, then three, finally six—they were moving more slowly, tracking instead of chasing, certain of their prey. Stuart nodded to himself. Then, afraid of what he might find, he checked over the rifle. The hammer was on half-cock, and a percussion cap clung to the nipple.

"Thanks, Ethan," he murmured, feeling a ridiculous sense of relief. It was only one shot, but it was one more than he'd had. Quickly, he searched through the saddlebags. He was quite calm, he assured himself, but he could feel his sweat drying cold in the wind, and he couldn't stop his hands from shaking. Finally, he found a cartridge pouch with a handful of balls for the rifle and a round box of caps. He had his own powder horn, and that was all he would need. Laying the caps carefully in a dry spot atop a rock, he glanced again at the riders, then drew out his pistol and bent over its cylinder.

He had reloaded two chambers, digging out the wet

powder, replacing it from his powder horn, and tamping a new ball down, when he decided the riders were close enough. His hands steady, he laid the pistol aside and took up the Hawken. It was too bad about Ethan, too bad about himself, more than too bad that he'd never see Jess again. But all that was behind him now. David Stuart was on trial for his life; the jury had ridden within rifle range. He drew back the heavy hammer, checked the cap, and breathed a silent prayer, hoping that Fairchild's perpetually poor shooting hadn't owed to the sights on his rifle.

There were eight raiders in the open now, strung out in a crescent and moving at an easy trot. Stuart chose the western flanker for a target, thinking it might be the Indian who'd come after him. With a hunter's concentration, he followed the man carefully for a couple of seconds before he pulled the trigger.

The rifle boomed and shoved hard against his shoulder. White smoke blossomed to give away his position. A second passed, time enough for Stuart to count two hammering heartbeats, and then the rider bucked in his saddle, leaned forward, slid off his mount in a boneless tumble into the mud. Stuart didn't see him fall; he was pouring powder down the barrel, ramming in a new ball with no time for a patch. He rolled back the hammer, found a cap, felt a chip of stone cut his face as a bullet slapped the rock beside him and whined away. He jerked the Hawken up, searching over the sights for a fresh target.

In the time it had taken him to reload, the scene below had changed. The raiders were coming on at a gallop, the horns of their crescent drawing in to surround his butte. A puff of smoke rose from the center of the line. Another bullet droned within inches of Stuart's head. Finding an instant to marvel at such marksmanship, Stuart slapped the Hawken's sights on the rider who had shot so straight. He was a big target, inside fifty yards now; his white hair making a mark to shoot for. Stuart steadied on that hair and shot much more quickly than he would have liked.

Even above the sound of thunder, he heard the whang

of the rider's voice, a cry like an axe against an iron gate. The big man threw a gloved hand across his face, roared again, wavered in the saddle. Stuart went to his pistol. He rested against the rock, chose the nearest rider, missed.

The big raider had plowed to a stop. One of the others screamed with a voice like a woman's. "Hold up, Kid! Plum! Hold off, all of you. Tom's been hit!"

The big man had not quit roaring. The woman rode up beside him, took his arm. In the pause, Stuart had the Hawken ready again, his sights on another rider. He managed not to shoot as his target turned sharply and kicked his horse back toward the others. Stuart led him a hair, pulled the trigger, and let the man ride into the path of his bullet. It took him high in the middle of his back, but he stayed in the saddle, swaying, until he had ridden past the man and woman.

Stuart fired at the pair as they, too, turned to get out of range. He couldn't tell that he hit either one. They disappeared into a fold in the ground almost too small to see. The others converged on the same spot and fell out of sight.

Stuart loaded the rifle, then poured powder into the empty chambers in his revolver. The new storm was rolling toward him, its shadow racing ahead across the ground, like the sword of judgment. He worked harder. There would be no loading in the dry once the storm struck. He wasn't worrying about getting wet. He was worrying about getting trapped on the rocky height he had chosen, about dying there with none to know.

Ten minutes later, in a sky-lighting flash of lightning, he saw movement a mile off to the east. Three or four riders came up out of the dry creek, crossed a little rise, and dropped out of sight again. Stuart knew there were more, wondered where they were, shrugged. He figured they had given him as good a chance as he was going to get.

He slid down off the ledge onto the waiting sorrel. For a hundred yards or so, he kept the horse to a soft walk.

He watched carefully for any flank riders the group might have left to ambush him. But even in the brightest of the lightning, he saw nothing. When he couldn't stand the suspense any longer, he dug his heels into the horse's flanks and rode headlong into the teeth of the storm.

Hours later, he walked the exhausted sorrel into a soggy, hail-beaten camp. Rain still fell in a sullen drizzle that made the month seem more like October than June. Drifts of sleet and a scattering of larger hailstones still littered the muddy trail. The children were mostly out of sight, presumably huddled in the relative dryness of the wagon beds. Among the battered wagons, men and women repaired gashed canvas covers, worked around smoky cooking fires, tended to mules and oxen injured by the pounding hail. Stuart could sympathize with the livestock. Caught in the open by the skirts of the storm, he and the sorrel had their own bruises to show.

In the early darkness, few noticed Stuart at first. Only the four Buttrell boys, stair-stepped from eight to seventeen, stopped what they were doing to gape at him. He turned the horse toward his uncle's wagon. He was wet and chilled and bone tired, but those weren't his biggest reasons for wanting to stay unnoticed for a while. During the long ride back, it had come to him that he would have to explain what had happened, first to Wagonmaster Thorne and then to the others. Worst, he would have to tell Jessica about Ethan.

"You! David Stuart!"

Resignedly, Stuart reined in the sorrel. Manasseh Thorne had turned from a group of men heaving a stuck wagon up to more solid ground. He was not tall but quite solid, a heavy man with bushy side-whiskers and black-button eyes glaring past a hawk's nose. He planted his fists on his hips and turned those eyes on Stuart.

"Stand down!" In Ohio, County Judge Thorne had been known as an orator, able to draw a crowd just by clearing his throat. Now the ring of his voice silenced the talk around the cooking fires. "Stand down and explain yourself, young Stuart!"

Stuart stood down from Fairchild's sorrel and turned loose of the reins. He faced Thorne, but from the tail of his eye, he could see others turning from their work to watch. He caught a glimpse of his uncle Douglas, his bearded face lined with concern. He didn't see Jessica.

"Mr. Thorne," he began.

The wagonmaster cut him off. "Every soul in our little community has a job, and every job is important." It was a speech Thorne had often made before, and Stuart was too tired to interrupt. "If we're to get to Oregon, every one of us must do that job. We all signed articles to that effect, even the youngest of us. When any man turns his back on his duty—" Thorne stopped abruptly. He was staring at the sorrel. "Where's Fairchild? I want him to hear this, too. I don't have time or patience to say it twice."

Stuart shook his head. "Ethan's . . ." He couldn't say it, not out in front of everyone like that. "Ethan's gone," he said, hearing the surprised murmur from around him. "We were attacked. We thought they were Indians."

"Indians!" Thorne snorted his disgust. "Indians! A child could make up a better story."

Stuart remembered that Thorne had warned them about Indians that very morning, but he didn't think it a good moment to remind the wagonmaster of that.

"Jessica was driving Ethan's wagon for him. She says you and Fairchild had words."

"Yes, sir."

"She says you two left your posts."

"Yes, sir."

"And that you then rode away from the train on some mission personal to the two of you."

"That much is true, but—"

"The truth is all I want, but I want all of that."

"We rode away from our posts." Stuart paused, pondering what he'd been pondering the last hour, how to put the best face on his folly.

"Well?"

"We fought."

"I can see that. Over what? What was important enough to take you two young bucks away from your duty?"

Somebody in the crowd broke the tense silence with a snicker. Thorne's cheeks flushed, but he didn't glance away from Stuart.

"A disagreement," Stuart said finally. "Our reasons were our business. What happened was, we'd no sooner exchanged blows than a party of Indians came whooping and shooting at us."

Thorne rubbed his whiskered cheek thoughtfully. "I heard no shooting." He looked around at the silent group. "Any of you hear shooting?"

No one answered for a time that seemed endless to Stuart. Then Caleb Sugarhouse plunged into the silence like a man kicking in a door. "I didn't," he said loudly. "Nor none of us did! Not unless it was cannons in the sky. They was a-plenty thunder."

"I did." After Sugarhouse's roar, Jessica's words were almost inaudible. "I heard the shooting."

Jessica Thorne had paled since Stuart saw her last. She seemed wan and frail, as if she had been ill for a long time. She looked once at Stuart, her wide blue eyes filled with fear and questions, then faced her father.

"I did," she repeated. "It was just before the storm broke. A long way behind us. I thought . . ." She stopped, not saying what she had thought, but her eyes questioned Stuart again.

"She could have," Sugarhouse boomed. "She was driving the back wagon."

"Fairchild's wagon."

Jessica Thorne stepped forward and put her hand on Stuart's arm. "Where is he, David?" she asked softly. "Where is Ethan?"

Stuart had been practicing his answer for an hour. *It's*

a shame, he'd intended to say, *but I guess it's what you'd call God's will. He got on my horse. Plain bad luck he did it. The Indians shot my horse first thing. Then they shot Ethan as they rode by. What? Yes, I saw him dead. You know he was. Else I'd never have left him.*

Staring into Jessica's eyes, holding his gaze on hers with an effort greater than any other he'd made that day, he couldn't remember his part. All he could think to say was, "Jess, I'm sorry. I couldn't help him."

He thought that Jessica screamed, that she split the sodden clouds with her scream. Her mouth had opened to scream. But she made no sound at all. Not a wail or a moan or a sigh.

Manasseh Thorne heard her silence, saw Stuart's face, put the puzzle together. "Girl," he said, still looking at Stuart. "How many shots?"

If she heard his question, she did not answer.

To Stuart, Thorne said, "If I was to look at your gun, I'd find that you'd fired it. That right?"

"Yes, sir."

"If I was to go back now and look—which into the night and the backwash of that storm I cannot—would I find that Fairchild had fired his?"

Stuart tried to remember, shook his head. "He never had the chance," he said.

Sugarhouse laughed. "I believe that," he boomed.

"Bide a bit!" Douglas Stuart pushed to the front, took a stand beside his nephew, black beard bristling with indignation. "This is not a trial!"

"It ought to be," somebody said.

"I want to see Stuart's gun. And that's Fairchild's horse. Why's he riding Fairchild's horse? And where's he been all this time?"

"Maybe we don't need a trial!" Sugarhouse's bellow rode over the rest. "We'll get to the truth here! Grab him!"

This time, Jessica did scream. With his mind still on her, Stuart began too late to struggle against the hands that reached for him. But Manasseh Thorne's voice rang out like a bell.

"Stand where you are. I am in charge here, as we all agreed, even you, Caleb! We'll have no flouting of that law! Let him go!"

A half dozen of the group protested, but Thorne stared them down. "I'll decide what action shall be taken," he said. "And I'll ask the questions." He waited while the men fell back, muttering. Then he looked again at Stuart.

"Did you kill your brother?"

"No!"

In spite of all that had happened, the question caught Stuart by surprise. Ethan was not his brother, of course; Thorne had made it part of their contract that all were to think of the rest as brothers. Stuart had been so deeply tied up in his own misery and Jessica's that he hadn't fully understood the reaction of the others on the train. Now he saw it. They believed—maybe even Jessica believed—that *he* had killed Ethan.

"No," he said again, straight to Jessica. "No. I'd never do such a thing."

Thorne cleared his throat. "But were you your brother's keeper?"

That question was harder to answer. He saw again the picture his mind had shown him a hundred times in the last hours: Ethan on the ground, soaked in his own blood, the Indians charging past the bodies of man and horse, himself turning to run. The rain had been heavy, the light uncertain. Was he *sure* he hadn't seen Ethan move just as the sorrel wheeled to run?

His own uncertainty made him angry. "I was! I tried. I killed two or three of them. If you're man enough to ride, I'll show you their bodies." He knew he had stepped beyond his bounds. No man among them dared speak to Thorne in that manner. Stuart was past caring. "I'll show you my horse. I'll show you Ethan's body, if that's what you want to see!"

Jessica Thorne put her hands over her face and began

to cry softly. Martha Thorne came up to put an arm around her daughter's shoulders. She would have led her away, but Jessica shook her head.

"No, I have to hear it, all of it."

"And I'll bring him back for burial. I'd never have left his body behind, if there hadn't been so many of them."

"Yeah?" Sugarhouse's voice was heavy with disbelief. "How many would that be?"

"Caleb!" Thorne's tone was a command. Eye to eye, he backed Sugarhouse down. Then, more quietly, he said, "My daughter's made a good point, David. We've kept you from telling your story through. Perhaps you'll be good enough to tell it now."

As well as he could, Stuart told them how he had seen the Indians coming and had warned Ethan, how each had gotten on the nearest horse, how the black had gone down at the second or third shot, how he had seen Ethan dead on the ground before he'd been forced to run.

"You left him there?"

"I led them away from the train!" he answered. Then he told about standing the Indians off at the butte, told them that up close the Indians had not looked like he thought Indians would look. He described knocking one out of the saddle, killing or wounding two more, driving them away before returning to the train for their help. "I might have expected you to be glad to see me," he finished with weary bitterness. "To be grateful one of us lived to tell you about it."

Jessica Thorne turned away from the group and wavered toward her father's wagon, her mother supporting her. Stuart turned toward her, took a step in that direction, but the group closed tight to block his way.

"Sugarhouse," he said to the one in front of him, "step aside. Don't make me move you. I have to talk to Jess."

Sugarhouse stood his ground. "You left him," he said flatly. "You turned yellow and ran from them so-called Indians and left your friend to die. That's it, ain't it?"

Stuart didn't even try to answer. He swung his fist with

all the anger and frustration and grief in his body, driving it straight at the sneering man's face. The blow didn't land. Strong hands—his uncle's hands—caught his arm and held it.

"Steady, lad," Douglas Stuart's soft burr said at his ear. "There'll be enough and more of such talk, from now until the trump of doom. You canna fight them all."

Stuart was willing to try. But Thorne had pushed between him and Sugarhouse. "David," he said, still quietly, "I'll see your powder horn."

Stuart unslung the horn and passed it to his leader without question. Thorne opened the big end, peered into the chamber, and turned it down. After a few seconds, a spoonful of thin gray mud dribbled out of the horn onto the ground between them.

The oldest Buttrell boy, Francis, remarked how near Stuart had come to running out of powder. That started a couple more trying to guess how many shots he must have fired to use up a horn's worth. Dr. Harris wondered aloud why a guilty man would have bothered to exchange horses and leave his good Colt's rifle behind when a simpler story would have done as well. All of them seemed impressed.

Thorne had made up his mind. Like a lawyer sensing the turn in a jury's thinking, he wheeled to Sugarhouse. "In olden days," he said in his orator's voice, "a man who charged another with a crime and failed to prove his case suffered the penalty for that crime. Are you prepared to meet that standard, Caleb?"

Sugarhouse scowled but didn't answer. "Any of you others?" Thorne demanded. "Very well. We know all we ever shall know of this matter. We know David Stuart to be a forthright young man, however headstrong and disobedient."

Thorne looked at Stuart. "In accordance with the ordinances of this train, I fine you the sum of one dollar for failure to keep your powder dry." He paused a second, and something human showed in his face, a grief that surprised Stuart. "Your disobedience of orders has been punished sufficiently, I think." Suddenly, his voice was a shout. "The rest of you," Thorne roared, "tighten your formation and get the camp cleaned up. This matter is closed."

Stuart hung his head, letting out a long breath. Then he straightened again.

"Sir? One thing. I'm going back after Ethan's body, with your permission." Or without it, he thought. Thorne might have read the idea in his eyes.

"You can't go back tonight," he said gruffly. "Nor can the train wait for you. See me in the morning. Perhaps it would be best to send back a party strong enough to resist an attack by Indians. See me in the morning, and we'll decide."

He turned away, toward his wagon and Jessica. Stuart would have followed, but his uncle's arm fell across his shoulders.

"Not now, boy," the older man said. "Rest yourself first. You'll do no good in speaking to the lass now. No good for her nor you neither."

Too tired to argue, Stuart let himself be led away. He was beginning to see, in a way he hadn't grasped before, just what had happened. He had left his friend behind.

He had seen Ethan fall, had known one keen cold second during which he might have whirled the sorrel to pick Ethan up or to fight and die by his side. Stuart had hesitated in that second, and his choice had gone by forever. He had stood between darkness and light and chosen the darkness. Now he saw he would carry the burden of that choice all the way to his grave.

3

       Ethan Fairchild had somehow kicked off the cover in the night. He was cold, as if it were February in Ohio rather than mid-June on the Plains. His teeth chattered. Hard, shuddering paroxysms of shivering racked his body. Worse, a rain must have blown up, and the wagon sheet must be leaking, because his clothes were wet and soggy. Half asleep, he groped for his blanket and tried to sit up.

But there was no blanket. A stroke of lightning seemed to split his head with light and a sound he couldn't quite hear and a fierce, blinding pain. But it was silence, not thunder, that crashed down in its wake, a silence broken only by the soft plash and swirl of falling rain, of water all around him.

Stu! There was something about Stuart he had to remember, something important. He would think of it soon, as soon as the lightning went away.

He put a hand to his head and sank back, until he realized he was lying in water, running water almost deep enough to cover him. He pushed himself up through shards of pain, then had to roll to the side while his stomach heaved and a bout of retching doubled him up.

After the sickness passed, he began to remember. He'd quarreled with Stu and they'd fought. Ethan had been winning when the damned Indians—or whatever they were—had come down on them by surprise. He remembered swinging onto the black horse, remembered the horse going down, remembered trying to shout as he was thrown.

He remembered thinking, "*Run, Stu! Don't stop for me!*"

He didn't know if he'd gotten the words out or not. It didn't matter. *By now they must have killed Stu.* And they would be back for him. The white-haired man had said so. Ethan had to do something, and quickly.

He couldn't identify any part of his body that didn't hurt. When he found the strength to roll over onto his side, he couldn't identify any part of his body that wasn't broken. The dark silence he'd come out of made another pass at him like the scorpion tail of a whirlwind. Its promise was tempting, but he refused it. He bent one leg far enough to find a knee. He got up on that knee, collapsed, tired again.

At first, he couldn't see anything. The time must have been near sunset. Or maybe dawn. The heavy dark clouds made it hard to be certain. Fairchild wiped his eyes, squinting in the half-light, and saw his own hands, saw the shimmer of water, saw a black shape humped up from its surface. He put out a hand and touched the rough coat of Stuart's black horse.

The animal had been dead when it fell. Again, he remembered what the white-haired man had said. They would be back for the tack and guns. *Be back!* he told himself. They haven't come *back* because they haven't done for Stu! I've got to give him a hand. The thought gave him a leg up on the wall of his pain.

He crawled to the horse, puzzled because its body seemed jammed and twisted in ways he couldn't understand. Giving up on that, he slid Stuart's rifle out of the boot. Then he fumbled endlessly with the brass buckles until he had unstrapped the saddlebags. After that, it was time to try to stand.

What wasn't broken didn't want to move. Panting from exertion and pain, he swayed on his feet, vomited again, stayed upright. After a minute he slung the saddlebags over his shoulder. If he lived, he'd worry later about what was in them.

The big black horse was lying on the canteen. Fairchild took hold of the strap and pulled. The effort cost him the return of pains he had put out of his mind. But the canteen came free.

Fairchild picked up his hat and limped away in the direction he thought Stuart had gone. In the clouded darkness, he couldn't be sure, but at least his path carried him up out of the rising water. At the low rim of the arena, he stopped. Not far away, a wall of grayish darkness defined the horizon all around him. He saw no horse, no man, not even the gleam of campfire or stars. He heard no hoof-beats, no shots, no creaking wagons. Straddling the low crest, Fairchild could have believed that the awful swirl of silence had left him completely alone in the world.

With no better idea, he crossed the rim and struggled a quarter of a mile across in the direction he thought would lead him back to the train. The going was rougher than he remembered, or maybe it only seemed so because of the aches in his limbs and the unceasing pain in his head. He stumbled into a shallow creek bed, floundering through water that reached his waist. On the other bank, he found tracks.

Horses had passed that way not long before, because the edges of the marks were only beginning to soften and settle in the rain. The tracks were cut deep, the horses running hard. A few yards on, the trail dissolved into confusion. Fairchild saw where a second trail crossed the first at right angles, several horses again, but now moving at a walk.

In the growing dark, he couldn't see more, and the rain kept him from striking a light. The message, though, was pretty clear. Either Stuart and the sorrel had outrun the pursuers, or they had run him down and dealt with him. In either case, the Indians had not headed straight back to strip the black horse.

Fairchild tried to fit it all into his aching head, but failed. Were they Indians? They had screamed when they charged. But one of them had white hair. One of them must have been a woman. He hadn't really seen the others. *Whatever they are, they may have killed Stu by now!* He could grasp the fact that David Stuart was almost certainly dead, for no better reason than wanting to fight over Jessica Thorne.

He had more difficulty grasping Jessica Thorne in his mind. He saw her opening her arms to him, but he heard her saying *Get away from me!* But he couldn't stop thinking about her. He stumbled blindly ahead, remembering, letting her memory take him away from the cold and the pain.

He remembered her in the moonlight, heard her voice in the daylight when she had denied her love for him and their marriage in the eyes of God. He knew that she loved him, that she was waiting anxiously for him to catch up to the wagons. He knew he loved her and that he would soon catch up to the wagons.

But then he realized that she would never forgive him slate-clean if he saved himself and came back without Stuart. He nodded and felt mud against his cheek. He realized he was no longer walking, that he must have fallen. Scrabbling in the mud, he found rifle and saddlebags and canteen, gathered them, pushed himself up, walked.

He saw the tracks now only as a darker shadow against the shadowed ground, but he followed doggedly. He had not come across any place where the horses had stopped, any blots of blood on the trail. He had not heard any commotion of gunfire.

Nor did he hear what his ears were most carefully tuned to hear—the sounds of his friends riding hard to find him and bring him safely back within the fold.

The train would be stopped for the storm. But he had no idea how far away the train might be. He did not know whether it had weathered the storm and was moving again. He did not think that he had been unconscious for a whole day, but he could not be certain. He worked on the things that were clear to him. He could not hope to find Stu or the Indians; the tracks he'd been following were puddling, would soon disappear completely. He could try to keep on in the same direction, but he couldn't be certain of keeping his way on that dark rolling plain.

What else was he sure of? He didn't know. All right. He was sure that he didn't know what else he was sure of.

Enough of that. He kept walking, down the long slope of a gully. At the bottom, he was wading in water a foot deep. Before he could cross the short run of the bottom and start up the far side, the water was to his knees, and a strong current tugged at his pants.

He used the rest of his strength climbing the wall of the gully, then lay exhausted on the low rim. Darkness was all but complete around him. He would follow the rim, he decided. Yes, he told himself, but what if you slip over the edge, fall into the water? You could drown in a minute! More important, where would the rim take you?

He thought of trying to cross the creek again, returning to higher ground. That was foolish. He thought of turning back in the direction he believed to be north, but he could not come up with a reason.

Without a lantern in that darkness, he dared not move far in any direction. He might fall in a hole, trip over a rock, lose his direction. He thought there had been a big rock at the rim where the creek curved back north. Was it a fact he could be sure of?

Ethan began to crawl in the direction he believed to be west. Now and then he stopped, found a fist-sized rock, and threw it off to his right. Each time he heard the rock plunk into water. He hoped the experiments meant he was following the rim of the creek bank fairly closely. More and more frequent displays of lightning assured him that he was. Finally, in the daylight of a broad sheet of lightning, he saw the gray outline of the boulder he was seeking.

When he came to it, he could not remember why he

had sought it. Had there been a reason? He thought so. He crawled around the boulder to the south and west until he nosed into a dense juniper bush. That was it!

Fairchild unslung his gear and thrust it under the edge of the rock. The bush was not quite as solid as a tin roof, but it gave him the illusion of shelter. Now that he was no longer moving, he began to shiver again. He took off his coat and spread it over the top of the bush. As he crawled under his airy, leaking shelter, he thought of an afternoon all of ten years ago, an afternoon when he and Stu had built a lean-to in the woods above the creek on his family's farm. It too had leaked, and the smoke from their little fire had sought out the lean-to like a starved homing pigeon. But there had never been a finer lean-to, just as there had never been a finer shelter than his current bush.

Feeling carefully inside the saddlebags, he found strips of jerky, a few sticks of peppermint for Stu's sweet tooth, other things he could identify in the morning. If he tried to check his powder, he would get it wet for sure. He drank from the canteen, poured out the rest of the stale water, and set the vessel out beside the rock to fill with rainwater. He stayed awake long enough to chew on a strip of jerky and eat one of Stuart's peppermints. Then he arranged himself as best he could under his tiny tent, and slipped gradually into a troubled sleep.

4

As was his custom, Manasseh Thorne was the first member of the party to be awake and abroad in the morning. He had slept poorly. He had been sleeping poorly ever since the train drew away from the settlements of Kansas, away from anything that might be called civilization. Tramping through the silent camp, Thorne shook his head to clear away the tatters of a familiar nightmare in which his wagons were trapped in the high passes, his people were starving, his wife and daughter dead and dying.

"Mud," he growled, half aloud, to banish the dream from his mind. The storm had cleared away, but the ruts of the trail would be deep in black, sticky mud. It would cling to the hooves of the oxen and the boots of the people. Mud. Hard on the stock. Hard on wheels and axles and all the thousand parts of a wagon that Thorne had never thought about before this journey started. Hard on the people—*his* people.

Some would want to stop, to take a day of rest while the ground dried out. Mentally, Thorne began preparing his arguments. It was getting on toward the end of June already, with less than six hundred miles behind them. The snows would begin in October if not in late September.

I will not stop for this mud.

He passed the Buttrell wagon, thinking of the children sleeping there. The Kenny wagon was next, and he would have to watch its off hind wheel today in the mud. Barbara Kenny—*Widow* Kenny, since their crossing of the Big Blue—had insisted on coming on alone after Sam's death, hiring the second Buttrell kid to drive for her now and then.

"There's nothing for me back home," she'd said. "I can find a new start in Oregon."

"Or a new man," Thorne murmured, remembering her words. Women would be at a premium there, and a man could do worse than Barbara Kenny.

At the edge of the circled wagons, he stopped and took off his hat. No hint of sunrise touched the sky. The clouds had blown away in the night, and the Milky Way arched overhead like a vast glowing rainbow. Thorne stood beneath it, his lips moving in his desperate daily prayer for guidance and grace to get the train through the passes before the snows came.

Shivering in the sharp predawn cold that seemed his only answer, he turned away. His train was beginning to stir. From some of the wagons came muffled voices, sounds of movement, once the soft creaks and whispers— this from the Holden wagon, Thorne noted with a smile, newlyweds—of a man and woman finding one another in the dark. Oxen stirred and lowed.

Down by the horse lines, unexpected movement caught Thorne's eye. He strode quickly that way, his hand seeking the unfamiliar butt of his pistol. Outside the circle of wagons, the sharp silhouette of a man angled black against the glowing sky.

"Who's there?"

"It's me, Mr. Thorne, Francis Buttrell. Davy Stuart and me."

Thorne was close enough now to see them both, the Buttrell boy holding a rifle and looking on while Stuart threw a saddle across the back of a leggy sorrel.

"Are you on watch?" Like a man shrugging into a familiar coat, Thorne clothed himself in gruffness and self-assurance and brisk efficiency. "You're away from your post."

"Yes, sir. It's all right. Orren's up on that little hump watching things."

"What's going on? Stuart?"

Stuart didn't answer. He finished tightening the girths. Straightening, he slung a pair of saddle holsters across the sorrel's withers. Each held a single-shot Dragoon pistol. Besides his holstered Navy Colt, Stuart had another revolver thrust through his belt. He looped the strap of a canteen around the saddle horn and started to mount.

"No," Thorne said.

"Don't try to stop me," Stuart said. "I told you last evening, I'm going back for Ethan."

"And I asked you to see me first," Thorne said. "If you go alone, we'll have two men lost."

"I won't risk another life."

"I'll go with him, Mr. Thorne," Francis Buttrell put in quickly. "I'm growed up enough. Pa says."

Thorne stared at him a moment. "All right," he agreed. "But after breakfast. And after first light, if you hope to find anything.

And with enough men to stand off . . ."

Manasseh Thorne hesitated. He hadn't liked Stuart's story about Indians. He did not like this young rooster that scratched after his chick. He hadn't liked Jessica's broken sobbing in the night when she'd thought everyone else was asleep. But he had not lived twoscore years and twelve by giving vent to his every thought. He had seen the truth in the matter at once: there would never be any way to know what really happened between Stuart and Fairchild. Thus Thorne had to choose. Privately, he would always hold the matter in doubt. Before others, he had to believe or disbelieve.

"To stand off any party you might encounter," he finished. He put his hand on Stuart's shoulder, tightening his grip when the younger man would have pulled away.

"Waiting won't hurt Ethan," he said, more softly. "And I wish you'd speak to Jessica before you go. She's upset."

For the first time, Stuart looked at him. The anger and rebellion died slowly out of his dark eyes. "All right," he said at last. "I'll wait. And I'll speak to Jess."

Thorne nodded and turned away. Walking back toward a newly kindled fire and the smell of fresh coffee, he thought of Stuart's haggard face. It gave the wagonmaster no comfort to know there'd been one man on the train that night who'd slept even less than he.

"I have to go, Jess."

David Stuart stood awkwardly by the tailboard of the Thorne wagon, holding the sorrel's bridle. At the cooking fire nearby, Mrs. Thorne bustled about her morning's business. The whole camp bustled, men yoking up the oxen, giving last-minute attention to greasing the running gear of their wagons and checking the iron tires, preparing for the day's run. A dozen yards away, Francis Buttrell and three others waited by their horses, careful not to show an interest in Stuart and Jessica.

"I have to go," Stuart repeated, as much for himself as for Jessica. "Don't worry, Jess. We'll find him."

Fairchild's sorrel lowered its long nose, nuzzled at Jessica's elbow. The girl put a trembling, pale hand on its white face. She looked frail and frightened. Stuart longed to put his arms around her, to assure her everything was all right. But everything wasn't, and she knew it, and he didn't know how she would react to his touch.

"I'm not worried." She raised tearful blue eyes to meet his gaze while she stroked the sorrel's rough coat. "Not about Ethan. Not now. It's you."

"I'm all right."

"I wish—" She bit her lip. "I wish you'd stay. Here. Where it's safe. With me."

Stuart shook his head. "Jess, I owe it to Ethan. I have to find him." Stuart stopped, realizing that he'd come very close to saying *I have to be sure he's dead.*

He was sure, of course. He had seen the blood, seen Ethan's still body beside the crumpled black horse. He would never have left him if there had been the slightest doubt. He was sure. But he had to bring back the body to prove to the whole train that Ethan was dead.

For the first time, Stuart saw the greater difficulty. *It'll be easy to prove him dead. But how will I prove that I didn't kill him!*

"I have to see he gets a Christian burial. That's the least he'd do for me."

"It's not worth your life," Jessica whispered.

Before Stuart could decide how to answer that, Martha Thorne came up and put a protective arm around her daughter's shoulders.

"Jessica, honey, best you get in the wagon now. You know Doc Harris told you not to overdo for a few days."

She looked at Stuart. Her eyes were the same blue as Jessica's, faded a little, but still quick and searching. "David, you be careful out there. Come back safe."

"Yes!" Jessica pulled free of her mother and caught Stuart in a quick, desperate hug. "Come back, Davy. I couldn't bear to lose you, too."

Stuart swallowed, standing tongue-tied as Martha Thorne shepherded Jessica back to the shelter of the wagon. Then he turned away, back to where the others waited. They'd been talking among themselves. As Stuart came up, he caught the end of what Milt Ames was saying.

"—got Fairchild's horse and his gun, and it looks like he's on his way to taking his woman, too."

"Hist," Tom Lee murmured, and Ames fell silent with a guilty glance at Stuart.

Anger flared through Stuart, hot and red, but he held it back. "You canna fight them all," his uncle had said. The idea still did not satisfy Stuart, but he swung onto the sorrel and started for the eastern trail at a trot, not giving a damn whether the others followed or not.

By eight o'clock the mud had slowed them to a walk. Milt Ames, leading the balky packhorse they'd brought for Ethan's body, fell behind, so Stuart called a halt on a low swell of ground overlooking the trail ruts. The point rider, Lije Holden, saw them stop and cantered back.

"Do you see the place, Davy?" he asked, drawing his stocky gray up alongside the sorrel.

"I'm not sure." Stuart had believed he could go straight back to the spot where he and Fairchild had fought, but he had not expected the flood. "It all looks different after the rain."

"Afraid of that." Holden squinted up at the sun. A rangy Kentuckian, he was one of the few on the train not hailing from the same Ohio county. He and his new bride had joined at Independence. "Was we to start back right now, we'd not catch old Thorne and the train by the noon halt. It'll be a long ride or a cold camp tonight."

"Start back now if you like," Stuart snapped. "I'm staying."

Holden raised his eyebrows. "Didn't mean no offense." He spat tobacco juice into a puddle, then straightened as Ames led the packhorse up. "Ready, Milt?"

"Goldanged worthless piece of flea-bait," Ames mumbled, yanking angrily on the lead rope.

"I'll spell you," Francis Buttrell said, and Long Tom Lee seconded the offer, but Ames shook his head.

"No, I've got onto the sleight of it now. But we ought to leave him for the buzzards, if we don't find Fairchild after all."

Another two hours brought them to something Stuart recognized. He remembered the low butte with its single juniper and led the party around toward the grassy arena where he and Fairchild had fought. He crested the high west bank of a dry creek bed they had crossed the day before, then reined up the sorrel in dismay. He'd hardly noticed the gully then, but now it was a river. On the eastern side, the bank was under a flood of swift, foaming water which covered the low ground as far as they could see.

"We didn't get this much rain in camp," the Buttrell boy said.

Holden let out a long whistle. "Most of it was off to the north," he said. "Must have rained a devil of a lot on the watershed up yonder on the plains. We ain't getting past this, not today, anyways."

"Not this month, looks like," Tom Lee added. "Not without old Noah gives us a lift, that is. Makes you grateful we got our wagons through here before the floods came."

Ames asked Stuart whether he was sure he had the right place.

Stuart frowned, trying to picture it as it had been without the water. "It must be," he said finally. "We crossed right about here. Maybe we can see more if we follow along the bank."

Dispirited, they rode slowly around the high curving bank, past the low arena in which Stuart and Fairchild had been ambushed. He identified the spot, now an eddy in the brown water, where he and Fairchild had stood when the Indians attacked. The others mumbled.

"That cut right there, behind the butte, is where they came down from. And I rode out over that saddle to the east."

"What kind of Indians?" Milt Ames asked suddenly.

"I don't know." Stuart remembered the one with long white hair, another who'd screamed like a woman. "Pawnee, I guess. They're supposed to be the wild ones around here."

"How many of them?"

"I saw six or seven. It was dark, raining. I heard others. I don't know how many."

Ames rubbed his chin. "You saw six or seven," he said. "You shot a couple or three and ran from the rest."

"We ran first." For the first time, Stuart realized how thin the truth sounded. "I found a place to stand them off maybe three, four miles east of here. That's when I shot a couple." He stared hard at Ames. "You want to say what you're thinking, Milt?"

"Seems to me we've had plenty of that kind of trouble," Holden interrupted. "You'uns want to fight, I'd be obliged if you'd do it when we're back amongst the train." He leaned forward and peered out across the tossing flood-water. "Was you riding your black horse?"

"I was. We got mixed up trying to get out. Ethan was on my black horse when he went down."

"Horse killed?"

"Yes," he said. "My horse was killed." He waited. *Ask me one more question, you son of a bitch, and I'll take you out of that saddle myself.*

The Kentuckian stretched out a long arm. "What do you reckon that is? Over there where the channel bends at them rocks. See?"

Ames stood up in his stirrups. "I see it!" he said exci*

edly. "Looks black, whatever it is. Tom, can you tell?"

Francis Buttrell had been fumbling in his saddlebags. He brought out his father's long spyglass and trained it on the object. "It's black, sure enough. Except the middle's brown. That's it, Davy. It's your black and that's his brown saddle!"

"Let me see."

Buttrell handed him the telescope. "He's dead all right. All bloated up. Water's deep enough to float him."

"Any sign of Fairchild?" Ames asked.

"Didn't see any."

Stuart scanned the water, hoping. The brown surface was streaked with ridges of dirty white foam. A pine tree, washed down from God knew where, swept along, its branches waving like arms as it rolled in the current. The black horse bobbed and swayed as the rushing water tugged at whatever held it.

"No," he said finally. "I don't see him."

"I'll try." Holden took the telescope, looked, shook his head.

"He'd've floated quicker, farther," Ames murmured. "Might be plumb down to the Platte by now."

Lee said, "Could a man maybe get on top of this wall, ride it far enough to spot the body?"

"Maybe."

"Maybe," Holden agreed. "If'n his horse had wings, and he had a week to follow along the bank looking, and if poor Ethan ain't already to the river, or fetched up under a rock someplace."

"I could ride it," Stuart said. "I'd have to go back west until the wall's clear of the water."

"Just this side of California," Lee said.

"I have to try."

"What for? Conscience?"

Stuart stared at him.

"Hell," Milt Ames said, "he means for the girl."

"..."

"..e's girl. He's got to do it for her."

"That's enough," Stuart snapped. He wheeled angrily, but Ames raised both hands, palms out.

"I didn't mean nothing by it, honor bright," he said. "But it won't do you nor her nor nobody no good for you to go get killed yourself over a dead man."

Holden put a lean hand on Stuart's arm. "He's got the straight of it, Davy," he said. "There's nothing we can do now but get back to the train."

In spite of the mud, Manasseh Thorne had pressed on hard after the noon halt. It was nearly midnight when Stuart and the others caught up to the train. The east guard welcomed them back without a question; the riderless horse told all. Stuart tried to thank his companions, but they shrugged him off.

"Don't hardly seem worth making a fuss over," Holden mumbled. "I got to get on over to Sarah. She don't sleep too good unless I'm nigh."

One or two light sleepers inquired of them while they were putting up their horses. Then everyone went back to sleep.

Everyone except Jessica Thorne. Keeping to the shadows and moving very quietly, she made her way along the outer sides of the circled wagons until she came to David Stuart's. He was exhausted but not yet asleep. He had gotten his boots and shirt off. In that state he was sitting on the tailgate, his shoulders slumped in weariness and defeat, when she slipped silently around the edge and stood facing him. Moonlight caught on the hopeless question in her eyes.

He shook his head, put out a hand to touch her cheek gently. She put her hands on his and turned her face to kiss his palm. He lifted her onto the gate beside him.

"I'm sorry," he whispered.

Her chin quivered as she shook her head, but she did not cry. "It's you I was worried about," she breathed in his ear. "I've had the day to think. I know you've done your best. I know it wasn't your fault."

He wasn't sure he should believe her, but he was glad to hear it. After a moment he put his arm about her shoulders, softly so that he could move it if she objected. She didn't. He thought it offered him an opening, an advantage for him in her words. He reached for it.

"I can't help thinking it was some my fault."

She shook her head.

"I mean, if I hadn't been jealous of Ethan and you and how I thought things were between you, I'd never have—"

She put her hand over his mouth. She had indeed left him an opportunity, but he mustn't overreach. She looked into his eyes and saw the sadness he wanted her to see. She lifted her face and kissed the back of her hand where it covered his lips.

"It's all right," she said softly. "It really is."

He waited for her to move her hand. Then he said, "Nothing's changed." He waited. "I mean I haven't. I'm the same in the way I feel."

He wanted to ask her whether she was the same, but he saw that her answer would not tell him what he wanted to know. He was all patience.

"What do you mean?"

He was afraid to say it, fearful of offending her. He smiled but held the sadness in his eyes.

"Do you mean—?" she started. "Do you love me?"

He was through the gate and he knew it. Still not wanting to speak, he nodded his head. Surely she wouldn't fault him for answering her question.

She didn't. Instead she put her slender hands on his shoulders and kissed him. Softly and briefly. But she did it.

He couldn't remember that she had ever done such a thing on her own. His heart picked up its pace. He was afraid that she would hear it and move away from him, but he couldn't quiet it. Fearing to return the kiss quite yet, he looped his arms around her and drew her closer to his chest. She did not resist the pressure but melted into his embrace.

"Davy?" Her voice was no more than a breath against his skin. "Davy, I'm cold. Do you want to go inside, to take me inside the wagon with you?"

It took him a moment to understand, and a moment longer to think through his answer, to conquer the raging blood that made him close his arms around her until she gasped for breath. Then he took her arms and gently held her away.

"Not tonight," he whispered, looking into her face, unable to believe his luck. "Not this way." He drew a deep breath and said, "When we're married."

"Oh, Davy."

He didn't know why she cried. For a moment, he thought it meant she would refuse, but then her arms circled him again and she burrowed against his chest.

"Davy, can it be soon? Very soon?"

"Sure, Jess," he breathed against her hair, holding her. "As soon as you want."

And through her muffled sobs, he heard what he'd been waiting for, the words he'd dreamed about. "Davy," she whispered. "Davy, I love you."

Then she was gone. Stuart sat for a long time on the tailgate in the cool prairie night, half naked, half exhausted, half elated, and wholly unable to sleep.

5

Thoman Silverhorn sat with his back against a crumbling limestone boulder. A bloody, crusted bandage covered the left side of his face. His hat lay in the yellow mud beside him, and he gripped and released the brim rhythmically with the pain that throbbed through his head. The pain came in waves of color, orange and red and dazzling white. Silverhorn could see the color like sheets of fire behind his eyes, but that was all he could see.

At first, he'd been half conscious, snarling curses as Grace and Plum kept him on his horse until they'd reached a campsite for the night. The night had been all right. But now it was day, time to be moving again.

"Tom?"

Grace. He heard her feet shift, a yard from him and a little to his right. He turned his head that way, covering his good eye as though it pained him.

"Goddamn you, woman, leave me alone."

"Thoman, we got to be moving." She was leaning closer. He waited for her to touch him, but she knew better. "The rain's stopped. Sky's clearing off."

"I know that." He did. He could feel it in the waft of the air against his face, the occasional warmth of sunlight. But he couldn't *see*, damn it all. "We'll move when I say."

"Those Dragoons that've been following us are—"

"Shut up."

"Listen, Thoman, Grace is right." That was Simon, oldest of the Whitley brothers. "We can't just sit around whilst you nurse your eye. Me and Gabe and Jonas, why, those soldiers wanted to hang us back there in Kansas. I don't judge they've forgot, just becausin' we've rode a few miles west of there."

Simon was a few steps to the left, sitting, his face toward Silverhorn. Jonas stood a yard or so to his brother's right, shifting his boots uneasily in the mud, but Gabe had gone down by the horses to console Middleton's woman. She'd console pretty quick, Silverhorn figured, would be Gabe's woman by the time he got back.

He had taken careful note of the Whitleys. They were the ones who would cause trouble. Blue Eye and Kills Running would stay or go according to the luck of the gang and their own ideas. They would take no part in any struggle for leadership, and big Plum, lost inside his own head, was too stupid to care who led. But Simon had been watching his chance. If he knew Silverhorn was blind, he might figure he had it.

"Shut up," Silverhorn repeated. A lesser man might have felt sorry for himself. Silverhorn was angry all the way into the marrow of his backbone. He let his anger show as he swung his head toward Simon. "You figure you're smart enough and mean enough to take over, Simon?" Silverhorn put his left hand on the big .44 caliber pistol in his waist sash. "Maybe you better say so straight-out, and we'll find out who's the best man, bad eye or not."

For a second, Simon didn't answer, and Silverhorn thought he'd seen through the bluff. Then he heard the soft scrape as Simon leaned back.

"Hell, Tom, I didn't mean nothing," he said. "I know that eye pains you."

"Middleton and the Kid got worse," Jonas Whitley muttered. "We done left them back in the mud. This ain't working out. Maybe Simon oughta be the stud bull in this herd."

"That's enough, Jonas," Simon said quickly. "You get on down to the horses and see what's keeping Gabe. Me and Tom, we need to be alone."

"You let Thoman rest," Grace said suddenly. "Go on down and saddle up the horses. Get ready to move. I'll make up an Indian poultice that'll perk Thoman right back up, and then we'll get on our way."

"I don't take orders from no woman," Jonas snarled. "Especially not no half-Indian whore."

Silverhorn lifted his head, half drawing the pistol as he turned toward Jonas. He heard Simon take a quick step.

"Easy, now," Simon said. "Let's us not have any bother while Thoman's ailing. That's a right good idea, Grace. Gabe and Jonas and me, we'll be ready. Plum, the rest of you, come on along, now."

Movement sounded all around Silverhorn. He leaned

his head back against the rock and waited until it went away. Someone was still there, though, and he tightened his grip on the pistol's butt.

"Simon," Grace said. "He suspects."

"Suspects what?"

"Hold still. Let me look at that eye." She touched his face, put his head back, spread open the eyelids of his right eye. "Can you see anything at all?"

"Light, sometimes." Silverhorn tried to blink. "Shapes moving, all streaky and dark."

"It'll get better. Nothing wrong with it. It's what's happened to the other that's causing you your trouble." She paused a second, then said, "The other one's gone. That bullet put it plumb out."

"Red whore," Silverhorn growled. "Don't you think I know that?"

Grace chuckled. "Figured you did. I'll have Plum bring your horse up. When we get on the trail, I'll ride beside you, up ahead. The others won't know it's me finding the way." She waited a second, then said, "Thoman? Why do you call me red? You got as much Indian blood as me, and it ain't nothing to be ashamed of."

"Shut up." Bracing his hand against the rock, Silverhorn got to his feet. "We'll do just what you said. Get my horse up here, and be damned quick about it."

Ethan Fairchild woke when the rain stopped. He tried to read his watch but could not see the dial for a film of fog inside the crystal. If his spirits had been higher, he would have cursed. So far, the silly skirmish with Stuart had cost him his rifle, horse, gear, and watch. Their monetary value was beside the point; Ethan had lost a great deal of what he depended upon to survive in this wild land.

I'd rather've lost the money, he told himself. But he couldn't complain, even if there had been someone to listen. He still had his life.

He thought of Jessica Thorne. And my love, he thought.

I have the two things that are important. Yes, especially my love.

After a moment, he arranged his coat in a slightly less uncomfortable way and went back to sleep with the hope that full daylight would bring him the strength and the luck to catch up to the train. In his dreams, Stu and Jessie came to find him and feed him and bind his wounds and take him back to his warm, dry wagon.

He awakened next to a broad, flat world of shallow mud. No one had come to help or to hurt him. From the top of his rock, he could see neither movement nor footprint no matter which direction he looked. The sky was clear, a watery, washed-out blue with no hint of clouds. Squinting at the sun, Fairchild worked out where north had to be. He would walk north, toward the Platte. When he reached the riverbank and the trail, he would turn west, in the direction he'd last seen the train. Anywhere along the way, he should run into the search parties Manasseh Thorne was sure to send out. With tolerable luck, he would be back with Jessica in time for supper.

His first efforts to walk resulted in slides and falls in the slick black mud. Before he'd made a hundred yards, his hands and clothing were caked, and balls of mud clung to his boots, making each step an effort. Worse, the action of Stuart's repeating Colt rifle was packed with it. Fairchild forced himself to rest in the shade until the blazing morning sun had worked on the ground for a couple of hours. By mid-morning, his clothes and boots were halfway dry. He had cleaned the rifle with his hunting knife and a piece of his shirttail until there was some chance it would shoot. The footing was a little better, and he set off slowly and carefully. At any moment, he would meet a rescue party coming back east.

Partly for that reason and partly because the mud was still slippery beneath his feet, Fairchild walked slowly. Had he been cataloging reasons, he would have included the soreness in every muscle in his body. The going was slow. Twice he had to turn aside from gullies that still ran

bank-full with muddy water. He couldn't guess how far
the detours took him out of his way before he found a
place to cross, but it was past noon when finally he came
to the edge of the broken country and saw the braided
brown ribbon of the Platte below him. Far off on the eastern horizon, the dark spire of Chimney Rock lifted against
the sky.

With a whoop, Fairchild broke into a shambling run,
sliding and scrambling down toward the valley until he
reached the deep-cut ruts gouged by thousands of wagons.
His own had been among them, he knew, and soon he
would be back with it, with the train, with Jessie and the
others. To celebrate, he drank some water, then took a
good long time chewing a piece of jerky and trying not
to wonder why no one had come to help him. As he
trudged along between the ruts throughout the long afternoon he could not avoid wondering.

At sunset he began looking for a better place to camp
than he had found the night before. It was a cold camp.
His matches had gotten wet along with his watch and
powder and gear. He ate half of the last strip of jerky with
a great deal less certainty that he would not need the rest
of it. He was confident enough to eat one more stick of
peppermint.

By the time the sun was only a hazy pink memory in
the west, he had gone twice through a litany of explana-
tions for his situation. The darkest explanation was the
simplest and he feared the most likely.

David Stuart had not escaped from the Indians. The
Indians had killed him. No one had brought word back to
the train, so that they hadn't known anyone was missing
until the night camp. The explanation was a dismal one
indeed, and it did not satisfy Ethan. When neither he nor
Stuart appeared for supper, Jessica would surely have told
her father what had happened. Then Manasseh Thorne
would have sent a party back to look for them both.

Of course, they might have come back, might have
found Stu's body, might have carried it back to the train.

There would have been no prints, no trail back in Ethan's direction. That made sense, providing his body had been much closer to the train, so that the rescue party had not come any farther. Tomorrow, at the latest, Fairchild would come to that spot where Stuart had fallen, where others had come on horseback to find him. At least tomorrow he would get past the unmarked plain of mud, would find someone's tracks.

He tried to sleep, but the thoughts wouldn't leave him. Even should he fail to find tracks, he would know which direction to take to catch up to the train. Making twelve or fifteen miles a day at the most, it had as little chance of outdistancing him as a lumbering buffalo had of outrunning a wolf. As soon as he was back on the trail, with better walking, he would catch up easily.

Still. The doubts niggled at his mind. Stuart might have lost his mount, might be dragging through the mud somewhere not too far from Fairchild. But no. That did not explain the absence of a rescue party. Had a party found Stu, he would have told them where to look for Ethan.

Could something have happened to the train? He did not want to imagine it. What could possibly have happened to immobilize the wagons and their outriders? The Indians? A tornado that dropped out of the clouds and struck the wagons? A huge crack in the earth that swallowed them up?

"That's crazy."

The sound of his own voice startled him, and somehow made the night seem quieter, more lonely than before. He knew his thoughts weren't making sense. He felt chilled, and he wondered if he was feverish. It was a new nightmare to imagine coming on the ruins of those wagons. He could not dwell on it for fear of Jessica Thorne's having been in such a storm.

Why—if no one else came looking—why had she not come on her hands and knees in search of him? He knew that he would have done so for her.

But that was silly. Why should she come alone in the

mud? And why would her father allow it? Fairchild laughed. The wagonmaster would shed no tears over Fairchild or Stuart, either. He guarded his daughter as if he never intended her to marry! Did that mean that Thorne would forbid any member of the train to backtrack in search of the two of them?

The whirling circle of thoughts filled Fairchild's mind well past midnight. Even after that, he slept poorly. He ached, his cuts and abrasions were festering, and even in sleep, his mind churned with fantastic dreams.

There, he acknowledged another explanation for being left alone in the land: The Indians might have been a larger party than he saw, they might have chased Stu into another gang of them, the whole group might have attacked the train. Each time that scene insinuated itself into his mind, he woke and sat upright. And each time, his mind was merciful enough to offer no memory of the dark screaming dream of the loss of his love.

He woke before daylight and ate half of the rest of his jerky. Following that regimen, he figured he would always have some of it left. The thought failed to amuse him. He slung his gear, shouldered his rifle, and set out walking with the determination to find signs of the train before dark.

Twice he saw antelope watching him, immobile as statues, pronged horns lifted in curiosity until they recognized his man-shape against the light and bounded away. He wouldn't starve. He could hunt, dry his matches, build a fire. But he would do none of those things while there was a chance he might overtake the wagons.

At noon he was still strong enough in spirit to believe that he would find the train or its ashes. In the dying ebb of sunset, he found tracks in the dried smooth mud where wagons had turned aside to make camp, the prints of dozens of oxen, the blackened circles of cooking fires. He sank down on a rock, glad that one fear at least had been laid to rest. The train was all right. Thorne and the others had camped here not more than two nights past.

Then why didn't they come back for me?

Against the glimmer of twilight he found part of an answer. Planted off at one side of the abandoned campsite stood a two-foot-tall wooden cross. At first, he didn't notice it in particular. There were many grave markers along the trail. His own train had contributed two, one for Sam Kenny at the Big Blue, and one for little Ella Lee, dead of a fever where they'd first struck the Platte. But this marker was new, Fairchild saw, the dirt around its base fresh turned after the rain.

"So," he said. His unused voice was dry, husky, cracking, grieving. "So! The Indians did get poor Stu."

Had Fairchild been thinking of himself at the moment, he might have supposed that the party believed him dead as well. The thought might have explained the exodus of the wagon train. But Ethan Fairchild was not thinking of himself. He was thinking of David Stuart, thinking of a fine young man brought down to death by savages, thinking of the ceremony which must have surrounded that grave. Then as he neared the cross, he saw that the ground had not been disturbed. Instead of a grave, there was nothing but an arm of the sea of dried mud.

Off to the east, a voice called a command. Riders were coming along the trail, a dozen at least. Fairchild looked up in search of the faces of his companions, perhaps even of Jessica Thorne. But the faces, what he could see of them in the half-light, were unknown to him. They looked hard and suspicious. He snapped to alertness, gripping the Colt rifle with both hands. It was just like a revolver with a very long barrel. He looked for cover, didn't find any, stood his ground, holding the rifle.

"Detail—halt!"

The lead rider stared at Fairchild, then looked carefully out toward the buttes, then toward the straggling willows along the river. He spoke quietly, and the men behind him spread into a line, facing Fairchild. The leader left the others and rode forward. He was bearded, dusty, streaked with the same mud that caked Fairchild's face and hands.

But underneath the mud and dust, his trousers had been light blue, the coat darker blue and faced with orange. Fairchild gaped at him like a child seeing an elephant for the first time.

"Thank God," he croaked. "You're the Army."

The stranger's bearded face split in a grin, which vanished as suddenly as it had appeared. "Some of it," he conceded, reining in a dozen paces away. "Cranfill, Oscar. Lieutenant commanding this detachment of the Second Regiment of Dragoons. You are?"

"Ethan Fairchild. My God, Lieutenant, but I'm glad to see you. Have you heard anything about my train?"

The officer raised a hand. "One thing at a time, Mr. Fairchild," he said. "If you're so pleased to see us, suppose you put down your rifle. Then we can talk."

"Oh." Feeling foolish, Fairchild let the Colt's barrel sag until it pointed at the ground. He remembered to lower the hammer to half-cock, then looked up into Cranfill's haggard face. "Sorry. Thought at first you were some of them that jumped us."

Cranfill leaned forward, suspicion glinting in his eyes. Fairchild realized the lieutenant wasn't much past his own age, but there was a spring-steel tension about the officer's movements that suggested he was a veteran even so.

" 'Us,' you say." Cranfill glanced around again. "Where are your companions, Mr. Fairchild? And your horse?"

"Lost," Fairchild said. "They killed my comp—my friend, David Stuart. And they killed my horse. Only it wasn't mine, Stu got away on him, and it was his they killed." Fairchild stopped, frowning as he thought over what he'd said. He could feel himself getting tangled in his own words, and he shook his head wearily. "Look, Lieutenant, this is going to take a lot of telling. Might you have some food? And maybe a cup of coffee you could spare?"

For a moment longer, Cranfill studied him. Then he turned abruptly.

"Sergeant, bring the detail in. We'll camp here for the

night. Picket the animals and get sentries on that rise to the south." Turning back toward Fairchild, he smiled, but the suspicion was still in his eyes. "And see about getting Mr. Fairchild something to eat."

"Indians, you say?" Lieutenant Cranfill filled a briar pipe without haste, then took a twig from the fire to puff it into life. "What tribe?"

Fairchild shrugged. He didn't like the question or its tone or the fact that two or three of the Dragoons, without making any big point of it, were always near him, watching. But he'd had two plates of the Army's salt pork and beans and all the strong sweet coffee he could drink and a chance to warm himself by the lieutenant's squad fire. He figured he owed a few answers in return.

"I don't know one Indian from another. And I didn't have a hell of a lot of time to study them." He held his tin cup out to Sergeant Neidercutt, who was pouring coffee from a mess tin. "Any more of that, Sergeant?"

The sergeant pushed his wide-brimmed civilian hat back and spat off to one side. "Sure thing," he said, filling Fairchild's cup. "If all them hundreds of Indians couldn't kill you, I expect a gallon of Army coffee won't."

"Seven or eight, you said." The lieutenant still stared at Fairchild. "Indians, you said. Can you describe any individual in the group?"

Fairchild wrapped his hands around the hot metal of the cup. He hadn't realized how cold he'd been until he had the chance to get warm. Closing his eyes, he tried again to picture the confused seconds that followed the first shot.

"I can." He opened his eyes, looked at Cranfill. "By damn, Lieutenant, I can! One of them had white hair—long, and flowing loose."

Neidercutt murmured something to the lieutenant, spat again. Cranfill nodded.

"Any others you recall?"

"What I recall," Fairchild said, "is forty others, members of the wagon train I was on. If I could get a horse from you, I'd like to report to them."

"The group you saw attacked an armed emigrant party? Forty strong? How many did you say were in the war party?"

"I said six or seven, but I didn't count them. They were shooting at me. I'm pretty sure there were more. No, they didn't attack the train. Not that I know of. I was a rear flanker."

The lieutenant puffed his pipe while he thought about that. "Was there a woman in the group?" he asked finally.

"A woman? I didn't see one." Then he stopped, puzzled. "But I think maybe I heard one. I think maybe she killed my horse."

The sergeant rubbed his stubbly chin and turned away. Fairchild heard murmurs from the Dragoons nearest him, felt a sudden tightening in the air. Lieutenant Cranfill tapped his pipe against the sole of his boot to knock out the ashes.

"Is that a fact?" His voice was very casual. "Where'd you see them last?"

"I saw them last coming straight damn at me, that's where!" Slinging the cup aside, Fairchild stood up quickly. "Then they shot my horse, and then I fell and didn't see anything else for quite a spell. Then I knew they'd killed my friend, and gone on to do God knows what to the train, and you won't tell me a damned thing about it!"

He wheeled toward Cranfill, only to look straight into the muzzle of Sergeant Neidercutt's long-barreled Colt pistol. From either side, a pair of burly privates grabbed his arms. Fairchild struggled for a second, then realized the futility and willed himself to stillness.

"Look," he said to Cranfill, "it's obvious you don't believe me. Why don't we stop this nonsense? I want to get some sleep and get an early start to catch up to my people in the morning."

Cranfill lifted a hand. "I believe you, Mr. Fairchild," he said. "Certainly I believe the descriptions you gave us are accurate. The fact is, we've been pursuing the very pack of wolves you describe. The sergeant thinks you might be one of them who got separated from the main party."

Fairchild looked at the sergeant, who still held his pistol ready. "Listen, Lieutenant," he began, "if you believe that—"

"If I believe that, we'd be burying you over by that other grave right now," Cranfill cut in, his voice cold and level. "But I haven't decided." He gestured to the troopers, who released Fairchild's arms and stepped back. "I don't think we'll need your revolver, Sergeant. Now, Mr. Fairchild, if you'll sit down, I have another question or two."

"Do I have any choice?"

Cranfill smiled. "Very damned little," he said. "This friend of yours, Stuart. What makes you think he's dead?"

Hunkering down again by the fire, Fairchild waved a hand around. "You don't see him, do you? If he was alive, he would've come back for me." *Of course, I thought the same about my friends from the train.* "I figure that marker over there is his, although you gentlemen interrupted me before I got a chance to look."

"I see."

"I damn well hope you do! Look, I've got a little money on me, maybe enough to buy a horse."

"Beggin' the lieutenant's pardon," Neidercutt interrupted softly. He had walked over to the wooden cross. Now he stood behind it, his eyes searching Fairchild's face. "What does this citizen say his name is, again?"

"Fairchild, Sergeant. Ethan Fairchild."

Neidercutt spat reflectively. "Ethan Fairchild," he said. "You sure? You sure it ain't maybe Lazarus?"

"I'm sure."

"What is it, Sergeant?" Cranfill interrupted.

"If the lieutenant would step over here, sir, I got me a marvel to show him." When Fairchild started to rise, the sergeant touched the butt of the Colt. "You just sit tight, Lazarus. We'll see about you in a minute."

Looking puzzled, Cranfill strode over to stand beside his sergeant. He looked down at the marker, and his face creased into a grin.

"Marvel, indeed," he murmured. "We might even say a miracle!" Looking up, he motioned to Fairchild. "Step over here, please. Maybe you can explain something to us."

Fairchild joined the two soldiers beside the rough cross, mystified by their words and the way they stared at him.

"Sure you don't want to give us another name, Citizen?"

"Strange as it might seem to you, Sergeant, I know who *my* parents were."

Neidercutt nodded. "They teach you to read?" he asked.

"Middling well."

The sergeant stepped back and gestured at the cross. "Then read us that, Lazarus," he said.

Fairchild bent to peer at the smooth wooden face of the cross. He was taken first by the fine clear lettering which he recognized as Jessica Thorne's. In the dancing firelight, he had a little trouble making out the inscription. Then a trooper threw an armful of sage on the nearest fire, and Fairchild stared in blank disbelief as the words leaped out at him:

> *In Loving Mem'ry*
> *ETHAN FAIRCHILD*
> *Born Pike County Ohio April 7 1839*
> *Killed by Indians June 26 1859*

6

           "I am the resurrection, and the life," Manasseh Thorne intoned. "He that believeth in me, though he were dead, yet shall he live: and whosoever lievth and believeth in me shall never die."

Gathered around the wooden cross in the first gray light of dawn, the people of the train gave a collective sigh. Thorne raised his eyes from the pages of the prayer book, frowning through his wire-rimmed spectacles.

"Our departed brother, Ethan Fairchild, lived by those words. We can't give him the Christian burial he deserves, but we mark his passing and pay our respects today, confident we will meet him again in that happy day of resurrection."

And what will I say to Ethan on that happy day? David Stuart asked himself grimly. *Sorry, Ethan. Sorry I got you killed with my damn-fool wanting to fight. Sorry I played the coward and left you. But it's turned out all right. No hard feelings.*

He bowed his head to hide a sudden impulse to smile. He had a pretty good idea how Ethan would answer that. Chances were, Stuart would wind up standing before the golden throne with a black eye and a split lip.

Wish you were here to give it to me, Ethan, he thought. As God's my witness, I wouldn't even hit back!

"—in the sure and certain hope—"

Raising his head carefully, Stuart sought Jessica Thorne's eye. But Jess stood beside her mother, her blond head bowed, too lost in her own misery to notice Stuart's.

It was natural for her to grieve over Ethan, Stuart reminded himself. Like Stuart, Ethan had been her friend, her suitor. In fact, over the past few weeks, Ethan had seemed to have the inside track with her, and it had been Stuart's blind anger over feeling her slip away that had driven him to fight.

But he must have been wrong. He, David Stuart, had been the one she'd come to last night, the one to whom she'd pledged her love, the one she'd wanted to marry soon, very soon.

"Tom, will you lead us in a hymn?"

The mournful notes of Long Tom Lee's fiddle startled Stuart. He hadn't realized Thorne was finished. His eyes still on Jessica's pale face, he sang with the others:

> Softly now the light of day
> Fades upon my sight away:
> Free from care, from labor free,
> Lord, I would commune with thee.

Jess lifted her head, and her blue eyes, wet with tears, locked on Stuart's. Her face was still. He wondered if she'd slept, and how much. He knew she'd been up early, earlier even that he, dipping a brush into a pail of tar used to caulk the wagons and inscribing Ethan's name and dates on the cross. It was all Stuart could do to keep from reaching out to her, but that wouldn't be right. Not here.

> Thou whose all-pervading eye
> Nought escapes without, within,
> Pardon each infirmity,
> Open fault and secret sin.

He saw Jess flinch on the last line, and her eyes wavered from his. Crying quietly, she pulled her shawl tighter around her shaking shoulders and bowed her head again.

She had to be thinking of him, of his open fault in leaving Ethan. And there were some who believed it was secret sin, who still suspected he'd murdered Ethan or abandoned him to die. Stuart had seen how the others in the train looked at him during the service. Some—his uncle Douglas, of course, Francis Buttrell, lanky Lije Holden—had made a point of standing with him. A few, like Caleb Sugarhouse and Milt Ames, were equally pointed about crossing to the other side.

"Let us pray," Manasseh Thorne said.

In the same tones he might have used to urge a reluctant ox, Thorne invoked God to welcome His servant Ethan Fairchild, to bless those still on the trail, to shelter them from Indians and pestilence, to guide them safely and rapidly through the wilderness.

"Amen," Stuart said with the others. Standing to one side with his pipes under his arm, Uncle Douglas began "Amazing Grace." To its tune, the emigrants started back to their wagons, a straggling procession with Thorne leading the way like a drum major.

"It's blessed near sunup," Thorne said to everyone in general. "Light's already on the buttes. Caleb, Doc Harris, it's your time on point. A couple of you Buttrells take the flanks. Time we were moving. Lije—"

Lagging behind her mother, Jessica Thorne fell into step beside Stuart. He leaned near to hear what she was saying under cover of Thorne's bellowing and the wailing of the bagpipes.

"I'm glad." Her voice threatened to break, and she stopped and swallowed. "It sounds awful to say it, but I'm glad that's done. It's over now. Now I can face it that Ethan's really—"

"Gone," Stuart finished for her, but she shook her head.

"No. Not gone. Ethan's dead. That's what I can face." She reached out and took his hand. "Ethan's dead and the rest of us have to go on."

Stuart squeezed her hand. He heard the angry muttered comment of somebody behind him. Not all the words reached him, but it was near enough to what Milt Ames had said the day before.

"—got Fairchild's horse and his gun, and it looks like

he's on his way to taking his woman, too."

Jess heard it, too. He could tell by the way she ducked her head, by the faint flush that lighted her cheeks.

"Jess, you know what people will think. If you want more time before we marry, I'll understand."

She shook her head. "No. I don't care what people think," she said with desperate intensity. "That's what Ethan's dying tells us. We don't know how much time there is. We can't afford to wait, not for anything." Half turning, she looked at him. "If you meant what you said last night. If you want to marry me."

"I'll talk to your father today. Fort Laramie's less than a week away. We can be married there."

"Jessica!" Manasseh Thorne called. "Get along, girl, you've got chores! Fine thing, if the wagonmaster's wagon is the last one ready to roll!"

Jess laughed softly and squeezed his hand. To Stuart, it seemed she was making the laugh a secret, just between the two of them. Then she released him and hurried away, while he turned toward his uncle's wagon. An hour later, with Thorne complaining vigorously because they'd not yet put a mile behind them, the train crept into line, shook itself out like a many-jointed snake, and rolled away west with the early sun at its back.

David Stuart sat astride Ethan's sorrel horse flanking the string of wagons. Just as if nothing had ever happened to Ethan, he thought, just as if this were my horse and my rifle. As if Jess had been mine when Ethan was alive.

He let it go. That train of thought would not take him anywhere he wanted to be. He thought instead of the future, and the future was a far brighter place than the past. He and Jess were, after all, going to be married. He was certain of it, though Jessica's father had shown no great enthusiasm for the idea. Stuart had spoken to him the very day he'd promised Jess, at the noon halt.

"Marriage? You and Jessica?"

"Yes, sir. At Fort Laramie, if there's someone there to perform the service."

"You've discussed this with Jessica?"

"Yes, sir."

"Have you, by God!" Manasseh Thorne's sunburned face grew a little redder, but he kept his voice low. Stuart understood. One of the things he hated about the train was the lack of privacy. Someone was always around. There was seldom a chance for a truly private talk, for an hour alone with a sweetheart.

Not even for a good fight, Stuart thought, tightening his lips. Not without leaving the train. Not without getting someone killed.

"I suppose she's entirely in favor of this—this madness," Thorne said.

"I believe she is, sir. She wanted to come with me to talk to you." Stuart hesitated, then shrugged and finished, "But I judged it better to face you alone."

Thorne glared at him for a moment. Then, slowly, his expression changed. He stroked his beard while his mouth struggled with a smile. "You did, did you?" he growled. "Thought you'd bell the cat yourself?"

"Yes, sir."

Thorne nodded. "Well, that's a sign of some gumption, anyway," he said. Then, as if he'd just thought of the question, he asked, "How do you propose to support my daughter, young man?"

"Well, I've learned a fair amount of gunsmithing from my uncle. I'd intended to go on as his apprentice for a while."

"I doubt you'd earn enough that way to support yourself and Jessica."

Stuart nodded. "Since talking with Jess, I've had another thought. You said something earlier about selling Ethan's wagon and goods at Fort Laramie."

"Yes," Thorne said after a moment. "There'll be mail service from the fort. Since Fairchild has no kin with the train, I'd thought to send the money back to his family. I mean to write them about his death."

"I'll match the best offer you get for the wagon and team," Stuart said. "If it's more than my savings, Uncle Douglas has agreed to advance me the rest. Ethan's farming tools will give me a start when we get to Oregon."

"You're not a farmer."

"I can be."

Thorne frowned and combed his fingers through his beard. Stuart suspected he was thinking of what Sugarhouse or Ames might say about that. *First his horse and rifle, then his woman, now his wagon and team. Surprised Stuart didn't pocket that wooden cross we set for Ethan, too.*

If that was on Thorne's mind, he didn't say so. "It's not a matter to be decided in a heartbeat," he said finally. "I'll think on it."

Stuart started to say more, then nodded. Thorne would have to think fast, but there was nothing to be gained by saying that nor by telling Thorne he meant to marry Jess no matter what the decision was.

That was how he'd left it with Thorne. After three days, that was where things still stood. For those three days, Stuart had ridden flanker like a schoolboy living for recess. He burned to be with Jessica Thorne, to tell her his thoughts and hopes and dreams. To his delight, she took every opportunity to seek him out, just as if she too had been anxious for recess. While he was with her, Stuart could think of nothing but Jessica. And while he was riding the flank, he grew fearful that such great happiness could not last.

And yet it lasted.

When he was alone he planned and rehearsed what he would say to her when he saw her next. When he saw her next he forgot some of his words. He was clumsy and stupid, regretful and anxious. He cursed himself for his forgetfulness. But Jess accepted every word and idea and protestation of love, and she seemed to expect no more than he brought her. At times he was struck dumb with fear that God was mocking him. Stuart knew it could not last.

And still it had lasted, until the day he'd been waiting for was almost there.

Stuart reined in the sorrel to look back on the plodding wagons. He didn't have much longer to wait. Thorne didn't have long to finish his thinking.

Ahead, the land rose and fell in grass-covered slopes that looked gentle until someone tried to drive a wagon up them. Off to the southwest, flat-topped hills rose tier on tier until they became the looming bulk of the Laramie Mountains, naked rock rising blue-gray above slopes black with pines. Tonight, Stuart knew, the train would camp not far short of Laramie Crossing, with the fort and his wedding just beyond.

As silently as ever she could, Jessica Thorne slipped from the tent where she normally slept. Her parents were in the wagon, and she stood motionless beside it, listening. She knew her father often lay wakeful, but tonight she heard his gentle snoring. She pulled her blanket tight around her shoulders, partly for protection from the thin night wind, but mostly to hide her white nightdress. Then she crept on silent feet around the circle of wagons.

The night was far along. The moon had set already, and all the stars God had ever made shone overhead. But Jessica took no time to look at the heavens. There was something she had to do, now, tonight, before she let Davy marry her in ignorance.

Once she froze as she heard voices. After a moment, she located the sound out on the far fringe of the circle. A sulfur match flared yellow, waxed and flickered above the bowl of a pipe, went out. In its momentary glow, she recognized Caleb Sugarhouse, on watch with another man she couldn't see. She heard them laugh together at whatever Sugarhouse had said, and then they moved across the skyline and out of her sight.

Shivering, she huddled motionless for a minute or more. Sugarhouse or the other man might come back. Someone else might be awake. Maybe she should go back. If anyone saw her, realized what she was doing . . . !

Coward, she scolded herself. She went on. Davy was sleeping in the wagon that had belonged to Ethan Fairchild. He'd told her all about it, how he planned to buy the wagon and tools, how they would get land in Oregon, how he could farm until something better opened up, how they would be happy together.

Before her resolve could fail her, she put her foot on the iron step and swung lightly up and through the curtain into the wagon. She crouched there for a second, her eyes adjusting to the greater darkness inside. Then she heard Stuart moan.

"No!" His voice was muffled and indistinct, barely loud enough for her to hear. "Ethan!" Then in another voice, "Come back. Don't leave me!"

Moving swiftly to his side, she knelt on the edge of the down comforter that was his bed. "Davy." She shook his shoulder. "Davy, wake up."

He rolled away, flailed an arm at the entangling blankets, stared up at her wildly. "Ethan," he said again. Then he blinked. In the starlight from the half-open curtain she saw his soul come back into his eyes. "Jess. I was dreaming." He reached out to touch her, and suddenly he was awake. "Jess! What are you doing here?"

She pressed her fingers to his lips. "Shhh. I had to talk to you, before tomorrow."

"But if anyone hears you, there won't be a tomorrow!"

"No one will hear." Irrationally, she felt an urge to giggle. "Anyway, we're an old engaged couple now." She bit her lip. "Davy, there's something I have to tell you."

Raising himself on one elbow, he took her hands in his. "You're freezing," he whispered. "Jess, don't you have a lick of sense? What's so important that it couldn't wait?"

She'd thought about how to tell him. The words weren't hard. She'd taken them right from her Bible, from the parts Martha Thorne clucked her tongue over, and she'd practiced them in her head. *Davy, Ethan and I lay together one night along the trail. I think I'm with child.* But now that the moment was here, she couldn't think how to say them. "Davy, it's about Ethan."

"You, too?" Stuart lay back in his blankets, putting his forearm across his eyes. "I was dreaming about him, Jess," he said. "It's the same dream, most every night. He's hurt, and reaching out to me, and I want to help him." He drew in a long breath through his teeth. "And then I ride away and leave him."

"Davy, don't," Jessica said. He looked up at her.

"Jess, it didn't happen that way. I swear to God it didn't, no matter what anybody thinks. But things like that hymn we sang when you put up his marker. Things like that make me feel guilty when I'm not. But if you don't want to marry me, now you know it, I'll understand."

"Oh, Davy." She put her arms around him and bowed her head against his chest. She'd thought it would be so easy. She would say her words, and she'd accept whatever names he called her, and she wouldn't cry. She knew her tears were hot against his skin. "Davy, it isn't that. I never thought that, never."

Then his arms came around her, drawing her body into him. His lips sought her blindly, kissing her hair, her wet eyes, her cheeks, finally her mouth, with a mounting hunger she'd never expected from quiet, reliable Davy Stuart. For just an instant, filled with doubt and fear, she hung back.

I have to tell him.

You can't!

All right, I can't. But I can do this.

She let go, freely, without reserve, hearing him swear he would love her always, hearing herself answer that she would never leave him, never harm him, never betray him if only he would love her, marry her. With hands as eager and clumsy as his, she helped draw aside the barriers of blanket and nightdress and clothing between them, imagining she could feel the barriers of fear and doubt and past memory falling as well. As his body pressed hers down onto the comforter, she clung to him, knowing she had been wrong about one thing. She had thought she would have to pretend, but when the moment came, she didn't.

7

"Hey, Dead Man!" A booted toe nudged at Fairchild's ribs. "Roll out for morning stables, farm boy. You're in the Army now."

"Like hell," Fairchild muttered, but he rolled out of his lone bed on the prairie grass and pulled on his boots. Around him, the Dragoon camp was stirring into life, urged on by Sergeant Neidercutt. Like the troopers around him, Fairchild folded his blanket and laid it across the saddle that had served him as a pillow. Digging into the Army-issue saddlebags, he found a brush and currycomb and went to catch his horse.

"You're in luck, Mr. Fairchild," Cranfill had told him the morning after the Dragoons found him. "Normally, we wouldn't have an extra mount, but we can shift the loads around on our pack animals and free one of them for you to ride."

"You have an extra saddle, too?"

Cranfill looked at him for a moment, then nodded. "As it happens, we do," he said.

His tone didn't encourage questions, so Fairchild didn't ask any. "I'm obliged to you," he said. "I figure I can catch up to my party in a couple of days with a good horse under me. I'll be glad to pay you what I have, and the rest as soon as I get back to my wagon."

"I'm sorry, but you'll have to put off going after your train. You'll ride along with us."

Fairchild shook his head. "I've got my wagon, friends, my girl to catch up to."

"That can wait a little while."

"*I* can't wait! Look, if you don't want to sell me a horse, I'll walk. I was doing all right before I met you."

"You were being stalked by a half-dozen young Cheyenne braves," Cranfill said. "The Indians along here are pretty well peaceful, but a man alone is always a temptation. They were moving along that ridge to the south, waiting for a chance to take you without losing any men. They rode off when they saw us."

Fairchild looked at the ridge, wondering if what the lieutenant said could be true. It didn't really matter, he decided. He had to get back. "You don't understand. My people, my fiancée, they all think I'm dead."

"If you try to go on alone, they'll damned well be right," Cranfill said. His voice hardened. "You will accompany our patrol until we reach Fort Laramie. Then I'll turn you and your story over to the commanding officer, and he will no doubt send you on your way with apologies. Is that clear?"

Fairchild shook his head. "You can't take me with you."

"Sergeant Neidercutt," Cranfill said.

"Sir."

"Mr. Fairchild will ride with us. Be sure he doesn't stray from the column during the march." Cranfill gave Fairchild a level look. "If he strays more than fifty yards, shoot him off his horse as you would a deserter."

"Yes, sir. With pleasure, sir."

"Shoot?" *With pleasure?*

"I hope you won't expect too much, Mr. Fairchild," Cranfill said with a thin smile. "Government mounts aren't the best in the world, and the pack animals are pretty near the bottom even of that barrel."

"I'll take care he gets the best of the lot, sir," Neidercutt said. The little sergeant spat on the ground and squinted at Fairchild. "You ride up ahead, Dead Man, just off to the right of the guidon. And remember, if I ain't got my eye on you, there's a dozen troopers that will have. Try not to stray."

Whatever else the sergeant might be, Fairchild thought as he settled in to curry the chestnut Neidercutt had picked for him, he was a good judge of horses. In only a few days, Fairchild had learned to hate this particular horse with quiet intensity. He was pretty certain that every trooper in the Army had rejected it as a mount.

The chestnut had one walled eye, a nasty disposition, and the keen intelligence to find that gait which would be most uncomfortable for its rider at any given moment. As he put aside the currying tools to spread the blanket on its back, it twisted like a snake to snap at his shoulder. Dispassionately, he clouted it across the nose and went back to arranging the blanket so it wouldn't gall.

"Hey, Dead One, you've a way with horses." Trooper Healy left off currying his tall black gelding to grin at Fairchild. "That plug would've killed any one of us by now."

"Grew up with horses," Fairchild said. "Back at home, we didn't groom them hardly as much as the Army does, though."

"Hah!" That was Schmidt, a round-faced German private who wore a bristling blond Dragoon moustache and a perpetual frown. "Likely you vould if your life depended on it, yah? Ve love these horses like they vas our brothers and sweethearts, yah?"

"There's truth in that, Dutch," Fairchild conceded, heaving his borrowed Grimsley saddle up and into place. In his time with the patrol, the troopers had accepted him with surprising ease. He didn't doubt any one of them would shoot him if the situation required, but in the meantime they were pleasant enough. Passing along the line to inspect horses and gear, even Neidercutt seemed as if he would no longer shoot Fairchild "with pleasure."

"That's good work for a Dead Man," he growled, tugging at the chestnut's cinch. He grabbed the bridle to look closely at the animal's eyes, then moved to check the fit of the saddle blanket. "You'll never gall a horse's back that way. Wish you could teach it to some of our recruits." He raised his voice. "All right, fall out. Ten minutes for breakfast, and then we're moving."

Later, Fairchild rode a dozen yards behind the guidon, conscious of eyes always on his back, while the patrol kept up a steady, monotonous pace. The column strung itself out to lessen the dust, the men talking or smoking as they chose. Fairchild didn't think it looked very military, but it did cover ground.

Lieutenant Cranfill, with occasional advice from Neidercutt or from the black-eyed Delaware scout, seemed to know exactly where he was going. And evidently he did. Three times they'd come upon the ashes of campfires, the droppings and trodden grass where horses had been picketed. And even Fairchild could see that the trail was growing fresher.

Try as he might, he could not see the tracks they apparently were following. All he could see was dust and deep rippling prairie grass that shifted from gray to green to brownish-gold as the arid west wind swept across it. Occasional deep-cut creek beds, dry and rocky, crossed their path, while the blue shadow of mountains grew daily larger and more solid ahead of them.

As nearly as he could tell, he'd been riding steadily southwest. Far enough, he thought, from the due west that would have taken him back toward the wagon train where his thoughts rested most of the time. Those thoughts had kept him awake much of each night he'd been with the Dragoons.

Even during the day, as he rode the mean-spirited horse, he considered the dozen actions Jessica might take now that she thought him dead. None of the actions was pleasant to contemplate. He had tried to convince himself that she would not do any of those things before he could catch up to the train. But he wasn't convinced.

"Hey, Dead One." Healy had ridden up alongside him, startling him out of his brooding. "Better wake up. We're likely to close up on them we're after pretty quick."

Fairchild raised his head, feeling a little hope. "What makes you think so?" he asked.

"Been gaining on them right steady." Healy swept a hand toward the mountains rising ahead. "They'll cut north or south before they've reached the Laramies. Less'n they want to be caught on open ground, they'll try and shake us off first."

"Suppose they don't? Suppose they go straight to the mountains?"

Healy grinned. "With luck, they'll do just that. Then we can go our way to Fort Laramie and leave them to the Sioux."

"Fort Laramie," Fairchild murmured. "That's where the train will be. Where my girl will be."

The flaxen-maned chestnut horse, sensing its rider's momentary inattention, threw its head back sharply into Fairchild's face. Fairchild curbed it hard, and it ducked and twisted to bite at his calf. For a few seconds, he forgot Healy, the patrol, the train, even Jessica, while he brought the dancing, balky animal under control. When the chestnut at last fell back into ranks with deceptive obedience, Fairchild looked up to find Healy's eyes on him.

"This nag would make a good cover for somebody's saddle," Fairchild said. "If your lieutenant will let me, I'll do the skinning myself."

Healy waved a hand as if to shoo away the words. "That tale you've been telling us all about your friend and your sweetheart and the Indians," the trooper said, frowning a little. "There's a bit of truth in it, then?"

"What? Yes, gospel truth, Healy. I'll prove it when we get to the fort." Fairchild was silent a moment, thinking.

"I still can't understand what made my people think I'm dead."

"Can you not?" The trooper paused to wipe his face with his orange neckcloth. He started to speak again, then shook his head.

"What is it?" Fairchild asked.

"Nothing, most likely."

"You've got something on your mind, Healy. If you still think I'm one of those damned raiders—"

"Oh, no," the trooper said quickly. "It's not that."

"But it's something. If you know something that would help, I'd be grateful to hear it."

Healy rode in silence for a minute or more. Fairchild waited. Finally, the Dragoon gave him a troubled look.

"That friend of yours, your best friend, as you said?"

"David Stuart. The raiders must have run him down and killed him. Else he would've come back for me."

"So you've said. But you'd fought with him."

"That's how they were able to sneak up on us."

"Over a woman."

"Yes."

"And those pilgrims who left your grave marker standing on the plain left none for him."

"That doesn't prove anything." Fairchild heard his own voice rising defensively. With an effort, he took a more reasonable tone. "Probably they buried him where they found his body. And they didn't look for me because . . ." He couldn't think of any way to finish that sentence. "Because they were sure I was dead, too," he said finally.

"Sure and that's probably the way of it," Healy agreed. He patted his big black on the neck and started to rein away.

Fairchild knew he should let the trooper go, but he couldn't stop himself from putting out a hand. "But you don't think so?"

"It's not my business. Some of the boys, around the campfire by night, they don't think so."

"What do they think?"

For a second longer, Healy hesitated. Then he shrugged. "Isn't it likely that this Stuart was glad enough to see you fall?" he asked. "Or that he didn't wait to question his luck, but raced straight back to the train?"

"Stu wouldn't do that!"

"And left you to have your bones picked on the plains?" Healy wiped his face again, then finished, "I'd bet he's there now, giving comfort to your sweetheart for her loss."

Fairchild leaned across and grabbed the Dragoon's shoulder. "You can't talk that way about my friend! He'd never pull a low, sneaking trick like that!"

Healy reined away from the clutching hand. The chestnut snorted and edged around, baring its teeth at Healy's black horse.

"I'd not have said anything, but that you asked," Healy said.

"Well, don't say anything else."

"Silence in the ranks!"

Cranfill's command rang down the column like a bugle call. A moment later, Sergeant Neidercutt wheeled his horse and came trotting back down the line, drawing up beside Fairchild and Healy.

"Healy, get out on the point and relieve Jenkins. Keep a sharp eye. We'll halt for nooning a ways up Lodgepole Creek." He watched as Healy spurred away, then said, "You, Fairchild, what's wrong here?"

Fairchild started to complain about Healy, then bit it back. "Nothing," he said at last.

Neidercutt spat in the dust. "Too much time at a walk," he said. "Makes a column nervous, men and horses, too— especially that devil of yours." He stood in his stirrups and cupped a hand to his mouth. "Permission to trot, Lieutenant?"

"At the trot, ho!" Cranfill's voice floated back.

As the chestnut jolted into a bone-jarring trot, the sergeant motioned to Fairchild. "Close up on the front of the column, Dead Man," he called. "I want you handy when trouble starts. And leave your rifle in its boot until I tell you different, understand?"

"Yes, Sergeant."

Fairchild spurred ahead and fell into place on Neidercutt's flank. He had to post the trot to keep the horse from shaking him to death. His calves and thighs, unused to the strain, began to tighten and ache. Fairchild hardly noticed. His thoughts were turned inside, toward Healy's words and the mark they'd left on his mind.

"I don't believe it!" he muttered, loud enough to draw a suspicious glance from Neidercutt. "I don't believe it. Not Stu. Nor Jess. I won't believe it of either of them."

The singing prairie wind carried the words away. "Well, I don't," he repeated, trying to make the words sound convincing. "I don't believe it."

He was grateful when Cranfill, after a mile or so, raised his arm to signal the column back to a horse-saving walk. Another mile went by with no apparent change in the landscape. Then, as if a great plow had turned a single furrow across the prairie, the land opened suddenly into a shallow, winding valley, bordered by steep, rocky-topped buttes and ridges. A stream ran swift and clear down its middle—Lodgepole Creek, Fairchild supposed.

Cranfill halted the troopers right at the rim. They dismounted, smoked, drank in swigs from their canteens, ate quick bites of bacon saved from breakfast—all without taking their eyes off the green floor of the valley. The scout and flankers came galloping back to the head of the column.

"Same tracks." The Delaware scout spoke first. "Nine, ten horses, going easy. Maybe two hours, maybe four." He pushed back the wide brim of his Mexican hat and nodded toward the creek. "Good cover. They maybe stop, wait, shoot us when we come along."

"Begging the lieutenant's pardon," Healy put in, "but I thought I saw a bit of smoke when first we came over that rise back there. It was gone before I could make sure."

The lieutenant nodded. "Thanks, Healy." He didn't look at any of them. He was studying the valley floor. "Boyce, what's it like upstream?"

"Looks like the valley narrows down, say a quarter of a mile from here," the second trooper said. "I could see lots of rocks cropping up along the creek like they was dropped by big rock cows." He hesitated a second, then added, "Scout's right, sir. It's a good place for them to lay for us."

"I see." Cranfill rubbed his bearded chin. "Well, we'll give them their chance." He looked up, his tone changing. "Boyce, you and Schmidt continue west along the rim. Keep us in sight, and fall back on the column if you come under fire. Go now."

Boyce drew his carbine from its boot and reined around. "Yes, sir. Come on, Dutch." When they were a little distance away, he added, "If we 'come under fire,' let's hope they're damn poor shots!"

"Sergeant, take a couple of men downstream until you can descend into the valley. Move along the creek so as to cover our left flank. The rest of us will follow the trail."

"Yes, sir. Healy, Jenkins, come with me." He started away, then drew his mount up. "With the lieutenant's permission, we'll take our guest along." He slouched in his saddle and smiled at Fairchild. "That all right with you?"

Caught by surprise, Fairchild didn't answer at once. He realized Cranfill and the others were looking at him, suspicion born anew on their faces.

"Mr. Fairchild?" Cranfill said.

Considering, Ethan Fairchild saw a choice between being shot in the front or back. He wished for more options, but damned if he intended the cocky little sergeant or anyone else to think he was afraid.

"Sounds good to me," he said, looking at Neidercutt. "I'll go anyplace you will."

Neidercutt spat to one side. "You'd damned well better," he said. He unhooked the flap of his holster so that the polished wood butt of the big Colt Dragoon showed. "If you try to go anyplace else, we'll see if you can rise from the grave a second time, Dead Man."

8

The whole train was moving faster now. They had passed the Fourth of July at Fort Laramie with a dance and a noisy celebration that included a salute from the garrison's cannon. Everyone, even worried Manasseh Thorne, seemed to enjoy the break from the endless days on the trail. But when Thorne rose to make his Independence Day speech, it hadn't been the eagle-screaming address everybody expected. Instead, Manasseh Thorne told them how much time they had to cross the mountains. Just that long and no longer, the devil take the hindmost.

"Remember the Donners," Thorne had said.

"That was years ago," Caleb Sugarhouse objected. "Besides, the Donners got caught in the Sierra Nevada, heading for California. We're taking the Oregon route."

"Then we have to cross the Cascade Range instead," Thorne said. "Does that strike you as a better place to die?" Riding over Sugarhouse's answer, he'd raised his voice to include all the train. "Make no mistake about it, any of you. There're mountains ahead, high and unforgiving mountains. They've got no food for malingerers, no warmth for latecomers. They don't take excuses. Unless we clear the passes before the snow flies, we'll all be wintering on Donner steaks."

That wasn't funny. No one laughed but the oldest But-

trell boy, and·he choked on it once the thought worked
its way into the tough gristle of his mind. Stuart, looking
at Jessica, had thought it especially unfunny, though
grudgingly he had to admit Thorne was right. It was July
already, with most of the journey still ahead. Thorne's
train had been lucky so far, with only three of its number
lost; but the mountains, as Thorne said, didn't care about
luck.

Fort Laramie had held a personal disappointment, too,
for Stuart and Jessica.

"Who would have thought there wouldn't be a preacher
at Fort Laramie?" Jessica asked.

"Who would have thought the biggest fort between Nebraska and the Pacific would have one company of infantry, commanded by a lieutenant?" Stuart countered. He
took her hand as they trudged beside the wagon that had
once belonged to Ethan Fairchild. The prairie wind blew
steady and dry in their faces. "Your father's the wagonmaster. He was a judge back home. He could marry us."

"But he won't," Jessica said. "He says it's not seemly."
She tilted her head to smile at Stuart from beneath the
brim of her sunbonnet. "I wanted to ask how seemly he
thought it was for me to tiptoe to your wagon midnights.
But I didn't."

"Thank God for that, anyway," Stuart murmured. "Listen, we'll be at Bradley's Oak in two or three days. The
sutler from Fort Laramie said there's some kind of
preacher there. Maybe, just for that long, we ought not to
be together so much."

"Tired of me already?"

"You know better. It's you I'm concerned about."

"My good name?" Jessica asked, with a bitterness in
her voice Stuart didn't understand. "My unblemished virtue?" She laughed and squeezed Stuart's hand. "I'll risk
it if you will, Davy Stuart. But I'll be glad when we reach
this Bradley's Oak."

There in the foothills north of the Laramies, wagon ruts
sliced deep into the soft limestone of the slopes. Trees

grew thicker than anywhere Stuart could remember since the train had left Independence. But they would thin out again. The grass stood in short dry bunches from the over-grazing of trains before theirs.

Days, the train plodded through a fine, dry dust raised by the wagon wheels. Evenings, oxen and horses and people drank eagerly of the cold sweet water of the North Platte, and the travelers gathered at their fires, remembering Ohio and looking ahead to Oregon, singing, praying, hoping the next day's march would be easier than the last. And midnights, Jessica Thorne tiptoed to David Stuart's wagon.

The Reverend Mister Elgin Bradley had taken ill in the spring of 1851. With his family, he had left the westward train they were a part of. He'd followed a clear, shallow creek a little way south to a valley where a great arch of stone spanned the stream and beaver worked in the deep pool on the far side. There, he'd driven his wagon beneath the shade of a tree he took for an oak and, with his family, had waited to die.

The tree was not an oak, and Elgin Bradley did not die. Neither did he recover. Instead, he hunted and worked and built when he felt strong and took to his bed when the sickness overcame him. The Sioux looked him over, debated whether to burn his first crude cabin, decided finally that this was some strange kind of white holy man, perhaps touched by the spirits, who should be left in peace.

Because any inhabited place exercised a pull, the trail humped itself like a snake and twisted a coil to run past his door. By 1853, he had thrown up a hostel with two little rooms shantied off the back, a small barn, a toolshed, and three sides of a corral. A year later, the map in Hempstead's *Guidebook for the Oregon Traveler* identified the spot, with unconscious irony, as Bradley's Oak. And by that name it was known when Marguerite Bradley came to its doorway to welcome Thorne's train to its camping place.

"Just pull right on ahead. There's a good spot to circle your wagons up by the grove. There's a spring there, and no other emigrants this week to drink it dry. I'll call my Annie to show you the way."

"Thank you, madam." Manasseh Thorne climbed down from the lead wagon and beat dust from his coat and trousers. He strode across the bare yard to stand before Mrs. Elgin Bradley. "I'm of the understanding that there's a minister of the gospel here."

"Yes. My husband."

Marguerite Bradley stepped out from the doorway and clung to the hitchrail. Tanned and dried by eight years of sun and wind, her skin reminded Thorne of fine, soft leather. The colors of her dress had bled together into the same toneless brown, and her apron was no longer white. Her eyes were green, though, and still shone with a fitful spark of light like a guttering candle. At a distance, he'd thought her hair looked perfectly white. Up close he could see the mingled black strands which had refused to give in.

She had watched him as he approached. "Do you have any medicine?" she asked.

"Medicine?" Thorne stepped back without realizing it, suddenly wary. "What kind of medicine?"

"Any kind."

"Ma'am? Are you ill?"

"My husband."

"What's wrong with him?"

She seemed to realize what was in his mind, for suddenly she smiled. "No," she said. "It's not the cholera. Nor smallpox, nor scarlet fever. It is a condition of some years' standing."

"I see." Thorne tried to hold back his sigh of relief. "Maybe we can help."

"Are you a doctor?"

"No, ma'am, but I've got something pretty close to one

with our party." He looked around, saw one of the middle Buttrell boys standing and staring. "You there, tadpole! Go find Dr. Harris and bring him here to the house. Hear? And get your big brother to come and handle my wagon."

"Yes, sir!" The boy scampered away down the line. "Francis! Hey, Francis, old Mr. Thorne says come!"

"I appreciate your concern," the woman said. "Oh, but I'm forgetting my manners." She turned. "Ann, dear! Annie! Please show these folks the way up to the spring."

Ann Bradley came to the door, and Thorne caught his breath. Perhaps eighteen, she was a picture from the past, a daguerreotype with color and shape, the portrait of her mother thirty years past. Her hair was long and black in every strand, her skin still unlined and supple, her eyes as bright green as stained glass in a lighted church window.

"Surely, Mama!" she cried, smiling in a way that made Thorne, not a poetic man, think of a lone wild rose growing bravely in a dusty graveyard. She ran lightly to the lead wagon just as Francis Buttrell came up to take Thorne's place on its seat.

"Hello," she cried. "Welcome to Bradley's Oak." Then she laughed. "There really isn't an oak, but perhaps that doesn't matter. Here, let me get up beside you. I'll show you where to turn."

Big and shambling and awkward at seventeen, Francis Buttrell stared and stammered. Finally, he managed to make room for her on the seat. She seemed unconscious of his confusion, pointing ahead.

"Up there. Just follow the trail. It splits off to the left, up about a hundred yards."

Staring at her in the intervals between handling the lines and the brake, the Buttrell boy promised God his life as a missionary to the heathens in a foreign land, on the single condition that he be allowed to take the green-eyed girl with him. Older men, struck by the girl's fresh loveliness and flying skirts, prayed other sorts of prayers to other powers.

"I wish you'd come on in and have a look at Mr. Bradley," the older woman said to Thorne. "He hasn't been doing at all well of late. And tell your ladies to come to the house." She smiled. "We'll have tea."

Manasseh Thorne watched a moment longer, stroking his beard, as the Buttrell whelp shook the oxen into motion. He remembered suddenly his own eager, awkward, embarrassing days of courting Martha, the row her father had made when Thorne had asked for her hand. Come to that, he'd not been all that much more promising a specimen than young Stuart.

"Mr. Thorne, is it?" Marguerite Bradley said uncertainly. "Could you come in, sir?"

"Yes, ma'am." Resolutely, Thorne turned his eyes and his mind away from Ann Bradley. "I see my wife, Martha, and some of the other ladies coming now. And I'll be pleased to meet your husband, Mrs. Bradley. I have a favor to ask of him."

He stepped onto the low creaking porch and followed the woman through the cave-dark doorway. A tall, spare man met them in the first room, leaning heavily on a stick cut from a young aspen.

"Elgin!" the woman cried. "You know you oughtn't be out of bed. You'll catch your death!"

Elgin Bradley's eyes were brown. All the rest of him—hair, beard, skin, and robe—was gray. It was Thorne's first idea that the family had embalmed Elgin Bradley a good long time ago, and stood him up for posterity's sake in the middle of the large hostel dining room. Thorne had time to think that the taxidermist had done a good job, before the nicely preserved corpse spoke.

"Mother," Bradley wheezed. Alive, the founder of Bradley's Oak trembled, faltered, struggled for breath after each tortured phrase. "We have visitors. This is no time. To give in to. Our human frailties."

"But, Elgin."

"Sir," he said to Thorne. "Elgin R. Bradley. Lately pastor in Illinois. At your service." He lifted his frail hairless hand but could not extend it to the horizontal.

"Manasseh Thorne." His visitor made up for the lack, gripped his host's hand. "Having the privilege of leading the people in this train toward Oregon."

"Privilege all ours," said Bradley, saving words and breath. He turned his long pale face toward his wife who finished for him.

"Welcome," she said in the Bradley's Oak tradition of hospitality with an economy of words.

Thorne said, "I had hoped, Mr. Bradley, that you might see fit to perform a ceremony for us. But I fear you aren't well enough. I've sent for our surgeon."

Bradley fluttered a skeletal hand. "Duty," he said. "You, sir. Wagonmaster. You understand. If you have need of my services. I shall serve."

Marguerite shook her head. "We would appreciate the attention of your surgeon," she said firmly. "We can speak of your ceremony later."

Thorne went to the window. After a moment he saw young Harris lugging his leather satchel toward the barn-like hostel. Fred Harris was another outsider to the company on the train. Virginia, he'd said when he joined at Independence, and recently graduated from some high-toned medical school back East. Thorne didn't trust him, wondering why a man who called himself a physician needed to cross the continent in search of patients. But the women of the train had been so eager to have a doctor along that Thorne had bridled his questions and offered Harris a place.

Certainly, Harris had been a blessing to have around. He'd lanced a swelling on Lije Holden's hand that might have led to blood poisoning. He'd pulled Caleb Sugarhouse through a bad bout of grippe, and he'd given the little Lee girl devoted care when she fell sick, though he hadn't been able to name her illness or save her life. Not least, he'd shown a real talent for nursing sick and injured oxen.

"He's here now," Thorne said, moving to open the door

before Harris could knock. To himself, Thorne growled that only a damned Southerner would knock and wait at the door of an inn. But he smiled at Harris and motioned him inside.

"Thank you for coming, Doc. We may have a patient for you."

"Very well."

Harris stared around the dark room like a puzzled owl. He reminded Thorne of a man-sized rag doll. His eyes were too small, mere dark buttons in a smooth linen face. Straw-colored hair hung beneath his hat brim in curls and strings in a way that probably was stylish in Virginia. His gait was so awkward and heavy that Thorne was certain the man would make noise tiptoeing on a cloud of feathers.

But the hands were real. They might easily be the hands of a surgeon as Harris claimed. They hung strong and brown at his sides, the long fingers of one lightly gripping the handle of the medical case. His hands were supple, flexible, coordinated to his intentions. They were powerful, probing, sensitive, kind.

Fred Harris bowed awkwardly toward Mrs. Bradley, looked at the ghost of her husband. He smiled slightly.

"It is my guess, sir, that you are the patient."

"A good eye. Young man. Elgin R. Bradley." Bradley put out a ghostly hand and breathed a few words of which only *service* was audible.

Harris maintained his grip on the hand and guided Bradley to a wooden settee. His voice too was kind and probing as he asked the older man about his pains and weaknesses and vision. Thorne and Marguerite watched as Bradley absorbed the attention like a sponge dipped in warm water. After a moment Harris produced a small bottle of pills, called for a glass of water, and gave Bradley one of the tablets.

Elgin Bradley swallowed, choked, swallowed again, and pronounced himself cured. He stood away from the settee, balancing with a long frail arm still in the doctor's grasp.

"I trust you understand," Bradley breathed. "The inn makes our living. But we haven't so much hard money. Your bill. I will do my best."

"Perhaps we can take it out in trade, sir," Harris said. His button eyes sought Thorne and he smiled. "I understand we're to have a happy occasion soon, if you feel up to it."

"What's that?" Thorne asked, his voice louder than he'd intended. He did not like losing the air of leadership, and he did not like surprises. Particularly, he did not like the idea that family business, his business, was a matter of common gossip.

Harris grew quiet. "My apologies," he said. "It seems I've spoken out of turn."

Outside along the train of wagons, the Buttrell boy kept tripping over his own boots as he tried to keep up with Ann Bradley. She heard him and she saw him as she saw everything within the compass of those bright green eyes, but her replies lacked the zeal which crackled in his words. But she studied the resting oxen as if they were winged creatures from a pagan poem.

"My goodness," she said. "Just look how far you've come. Think how far you've yet to go. It must be the most exciting thing in the world to travel!"

Francis Buttrell glanced at the ponderous dust-covered, fly-ridden oxen at rest. He stared again at the girl and saw in the background a half-rotted wagon with its wheels silted a hand deep in loam beneath a large tree. The reason for her excitement escaped him.

Ann Bradley went on along the string of wagons, taking each one in with a fresh and lively hunger. She came to the end of that line of wagons and started around the rear to see the other side. Rounding the last wagon, she stopped abruptly.

"Oh! Pardon me." Her tanned cheeks took on a pink tone. "I didn't mean to intrude."

Francis Buttrell came up behind her. "Oh," he said, in somewhat the same tone, although he didn't blush. "Miss Bradley, this is Mr. Stuart and Miss Jessica Thorne."

The couple separated to arms' length, still holding hands like dancers ready to twirl. The young man smiled at Ann. "Hello," he said.

"Hello," Miss Thorne echoed. She went back into his embrace with an air of slight jealousy.

"I'm Ann Bradley. Welcome to Bradley's Oak." She stared at them with bright green eyes full of awe. "What a joy it must be to travel in such a big, new wagon!"

Now Miss Thorne's cheeks colored a bit. "We're not traveling together." She smiled up at Stuart. "Not yet." She moved away from the man's grasp and came to Ann. "My name is Jessica Thorne. I'm very pleased to make your acquaintance, Miss Bradley."

Ann smiled, blushed. At last she bowed to them in an old-fashioned curtsy. "You're most welcome here. How may I serve you?"

David Stuart raised his eyebrows and opened his mouth half in surprise and half as if to answer the question. Jessica Thorne turned to him immediately and gave the tender inside of his arm a vicious pinch.

"Don't you dare!" she whispered loudly enough for the others to hear. "Miss Bradley, I'd like you to meet my fiancé, David Stuart."

Miss Bradley seemed honored, pleased, excited beyond measure. "My father sometimes marries people," she offered.

Suddenly privy to information he had no business possessing, Francis Buttrell looked at his boots. Everyone in the train knew that Jessica had been keeping company with Stuart. But Francis was confused. He knew that Jessica had been keeping company with Ethan Fairchild, close company. Francis had seen them slip off from the train together more than once.

That Jessica had so quickly shifted her affections to Stuart was more than Francis could understand. He hadn't known or thought much about love until he saw Ann Bradley run out of the ramshackle hostel toward the wagons. But he knew now that love was forever.

Seeing his surprise and embarrassment, Jessica Thorne went to Francis, took his arm in a familiar fashion as if he too were a possible suitor, and smiled at him so warmly that he grew even more confused.

"Francis," she said quietly. "You mustn't be upset. David and I have been friends a long while. And now we've decided to marry. In a few years you'll understand."

"I understand now," he told her.

"Yes. But then you'll know how we feel."

Francis Buttrell looked at the green-eyed girl whose dress was too young for her, a bit too short, outgrown as she strained toward adulthood.

"I know now how you feel," he insisted. His face flushed beneath his hat as Jessica Thorne took his arm and smiled. She followed his eyes to the girl. "Perhaps you do." She squeezed his arm again in a way that embarrassed him and returned to Stuart.

Ann Bradley curtsied to them and started up the far side of the train with undiminished enthusiasm. She stopped to pet the goats and speak to the children and admire the same oxen from the other side. Francis Buttrell followed her as if she were playing a pipe. Halfway back to the lead wagon, he hit upon the plan of introducing her to each family. Thus he assumed the attitude of proprietorship. At last he dared ask her to show him the famous Bradley's Oak hostel.

"It's on our map," he explained.

"Is it really? I never thought we'd be part of a map."

"I've been looking forward to seeing you, I mean to seeing your inn ever since we left Independence. But I didn't have no idea then you'd be here." He heard the echoes of his words and saw no way to salvage the jumble he'd made of them.

"Well, you knew *someone* would be. They don't put places on a map if no one's there."

"But I didn't expect it would be someone like you."

She laughed. "It seems like I've *always* been here." She led him into the dimness of the large front room which was open to the public. She pointed toward a group of tables in front of the fireplace on the other side of the room. "Down at that end," she said, "is where people eat."

"I see."

She excused herself and went through a split curtain into the Bradley family's private quarters.

Immediately, Manasseh Thorne emerged through the curtain, took Buttrell by the elbow, and headed him back outside.

"Harris is busy in there," he explained. "Go find David Stuart and send him to me over past that wagon." He gestured toward the ruin Francis had seen earlier. "Go on, now. What are you looking back for? Get. And tell my Martha to bring the ladies along in here. There's tea and gossip."

Fred Harris put a little bottle of pills into Marguerite Bradley's hand as the two of them watched Elgin Bradley hobble out to welcome the rest of his guests.

"He'll be all right," Harris said. "The excitement of guests may be good for him, build him up."

"If it don't kill him."

Yes, Harris thought, like all medicine. It has both powers. He pursed his lips and looked at Mrs. Bradley thoughtfully.

"This medicine will help him breathe, but only for a little while, an hour or two after each tablet. I'm afraid it can't work a cure."

She nodded. The light in her green eyes was very dim. "I thought as much," she murmured. "Do you know what it is?"

"Your husband suffers from a progressive congestion of the lungs," Harris said. "It's not consumption, though some of the effects are similar." He spread his hands helplessly. "Aside from that, we know very little about it."

He stopped. Marguerite Bradley looked up at him. "When we first came here, he recovered his strength for a while."

"The altitude and the dry air were good for him."

"But it didn't last." She gestured at the window. The poles for the fourth side of the corral lay warping in the wagon which still stood in a sea of weeds beneath the oak that wasn't an oak. "But lately, he's been down more and more. He can seldom work for more than a few days at a time, and then he'll be poorly for weeks."

Harris nodded. "That's typical of the course of his condition." He hated himself for the distant, impersonal tone, but he couldn't say what he meant: *It will go on that way until he dies.*

"I see."

From her eyes, he saw that she understood, that she'd known for a long time, that he'd ended the last bit of hope she might have had. He licked his lips. He had worse to tell her. "Ma'am, I hesitated to say it, but your own health is not as good as it might be."

She looked at him quickly. "I'm all right," she said. After a moment, she shrugged. "I'll last as long as I need to."

"I wouldn't have said anything," Harris told her. "But in this case, well, you have a daughter as well."

"Yes," she interrupted gently. "In this case, there's Ann." She turned toward the window, hugging herself with her thin arms. "I do worry about Ann."

Fred Harris sighed. There was so much that medical school hadn't taught him, so much he didn't know about these complicated mechanisms he'd chosen for his life's work.

"I'm afraid you have cause to," he said.

9

"They're coming," Grace said.

Silverhorn opened his eye. "How many?"

"I saw three. Out front, scouting. There's more behind them."

"What are they?"

"Cavalry."

"The hell you're telling me!"

He heaved himself to his feet. Simon Whitley was up just as quick. Gabe and his woman had gone off into the willows someplace, but the others were gathered around the small fire near the creek, picking the last bones of the antelope Blue Eye had shot the day before.

"Soldiers?" Jonas Whitley stared at her, his eyes showing white. "They can't be!"

"Where's my telescope? How far are they?"

"Just barely into sight." Grace slipped off her stocky Indian pony, letting the reins drop. "They're coming on at a walk, looking sharp. They got an Indian in front, tracking us like we was leaving wagon ruts a foot deep."

"Lord God a'mercy!" Simon Whitley breathed. "I made sure we lost them soldiers away back. They can't still be on our track."

Silverhorn snorted. "You made sure of that, did you? So you wanted to stop for nooning and have a rest and a drink of creek water and a chance for Gabe to roll his slut in the grass." He caught the reins of his horse. "Kills Running, lead them horses out of sight amongst them willows. The rest of you get ready to move, smooth and quiet as a silk grandmother. I don't want to hear a snort or a whinny."

"Don't show yourself," Grace told him. "I seen the sun on their telescopes. They know we're close."

Silverhorn swung up onto his horse. "Douse that fire, Red Whore. And don't send them any damned smoke signals while you're doing it! Wait for me here."

He rode away fast, heading for the low, rocky rim of the valley. Grace took off her coat, poured creek water on it, and covered the tiny fire. Then she dumped the rest of the water on the steaming coat. Simon and Jonas Whitley stared after Silverhorn, fingering their weapons, while Plum and Blue Eye helped with the horses.

At the valley rim, Silverhorn reined in his horse just below the crest, lay on his stomach, and stretched out his telescope. The riders jumped into view across the rolling grassland, appearing and disappearing in the gentle folds of ground, looking almost near enough to touch. He could see all of them now. They were tricked out like shirttail farmers at threshing time, but they held a disciplined formation and were led by an officer in uniform. Out ahead were a scout and a couple of flankers, all aiming for the cut where his party had come down to the creek. In half an hour, maybe a little more, the scouts would be at the valley rim.

"Hell," Silverhorn muttered.

Immediately, he slid back and dropped into the saddle, kicking into a gallop to get back to the others. The Whitleys were bunched up, Gabe's woman clinging to him. They yapped at Silverhorn like a pack of hounds when he dismounted, until Simon cuffed the younger two into silence.

"Well?"

"It's the Army, all right," Silverhorn told them. "They're close and coming along, just like Grace says, more than a dozen of them."

"We got to run for it," Simon said. "What are you waiting on, a pillar of smoke? We got to get mounted and ride for our lives."

Silverhorn shook his head. "Blue Eye says there's nothing but open country ahead. If they catch us out on the prairie, they'll ride us down one at a time." He looked at Jonas, smiling a little. " 'Course, the ones that's fastest might get away. It'll be devil take the hindmost."

Jonas turned pale. He was built thick and heavy, and he knew as well as anybody that his horse would tire early. "Simon," he said.

"What're you saying, Thoman?" Simon asked.

"I'm saying we'd do best to make our stand right here."

The men growled. Grace stared at Silverhorn. "You sure?"

"Where else? Up there in those little dome hills? This is the best place."

"Maybe not the best time."

"By God," Silverhorn said. "It's the only time we'll have." He waved an arm. "Plum, Blue Eye, come on out here and listen. Here's how I see it. We'll three or four of us settle down in the creek bottoms where there's good cover. When the soldiers get close, we'll loose off at them."

Gabe Whitley cocked a suspicious eye at him. "Then what?" he asked. "Then them three or four gets killed?"

"You know how it is with Dragoons. They'll dismount, make a line, send their horses back." Silverhorn pointed upstream where fallen boulders dotted the ground beside the stream. "The rest of us will hide out in them rocks. Once the soldiers get down in the grass, Blue Eye and Kills Running will go for their horses. They won't be looking for that. While we've got them betwixt and between, we'll gallop down on their flank and shoot them all to pieces."

Silverhorn looked from one to the other. Grace grinned at him, and he swept his eye quickly past her. Plum had his thick lips pursed, frowning, almost like he understood. Blue Eye nodded once; he had liked the part about the horses, as Silverhorn knew he would. Gabe and Jonas

Whitley looked puzzled, angry, suspicious, but they waited for Simon to speak.

"Blue Eye, you best get up and keep watch. Warn us when they get nigh," Silverhorn said. Then he turned to Simon Whitley. "What say, Simon? We don't have a lot of time."

Simon fiddled with the lock of his rifle, frowning. "*We'll* gallop down on them, you said." He scowled at Silverhorn. "That's me and Gabe and Jonas, is it?"

Silverhorn raised his eyebrows. "Why, I'd thought so," he said, sounding surprised. "It only makes sense. The Pawnees to go after the horses, and me and Plum and the two women down in the bottoms. Gabe's woman won't be much shucks in a fight, but she can load for the others of us."

"Gabe?" The woman tugged at his arm. "Gabe, I don't want to leave you."

"There's twice as many soldiers as there is of us," Gabe said.

"I don't trust him, Simon," Jonas added.

Silverhorn spread his hands and smiled. "Why, listen," he said. "We don't have to kill them all. If we can run off, kill, cripple a few horses, they won't be able to follow us no more." He looked from one to the other of the Whitleys. " 'Course, if you don't have the stomach for it, you can ride out in the open with me."

"I'll tell you what we've got the stomach for," Simon said. "It's me and Gabe and Jonas will be down in the bottoms with the womenfolk. You and Plum can do the riding down on the flank."

"I go with Tom," Grace said.

"Grace comes with me," Silverhorn said at the same moment, then scowled at her.

"You and Grace, then." Simon stopped. A crafty look came into his eyes. "Then maybe Plum better stay with us. Jonas can ride along with you, just to be sure you don't forget your part. All right, Jonas?"

Jonas laughed. "You bet, Simon." He lifted his pistol halfway out its holster. "That old buzzard tries anything, and I'll shoot that other eye of his out."

Silverhorn looked at him steadily for a few seconds then turned away. "That all right with you, Plum?" he asked. "Staying down with old Simon, here?"

Plum's round face worked in surprise and consternation. He wasn't used to being noticed. "Well, sure, Tom. Certain sure." He made a shooing motion with one big hand. "I'll do whatever you say. Just tell me what to do."

"Why, thank you, Plum," Silverhorn said. "If I had ten men as smart as you, I'd never worry about a thing." He looked at the Whitleys, and his voice turned hard again. "Simon," he said slowly and calmly, "I've told you before that I'm the leader here. You'd be a power better off, a power better to do this like I say."

Whitley shook his head. "We'll do it like *I* say." He laughed. "Losing that eye's took some sand out of you, Thoman. Time was, you'd've swelled up like a poisoned hog if we questioned your plans. Maybe it's time I take over, after all."

The cackling cry of a prairie hen caused them all to turn. Blue Eye was coming back, riding low on his pony, swinging his arm back and forth over his head in the sign for enemy.

"All right!" Silverhorn's voice rose like a trumpet. "Enough talk. Get mounted, them that's coming with me. We got work to do!"

From the saddle, he paused to look down on Simon once more. "We'll talk about you taking over, Simon," he murmured. "Just as soon as this little scrap's over, we'll surely talk that out."

The patrol had taken the best way down. Neidercutt skirted the valley rim eastward for half a mile or more before he found a break, a steep, dry gully leading down to the creek.

"This way," he ordered. "You first, Dead Man."

The chestnut horse didn't like the idea much more than Fairchild did, but a hard cut from the sergeant's riding whip sent it over the edge, sliding stiff-legged in the crumbling dirt. Jenkins and Healy followed, Neidercutt coming last.

They had left the black sod of Nebraska behind, Fairchild saw. The soil here was dry and hard, a deep blood-red streaked with bands of grayish clay. He wouldn't have thought any plant could live in such ground, but cotton-woods and thick tangles of willow grew along the banks of the creek, and the deep grass of the valley floor was greener than anything he had seen for days.

He could imagine a plow biting into the flat grassy benches above the flood-line, could picture how they would look planted in stands of corn or summer wheat. Maybe this was what Oregon was like, he thought. Maybe he and Jess would—

"Pistols," Neidercutt said, his voice not much louder than the murmur of the creek.

The two troopers drew their revolvers. Neidercutt already had his out, the hand holding it resting on the pommel of his saddle.

"I don't have a pistol, Sergeant," Fairchild said.

Neidercutt looked as if he wanted to spit, but he didn't. "Maybe you *are* telling the truth," he said. "It's sure a greenhorn enough stunt to get caught in the open without a sidearm. Draw your rifle and keep quiet. We'll cross the water here. Move!"

The horses pushed through the willow thickets and clopped into the shallow stream. Healy's mount dipped its nose to drink, but the trooper yanked its head back. Fairchild's chestnut pranced, its head high, stepping carefully among the rocks of the creek bed. Fairchild could feel the animal trembling, though he couldn't imagine it was afraid.

Jenkins bit off a chew of tobacco and wiped his moustache with a leather gauntlet. "Now, then," he whispered to Fairchild, "ain't you glad you came along with us?"

"Wouldn't have missed it for the world."

"Silence in the ranks." On the far bank, Neidercutt made a quick, nervous gesture with his left hand. "Line abreast, Jenkins on the outside flank. Dead Man, you stick close to me."

Neidercutt was right about the revolver, Fairchild thought. A greenhorn stunt. He gripped his rifle tightly, wondering how he'd ever manage to fire it from horseback, especially from the chestnut's back. He'd ragged Davy a time or two for packing around that big Colt's pistol, but now he saw how wrong he'd been. Maybe the two of them, both armed with pistols, could have stood off the raiders that day. Fairchild promised himself that was one mistake he'd never make again.

Line abreast, they rode up the south bank of the stream. Jenkins watched the open grassland and the valley rim to the south, while the others kept their eyes on the willows and the dark shadows under the cottonwoods. Fairchild couldn't see any sign of Cranfill and the patrol. It might be anywhere, but presumably was moving along the opposite bank. He expected any second to see white smoke burst from the willow thicket or the rocks of the rim, to hear the boom of a rifle and the air-splitting buzz of a big bullet. But nothing happened.

The rim was maybe two hundred yards away. At that distance, he would have had only a breath to think about it between a shot and a bullet whistling at his door without his ever hearing the report. He cocked the rifle with a click that made Neidercutt swivel to look at him. The sergeant made a palm-down, patting gesture with his left hand, then turned back to scan the willows. Death from there would come even quicker, Fairchild thought, no time to consider it at all.

The creek mumbled and splashed over the round, smooth cobbles of its bed. A bluejay scolded from the high limb of a cottonwood. The chestnut, its tricks forgotten, swung through the dappled shadows as smooth and silent as a cat. A high sun looked down on them, warm but not hot enough to cause the sweat that trickled down between Fairchild's shoulders. Somewhere up ahead, a dead limb snapped sharply. Fairchild thought the lieutenant's patrol must have been pushing through the brush to cross the creek, because the first sound was followed by a sharp crackle—

"Mounted action!" Neidercutt bellowed. "Forward, trot!"

The chestnut horse swung to a trot on the command, almost dumping Fairchild in the grass. Cursing himself for stupidity, Fairchild hung on. What he'd taken for breaking branches had been shots up ahead, the bark of pistols and the deeper boom of long guns. Somewhere in the willow thicket, the patrol was engaged; and Neidercutt was bringing his force up on the flank, pulling Fairchild right into the middle of a fight.

The rattle of firing grew louder. Ahead, Fairchild could see nothing except the open, gentle slopes of the valley floor. Along the creek were the thick boles of cottonwoods and dark shadowy dells and the screen of willow leaves. There was nothing to shoot at. Fairchild clung to the reins, trying to manage the awkward length of the revolving rifle one-handed. If I ever get out of this, he thought, I'll never be without a handgun again—awake, asleep, eating or praying, drunk or sober.

Unexpectedly, the detachment plunged into the open onto a wide gravel bar in the stream where the banks were rocky and bare. Clearly, as if the scene were etched on a tintype, Fairchild saw everything in a scattered instant: the Dragoons on foot, strung out in a skirmish line, bending low like men walking into a hailstorm; horseholders dragging wild-eyed troop horses to the rear; Cranfill rising from the grass, revolver in hand and blood streaming from the side of his face, to wave the line forward; gray-white powder smoke spurting from the willows across the clearing, already hanging in a haze over the creek while the sound of the gunfire rose to a roar.

Then the barrel of a rifle poked from the brush dead in front of Fairchild. The gun boomed. From the tail of his eye, Fairchild saw Jenkins suddenly enveloped in a cloud of red spray, and then the trooper was gone, fallen from the saddle and left behind.

"Down! Take cover!"

He heard Neidercutt's frantic shout dimly, as if the little sergeant were a long way off. He didn't understand the command, and it wouldn't have mattered if he had. The chestnut put its head down and plunged into a gallop, straight at the wall of willows where the rifleman crouched.

Fairchild hunched down in the saddle, throwing up his left arm to protect his eyes. Willow withes lashed like whips across his forearm and his hunched shoulders, tore off his hat, slashed at his cheeks. Almost beneath the chestnut's hooves, a man sprang up, throwing aside his rifle and scrabbling for a long single-shot pistol, his mouth opening in a desperate shout.

"Simon!"

Then the chestnut drove into the man with a shock that jolted Fairchild from stirrups to clenched teeth. He recovered, jerking the Colt's rifle up as the horse plunged past the fallen man and momentarily into the open again. A huge, moon-faced man was rising from behind the trunk of a fallen cottonwood, a pepperbox pistol in his hand, his eyes round in clownish surprise as Fairchild and the chestnut burst from the trees.

Fairchild shot him.

At that range, and with the Colt's long barrel, Fairchild's marksmanship was good enough. The big .44 round took the man low in the belly, staggering him back against the cottonwood trunk. Still looking surprised, he steadied himself and raised the pepperbox, squinting one eye to aim dead at Fairchild's heart. Fairchild drew the Colt's hammer back and fired again. He saw the man go backward over the log and swung the rifle to the off side, snapping a third shot at a figure that rose screaming from the grass.

He had forgotten the reins and any hope of controlling the chestnut, but the horse didn't seem to need his help. It planted its hooves in a skidding turn and wheeled back on the first man who'd fired from the willows. He was up on his knees, trying to raise his pistol. He started to shout as the horse bore down on him. Fairchild fired, heard the smack of the bullet and the choking end of the cry. Then the chestnut reared with a high whinnying squeal Fairchild had never heard from a horse before. Its forehooves slashed down with a horrible, wet crunching noise and the pistol went flying.

The horse wheeled again, snorting and tossing its head. It stood still, legs braced and trembling, snakelike neck darting this way and that while wicked wide white eyes searched the brush. Swaying in the saddle, Fairchild cocked the Colt's hammer and looked for another target. A man he hadn't seen before lay just in front of him, his face in the grass and his straggly graying hair soaked with blood.

Fairchild didn't know whether a minute had passed or half an hour. During the confused fight he had been vaguely conscious of cries and shots, the snap and rattle of bullets cutting through the branches around him, the sounds of other men and other horses. Now everything was suddenly quiet.

In the silence, Sergeant Neidercutt's voice rang like the trump of doom. "Damn you, Dead Man!" The sergeant kneed his horse in close to Fairchild's, and the chestnut swiveled and slashed at Neidercutt's mount with its teeth. "Get that damn devil horse under control! Didn't you hear my orders? If I hadn't shot that last one, he'd've killed you dead. Who the hell do you think you are, Lighthorse Harry Lee?"

Fairchild stared at him dully. He didn't know who Lighthorse Harry Lee was. Just then, he didn't care. He tried to say something, but all he could manage was a dry croak. His throat ached and burned with the taste of gunpowder. He started to reach for his canteen, then changed his mind and slid down out of the saddle. Dropping the chestnut's reins, he walked over to look at the people he'd killed.

The horse hadn't left much of the first man, but Fairchild could see he'd been young and slender, with heavy dark hair and beard. Healy was already bending over the one who'd screamed. The trooper stared at Fairchild.

"Blessed Mary preserve us," he whispered, his hand sketching a cross. "This one was a woman!"

Fairchild didn't answer. He'd seen the man Neidercutt shot. Keeping the rifle ready, he stepped around the fallen cottonwood to find the last one.

The man lay on his back, his arms askew, one leg cocked up onto the log, his face a portrait of agony. He raised his head, looked at Fairchild with round, puzzled blue eyes, looked at his own gun lying in the dirt by his hand. Fairchild saw the effort in his eyes, but no muscle moved below his shoulders.

Fairchild didn't recognize any of the men, but they'd had a woman with them. He was satisfied that the bushwhackers were the ones who had shot the black horse from under him, who probably had killed Stuart as well.

"Where are the others?" he asked. "Where's the Indian? And the one with white hair? Where are they?"

He saw recognition in the man's eyes.

"Thoma!" It sounded like that, anyway. The voice was no more than a husking growl. "Tom—kill—" The big man stopped, gurgled, made a great effort. "Plum!" he said.

A gush of blood drowned the last word. He choked, turned his head, his eyes growing wide and frightened. Fairchild raised the rifle.

"No!"

Neidercutt's shout was lost in the roar of the Colt. The big man jerked once, then was still. A moment later, the sergeant, eyes blazing, snatched the rifle from Fairchild's hands.

"Damn you, were you trying to keep him from talking?"

"He'd talked enough," Fairchild said.

"Listen, you civilian son of a—"

"Sergeant." Cranfill's voice cut the sergeant off like a knife. "Report!"

Neidercutt turned, bracing to attention. Cranfill had come through the screen of willows with a half-dozen troopers behind him. They stared at the dead men, then at Fairchild, with wide and wondering eyes.

"Jenkins is dead, sir," Neidercutt said. His voice sounded as harsh and cracked as Fairchild's. "Shot down. There's four of the enemy dead here. One of them a woman, Healy says. Truth is, this civilian charged them like a wild man, shot down three in a heartbeat. We'd likely have lost more men, but for him." He paused a second, then added, "We did have a prisoner, but this dead man killed him, too."

The lieutenant's eyes came to Fairchild, hard and level. "And why was that, Mr. Fairchild?" he asked.

"He was afraid," Fairchild said. It wasn't a good answer, but it was the only one he had.

"He might have told us something."

"He did tell me something." Fairchild raised his head. He tried to swallow. "They're the ones. The ones that jumped Davy and me. But this isn't all of them. There's the one with white hair—I think he must be the leader. And an Indian. I remember an Indian."

"I see," Cranfill said. "Very well, Mr. Fairchild. Sergeant, take charge of the wounded."

Fairchild caught his arm. "Wait," he said. "We can catch them. They can't be far. We can kill them all, every damned one of them, just shoot them down like the dogs they are."

Fairchild was surprised at himself. He felt his voice rising, his grip tightening on Cranfill's arm, but he couldn't stop. He wanted to catch up to Jessica and make their marriage real in the sight of society. But he felt a pull toward the white-haired man they called Thoma. He felt a pull toward a revenge he could not have defined. The pull was deeper than any positive desire for Jessica; it was ugly anger and blood lust.

"We need to go after them!" he said. "If we don't go now, we'll lose a day. We can get them, I know we can. We can get every damned, murdering one of them.".

"Easy, man." That was Healy's voice. His arms were around Fairchild, holding him back. Another trooper had hold of him, too, pinning his arms while Healy spoke in a soothing murmur. "The lieutenant knows best. We got one dead and three more wounded, and we got horses dead or hurt that can't travel just now. You just sit a minute and have you a drink of water and it'll all come clear."

"But we'll lose them!" Fairchild made one last pull back toward Cranfill. "They'll get away, sir. But we can get them if we hurry!"

Cranfill was looking at him strangely. He saw the same expression on other faces, heard the Dragoons murmur among themselves.

"I'm sorry, Mr. Fairchild," Cranfill said. He sounded as if he meant it. "Healy, look after him. We've got wounded men to tend and graves to dig."

At the first ripple of gunfire, Jonas Whitley came scrambling down from the tall rock where he'd been keeping watch.

"It's started!" he said. "They's after Simon and them. Let's go."

None of the others moved. Grace, perched halfway up the rock, her skirt hiked up so high that she might as well have been naked, grinned at him. Blue Eye and Kills Running squatted under cover with the horses' reins in their hands. They looked at each other and then at Silverhorn, who lounged on the grass with his back against a boulder.

"Just where was it you was reckoning we should go, Jonas?" he asked, slowly uncoiling himself.

"Why, down on them soldiers!" Jonas waved a hand toward the confused babel of shots and shouts and screaming horses. "It's time! Send them Indians after the mounts! Us'uns ride down on the flank, like you said!" He took a step toward Silverhorn. "I won't hold back, no matter what Simon told me. I'll be right with you, shooting them to pieces."

"That's mighty generous of you, Jonas," Silverhorn said. He rose, stretching his long arms. "That's as handsome an offer as I ever heard. But the fact is, I been studying on this."

"We got to hurry!"

"That brother of yours, Simon, he's mighty anxious to run this outfit. So I done decided that he can run this part of it all by his lonesome."

Behind him, Jonas heard Grace chuckle and shift position. Blue Eye said something in Pawnee to Kills Running, and both laughed.

"Damn traitor!" Jonas yelled, snatching at the brace of pistols in his belt. Silverhorn was loose, relaxed, not ready at all. Jonas knew he had the one-eyed man, had him cold, and he started a yell of triumph as he rocked back the hammer on his right-hand gun.

Something landed on his shoulders like a catamount, clawing for his eyes, biting, ripping a deep scratch across his throat. Grace. He hunched his shoulders and shook himself, threw her aside. Quickly, he turned back to Silverhorn. Silverhorn still hadn't started his draw. Jonas had him cold, except that he couldn't lift his pistols. Then the white-haired man seemed to waver before his eyes.

"Silverhorn!" he said in his mind, but the only sound he could make was a breathy sigh. He dropped his left-hand pistol and clapped his hand to his throat, staring in wonder at the dripping red spray that covered his palm. Then he pitched forward on his face in the grass.

"That was right nice, Grace." Silverhorn bent to take the reins of his horse from Blue Eye. "Day or night, you know just what it is that a man wants."

Grace slipped the long Arkansas knife back into its sheath and grinned at him. "I'm always trying to please," she said.

Kills Running handed the reins of the other horses to Blue Eye. He went to kneel beside Jonas, went through his pockets quickly, taking money, a clasp knife, a silver dollar which he held high. He tucked both of Jonas's pistols in his own belt. Then he caught the dead man by the hair, lifting the head while he looked at Grace.

"Scalp?" he asked Grace. She shook her head, and he looked to Silverhorn. "Boss? You want?"

"Help yourself," Silverhorn said. He swung up into the saddle. "Best we move on," he said over the crackle of gunfire. "I figure them troopers and Simon will keep one another busy for a little while, yet. Let's us cover some miles before anybody thinks to look for us."

Kills Running made a quick cut, pushed the bloody scalp into his possible bag, and ran to get his horse. Silverhorn reined up, looking back toward the sounds of the fight as the others mounted.

"Too bad about Plum." The two Pawnee had ridden on, and only Grace heard him. He shook his head. "I'm going to miss Plum," he said.

10

"We can't afford to stop for more celebrating," Manasseh Thorne said. "I'd figured we could make another six miles before dark. We're still two weeks from South Pass, and that's only the beginning."

His wife patted his arm. "We know you're worried, Man," she said. "But it's only one day and only one very special celebration."

"One day is one too many, Martha. Unless we keep on, we'll all be wintering—"

He caught himself assuming his courtroom tone and stopped in mid-stride, just as both Martha and Jessica put fingers to their lips. From Thorne's viewpoint, the worst thing about a covered wagon was that family arguments had to be conducted very quietly, or they became everyone's business.

"I'm sorry, Father," Jessica said. "Davy and I didn't plan anything like this." She squeezed Stuart's hand, mostly, Thorne suspected, to keep him quiet. "But when Mrs. Buttrell and the other ladies found out, they just took over."

They just behaved like women, Thorne thought. But he did not say so. Instead, he tugged his beard and glared at the young couple sitting against the tailboard of the wagon. "I never gave my consent," he said.

"Sir," Stuart began, but Jessica squeezed his hand again.

"Davy talked to you about it ten days ago," she said.

"Yes, and I told him I would have to think on it."

"You didn't ever say no."

"I hoped you two would come to your senses."

"You've always said, under the law, silence gives consent."

Thorne chewed his beard, frowning. Not for the first time, he had the thought that, had she been a boy, Jess would probably have done better at the bar than he.

"That's different," he said, but he recognized the signs. He'd seldom won an argument with both Jess and Martha arrayed against him, and he sensed he wasn't going to win this one.

"Manasseh Thorne, I'm ashamed of you," Martha said. "Here our only daughter is about to wed a fine young man." Her voice caught for a second. Thorne knew that

Martha had loved Ethan Fairchild like her own, had none too secretly hoped he would claim Jessica's hand. But she hurried on without a sign. "And you're growling like an old bear because your pride is hurt." She waved a hand vaguely at the world beyond the yellowing canvas cover of the wagon. "Why, everyone else is just as happy about it as can be."

That was true. Half the train was out preparing for the wedding supper, making pies and barbecuing goats and skinning antelope to roast and sending the little ones to gather wildflowers and God alone knew what else. Whatever scandal there might be over Jess marrying so soon after Ethan's death, making a public fuss would only make matters worse. Thorne began to look for a good way to back down.

"Jessica, is this your considered decision?" he asked.

It was Stuart who answered. "It's our decision, sir."

"Father," Jessica said. With her free hand, she reached out to clasp his fingers as she'd done when she was a little girl. "I've chosen David. You've often told me Mother left her family in Kentucky and came to make her life with you. It didn't mean she loved her father less. Nor that I'll love you any less."

Thorne sighed and reached out to slap Stuart on the shoulder. "You have my blessing, David Stuart," he said. "And God help you. You're getting a young lady who could argue the horns off your uncle's billygoat."

As soon as she'd heard the news, plump Mrs. Buttrell had lifted her skirts six inches off the ground and run to the Buttrell wagon. She knew the Bradleys had meat and eggs and fresh vegetables from their garden, but she reasoned they might be short of other things. Digging in the long box that was her larder, she brought out a precious pound of butter for the cooking.

"A wedding," she panted when she reached the Bradley

kitchen. "Jessica Thorne and that nice Stuart boy! Who would have thought it?"

Lena Ames pursed her lips. "Anybody who lies awake much at night might have suspected it, Alathea." She stirred her pot of beans. "Lord knows, they've been acting the part. My, it's a pleasure to cook on a real stove again. I just don't know what Jessica Thorne can be thinking. And we have real wood for the fire, not those awful buffalo chips. We'll have a good supper for everyone, though I won't be able to eat a bite, thinking about her marrying, with that poor Ethan Fairchild not cold yet in his grave."

Barbara Kenny looked up from the dough she was rolling out. "I didn't know you were so fond of Ethan Fairchild, Lena," she said.

"It's not that I was fond of him. Maybe I need just a little more salt pork to give these flavor. But it's not *entirely* certain that David Stuart is as innocent as he says. Here, Alathea, let me help you with that water bucket. And I'd think that girl would at least wait a decent time before she goes traipsing off with another man."

Barbara felt anger rising in her, tightening her throat as she spoke. "And what is a decent time, Mrs. Ames?" she asked. The black cloth band on her sleeve seemed to tighten around her arm like a snake. "How long should a woman wait before she can go on with her life?"

Lena Ames looked across at her, surprised. "Oh, I never meant anything about *you*, dear," she said. "Does Mrs. Bradley have any onions from that garden, I wonder? We all think it's so brave of you to go on after losing your dear Sam that way, and married such a short time, too."

"Thank you," Barbara said. She put down the rolling pin and went to the back door of the hostel. "Alathea, can you finish for me, please. I feel—dizzy—all at once."

"Surely, dear." Alathea Buttrell patted her shoulder with a dimpled, floury hand. "You just go get a breath of air. We'll be fine."

* * *

Jessica Thorne realized she had not been alone with her own thoughts for an instant since her father had agreed to the wedding. Her mother had bustled her immediately into one of the sitting rooms of the inn, bearing the dress she herself had worn to marry Manasseh Thorne. A group of ladies had gathered as though by magic to fit Jessica into the dress and to bombard her with the duties and cautions of being a wife.

"You just never fear about that first night, sweetie," Becky Miller consoled as she deftly pinned up the hem. "It'll all be over in the morning."

"And then you can start making something out of him," Helen Coates added. "Not that your Mr. Stuart isn't something now. But the men all need a woman's guiding hand, my dear."

Mrs. Coates confided to Jessica certain secrets of cooking to please a man without working herself to death, and then Mrs. Miller offered some whispered advice about doing her wifely duty, distasteful as she might sometimes find it, without getting herself with child.

"I hadn't noticed it was all that much bother," Sarah Holden blurted out, then blushed as all the others laughed. Black-eyed and pert as a mountain cardinal, Sarah was at least a year younger than Jessica. "I mean, Lije pretty much takes care of everything."

Jessica Thorne watched a male sparrow with his bright black cravat carrying straw from the oxen's feed to a new nest in the tree just outside the window. Female sparrows were the lucky ones. Their brightly banded little men did their courting without jealousy or anger. They didn't worry about what their neighbors might think. They didn't worry about bringing their young into the world with no nest, no name. *The birds of the air have nests.*

David Stuart would be good at building a nest. And she did have feelings for him. It was not as if marrying Davy would make her a harlot, a camp follower. If Ethan had not happened upon her at such a vulnerable time, why, she might have chosen Davy instead. He might have been

the father of her child. She sighed. That it was true did
not change her situation.

She wondered if the lady sparrow had rejected or lost
other suitors. There were no cats here—no tame cats, anyway—but she'd seen hawks and snakes. And a prairie
storm with wind and hail could smash a sparrow to earth.
One sparrow shall not fall to the ground without . . . without God's knowing it. But if the male flew away one day,
or fell behind and never came back, the female would
never know what God knew, would never be sure.

She could not help wondering if Ethan was watching
somewhere, listening, aware of what she was about to do
to his memory in order to give his child the wrong name.
Forgive me if you are, Ethan, she thought. Dear God,
please forgive me. I'm doing what seems best. Please help
me carry it through. *I watch, and am as a sparrow alone
upon the housetop.*

"What?" she asked suddenly.

Mrs. Coates clucked her tongue. "Why, child, you
might as well be at the altar now, for all the attention
you're paying," she said. "You haven't heard a word."

"Oh, I have. I'm listening."

"I was saying we'll need to let these seams out a little
at the waist, don't you think?"

Jessica Thorne took a breath, drew in her stomach. "No,
I was just slouching." She stood straight, pulling her
shoulders back. "How's that? Won't that do?"

"It might do if you don't eat a bite all evening! But
there's no need to be uncomfortable on such an occasion
as this."

"I should say not," Becky Miller seconded, inspecting
the fit. "You've caught your young man now; no need to
keep a wasp waist." She patted her own comfortably
plump stomach. "One or two young ones, and you'll say
good-bye to all that anyway. But you won't have to worry
for a while, yet."

*   *   *

Francis Buttrell knew where to find Stuart. He had helped his father build the fire down in the hollow behind the barn. Will Buttrell and Sugarhouse and Hiram Miller had spitted two goats and an antelope above the coals to roast, leaving the job of turning the spits and basting the meat to the Miller twins. While their wives were busy elsewhere, most of the men from the train had gathered in the hollow to smoke and talk.

Francis suspected Lije Holden had made the wedding celebration an excuse to uncork a fresh jug of the mountain whiskey he'd brought in some quantity from Kentucky. Holden didn't seem to drink much of it himself, never enough to affect his speech or his judgment, but not everyone in the party showed the same restraint.

If whiskey was present, it meant that Manasseh Thorne was not part of the group. Normally the same would be true of Douglas Stuart, but this time he stood near his nephew, watching with Presbyterian disapproval while Warner Espy pressed a long finger into the middle of Davy Stuart's chest.

"Be the boss from the very first minute," Espy was saying. "You hear? You got to be the boss. Because if you don't, she'll lead you around the rest of your life the way you lead a bull by the ring in his nose."

Buttrell saw Stuart nod and glance around the group as if he were looking for a way out. Most of the others were busy, drinking loop-fingered from the jug, playing Napoleon or casino, bound in tight knots of conversation about the state of the trail or the war in Kansas or farming in Oregon. A few sat on the ground listening to Stuart's schooling. Joe Coates snorted at Espy's lesson.

"Going to lead him around by the what?" he asked. The men nearest him laughed loudly.

"You mean the way your woman leads you?"

"Don't he wish!"

Milt Ames said, "Here, Davy, better have a drink of this tanglefoot. Man needs a little something to get him through a day like this and a night like you got coming."

"You listen to Milt, son," Espy put in, swaying a little. "He knows all about how and when and where."

The crowd laughed again, though Francis couldn't see what was funny. He wished he did not innately understand a kind of talk he had never heard before. It made him uneasy. He felt ashamed, ashamed of his own father, ashamed of all these men who seemed to him to be violating a sacred trust between themselves and their wives. It made him want to turn and go back to the hostel.

But one of the Miller twins had brought him a message from Stuart. Buttrell saw his chance to stay out of the smoky hollow. He waved his hat, got Stuart's attention, motioned for the bridegroom to come up. Stuart saw him, spoke earnestly to Espy for a moment, and came out of the hollow in long strides. His uncle followed more slowly.

Francis said, "Boaz Miller told me you wanted to see me."

"Not here," David Stuart said quietly. He turned back to his uncle. "Make some excuse for me, will you? I have to get away from that bunch."

"Aye," Douglas Stuart said. "Don't take them to heart, lad. They mean no harm." He drew a large silver watch from his pocket and opened its case. "Best be back at the wagon in an hour. You'll not want to miss the ceremony."

Unwillingly, Stuart laughed. "No danger of that, Uncle," he said. "Thanks. Francis, step over here with me, please. Lead the way, like it was your idea."

"Over in here," Francis said, loudly enough for the men to hear if they were interested. Then he headed into a stand of bushier woods that Elgin Bradley had never gotten round to clearing.

Stuart passed him, kept going. "Damned old drones," he said, perhaps to Buttrell, perhaps to himself. "They talk about love like people were cattle. 'Bulls and heifers.' My God!"

"I guess you was ready to get loose from them, then."

"I hope you didn't have to listen to much of that."

Buttrell looked away. "I didn't get close enough to hear it," he mumbled.

"I'm glad." Stuart stopped, turned, put a hand on his shoulder. "Francis, I haven't thanked you," he said. "That day I went to look for Ethan, I mean. You were the first one who volunteered to come, the one who believed my story."

Francis Buttrell bit his lip. He felt as if he were taking credit that belonged to someone else. It wasn't that he'd believed Stuart or thought especially well of him; he'd wanted to help Jessica Thorne. He'd thought then that he loved her. Now he knew better, of course. He knew it was Ann Bradley that he loved, would always love, would come back someday to marry.

"It wasn't nothing special," he mumbled.

"For me it was," Stuart said. "You played the man that day. What I'd like is for you to stand up with me."

"What?"

"At the wedding. My uncle Douglas will be with me. I wish you would, too. Could you do that?"

Francis saw a picture of himself, standing tall and strong beside Stuart, not caring what Ames or old Sugarhouse or any of the others said. Maybe someday, then, Stuart would stand by for him that same way when he married Ann Bradley.

"Francis?"

"Sure," Francis Buttrell said, unconsciously pitching his voice a little deeper. "I'll be proud to."

Fred Harris had been in the hollow for a few minutes, drawn along by the general sway of the group. He'd had one quick pull from Holden's jug, had hung on the fringe of two or three conversations without taking part. Soon, though, he left the clandestine gathering to wander farther into the woods, alone. He saw Stuart go off in another direction with young Buttrell. He might have come round to intersect their path, but he shied away from intruding upon some business of theirs.

He was a man tuned to aloneness. He had come home from medical school with a mind to helping his parents live forever. If that proved too ambitious, he was sure he could at least make their last years more comfortable. Even now, walking through the afternoon woods two thousand miles and another lifetime west of Fairfax Court House, Harris remembered how his parents had sacrificed to help him through his studies. But nothing in his studies had taught him a cure for yellow fever. He saw but did not appreciate the irony that his first lesson in how little doctors really knew had come through the deaths of those he'd wanted most to save.

He recognized the onset of the melancholy that often gripped him. Physician, heal thyself, he thought, and consciously picked up his pace. Sunlight came in rags and tatters through the branches of the spindly pines around him. The ground beneath his boots was deeply covered with dry, springy pine needles, so soft and silent that even his clumsy feet could move quietly. He thought he was alone in the woods, but when the trees opened suddenly into a clearing blooming with mountain iris, he saw he was not. Near a thicket of aspen saplings perhaps fifty yards away, he saw a strange phenomenon, a woman alone.

When Barbara Kenny left the kitchen, she walked straight to her wagon. She bathed her face in the cold water one of the Buttrell boys had brought from the spring and gradually worked herself past her urge to tear out Lena Ames's hair. That done, she stood staring into the woods that started beyond the circle of wagons. Judge Thorne had warned them all, the ladies especially, never to wander away from the train. And certainly not unarmed.

"I'm not really *wandering*," she whispered to herself. "Not so long as I go in a straight line."

But her conscience pricked her at that, so she found the little ring-triggered pocket revolver that had belonged to her husband. She was a much better shot with his rifle, but the rifle wouldn't slip into the little clutch bag that she took from the wagon.

"There," she said. "Now I'm armed. And still not wandering."

No, she was headed straight and far away from Lena Ames and her gossip and the kind of thinking she represented, though she knew she couldn't get far enough away to help. Ahead, she could hear men already whooping and carrying on down behind the barn. She could even smell their homemade whiskey. She angled farther away from them, for that was more of what she wanted to escape, until she was headed for the creek and the deep pool behind the beaver dam.

At the edge of a clearing, she stopped, one hand resting softly on the slender trunk of an aspen. The bright leaves fluttered silver-green in the wind, their murmur blending with the rush of creek water past the head of the dam. Thirty yards in front of her, a doe stepped into the clearing. It posed for a moment, motionless, before curving its neck downward to nose at the grass between its hooves.

"Yes," Barbara whispered, as if in answer to a question. The doe raised its head, its long ears cocked alertly forward, then resumed its grazing. Barbara stood entranced, overcome by that same kind of joy which she had found unbearable during holidays.

She'd come out here to purge her mind of the past, to draw out and discard every memory of her dead husband, of her label as old maid before the marriage and of widow since, of people like Lena who kept watch to be sure the labels stayed in place. She realized now that along with the pain, her mind held memories that were sweet, precious, that she could not live without.

"Sam." This time the whisper wasn't loud enough to disturb even the deer. "Damn you, Sam. Why did you have to die?"

The doe threw its head up abruptly and looked off to the right. For an instant, Barbara looked straight into the liquid black eyes, and then the deer was gone as though it had dissolved into the background of trees.

Behind her and off to her left, someone was moving softly through the brush toward her. The passage which had frightened the deer was soft and quiet to the woman's ear. Barbara Kenny felt a ripple of pleasantly fearful excitement. A man from the train? A stranger? An Indian who would spirit her off to his lodge? Probably, she thought with a smile, Manasseh Thorne to chide her for wandering. She did not turn but waited, content to meet whatever adventure came, until Dr. Harris walked around in front of her.

"Hello," he said, inclining his head in the hint of a bow. "I saw you out here alone. Can I be of service?"

"I *was* watching a deer," she told him. "It's gone now."

"Do you mean that I drove it away? I'm sorry. I had no wish to intrude on your privacy."

She smiled. "It was time someone intruded," she said. "I was becoming silly. I'm glad you came."

"But I regret that I spooked your game. I know what it's like to have a buck in your sights and lose it."

"This was only a doe."

Harris raised his brows a little, and she saw her meaning register in his mind. "I'm sorry," he said. "I meant no slight; neither to the doe nor to yourself. There is no more graceful creature in a forest glade."

"Than a doe?"

"If you wish."

"Is that Virginia gallantry, Doctor?" Barbara asked, matching his half-playful tone. It seemed a long time since she'd been playful with anyone. "If so, I could come to like it. But you seem to be alone, too."

"I was. Until now, if I may be so bold as to join you."

She looked at him appraisingly. "You have a quality of solitude. So much so that I sometimes see you completely alone in the midst of a crowd."

"I've had much the same impression of you," he said, and now his voice was quite serious. "Maybe we have that in common."

"We may. But it was not always so. I have been married. I wonder, Dr. Harris, whether you could venture that far outside yourself?"

She saw him frown for the briefest moment. "And is your interest that of the scientist?" he asked. "Or have you some more personal curiosity?"

"Wouldn't it be nice if every choice were so simple? But you know better. My motive is neither purely white nor yet purely black. My interest is gray."

"Gray is my favorite color."

Harris moved a long step toward her. She stood away from the tree and waited to see if he would bridge the gap between them.

Late in the afternoon Jessica stepped down from her father's wagon wearing her mother's wedding dress. For a moment, that sight was more than Manasseh Thorne could manage. Then he shifted his mind back into its wagon-master mode.

"We ought to be six miles farther along by now," he muttered, too softly for anyone to hear. "And I'll bet we've used up a week's supplies on one damned spree."

Then he bit sharply at the beard-hidden corner of his lip, and offered Jessica his arm. They marched in serious ceremony from the wagon across the yard and onto the porch of Bradley's Oak Inn. Stiff as a British grenadier, Francis Buttrell stood holding the door. Inside, virtually every soul from the inn and the wagon train encampment waited for the ceremony to begin.

The crowd left clear a narrow aisle from the door to a point near the broad fireplace. There, someone had cobbled together a rough arch of slats and pine boughs. Standing beneath it without his cane, Elgin Bradley awaited the father and bride. To one side David Stuart stood in his black Sunday best, his uncle Douglas at his side. On the other side, Sarah Holden waited, flanked by all the young girls of the train with bouquets of wildflowers.

Shaken, Jessica hesitated before she reached the arch. But it was too late to hesitate, too late to change her mind, too late to tell Davy the truth, too late for anything. Maybe it had been too late from the start, from that night with Ethan along the river.

Responding to her father's gentle pressure on her arm, she smiled at Stuart as bravely as Joan of Arc going to the stake and moved forward. Then David stood beside her before the tall pale apparition of their host.

Elgin Bradley opened the small blue prayer book to a spot marked by a silken ribbon. "Dearly beloved," Elgin Bradley began in a tone surprisingly strong, "we are gathered here in the presence of God and in the face of this congregation to unite this man and woman in marriage."

He went on, explaining the sanctity of marriage, pointing out the solemnity of the occasion, invoking blessings on everyone gathered there. Jessica Thorne lost track. Without lifting her eyes she looked at David Stuart and saw Ethan Fairchild standing in his place. She thought of the life within her, of the joy which might have been hers and Ethan's if she had not spurned him the day he rode away to fight over her. To fight and die because of her.

She heard the minister's words without understanding them, heard her own voice making the required responses at the right time. Just when she knew she would faint, she heard her father giving her away. To David Stuart.

She lifted her eyes to his. This time, she saw him, not Ethan. She saw a man with a deep-running humor and impetuous spirit. She saw a kindness hidden behind his dark, serious eyes.

Ridged against those traits within him, she saw the determined set of his jaw and shoulder. And in all those things she recognized the strength and the certainty and the love that she knew she would need. Always.

11

Ethan Fairchild sat on a flat rock, carefully recharging the cylinder from the Colt rifle. For luck, he drew the load on the one chamber he hadn't fired and replaced the powder and cap. Cranfill had two troopers on watch on the valley rim. Others moved around, gathering the horses and effects of the dead bandits and tending to the two wounded men.

"Hill's pretty bad, sir," Neidercutt told the lieutenant. "Probably we'll have to rig a travois for him. Teague's not much hurt. I sent Schmidt on west with the scout, looking for tracks of them that got away."

"Very good, Sergeant. Carry on."

Trooper Healy seated himself beside Fairchild and began sharpening a spade from one of the packs. "The remains of the deceased soldier," he said softly between strokes of the file, "may be interred at the place of death, should the commanding officer deem such burial to be proper. A report of the fact will be made to the adjutant-general of the Army." Healy looked sideways at Fairchild. "We're three days and more from Laramie at the pace we'll be moving. I expect poor Jimmy Jenkins will sleep right here."

Fairchild set the Colt's big hammer on half cock and laid the rifle across his knees. "I'm sorry," he said.

"Soldier's pay." Healy shrugged. "That charge of yours likely saved us a man or two."

"I didn't do so much. Mainly, it was the horse."

"All right, you that's not working!" Neidercutt's voice was pitched in a parade-ground tone. The troopers and Fairchild stopped what they were doing and turned toward the sergeant, who stood on a grassy bench up past the creek's high-water mark.

"We got five dead. That's five graves to dig, right up here on this flat. Healy, looks like you're ready. Some of the rest of you, get yourselves a spade and help out."

The Dragoons hesitated, looked at each other, murmured among themselves. Neidercutt put his hands on his hips and glared at them.

"Well? Has a little fight made you hard of hearing? Boyce, what's holding you back?"

Boyce licked his lips. "Sarge, it ain't right," he said. "It's orders, if you say so, but it ain't right."

"Boyce!"

"A moment, Sergeant." Cranfill had been seated on the bank, writing with a pencil in his order book. He got to his feet and came over beside Neidercutt. "What's not right, Boyce? Speak up."

"Well." The trooper looked at the others as if hoping for support. They shrugged, muttered, stared at the ground. "Begging the lieutenant's pardon, it ain't right to bury renegade trash alongside as good a soldier as Jenkins. If it's orders, I'll do it, sir, but I'm not wanting to dig no graves for them."

The sergeant, his face like a thundercloud, started to speak, but Cranfill held up a hand.

"I see," he said. "One's a woman."

"Renegade trash, same's the rest," Boyce growled, then added, "Sir."

Cranfill looked at Boyce, then at the others. They studied the ground, all but Healy. Cranfill bit at a thumbnail and nodded.

"Abstract justice isn't my department," he said. "I trust that's handled by more competent authority. But I won't order any man to help. Sergeant, ask for volunteers."

"If the lieutenant would just go inspect the horses, sir," Neidercutt said, "I'll find him all the volunteers he needs. This whole collection of barracks lawyers will be dying to volunteer."

"That'll do, Sergeant."

Neidercutt sighed. "As you say, sir." He faced the troopers. "Volunteers for burial detail."

"I'll make a place for Jenkins," Boyce said promptly, and another man seconded him.

"Get to it, then. Who else?"

Healy stood up, testing the edge of the spade with his thumb. "There's none so bad, man or woman, as deserves to lie unburied and unmourned," he said.

Fairchild said, "Hell, I'll do it."

Both Neidercutt and the lieutenant looked at him in surprise. He grinned at them and shrugged.

"I killed a couple. Guess I can bury them."

"Very good, Mr. Fairchild," Cranfill murmured, looking at him with a little frown. "Boyce, get Mr. Fairchild a spade."

Fairchild knew how to dig, and he'd never considered physical work an insult or burden. The digging was good. The sharp spade cut cleanly into the dry, hard soil. The hard dirt resisted the blade but gave in to his doggedness, and he felt the simple joy of conquest begin to wash away his reaction to the fight.

He'd never killed anyone before. Up until that day, he'd never even seen a man dead by violence. Then, in less than a minute, he had shot two men and a woman, though he hadn't known about her at the time. Looking inside himself, he found a lurking sickness, a stunned wonder that was already wearing off, a kind of sneaking relief that it had been they and not he who'd stopped the bullets and who now lay waiting for a grave.

That was all. No remorse. No feeling that he'd sinned against God or man. Once, back on the farm, he'd shot a wolf that had raided the henhouse. He had admired the thick gray coat, had felt a touch of sympathy about the hunger that drove the animal down among its enemies. And he'd never wanted to kill another.

But he wanted to kill the man with flowing white hair. He intended to kill him, if he had to track him to the end of the earth, if he had to kill all the survivors of the gang to get to their leader. It was that man, not David Stuart, who was responsible for all that had happened, who had probably killed Stuart, too. Fairchild wanted to kill him for that.

He saw himself riding to the edge of a low bluff only vaguely aware of the troopers on his flanks. As if alone he looked into the basin below. There Whitehair and his woman stood fighting back to back. The rest of the gang sat their horses as if they were carved from ice.

Fairchild urged his horse on. It soared off the edge of the twenty-foot bluff and landed softly in the basin. He rode through the mounted gang, shooting left and right, until he came to the fighting couple. Without concern, he shot down the woman, laughed as Whitehair turned at bay, fired his last shot into the renegade's belly.

"Hey, miner!"

Whitehair and his Indian maiden and the rest of the reverie disappeared like smoke on the clear warm breeze as Fairchild looked up. He was waist-deep in a good-sized grave clanging his shovel against solid rock. Sergeant Neidercutt stood on the brink, frowning down at him.

"That's as far as you're gonna go without blasting powder. Suppose you move over a little and start another one. Turns out we're going to need one more than we planned."

Fairchild climbed out of the hole and leaned on the handle of his spade. Trooper Healy, just started on his second grave, straightened and looked at Neidercutt.

"One more," Healy repeated. "Is it Hill, then?"

Neidercutt shook his head. "No, Hill's better. With luck he'll make it back to Laramie." He spat into one of the graves. "It's another of them damned wolves, I expect, though he's maybe just an unlucky citizen like Fairchild, here. Dutch and the Delaware found him upstream a ways, and tracks where five or six more rode off."

"Who killed him?" Fairchild asked.

"Likely he had a little misunderstanding with his friends. Throat cut, stripped, and scalped." Neidercutt snapped his fingers. "Reminds me, Mankiller, the Delaware wondered if you want the scalps of them four by the creek. Said he'd be glad to do it for you before we bury them."

Fairchild's stomach seemed to roll over. He pressed his lips together and swallowed. "One's yours," he said, keeping his voice flat.

"Don't take them, myself." The little sergeant grinned. "Give you something to show that little gal you're so sweet on, though, if you ever catch up to her again."

Immediately, Fairchild was back in the basin—reloading his Colt to put six more leads balls into Whitehair's squirming body. Calmly. Without haste, without regret. Just pointing the gun, cocking the hammer, pulling the trigger, cocking the hammer, pulling . . .

He looked at Neidercutt, felt his mouth twist into a sort of smile. "Sure," he said. "I'll take them. Tell him thanks for me."

The sergeant raised his eyebrows, nodded. Standing in the half-dug grave, Healy straightened and crossed himself.

"Holy Mary," he said. "Think what it is you're doing. That's no way for a civilized man to be behaving."

"I imagine not."

Neidercutt nodded. "I'll tell him," he said. He turned his head and spat. "Don't know as I'd mention this to the lieutenant. He might not understand it the way we do."

The prayer book looked like the one Manasseh Thorne had used, small and blue with limp leather bindings. But Fairchild could see that Cranfill's copy was battered and rolled up from riding in a saddlebag, its back broken, its covers bound with twine to hold loose pages. It fell open easily to the place the lieutenant wanted.

Trooper Hill lay on a blanket by the creek, breathing fast and shallow, his hand pressed to the bandage on his wounded side. The Delaware and one private were on watch, but the rest of the men gathered in two careful lines at the head and foot of the six rocky mounds, hats off, hands folded in front of them. Cranfill stood at the edge of Jenkins's grave and looked at them one by one, saving Fairchild for last, before he began to read.

" 'I am the resurrection and the life—' "

Fairchild knew the words of the burial service well. He'd heard them twice before on the trail, once for Sam Kenny and once for Etta Lee. Unlike Thorne, the lieutenant merely read from the book without adding his own ideas, but Fairchild couldn't tell that it hurt the service much.

For the first time, it occurred to him to wonder if Thorne had read those words over Fairchild's empty grave, what thoughts the wagonmaster had added, whether Jess had cried, whether the others had comforted her as they'd comforted Barbara Kenny. Somehow, the picture made him feel twice as alone and abandoned, twice as *dead* as he'd felt before.

With the amens said and a carbine volley fired over Jenkins, Cranfill dismissed the patrol to boil coffee and gnaw at salt pork and hardtack before starting on their way again. Fairchild started for Healy's squad fire, but Sergeant Neidercutt intercepted him.

"The lieutenant's compliments, Mr. Fairchild, and you'll kindly join him at his headquarters, that big cottonwood by the creek. Let's go."

Fairchild didn't know exactly what to expect. What he got was a smile from Cranfill and the offer of a tin cup of strong black coffee. He sipped at it eagerly, burning his tongue and not caring much.

"Sit down, Mr. Fairchild. You, too, Sergeant." Cranfill waved a hand at the hardtack crackers toasting by the fire. "Help yourselves. You did well in the fight, Mr. Fairchild. On behalf of the Army, I thank you."

"The Army's welcome." Fairchild lowered himself to a seat with his back against the rough bark of the cottonwood. The leaves whispered softly overhead, flashing silver in the sun as the wind ruffled them. "It all happened pretty fast. I don't think I did anything extra special."

Cranfill gave his brief grin. "Sergeant Neidercutt thinks you did, and he's a pretty good judge of such things."

Fairchild looked at the dour little sergeant in surprise, almost missing the next thing Cranfill said.

"We can't move fast with Hill on a litter, and we need to get him medical attention as soon as possible. I'm sending a couple of men crosslots to Fort Laramie, fast as they can march. They'll bring back an Army ambulance and escort. If we're lucky, the post surgeon will come, too."

The lieutenant paused to gnaw off a bite of cracker and bacon, then looked at Fairchild.

"I know you're eager to get back to your wagon train and your young lady. Would you like to volunteer for the party going to the fort? There will be some risk, but you'll save several days," Cranfill said.

"Risk be damned. Sure, I'll go."

"And you need not return with the detail from the fort."

"Yes, sir, Lieutenant. I'm your man."

"Good." Cranfill rubbed his chin. "As I said, there's a risk with only two men. That rifle of yours is certainly adequate. Wish I had enough for my whole command. But you really need a handgun. Sergeant?"

"Well, sir, the best thing we captured from them renegades is this." He held out the pepperbox pistol that had belonged to the round-faced man. "We found a bullet mold and fixings for it in the late owner's saddlebags. And Fairchild kind of earned it, seeing he killed the jasper what was using it."

Fairchild accepted the pistol gingerly, turning it in his hands. It had six barrels and looked to be about .30 caliber. "Better than nothing, I guess," he said.

"Not much. It'll do for close-in, and you don't have to take time to cock the hammer. But for anything farther away than three, four feet, say, you'll need something a little different." Neidercutt cleared his throat, squinting at Cranfill. "Now, if the lieutenant was to decide that Jenkins's old Colt Dragoon was lost in combat . . ."

He let his voice trail off. Cranfill laughed aloud, startling Fairchild.

"The lieutenant would probably end up buying it out of his pay," Cranfill said. "And he'd probably make his sergeant's life miserable during the process."

"Yes, sir. Standard military practice, sir."

"Do you happen to have that pistol handy, Sergeant?"

"As it happens, I do, sir."

He reached behind the log where he was sitting and drew out a black gunbelt with military holster and cartridge box. Cranfill took it from him, opened the holster flap to touch the smooth walnut butt of the Colt, then passed the whole assembly across to Fairchild.

"Lieutenant, I thank you. I want to pay."

Cranfill held up a hand. "It's not for sale. This gun belonged to a good soldier, Mr. Fairchild," he said. "Remember him when you wear it. Now, I can't make you a present of an Army animal or saddle, but we took four good horses as spoils of war. Since the sergeant tells me you're not too fond of the mount he chose for you, you can pick one of them, saddle and all."

Fairchild started to answer, then hesitated. He knew, if no one else did, that the chestnut horse had been the real hero of the fight. A horse like that, he reasoned, might come in handy, especially if he meant to look for Whitehair.

"Thanks, Lieutenant, but I'd rather keep that chestnut if there's any way around your regulations. Truth is, I've kind of gotten attached to him."

"It's an Army horse."

"Begging the lieutenant's pardon," Neidercutt said quickly, "but he got that flaxen-maned devil from the pack string. If the Army needs paying for him, me and the boys would take up a collection."

Cranfill sighed. "They don't teach you about these things at West Point," he muttered. He pulled out his order book and scribbled quickly, then tore out the page and handed it to Fairchild. "Here. This'll keep the commandant at Fort Laramie from hanging you as a horse thief. At least I think it will. The sergeant will find a volunteer to accompany you. Get a saddle on that animal and be ready to leave in ten minutes."

Fairchild took the paper and folded it into his pocket, then held out a hand to Cranfill.

"Lieutenant, I don't know how to tell you thanks."

Cranfill shook the hand. "Maybe you'd better get to Laramie alive before you get too grateful," he said with another quick grin. "Good luck, Mr. Fairchild. Catch up to your wagon train, marry that girl, and forget all about your adventures here. All right?"

"Sure," Fairchild said. "That's what I'll do."

He thought of Whitehair, of his vision of revenge, of the hatred that had gripped him just after the fight, when he'd wanted to see all the renegades dead. Half ashamed, he remembered the four scalps that the Delaware had wrapped in deerskin and tucked into his saddlebag. He would have to get rid of those before anyone civilized saw them.

"That's what I'll do," he repeated.

"Sure you will, Mankiller." Sergeant Neidercutt spat toward the stream. "Move along, now. You've got two hard days to Fort Laramie, and Sioux to dodge the whole way."

Despite the dire warnings from Cranfill and Neidercutt, the ride to Fort Laramie was uneventful except for long stretches at a trot, even longer stretches of walking and leading the horses, dry camps, mountains looming to the west, rolling grassy hills where startled antelope bounded away from the men and buffalo grazed. There may have been Indians around as Private Boyce assured him that there were; but he didn't see any until late afternoon of the third day, when the log buildings of Fort Laramie came into sight.

"There you go." Boyce pointed. Between the fort and the banks of the North Platte, a dozen or more buffalo hide lodges lay wrapped in drifting woodsmoke. "Indians. Them's Snakes, Shoshone, from over west a ways. Come down to smoke and talk and see what they can steal, most likely."

"Aren't they dangerous?"

"Nah. Snakes is friendly. And they hate the Sioux." Boyce shaded his eyes. "No wagons around. Guess that train of yours has done moved on." He glanced quickly at Fairchild.

Fairchild knew that Boyce wasn't sure there'd been a train, but it no longer bothered him. "I've fallen a good week behind them, probably ten days," he said. "I don't figure old Thorne stopped anyplace for long. Most likely, they're at Bradley's Oak by now, or heading for Platte Crossing." He shrugged. "No matter, I'll catch up. I figure I can go twice as fast as they can."

Boyce nodded. "So if you're ten days behind now, you'll catch up to where they are in five days," he said. Then he frowned. "But then they'll be five days farther on. And when you get there, they'll have gone on two days and some." He mopped his forehead, his lips moving as he worked back through his calculations. Finally, he shook his head.

"I don't know, man. Looking at it like that, blessed if I see how you're ever going to catch them."

Fairchild didn't understand the mathematics, either, but it didn't affect his assurance. "I'll catch them," he said. "Never fear about that. I'll write and let you know how it goes."

"Probably no need," Boyce said morosely. "Barracks talk is we'll be patrolling toward Fort Hall. Might be we'll run across you again."

They had been riding as they talked. Now they drew

up at a sentry's challenge. Boyce answered, and they rode inside the open fort. Fairchild was surprised at the lack of activity. Not more than a dozen blue-clad soldiers were in sight, and none of them moved with much enthusiasm. Boyce saw it, too.

"Not much doing here," he said as they tied their mounts in front of the log headquarters building. The chestnut snaked its head around to snap at Fairchild and he laughed and batted it on the nose.

"Don't see why you choosed that horse," Boyce said. "Let's us get reported, and then you can get along your way."

A sergeant at a crackerbox desk listened to their report, went into another room for a minute, then motioned Boyce and Fairchild inside. A lieutenant, shaved and looking even younger than Cranfill, greeted them with no special enthusiasm.

"Well?"

"Boyce, Second Dragoons, sir." The trooper came to something pretty close to attention. "This is Mr. Fairchild, civilian scout. Report from Lieutenant Cranfill, sir."

The lieutenant took the sheaf of papers from Boyce. He read through it quickly, then went back to study the close-written pages more thoroughly.

"Wounded," he muttered. "Army ambulance. Escort. With half the damned garrison ready to desert? Surgeon? My God, why doesn't he ask for the presidential carriage, with the secretary of war to drive it?"

"I don't know, sir," Boyce said.

The lieutenant glanced at him. "Shut up," he said. "Now. This trooper. Hill. Hurt bad?"

"Shot through the body, sir."

"I see." He raised his voice. "Grayson!"

"Yes, sir." The sergeant appeared in the doorway again.

"Detail six men, plus the surgeon's striker. Get an ambulance wagon ready to go. Week's rations. These men will guide it. You'll command."

"Yes, sir."

"Begging the lieutenant's pardon," Boyce said, "but I'll guide it. Mr. Fairchild's trying to catch up to his friends."

"Friends?" The lieutenant's glance fastened on Fairchild. "Miners?"

"No," Fairchild said. "Why do you ask that?"

"Rumors. Big silver strike, they say. California, someplace, or maybe Nevada. Probably just talk, but half the garrison's ready to desert to get to it and get rich."

"It's a wagon train I want. From Ohio." Fairchild caught himself lapsing into the same staccato speech as the lieutenant. "I was lost from it back near Scott's Bluff. The man in charge is named Thorne, Manasseh Thorne. Do you remember it?"

"Wagons. Civilians." The officer waved a hand in dismissal. "No. Wait a minute. Thorne. Sold off a lot of goods from some wagon. Here for the Fourth celebration. Looking for a preacher."

"That's them."

"They left on the fifth."

Fairchild calculated it in his mind. "What's today's date?"

12

Jessica Stuart gently eased her husband's arm from around her shoulders. When he didn't stir, she slipped out from beneath the down comforter they shared in the wagon bed and smoothed it back over him. He murmured something in his sleep. Jessica reached out to stroke his hair as if he were a sleeping child. After a moment, his breathing resumed its regular pattern and Jessica crept softly to the curtain at the front of the wagon's cover.

She wasn't sure of the time, but thought it somewhere around three in the morning. Drawing back the curtain, she breathed deeply of the crisp night air and peered around for signs of movement. Oxen shuffled in the rope corral at the center of the wagon circle. The tall peaked wagon covers loomed like clouds, frosted silver by the cold moonlight. A guard she took to be Sugarhouse came from between two wagons and went out toward the picketed horses, holding his rifle stiffly before him.

Like old times, Jessica thought, and stifled the impulse to giggle like a child. Since the wedding at Bradley's Oak, she'd had no reason to leave her own bed at night. Only now did she realize how much she'd missed the excitement of prowling like an Indian through the sleeping train.

She put on her slippers and wrapped a heavy robe round herself. Then she climbed softly out of the wagon, careful not to wake Davy. Even if he should wake now, it would be easy to give a reason for being out. *Nature called.* It would be no more difficult than that. And nature *was* calling in an old and familiar way that she had not expected at all.

Smiling to herself, she moved swiftly and quietly as a shadow along the inner circle of the wagons until she came to the one driven by Fred Harris. Within the circle an ox gave a muffled moo of protest, clumped its hooves and jostled for room, fell silent again. She waited, holding her breath, but the guard didn't return.

"Doctor?" She peeked into Harris's wagon, saw nothing but darkness. "Dr. Harris," she whispered. But he did not reply. Thinking him deeply asleep, she climbed over the tailgate into the wagon and put out her hand to find the foot of his bed. He was not in it.

She sat a long minute wondering, then looked out into the moonlit circle of the wagons. Sugarhouse came back, made a turn around the corraled oxen, paused to gaze up into the night sky. She smelled the smoke from his pipe. Two wagons back, an axle spring squeaked. Sugarhouse looked that way, startled, gripping his rifle. Then he laughed softly at himself and walked back toward the horses again.

The moment the guard disappeared, a man slipped away from the second wagon as smoothly as a shadow and moved toward Jessica. She drew back into the darkness of Harris's wagon and held her breath. Her heart fluttered her robe in quick little thumps. What would anyone think if she were found in Harris's wagon in the middle of the night!

But it made no sense that a man would have come from that wagon. It belonged to Mrs. Kenny. Then she heard someone outside, not two feet away from her hiding place. A moment later he slithered over the tailgate like a snake and knelt beside her looking back into the circle.

She kept her voice low. "Dr. Harris?"

He jumped, twisting around and away from her as if she'd been a rattlesnake. She caught a flash of his staring eyes in a shaft of moonlight before the curtain dropped across the tailgate.

"Great God Almighty!" he said in a rasping whisper. "Who is it?" She could feel him shaking, but after a second, he gave a quiet chuckle. "Jessica, you scared the devil out of my soul," he whispered.

"I'm sorry. I just got here. I wanted to talk to you."

"I hadn't been gone a minute. Nature called." He was embarrassed.

"Me, too," she began. Suddenly she understood. Harris had been in Barbara Kenny's wagon. It was not so different from her own experience, except this time the man was doing the tiptoeing. "It doesn't matter now," she breathed, holding tightly onto herself to keep from breaking out in helpless laughter.

"Of course it does." The doctor's voice was calmer as he worked his way toward composure. "I assume you had a medical question to discuss."

"Yes."

"It's a little outside my usual office hours."

Jessica pressed her lips together primly until she judged

it safe to speak. "Yes," she repeated. "I'm sorry. I had a very private question. I was wondering about having a baby."

"Oh," he breathed. She could feel the smile in his words. "Already? It's a little soon to be thinking of that. How long has it been since your last time?"

She felt her face burn and was glad he couldn't see her in the darkness. "Late in May," she said. "But that's just the thing. Now I find I've begun again."

"I see," he said in a different tone. She was certain she knew what was in his mind. *Late in May. Fairchild was lost in June. And the wedding was July twelfth.* "Begun again," he said. "The menses?"

"Yes."

"Well, then, that answers your question. You won't be having a baby quite yet."

"You're sure?"

"It's a pretty definite sign," he said. "You don't have to be as good a doctor as I am to make that diagnosis. If it persists more than a day or so, it will be a normal denial."

She hesitated, but there was no reason not to be honest. "Then I'm not sure. It's only been today."

He took her hand. "Don't worry. And don't worry Stuart. You can be sure in another day. Now, you'd better get back to your wagon, before somebody gets all the wrong ideas."

Even in the darkness, she could tell he was smiling. She slipped out of his wagon without making the springs squeak, and hurried back for her own. Stuart had turned over, was awake, had missed her.

"Jess? You all right?"

She shrugged off her robe and snuggled in beside him under the covers, pressing tightly to the warmth of his body. "I'm fine," she told him. "I've never been more fine."

"You're colder than a winter fish. Especially your feet. But I'm glad you're fine."

"Are you fine?"

"You're being silly."

"Are you?"

"Yes. Can't you tell?"

"Don't do that. Not now. Let me do this instead."

"Wanton woman." He caught her hand. "You've been so serious these past weeks. What's made you so flighty tonight?"

"Counting chickens," she said. "Before they hatch. Sometimes they don't. Hatch."

The laughter that had been bubbling inside her finally broke loose, though she couldn't share the joke with him. She giggled helplessly, and he kissed her to quiet her giggling, and she kissed him back until he released her hand, and after a while he said, "Your father's planning to start up his law practice when we reach Oregon City. He asked if I wanted to read for the law in his office."

"Ummm. Do you?"

"I've never thought of myself as a lawyer."

"You're very persuasive."

"So are you. Are you going to let me get back to sleep?"

Jessica Stuart smiled, a smile of peace and joy and freedom, as she slipped her arms around her husband's neck. "Eventually," she said.

Yawning, David Stuart dropped his tin plate and fork into the hot water where Sarah Holden was briskly washing breakfast dishes. She looked up at him with an impish smile.

"Sleep poorly, Mr. Stuart?" she asked, her voice innocent as the dew. "Funny thing, wakefulness. My Lije is took that same way some nights."

Stuart tipped his hat to her and mumbled a good morning, reminding himself as he walked away that there were damned few secrets on the trail. Jess, all brisk efficiency, was helping some of the other women stow the pots and pans. Stuart started that way, then saw Dr. Harris strapping up the tailboard on his wagon.

"Morning, Fred."

Harris glanced up and waved a hand. "Stuart." He yawned and gave the tailboard a yank to be sure it was secure. "Ready to roll. How are you?"

"Asking professionally?"

"What?" The doctor glanced at him, frowned, then laughed. "Oh, I see. No, I'm not looking for customers."

"I could use some advice, though. Jess and I were talking last night."

Harris nodded. "About a baby."

"No, about the law." Stuart stopped suddenly. He frowned at Harris. "A baby? No. What made you think of that?" He realized how that sounded and said, "I mean, it's too early for that, isn't it?"

Fred Harris seemed to shake himself, and suddenly his attention was all on Stuart.

"Oh. Yes, of course," he said. "Sorry, I was thinking of something else. Sorry." He looked away. "Advice, you say. What sort?"

Stuart explained about Thorne, the law office, his concern about law as a career.

"And there's the idea of working for Jessica's father," he finished. "I'm not sure how that would turn out."

"Wife's family. Yes," Harris murmured. "I expect that could be awkward. No experience myself."

Stuart followed Harris's glance across to the Widow Kenny who was yoking her team like a man. She led the lines back to the wagon box, paused, and looked across toward the two of them. Stuart saw her smile.

"The thing is, act while you have the opportunity," Harris said suddenly. Stuart glanced at him in surprise. The doctor usually didn't sound so definite or assured. "Don't wait your life away trying to find just the right thing. It'll come along."

"How will I know it's the right thing?"

Harris watched Mrs. Kenny lift her skirts to climb onto

the wagon seat. "You'll know," he said. He turned suddenly and clapped Stuart on the shoulder. "You'll know it when you see it, that's all."

Thoman Silverhorn sat his horse on the low bluff outside Taylor's Crossing. It was no more than a half-dozen shacks, thrown up beside the deep ruts that ran between Cherry Creek and Fort Laramie, built mainly by discouraged refugees from the Pikes Peak gold rush. Silverhorn thought it odd that a town should be named for a shallow spot in a creek, and even odder that a wart of a place like Taylor's Crossing should have a name at all. But, such as it was, it was just what he needed.

"Give me an hour," he said. "I don't know how long that doctor will take. See if Willard's got a watch."

"None of them's got a watch," Grace said.

"How do you know?"

Grace laughed. Silverhorn looked at her for a moment, then drew out a big silver hunter-cased watch by its chain.

"You can use mine." He flipped the case open to check the time, frowned, wound his watch, shook it. The second hand wasn't moving. He shook the watch again, then held it to his ear. "Hell," he said. The way he figured it, a man needed reliable weapons, hot food once a day, a warm woman at night, and a good watch. He was short the watch.

"I can tell when an hour's up." A tall, gaunt, scragglybearded man had come up beside them. "I don't need no goldamned watch, nor no goldamned woman to read it for me."

Silverhorn turned and squinted his good eye at him. "Willard," he said "there's nobody told you to come up here along of us. You're supposed to be down with the horses."

"That's no job for a man with brains," Willard said. "Them two goldamned heathen Indian savages can watch the horses. And them other two can watch them watch."

Silverhorn took off his hat and combed his fingers through his white mane of hair. He put the hat back on. "Willard," he said quietly, "it's not so long ago that I had me another helper that thought he had some brains. He got so's he didn't want to do what he was told. After that, he got so's he considered he had more brains than me."

"Hell, Thoman, I never had a goldamned idea like that."

"Last I saw of him," Silverhorn said, a little louder, "he was lying in the mud with his throat cut." He unbuttoned his coat and wrapped his hand around the handle of one of his big Colts. "Do you take my meaning, Willard?"

Willard looked at Silverhorn. He looked at the revolver with Silverhorn's hand on the butt. Then he turned and looked at Grace, who grinned and blew him a kiss.

"Why, sure, Thoman," he said, smiling to show three crooked teeth. "Never meant no offense. I'll just wait down by the horses until you tell me what to do."

"Thank you, Willard. You just do that."

"He's the best of them," Grace said, watching his back as he rode back down to join the others. "He's the best, and he's not worth skinning out for the hide and tallow."

"It's hard to get good help," Silverhorn said.

He had picked up three new men. Willard was on the run from something that had happened back in Missouri. He claimed it was a killing. Farley West had been run out of a mining camp. He wouldn't say why, but somebody had crisscrossed his back with twenty lashes from a bull-whip before they'd sent him on his way. Rafe Longdon had deserted from the Army to find gold, then had discovered digging for gold was more work than soldiering.

Silverhorn didn't know as yet whether he could trust them or whether they would be any good when it came time to go to work. He had fed them. Now he was ready to see them earn their keep. At least he could depend on Blue Eye and Kills Running. And Grace. He could always depend on Grace.

"Here." He drew his telescope from his belt and handed

it to Grace. "Keep an eye peeled. When you see me come out from the doctor's you bring them in."

"Sure, Tom." She grinned at him. "You have a good time down there, hear?"

Silverhorn left his mount tied at the edge of the settlement and went first to the little building whose sign advertised Professor Horace Holderman, Doctor of Phrenology. The sagging wooden door creaked open under his hand. To his surprise, the shack had two rooms. The first was empty except for a rough wooden table and two cane-bottomed chairs. Silverhorn crossed to the door marked Private, pushed it open, and went inside.

"What? Who's that?" A small round man with red cheeks, spectacles, sparse graying hair, turned to Silverhorn. "Can't you read, sir?" He peered through the spectacles at the dirty scarf that swathed the right side of Silverhorn's face. "Ah, a sufferer in distress. If you'll seat yourself outside, sir, I'll see to you presently. At the moment, I have a patient."

He gestured vaguely toward a broad, slope-shouldered man sitting naked to the waist on a leather-topped table. "What the hell!" the patient rumbled.

"Nothing wrong with him you can't cure with a bath and a gallon of whiskey," Silverhorn said. "My eye pains me. I need you to work on it."

"But I'm busy." Seeing no sign of apology in Silverhorn's eye, the doctor said, "I have a responsibility here. I'll get to you presently, if you'll just be patient."

"Patience ain't my longest suit as a general thing." Silverhorn jerked his head at the patient. "Get out."

"Like hell!" The slope-shouldered man lurched to his feet, balling his fists. "We'll see who gets put out of where."

Silverhorn opened his coat and gripped the pair of heavy pistols at his waist. "Follow suit or trump," he said. "It's all one to me. Get your gear and get out."

The doctor said, "Gentlemen, please, no violence." He took down the patient's coat and a dirty gray shirt from a peg on the wall. "Virgil, you go along now. We'll continue your treatment later."

Virgil grabbed his shirt and coat, hitched his long underwear up, and stalked to the door, pausing there to level a finger at Silverhorn.

"I'll see you again, mister."

"Now, I'll just count on that."

"All right." Dr. Holderman pushed the door closed behind Virgil and turned to Silverhorn. "Now, sir, what's wrong with you that couldn't wait five minutes?"

"Eye." Silverhorn took off his hat, shook out his white hair. Plumping himself down on the leather cushion, he unwound the bandana. He saw Holderman's face change. The doctor turned the shade of the lamp so that it cast more light on Silverhorn's face, then leaned close to look. His breath smelled of peppermint.

"God above, man, how did this happen?"

"Mosquitoes. Question's what you can do about it."

Horace Holderman licked his lips. "I can't fix it so's you'll see out of it again," he said. He looked at Silverhorn fearfully. "I can't. No doctor can. It's gone."

"I know that. Are you a sure-enough doctor?"

"Sir, I've treated the crowned heads of Europe. Only through the most distressing circumstances have I come to this rural spot."

"Got any more of that peppermint?"

"I can clean the wound, dress it for you. It will heal with only the slightest scar. You can keep the eye, but you'll never see out of it again."

"What good's a goddamned eye that don't work? Dig it out." Silverhorn shrugged irritably. "What good's a doctor that can't fix a man when he's hurt?"

"If you'll sit very still, I'll take care of it. The operation. And a clean dressing. Then I'll give you some salve that'll ease it some until the socket gets over the insult."

"Insult?" Silverhorn laughed. "Insult?"

"This will hurt," Holderman said. He selected a scalpel from an untidy stack of instruments and wiped it clean on his cuff. "Very considerably, I should think. Let me get you something to bite on."

"I've already done asked you once. Do you have any more of that peppermint?"

Silverhorn left with a clean white bandage covering his eye. Behind him, the office was silent. He pulled the door closed and lit a cigar, looking up toward the ridge where Grace should be. His vision swam. He couldn't tell if she was up there. With a shrug, he crossed to the general store.

The clerk was young, enthusiastic. "Good morning, sir. What can I help you with today?"

"Cigars."

"Do you like the kind you're smoking?"

"Rather have better. Give me a dozen of them cheroots."

"Yes, sir. Could I interest you in groceries, gunpowder, notions for the little woman?"

"Oh, yes, you can interest me in all that. But first I'll see your watches."

"Yes, sir. We don't carry but one kind. The best. Here you are." The young man looked at the clock on the wall, set the watch, and wound it. "Made in Waterbury. That's in Connecticut, away back East. Brought all the way out here for our customers."

Silverhorn took the watch, shook it, dropped it on the counter.

"Sir?"

Then he picked it up, listened to it, nodded, and put it in his pocket. "How much?"

The young man had already added the figures in his head and calculated the change, depending on the currency. He took Silverhorn's money and had opened his cash drawer, then hesitated at the sound of hooves outside. Five men and a woman had ridden into the middle of town.

"Tough-looking lot," the clerk observed.

"Not as tough as they look."

"A woman, too. Looks as tough as the rest, if you ask me."

"Tougher."

The clerk shrugged and counted out Silverhorn's change like a gambler dealing out a hand. Silverhorn smiled. The change was a dollar short, though the clerk's count had come out right.

"Anything else?"

Silverhorn nodded toward the shelves. "Give me one of those."

The clerk turned smiling to look, and Silverhorn rapped him smartly across the back of the head with the butt of his left-hand Colt. Casually, he stepped across the fallen man, scooped the money from the cash drawer, and gathered up the rest of the cigars.

Outside, Grace and the men were shooting. They were making a lot of noise to impress him, but he already knew there were not more than half a dozen folks in the whole town. He went outside to see that none of them were getting away.

Willard and Rafe Longdon had gone into the other buildings and were wasting a lot of good powder as far as Silverhorn could tell. Grace and the two Pawnee were back at the livery barn. Silverhorn called after them to throw a saddle on one of the extra horses. Behind him, West was at the door of the doctor's office.

"I've done for the doc already," Silverhorn told him. "You help with the horses, then go clean out the store. See you get everybody a watch."

West gaped at him. "What for? I can't read a watch."

"Because I goddamned well say so! Move!"

A slope-shouldered man ran barefoot from one of the shacks. He sprawled in the street, then gathered himself up to run again. Silverhorn recognized the doctor's last patient.

"You!" he roared and drew one of the Colts. Before he

could fire, Willard stepped from the door of the shack and shot first. The bullet hit the man in the back of the head, driving him down into the dirt again. Willard laughed and fired another shot into the body. He was gnawing on a hunk of ham.

"Willard!"

The new man looked at his boss, did not show the respect of lowering his gun.

"Time'll come you wish you had back that wasted powder. Get on with your work. Help West with the store!"

"We ain't left nothing in there that can be ate or drunk or shot."

"That ribbon clerk's alive yet. Drag him out here and tie him on a horse. Alive."

"That storekeeper? What the hell for? You saving him for Grace to have some fun?"

"Do like I tell you, or it'll be your hide she's having fun with. Do it, and be quick. We got to be away from here."

Willard grinned, bit off another mouthful of ham. "Sure," he said. "Anything you say, Thoman. You got the brains."

Half an hour later, Silverhorn looked with satisfaction on a job well done. His force was mounted on fresh horses, a string of pack animals carried all the supplies they could handle, and he had more than eight hundred dollars in notes and coin bulging the sides of his possible bag. The ribbon clerk swaying on the back of a tall black gelding moaned and hunched over the saddle horn.

Grace said, "We don't need another mouth."

"Not so long as we got yours," Silverhorn said. "Shut up." To his new men he said, "What you don't want to do is try my patience. Burn it."

They rode, one to each building, and tossed torches into the open doors. By the time the fires began to catch, the clerk was awake. Silverhorn walked up to him. "You're joining up with us."

The young man looked round him at the burning buildings, the dead lying in the street, the rough-looking riders on all sides of him. "Like hell," he said.

Somewhere a baby began to cry. Silverhorn said, "If you hadn't tried to overcharge me, you'd be dead. Since you've showed some character, I'm minded to give you a chance to make your way in the world. Willard, take his reins."

Grace rode her horse close to Silverhorn and leaned down toward him. "Listen. That's a baby."

Silverhorn got on his own horse. "I hear it."

"I didn't see no woman."

"Too bad about that. That's one thing we're almighty short of."

Grace moved her horse toward the burning house.

"Hell," Silverhorn bellowed. "Get back here. Where do you think you're going?"

"We can't leave a baby."

"You're the one said we didn't need another mouth."

She reined back around to stare at him. "But it's a baby, Tom," she said. "Not big enough to do for itself."

"You going to do for it?"

"We *can't* leave it."

"You're right. We damned well won't."

Silverhorn rode up onto the porch of the general store. Leaning down, he heaved up something they hadn't been able to pack.

Then he spurred his spooked horse as near the burning house as it was willing to go. The baby wailed. Heaving his burden up over his head, Silverhorn hurled it through the open doorway and into the fire.

"Tom!" Grace screamed. "No!"

"Good lordy mercy!" West yelled at the same moment. "Ride like hell!"

All of them had recognized what Silverhorn held when

he swung it up to throw. It was a twenty-five-pound keg of gunpowder. They rode like hell.

A few seconds later the building broke up with a glare and a great, echoing boom. A gush of bright flames disintegrated it. Burning boards and bits of things that did not burn as readily flew out in all directions. No further human sounds emanated from the little town of Taylor's Crossing.

At the bluff, Silverhorn drew them up to look back on their work. Grace stopped apart from the rest. She sat her horse heavily, staring down in the opposite direction from the others.

They watched the gray smoke rolling from the town. "You, Grace," Silverhorn called. "Get over here."

She didn't look up, didn't move, didn't acknowledge his presence.

"Red whore," he muttered.

The main knot of men had the clerk in tow; all were quiet. Willard was staring thoughtfully at the conflagration below. He sidled up close to Silverhorn and whispered hoarsely, "Time'll come you wish you had back that wasted powder."

Silverhorn looked at him hard enough to break a lesser man, began to shake, and then broke into loud, hoarse laughter. Now he was satisfied that Willard would do.

13

With his back to the early morning sun, Fairchild headed out at a trot. Rough as it was, it seemed to be the chestnut's smoothest gait. The saddle he'd picked from the patrol's spoils fit him well, and he could ride almost comfortably.

Dead man's saddle, he thought. Dead man's pistols, dead man's gear. Dead man's horse? Probably. If the chestnut devil hadn't killed a rider itself, it had probably lost one or more in its career as a troop horse. Riding in the clear morning with the sun beating on his back, Fairchild felt more dead than ever.

He allowed the horse its head. There was no way it could stray from the deep-cut highway of ruts bordered by wide brown shoulders from years of overgrazing by countless mules and oxen. A curtain of whitish dust, visible far behind each time he topped a rise, marked another train creeping west; but he hadn't seen a human shape all day long. Still, he would have to be careful. The wagon road was as likely to lead him to Whitehair's bunch as to a fort or settlement.

"Damn them," Fairchild muttered. Then, to the white-haired man specifically, "Damn *you!*"

The night before, he'd heard wolves calling in the next canyon. That's what Whitehair and his bunch were. Wolves. A pack of wolves that single out the weak and work them away from the herd, just the way they did me! Just the way they'd do it again, unless somebody stopped them.

Fairchild hoped to reach Bradley's Oak by dark. Secretly, he hoped to find the train still there. Sickness, bad water, straying of the oxen, anything might have held them up. He would ride up past Thorne's wagon, and he'd find out what happened to David Stuart, and Jess would come running out to meet him. Everything would be as it had before. Before he'd died.

His progress seemed so slow that he found himself singing through every song he could think of. Then he recited all the poems he could remember. That did not take him long. He tried Bible verses. Less time still. In his mind he went as slowly and carefully as he could through his warm, romantic tryst with Jessica Thorne. It pleased him to think that she might be remembering it, too.

But no. She wouldn't be daydreaming about making love to a dead man. "Dear God, I have to catch up to her. I have to show her I'm alive!"

That evening at just about the time he would have counted it too far past sundown to hunt, Ethan Fairchild saw a glimmer of light in the western distance. The chestnut didn't need instruction or encouragement; with dreams of a stable and a bait of oats and other horses it could kick and bully, it headed toward the light.

As he drew nearer, Fairchild determined that there was not one light, but several. In the heart of the clearing, a curtained window glowed like a star from the east side of a barnlike log building. Farther along, campfires cast orange circles on the ground and threw black dancing shadows back among the trees. With a leap of his heart, he saw the high loom of wagon covers painted with red and orange by the firelight.

Rising in his stirrups, Fairchild gave a whoop that made the chestnut buck and kick. He'd found the train! Spurring the unwilling horse past the building, he pounded down toward the wagons.

"Halloo the camp!" he called. "Jess! Doc Harris, Mr. Thorne, Stu! Jess, I'm alive!"

He reined the chestnut up hard by a rope corral, spooking a dozen drowsing oxen. Piling off the horse, dodging a wicked cut from its teeth, he ran toward the nearest campfire. He could see the people around it scrambling to their feet, hurrying to meet him.

"Hey, where's Manasseh Thorne? Where's Jess? It's me, Fairchild. I'm alive!"

"Stand where you are! Hands up!"

"Wait! You don't understand."

The racheting click of a rifle's hammer coming to cock brought Fairchild to his senses. He skidded to a halt, putting out his hands.

"Wait! It's me, Fairchild, Ethan Fairchild."

"Silence."

Fairchild didn't know the man who came toward him. He was of an age and a size with Manasseh Thorne, with the same spreading beard and the same air of authority. But he wore a somber black coat and trousers and an odd, tall, round-crowned hat. Behind the beard, his face was closed and hostile, and his hands held a new Sharps rifle, cocked and leveled at Fairchild's chest.

"What are you? What do you want here?"

In the fringes of the firelight, Fairchild could see a dozen or more men, older or younger copies of the spokesman, all with rifles ready and aimed at him. Behind them, a gaggle of drably attired women peered and pointed and whispered. All of them were strangers to Fairchild.

"But who are *you*?" he faltered. "I thought this was the Thorne train."

From the darkness behind him, he heard the chestnut's fighting squeal, followed by a bellow of pain. He spun that way, only to find more sentries closing on him from that direction. Helplessly, he turned again to face the bearded man, who had been waiting impassively.

"We are the Lord's anointed, the chosen ones of the great Jehovah," the first man declared, to a murmur of assent from the others. "We flee the persecution of Pharaoh to follow in the footsteps of the Prophet to the promised land of Zion."

"Oh," Fairchild said. "Mormons."

The spokesman took a step forward. "Some call us that," he conceded in a softer voice. His rifle did not waver. "Now, what is your name and your station and your reason for disturbing our peace? Speak up!"

Fairchild hung his head, all the strength in him seeming to flow down into a puddle of bleak disappointment. "I'm sorry," he said. "I got lost from my train, back a couple of weeks ago. I've been trying to catch up. When I saw your wagons camped here, I thought I'd found them."

"Elder, he lies," one of the men in the crowd said.

"He comes heavily armed," another pointed out.

"His horse bears the brand of Pharaoh," said a third. One sleeve of his coat hung in tatters where the chestnut's teeth had slashed it. Blood rilled down his forearm and dripped from the tips of his fingers. "And its soul is possessed by Satan himself."

"He's a spy!"

"A betrayer!"

"A Philistine."

"A Jebusite and a Hivite!"

"I'm a Baptist," Fairchild protested, but that didn't seem to help. The men pressed grimly closer, surrounding him, hands clenched on their rifles. "Look, if you start shooting, you're more likely to kill one another than me."

"Stop!" The first man's voice cut through the angry accusations. "Stand back, brethren!"

"But Elder—"

"Silence!" The elder dropped the hammer of his Sharps to half-cock. "We're still in the land of Egypt, and bound by its laws and customs. Lower your weapons!"

Slowly, the crowd did so, some of the younger men in obvious disappointment. The leader stepped up to face Fairchild.

"You've come to the wrong place, stranger," he said.

"I can see that."

"You will find others of your own kind in the inn, there." For a moment, the stern face softened a little. "I hope you find your friends," he said. "Go in peace."

"Sorry to have troubled you," Fairchild said. He touched the brim of his hat. "Good luck on your way to Zion."

He led the horse back to the log inn, feeling the stares of a half-dozen Saints still on his back. Roused by the commotion, three people had gathered on the porch, two of them women. They looked at him as he tied the chestnut to a rail. The man raised a lamp to peer at Fairchild. In its light, he was tall, spare, colorless. He leaned heavily on a cane held in his other hand.

"Elgin Bradley," he husked in Fairchild's direction. He spoke in a curious, halting wheeze. "At your service. You can take your animal—around to the stable. The ladies will—have your—supper ready—presently."

Fairchild touched his hat again. "Ladies," he said. "I'm Ethan Fairchild. It's very kind of you."

In the light, he could see that the women were mother and daughter. Framed in soft lamplight, the daughter smiled at him, leaning forward gracefully like a rosebud yearning into the darkness. Her long dark hair hung round the collar of a flowing woolly robe. Fairchild looked at her and saw green fire where her eyes caught the light.

"Kind?" Elgin Bradley said. "Not at all. Bradley's Oak—is a public inn. All are welcome. Day or night. My wife will prepare—your room. Take this—lamp—light your way—to the stable. Ann will serve—your meal—when you're done."

"Thank you."

Fairchild led the chestnut around to the barn, heaving back the sagging door. The whole building seemed to sag in the same manner, but Fairchild found a stall that seemed dry and tight. Immediately the chestnut whinnied and tossed his head. Another horse answered from some darker corner of the barn.

"Leave him alone," Fairchild told his Devil. "You're company here." He unsaddled the animal and rubbed it down with handfuls of hay, getting a nip on the calf for his trouble. Leaving it munching oats scooped from a half-rotten bag in one corner, he made his way back to the house.

In the cavernous dining hall, he spoke to Bradley. "I do appreciate your hospitality, sir. I haven't had a home-cooked meal or slept under a roof for weeks. But I should tell you that most of my money is in my wagon."

"No matter," Bradley wheezed. "First you must be fed." He waved toward his daughter. "Do you mind if I—sit—with you—whilst you sup?"

"I'd welcome the company." Fairchild watched as the

young lady worked at the heavy cookstove. Even as he visited with her father, he could not keep himself from watching her. It was as if he could see the warmth of life burning high in her eyes.

That flame burned very low in Fairchild just then. His disappointment at the encampment of the Saints had settled into a dull despair, a growing conviction that he would never catch up to the train, or worse, that he would overtake it to find Jess no longer interested in him. He tried to picture Jessica, to imagine her face, her eyes, the way she'd looked at him that night along the river. But it was hard to hold her image before him while Ann Bradley went about the warm animal actions of work. She turned, met his eyes looking at her, and smiled.

"Did I—understand—correctly," Elgin Bradley asked, breathed, waited for breath, "that your—wagon is outside? I had thought you—alone—on horseback."

"No. I mean, yes," Fairchild replied. "You're right. I'm alone, and horseback."

"But you mentioned—a wagon."

"My wagon would have been here a few days ago, not now."

"A few days ago?"

Ann Bradley laid out a plate and cup and silver for him. Next she set before him a big steaming bowl of stew. When she leaned across the table with a pot of coffee and a bowl of cobbler, she smiled again.

"Did I understand you to say, Mr. Fairchild, that your wagon was here before you?"

Ethan Fairchild had his mouth full of beef from the stew. He nodded but did not try to speak. The girl smiled more brightly. He washed down the mouthful of meat with a cup of coffee that was hot enough to blister his tonsils. For another long moment, he could not make a sound.

Elgin Bradley said, "The last wagons we had here— before the Saints came—were led by a Mr. Hagewold. The party before that hailed from—Ohio." He smiled at his own slight joke. "By way of Independence—of course."

"That would be right," Fairchild said glumly. "Thorne's train? Manasseh Thorne, big beard and a big voice?"

Elgin Bradley gave a gasping chuckle. "Exactly—sir." He patted a hand lightly on the tabletop. "Big beard—big voice—oh, ah-ha—exactly!"

"How long ago?"

"Daughter?"

"You just missed them," Ann said. She gave Fairchild an encouraging look. "They left, oh, not more than a week ago, very early in the morning."

Fairchild risked another swallow of coffee and looked from father to daughter. "How were they getting along? How were the Thornes?" He did not wish to blurt out his interest in a particular Thorne. "My wagon was probably at the very rear. Usually was."

"Not this time," Ann Bradley assured him. "No, I remember distinctly. The last wagon belonged to the bridegroom." She clapped her hands. "Oh, I remember now! They left on the twelfth, the very morning after the wedding. I remember because I remarked on what a short honeymoon they had—"

"Ann!"

She stopped suddenly, putting her hand to her lips. Her cheeks grew pink under their tan. "Oh, I'm sorry." Then she smiled again. "But it was such a lovely wedding. Right in this room. We almost never have anything like that."

Fairchild interrupted her. He couldn't help himself. "Who was the happy couple?" he asked harshly. "Their names. Do you remember?"

"Oh, yes," Bradley whispered. "Performed—ceremony—myself. Had to know. Wrote it—in my book." He stopped, looked up suddenly at Fairchild. His watery eyes went wide. "My book," he repeated. "Yes, that's where I've heard—your name."

"No, not mine. The couple you married. What were their names?"

"Strong dark young man," Elgin Bradley said. He put his hands flat on the table and started to push himself up. "Must get—my book. Look in—my record for—"

"His name was David, Father," Ann said brightly. "You remember, surely, don't you? David Stuart."

Fairchild took a breath. Then he asked his question, though he hoped he would die before he heard the answer. "And his bride?"

"Daughter—"

"I remember that, too," Ann said. She smiled. "I thought her maiden name was so beautiful. Jessica Thorne." She looked seriously at Fairchild. "I don't think Jessica Stuart is nearly as pretty, do you?"

At bedtime, Elgin Bradley called Fairchild into his bedroom. "I'd like you to see—the record," he said.

"The what?"

"My book—of record." As if it cost him infinite effort, Bradley opened a flat metal box and lifted out an old, leather-bound ledger book. He laid it on the bed, opened its cover, turned the pages. "I—keep a record—of all that happens here." He nodded toward the box. "Keep it—under the floor—there's a stone-lined chamber. All the happy events—"

"Like weddings."

"—all my visitors—all the sadness. Deaths. Births. And weddings." He found the page he wanted. "See, Thorne's train, July tenth. It may help you—understand."

"I understand," Fairchild said. He understood all right. The name should have warned him. David. In the Bible, it had been King David who had let his friend be killed so he could enjoy the friend's woman. He'd even married her.

"What?" He'd missed part of Bradley's ghostly whisper. "How's that?"

"The young bride—Jessica. In a private moment—the young bride came to me. Asked that I record—a death."

Bradley put a long, trembling finger to the page like a deacon prooftexting his claim. The line read *Ethan Fairchild of the Thorne train. Killed near Scott's Bluff. June 26, 1859.* Then, in Jessica's rounded handwriting, *Rest, beloved, never forgotten.*

"All legal," Fairchild said heavily.

"She wanted it—known, recorded—official—what had become of—Ethan Fairchild. Wanted it entered—above the record—of her own marriage—writ down."

He drew his finger farther down the page to the record of the marriage. Fairchild read it all.

"The name is wrong," he said.

What should it have been? David and—and Bathsheba, that was right. She'd been in on it, too. Had Jessica known? How much had she known of the way Stuart left him to be killed?

"The name?"

"Was she happy?"

Bradley sighed. "That's maybe too pretty a word for it. But the deed is done. I thought it might help you to see it in ink."

He saw it in blood, in flames. He intended to take David Stuart, groom, along to hell along with the white-haired man, along with himself. It showed in his face.

"What God has—joined together—is not for man—not for you—to put asunder."

"Joined together!" Fairchild laughed harshly. "And what of those that man has left to die?"

"I couldn't say."

"Are you not God, then?"

Elgin Bradley said, "No. I'm naught but—his poor agent in—this lonely land." He looked at Fairchild, his watery eyes deep and steady. "Are you?" he asked.

Fairchild tried to answer, felt the words stick in a tightening throat. Slapping the ledger closed, he turned and went out of the room.

14

A while after mid-morning, David Stuart reined his lathered sorrel up the gentle slope of a rise so that he could look down upon the laboring wagons. Taking off his hat, he wiped a sleeve across his forehead, blinking the sting of sweat from his eyes. He felt almost as lathered as the horse. The days since Bradley's Oak had alternated between sudden, drenching thunderstorms and clear, hot, sunny stretches when the dry wind sucked moisture out of people and animals.

In spite of that, they'd made good time, although he knew better than to tell that to Manasseh Thorne. They had crossed the Platte on the new bridge at Mormon Ferry, pushed on past the great brown-red dome of Independence Rock, and managed the three crossings of the Sweetwater with nothing worse than a day's delay and two oxen lost to quicksand. Now the wagons moved in a deep cut, not a canyon exactly, but a gully eroded by thousands of wagon wheels down to a hard, uneven floor of rock. Dust hung heavy in the cut, so that the high white wagon covers seemed to sway and waver above a brown fog. Mopping his dirty face, Stuart felt a moment's guilt at the luck that had put him on point that day instead of fighting the dust with Jess and the others.

"Davy! Davy Stuart!"

Stuart turned to see a rider plunge hell-for-reckless up out of the dust. He spotted Stuart on the slope, waved, and spurred his horse like a cowboy, drawing up with a clatter of hooves near enough to make the sorrel shy away.

"Who's that?" Stuart asked. "Francis, that you riding like a madman?"

"Judge Thorne, he said hurry and find you," Francis Buttrell panted. He pushed back his hat and drew down the bandana that had covered most of his face. "Said for you to report back to him right away." He grinned, teeth startlingly white against his dirty face. "Told me to take over your duties, too, so I get to ride up where there's some air moving for a spell."

"What's the trouble?" Stuart scanned the wagons anxiously, but everything looked normal as far as he could see. "Somebody broken down again? I was worried about the Ameses' near hind wheel, but I can see it's all right."

Buttrell shook his head. "Not that. There's another train behind us, eating our dust. They want to pass."

"Here? A snake couldn't slither by us in this cut."

"That's what I said, and their scout, he give me a good cussing and I told Mr. Thorne and Mr. Thorne said find you and send you back on the jump."

Stuart laughed. "Guess I'd better jump, then." He pointed. "Lije Holden's maybe a half mile ahead on the right. He cut some Indian sign up there, so go easy and watch yourself. See you at noon."

"Right, Davy." Buttrell touched his hat in acknowledgment. "I'll look sharp."

He galloped away. Stuart watched until he saw Buttrell drop back to a trot at the crest of the ridge and lean to draw his rifle from its scabbard. Then he turned and rode back along the line of the train.

Down inside the cut, the dust was as bad as he'd feared. The high banks shut off even the dry west wind. He pulled his neck-cloth up over his nose and mouth, passing other emigrants who trudged or rode with heads bowed and hats or bonnets pulled down, until he came to the Thorne wagon. Martha and Manasseh Thorne sat hunched together on the high seat, swathed in an old bedsheet.

His smile hidden behind the neckerchief, Stuart tugged at the brim of his hat. "Is it right what Francis told me?"

he called. "Some idiot wants to pass us in this hole?"

"Seems likely," Thorne rasped. With the sheet draped around his head and shoulders and his beard streaked in dust, he looked like a Hebrew prophet. "They're mule-drawn, faster than us. They must have camped back behind us a ways last night and caught up since breakfast. Now Buttrell says they're wanting by."

Martha Thorne said, "They want to beat you to the next grass, Manasseh."

"I understand that, Martha!" Thorne snapped. Immediately, he looked contrite. "Sorry." He patted her hand. "It's this blamed dust. Make an archangel cuss. Truth is, we can't tell just what they want. That's why I sent for you."

"Well, I can't make this cut any wider. And they can't get by."

"I'd guess they'll want us to pull over once we get out on clear ground. What's up ahead?"

"Ground's clear enough. Looks like half an hour to a pretty good nooning spot. Water, some grass, about the way the map shows it."

"They'd know that, too, I expect. Look like enough for two trains at once?"

"Light grazing, maybe. I wouldn't bet on the spring offering enough for us all."

"I see." Thorne coughed and tugged his beard. "Martha, look in the guidebook, please. See if it mentions water farther along." He frowned at Stuart. "Did you see anything beyond the nooning ground?"

"There's two, but I didn't get much of a look at the second. Lije says a party of Indians spent last night there, then moved out south. I figured it was a good idea to stay close together."

Mrs. Thorne held up the dog-eared copy of Hempstead's. "Here's the other spot," she said, pointing to the page. "Just a mile farther on."

"Water?"

"Water uncertain. Grass if there's not been too much traffic."

Thorne grunted. "That'd be their reason for wanting to beat us to the first spot."

"Want me to ride back and talk to their trainmaster?"

"I'd appreciate it. You can speak for me."

Stuart grinned, blushed a little. Nodding, he said, "All right, but what should I say, for you?"

Thorne laughed. His wife looked at him sharply. "Son," Thorne said, "if I knew that, I'd go myself!" Then he laughed again.

"Manasseh?" his wife asked.

Stuart smiled, uncertain whether he should laugh.

Thorne stroked his beard. "Just joshing," he said. "I trust you to work it out in an amicable fashion. We can't very well expect them to breathe our dust all the way to Oregon."

"You want to try to hold them off until we reach that nooning spot?"

"Try this. Explain them the situation. If their man's reasonable, ask him what he thinks is fair."

Mrs. Thorne continued to look at her husband as if uncertain whether she was on the right wagon seat.

Stuart nodded, turned his horse east, rode back along the train. He set the sorrel a leisurely, thoughtful gait and nodded to each wagon driver he passed. At his own wagon, he paused long enough to lean across, extend an arm, grip Jessica's gloved hand a moment as he explained his new duty.

Then he moved on toward the end of his train. "What the hell's up?" Caleb Sugarhouse wanted to know.

Stuart realized that every wagon was shut off from news of the others. Normally, they would have communicated by shouting or by walking up and down the slow-moving line, but in the deep dust fog of the cut, each wagon moved in isolation, every driver unable to speed up, slow down, or move aside.

"Another train behind us," Stuart told him.

"What train?"

Stuart shook his head. "I'm going back to find out."

The front span of a mule team was close enough to the last Thorne wagon to eat from its tailgate. The scout for the mule train lazed along on the north side of that front team of mules. A raw, spare man with sharply angular features, the scout was biding his time rather than riding on past the Thorne train to scout beyond the canyon. The strain of that exercise of patience showed in his appearance.

Stuart drew his horse up in the narrow space on the south side of his last wagon and waited for the mule-train scout to come up beside him. The axe-faced man looked at Stuart across the backs of the mules, then lifted his hand and touched his leather hat brim in a two-fingered salute.

Stuart returned the salute, gave his name.

"Pleased to meet you," the other said. "I'm Drexel." He said it as if it were enough.

"Where you out of?" Stuart asked.

Drexel smiled, his mouth as straight as a blade cut. "Independence," he said. "Every mortal time."

Stuart began to understand. Drexel was a professional scout, a man who made his living traveling the Oregon and California trails, a man who knew every bend in the road and every patch of grass fit to graze between Missouri and the Pacific Coast.

"Where you bound?"

"I'll ask you one instead," Drexel replied. He cut a plug of tobacco with a long double-edged knife and carried it to his mouth on the knife blade. "How long you figure to hold us up with them oxen?"

"Not a minute longer than we have to." Stuart gestured at the walls of the cut on either side. "I expect we'll be clear of this in half an hour or so. Don't see what we can do about it until then."

"You can haul them ox-wagons plumb over to one side

and stand fast. I calculate we could get by you on the other."

"Might be, unless we spill a wagon getting it up out of the ruts and block the trail for everybody," Stuart said. "We could get the two trains so tangled up in here that we'd both lose a day."

"Mortal greenhorns," Drexel said. "If you can't handle them wagons, you should've stayed home in Ioway, where you belonged."

"Ohio-ay." Stuart thought about telling Sugarhouse he'd have to pull his wagon aside and sit in the dust-fog while the other train passed. He didn't smile, though he was tempted. "We'd lose more time than we gained just convincing people to get the wagons moved."

Drexel's face hardened. "I might convince them pretty mortal fast," he said, running a thumb along the edge of the knife. "I don't much take to a lot of back talk from your kind."

Stuart felt his face growing hot. He remembered what Thorne had said about reasonable men, but he didn't seem to be finding many today. *Work it out in an amicable fashion.* Biting back the first answer that came to him, he gained a few seconds by reining the sorrel clear of the lead mules. When he looked back at Drexel, his voice was carefully good-natured.

"How long have you been scouting for trains, Mr. Drexel?"

"How long?" Drexel frowned at him as if looking for a trap in the words. "Started out in '47," he said finally. "Made the passage every year since then."

"I'll bet this isn't the first time you've gotten held up by a slower train."

"Gospel truth, worse luck. More mortal greenhorns every year."

Stuart nodded. "Ever gained anything by arguing about it?" he asked.

For the time it would have taken Stuart to count ten, the scout stared at him across the ears of the lead mules.

Then Drexel's slash of a mouth turned up at one corner.

"Sometimes," he admitted. He flipped the big knife around in his hand and slipped it into its sheath. "Can't never tell what you can chivy a greenhorn into, less'n you try."

"We'll be clear of the cut soon," Stuart said. "We'll pull aside then."

Drexel nodded. He jerked his head back toward the mule train. "Wagonmaster says see if I can't hurry you up. All these folk in a mortal hurry. Afraid all the silver'll be gone before they get there."

"Silver?" Stuart said.

The scout clapped his mouth shut as though he regretted unbending for the moment. "Maybe you want to talk to the wagonmaster," he said.

"As a matter of fact," Stuart said, "I do."

Drexel spat between his horse and the mules, then gestured toward the rear. Stuart had paid little attention to the rider a couple of wagons back on his own side of the narrow road. He slowed the horse until that rider came up beside him. "T. K. Hagewold," the rider said. "You the master of this ox train?"

"No," Stuart told him, "I'm just the scout." He glanced across the backs of the second team of mules to see that Drexel had dropped back even with them.

Hagewold said, "You're holding us up. You want to go back and point that out to your master?"

"Mr. Thorne understands the situation," Stuart said with what he figured was an amicable tone. "We're not holding you up. This canyon is."

Hagewold's eyes narrowed as he smiled. "Some truth in that," he said. "How much farther would you judge until we're through it?"

"I'd judge a mile. Maybe less."

Drexel said, "More like a half mile."

It came to Stuart as he looked at the angular man whose voice was as sharp as his features that Drexel had no home at either end of the trail. He spent his life riding now west and then east along that twisting road they called the Oregon Trail. There was no more room to dislike the man, though maybe a bit to pity him. Stuart let it go.

"You say you're the scout. You been on down the road past this canyon?"

Stuart said, "I have."

"How wide's the road out there?"

An idea occurred to Stuart, one that surprised him. It was the sort of thing his father might have come up with. He hesitated a moment, looking at it, then said, "Wide enough for a head-up even race."

"What?" Hagewold said.

Stuart could feel Drexel's eyes on him, too. "It's not more than a couple of miles to the spot we'd picked for nooning and a little grazing," Stuart said. "I guess you know about it yourself. We're not sure there's water enough for a train the size of ours, so we figure to push on to the next one. Our spirits are down some. Mr. Thorne thinks it might do us good to have a little race to that second spot, our train against yours."

Hagewold took off his hat, wiped at his brow, thinking about the offer. "Son, we're rolling along here now with our noses up the ass end of your train because of those oxen of yours. I don't see that it would be a very fair or profitable race between us."

Stuart looked crestfallen. "Well," he said glumly, "I don't know then how we ought to work it out, with both of us needing to noon at the same spot two miles down the road and that spot probably not holding enough water for both groups of us." He heard Drexel spit against the far wall of the cut. "But my wagonmaster, Mr. Thorne, he told me you'd be a reasonable man and would propose us an idea of how to work it out fair."

"God have mercy!" Hagewold said, as much to God as to anyone else. He glanced at Drexel, but the axe-faced scout was facing as stiffly forward in his saddle as a wooden Indian. After a moment, Hagewold said, "Well, then, you go back and tell Mr. Thorne I'll be thinking about it."

Stuart thanked him and turned his horse back toward the western end of the canyon, picking up quickly to a pace that would prevent his having to discuss the matter with each driver he passed. That did not keep Sugarhouse from asking about the mule train. Stuart called back to him, "They want to race."

"Race what?"

"Their fastest wagon against yours!"

Sugarhouse's reply to that idea contained the word *hell* used in a context lost on Stuart as he rode out of earshot. A couple of minutes later, when he caught up to the lead wagon, the western end of the canyon was in sight.

Thorne said, "Was he a reasonable man?"

"Yes. Mr. Hagewold was perfectly reasonable."

Thorne seemed relieved. "Hagewold?"

"Out of Independence. I didn't find out when they left."

"What's his proposal?"

"He's thinking about it until they pull up even. I guess he'll let us know then."

Thorne looked up sharply. "What was it made you think he'd be reasonable?"

"He said something about a race."

Mrs. Thorne said, "Race?"

Thorne said, "Race?"

Stuart winked at them. "They're going to pass us once we're out of this canyon. That'll be that. I thought we might have a little fun with them about the race."

"*You* thought? You said the race was Hagewold's idea."

"It's hard to remember who mentioned it first."

Mrs. Thorne said, "What kind of race? You don't mean a race with these wagons?"

"It wouldn't be much of a race," Stuart admitted, "our oxen against their mules. Chances are they'd beat us to that first nooning spot hands down."

"I expect you're right," Manasseh Thorne said, playing with the idea, considering what he'd been told about the nooning spots. "But we ought to make a little effort."

"Ought we?" Martha Thorne said. "Are you sure?"

They broke free of the canyon. The road widened at once as if it had felt constricted within the narrow walls. Stuart slacked off, rode slowly enough to drift back wagon by wagon, letting each driver know that a mule-drawn train of wagons was going to pass them pretty soon.

Caleb Sugarhouse grinned at him when Stuart drifted past. "You and your damned funning!" he said. Stuart nodded, grinned back at him, let his wagon roll on by.

Then Drexel rode by like a lean, sharp leather shadow on the other side of the wagons. Stuart watched him, wondered how far ahead he would scout before noon, then turned his attention back to the next rider. "Mr. Hagewold," he said. "Mr. Thorne is driving our lead wagon. I've come to invite you up for a visit."

Still viewing Stuart with a certain suspicion, Hagewold said, "Good enough." They rode along at a good rate until they came to the front of the ox-drawn train.

By that time, Stuart noticed as he looked back, three or four of the mule-drawn wagons had pulled out to the side of the wider roadway and were following their wagon-master toward the head of Thorne's train.

As each of the faster wagons drew even with an ox wagon, the drivers and passengers talked to each other animatedly. Members of each train had standard sorts of questions for each other: Had they seen any Indians? Suffered any outbreaks of illness? Where were they bound? Where had they come from? Did they know a certain family back in Ohio or Illinois or Missouri?

But the people of Hagewold's train all had one topic uppermost in their thoughts. By the time the two lead wagons were even, virtually every soul in the Thorne train had heard of the great silver strike at Caldwell's Spring, down in the western corner of Utah Territory near Carson City. There was silver clinging to the roots of the grass, silver nuggets as big as hen's eggs and just as easy to gather. Hagewold's party had been bound for southern Oregon, but they'd voted to go and get rich instead, and didn't Thorne's people want to come along?

"We're taking the Lander Cutoff up the trail a ways," Hagewold was telling the Thornes. "Saves a hundred miles and more." He winked at Thorne. "Think about it yourselves. It'll get you to Fort Hall ahead of some faster trains, give you a jump on the silver."

Drexel, lounging on his horse on the off side of Thorne's wagon, spat tobacco juice. "Not so good for an ox train," he said, as if each word he spoke without being paid hurt him. "Some long stretches with no water. Have to cross them fast."

"We'll hold to our course," Thorne said. "But we wish you Godspeed."

"You're ready to race, then?"

"We'll give it a little try."

"A little try?" Martha Thorne said, but no one paid her any attention. The lead mule-drawn wagon of the Hagewold train was just even with her. She pursed her lips as her husband readied his whip. Stuart raised his handgun to waste a charge of powder.

The gun went off with a boom and a great cloud of white smoke. Thorne cracked the whip. The heavy oxen broke from their normal plodding to a slightly faster pace, jolting the wagon forward. Manasseh Thorne cracked the whip again.

"Hey-yah!" he cried, getting into the spirit of the occasion. "Hup!"

The lumbering beasts stumbled into a halfhearted trot. But Hagewold's wagons were rolling steadily past them, the mules switching their long ears and pulling without apparent effort.

Martha looked back, saw surprise and consternation on the face of Will Buttrell, driving the second wagon and falling quickly behind his leader. No one had thought to tell him they were racing the other train. She listened for the crack of her husband's whip, turned back to him, saw him putting the whip in its stand.

"A *very* little try!" she said, loudly enough this time that Thorne turned to look at her. Stuart, her normally levelheaded son-in-law, had whirled his horse and torn on off along the road west, keeping pace with the feisty mules which seemed to have no trouble at all making their competitors' wagon wheels sing.

"Manasseh," she said, "what are we doing?"

"We're watching a faster train work up a sweat and a powerful thirst."

"It's what I thought." She shook her head and sat back then and watched the wagons roll by. Dust lingered in the air after the last had gone by, but now that they were clear of the cut, the prairie wind rapidly swept the air clean.

By and by, the Thorne train lumbered to the first nooning spot. The Hagewold train was a distant line of wagons, half hidden by its own dust, bound for the second campsite. Thorne took up his whip and cracked it softly above the broad backs of his sturdy oxen. As if they knew he didn't mean it, they ignored him. Looking west, Martha saw her son-in-law waiting for them a hundred yards up the road. He sat there, resting his horse, with his hat pushed back on his head like a kid until they caught up to him.

"Well?" he asked his father-in-law.

"We lost."

Stuart shook his head. "Just as well we didn't put any money on it."

Martha watched the two of them as Stuart urged his horse, fell in beside them, and rode along as if he had no serious duties as lead scout. Her husband said, "How's young Buttrell doing, when he's not mooning about that Bradley girl?"

"Doing very nicely. He came back to report to me. He's waiting for us over by the spring. Says we might even have enough spring water to wash off the dust."

"Water?" Martha asked.

Stuart looked culpable. "I guess I may've told Mr. Hagewold wrong about which spot was better for nooning. I haven't had much experience at scouting."

15

Ethan Fairchild was up and dressed by four-thirty. He strapped on the military belt with its holstered Colt and left the inn quietly. Out in the chilly morning twilight, he walked south round the barn and into the woods without direction or intent. The Mormon camp was busy with life, the Saints already finishing up with breakfast and starting to goad drowsy oxen into their yokes.

Old Thorne should have been wagonmaster to that bunch, Fairchild thought. They're on the move early and brisk enough to suit even him. Maybe if he hadn't been in such a hurry, he wouldn't have left me behind.

Maybe. Maybe if he and Stuart had finished their fight, Stu would have come to his senses. Maybe if the raiders hadn't attacked, the two of them would be sharing a bite of breakfast and a funny story right now. Or better, maybe he would be just waking, sharing a wagon and a bedroll and a new marriage with Jess.

Maybe Stuart wouldn't have left him to die. *Maybe I'd still be alive!*

With no wish to bump into the Mormon sentries again, Fairchild turned hard to his left. He paced down through a wooded draw pocked with human prints, then up the curving far wall into heavier brush which snatched at his boots and trousers. Ahead of him, and then to his right, running water murmured a little louder than the rustle of the leaves. He did not notice.

He was torn that morning in two opposite directions, for during the night he had pondered his situation until it became clear to him. He called himself foolish for not having seen it before. A child, he told himself, a little child could have figured it out! Trooper Healy had figured it out easily and had tried to show him the truth; but Fairchild in his blind, wrongheaded loyalty to a false friend, had refused to believe.

When that gang attacked us, David took my horse because it was faster. He looked back and saw me down.

Fairchild frowned. Was he imagining that part, or had he taken the first horse he came to? He couldn't be sure, but his thoughts plunged on past the question like water washing around a cottonwood stump.

Looked back and saw me fall and rode right on and left me to the heathen. Of course he did, the dirty bastard! He hightailed it back to the train and told them I was dead!

He could picture Stuart now; could see in him the devious, hypocritical coward he'd never been smart enough to notice before; could imagine him sidling up to Jess to console her. Suggesting that she make a marker for her poor lost love, since they'd never be able to dig him a proper grave. Taking her in his arms to comfort her when she cried. Finally even taking Fairchild's place as husband in her bed!

That dirty bastard! He made a fist as he said it in his mind, and struck his other palm hard enough to bruise it. He did not notice.

But none of it would ever have happened except for those rotten renegades with their white-haired leader. I was whipping David, about to beat the meanness out of him, when they set on us. That gave him his chance. But for the temptation they offered, he might never have showed himself for what he is.

Then the Dragoons had kept him from catching up to

the train. Maybe they saved him from the Cheyenne, as they said. Either way, they had made Stuart's word good and kept Fairchild from getting back to the train.

And Jessica. Jessica ready to marry Stuart. *Marry Stuart*, for God's sake! Where was the justice in that? Jessica had changed her mind mighty damned quick. If she changed it. If she hadn't known all along. If she and Stuart hadn't cooked it up between them somehow.

Fairchild stopped for a moment, resting a hand on the smooth silvery trunk of an aspen. Two or three small ants raced to investigate his fingers. When he didn't move, they ventured onto the back of the invading hand. One stung him. He shook them off and rubbed the spot absently, hardly aware of the pain.

There was something wrong with the way he was thinking. He couldn't quite see what it was, and after a moment, he brushed the idea aside as he had the ants. It didn't matter. He could never be certain that Jess had played the harlot with him. But he could never be certain that she hadn't. He would never know, and it was all because of David Stuart and that white-haired son of a whore.

Fairchild's laugh was like the bark of a fox. Maybe Stuart already had him a-moldering in the grave, but he would have a surprise or two coming, him and that white-haired killer, both. It was just a question of which one to go after first.

"Mr. Fairchild?"

He started, half convinced that Stuart or Whitehair had come to find him, hoping they had, ready at that moment to kill either or both.

"Mr. Fairchild? Is that you?"

The voice belonged to Ann Bradley. "Yes," Fairchild said sheepishly. He stared through the gloom of a morning fog that had risen while he walked. She was no more than a darker shadow among the shadows of trees and bushes. "I'm sorry. I didn't mean to alarm you."

"Breakfast won't be ready for a good half hour yet."

"Won't it?" He strained to see her, half expecting the green fire of her eyes to shine through the mist like the eyes of a wildcat or a wolf.

"No. I haven't even started it."

"But why have you come all the way out here in the woods at this hour?"

"Pardon me?"

"Is it safe for you?" He came a step or two nearer, at once wanting to see her face and resenting her intrusion upon his recitation of close-held pain.

"Safe?"

He could hear a smile in her voice. When he saw her clearly, she was standing on her own front porch. It took him a moment to believe that he had headed away from the inn and walked full circle round to come back to it. I'm a hell of a woodsman, he told himself.

"Out here by yourself in the dark," he said lamely.

"I came to enjoy the morning."

Fairchild remembered getting up before the others and going out into the dark new morning. He understood her. "It's going to be a nice one," he said.

As he drew nearer, she met his eyes. Her smile vanished and she took a quick backward step, one hand reaching behind her for the door latch. "I'd better go and start the fire."

"I'll help you," Fairchild offered.

"No!" She opened the door and stepped inside. "That is I can—no, no, thank you. I can manage."

She didn't close the door in his face, but he thought that she wanted to. Sensing her alarm, he said, "I believe I'll walk down to the stream, then. Good morning, Miss Bradley."

"Yes." She hesitated, her hand on the latch. "Breakfast in half an hour. I'll see you then, Mr. Fairchild."

He turned away, rubbing his chin thoughtfully. His fingers touched the unkempt beard he'd allowed to grow while he was on the trail with the Army. He was dirty, unshorn and unshaven, all in all as rough-looking a lot as any of the renegades he'd seen dead. It was no wonder that he'd frightened a delicate thing like Ann Bradley, although he wasn't sure it was his appearance that had bothered her.

On impulse, he turned. "Miss Bradley?"

She reappeared in the doorway so quickly that he knew she hadn't gone far.

"Yes?"

"I might come back a little earlier."

She stared at him. "Yes?"

"Do you think I could have a little hot water? And maybe your father would have an extra razor I might borrow?"

At the deep water behind the beaver dam, Fairchild took a moment to be certain he was alone. He wasn't worried about any of the Bradleys coming by, and the Mormon train had pulled out, leaving only tracks and a scattering of manure where their corral had been to show they were ever there. It would be embarrassing, though, to be interrupted by a bear, say, come down to drink at the pool.

Satisfied, he hung the gunbelt on a low branch, then peeled off his grimy trail clothes. There wasn't much he could do about the clothing, at least not right then. He'd spent the few dollars in his pockets on supplies at Fort Laramie, and clothing hadn't seemed important.

That brought up the matter of his lodging with the Bradleys. He put that question aside for the moment and eased his body into the stream, doing a moderately thorough job of scrubbing himself down. Before he was done, his teeth were chattering and the numbing bite of the icy water had convinced him he was alive, no matter what the people of the Thorne train might think.

He dressed quickly and went back to the inn. By breakfast time, he had used up the bowl of hot water Ann Bradley provided and had dulled Elgin Bradley's second-best razor. He brushed his ragged clothes, wished for a change from his own wagon, and felt better than he had felt since he'd last seen the train. Then he went in to breakfast.

In broader society, Marguerite and Elgin Bradley might not have recognized him. But Ann Bradley showed the greatest surprise. Her mouth fell open and she stopped in mid-course across the space between the great warm stove and the table where Fairchild stood, waiting politely for the rest to be seated. At last she came on with her platter of eggs fried over easy, fatback bacon, and biscuits.

"Good morning," she said as if she had never seen him before.

"Miss Bradley," he said. He smiled, and this time his smile seemed not to frighten her. Taking his seat, he bowed his head for Elgin Bradley's whispered grace and began to eat.

He thought the breakfast the finest he had ever tasted and said so. No, he insisted, he did not think it because he had been away from civilization for so long. The breakfast was fit for royalty and it was his humble privilege to partake of it.

"You have a way—with words—Mr. Fairchild," Elgin Bradley husked, perhaps a little flattered that a visitor would use a kind of language he appreciated. His sharp glance showed he knew whom the words were intended to impress. Marguerite accepted credit for the big steaming biscuits. Finishing his fourth one, Fairchild leaned back and looked at his host.

"You've been most generous," he said. "I hesitate to ask more. But I must ask one other favor of you."

"You have—but to name it. If it lies—within our power—it is granted."

"I want to work."

"I beg your pardon?"

"I told you last night that I had no money, but you consented to let me stay anyhow. The least I can do is earn my keep. If it wouldn't offend you, I'd like to tidy up a few loose ends about the place."

"Sir?"

"If you will be kind enough to allow it."

"But you are our guest."

"Father," Ann said quickly, "you gave your word to grant Mr. Fairchild's request." She smiled at Fairchild. "And we shall. As soon as I've done with the dishes, I'll show you the toolshed."

Fairchild thought about it. "It would be my pleasure to help you with the dishes."

Marguerite Bradley stood up from the table. "Certainly not," she said, with surprising vehemence. "Mr. Bradley and I will see to the dishes. You children run along. Ann can give you some ideas where to start, Mr. Fairchild." Fairchild stood, too.

"I?" Bradley said.

"You," she told him. "The young people are going outside to work in the warmth of God's fresh new morning."

"I see."

Ann kissed her mother on the cheek, whispered, "Thank you." Then she turned to Ethan.

A look was all he needed. He followed her, trying at first not to watch her walk, then helplessly rapt in her movements. Had anyone been privy to his musing to remind him that his heart was broken, he would have paid no heed.

Outside, the sun was just lifting itself free of the entangling trees. The air was fresh. Fairchild ached to make himself a part of it. The girl unlatched the shed and opened the door on creaking leather hinges to show him the tools.

He gathered up a shovel, hammer, handsaw. "Do you have any oil?" he asked. "A grindstone? Or a file?"

"Oh, yes. We have a grindstone some people from Council Bluffs left us last year. One of their mules died, and they had to lighten their load. They left it for us." She stopped, her cheeks coloring a little. "I'm sorry. I do rattle on so when there's someone to talk to. The file's on that shelf. And we have some whale oil for the lamps."

Fairchild began by replacing the hinges with new

leather from a tangle of old harness he found in the barn. By the time he'd finished, Ann was back with a little pitcher of clear oil.

"We have to order it from the post at Fort Laramie," she said. "The supply wagon's not due for a week. There's only one keg left."

"I won't waste any." He wiped down the hammer and saw to slow the rust. The hoes that the woman used in gardening were passably sharp. The plow needed attention, but that could wait. Fairchild settled on a stump, held the shovel with its handle between his knees, and began to sharpen its blade with the file.

The girl watched as if at a show. "I've never seen anyone sharpen a shovel."

"A shovel is just like a plow. It cuts better if the blade has a keen edge."

"Cuts? The dirt."

"Yes."

"I think of cutting wood or weeds or material or meat."

"I'm a farmer." He considered it as he plied the file in long, heavy strokes along each angle of the shovel blade. "I *was* a farmer."

"What are you now?" Ann asked.

"Dead," Fairchild murmured. He looked up quickly, catching surprise and apprehension in the green eyes. "A joke," he said. "A private joke. I don't know just what I am now."

"Don't you?"

"But I'm looking forward to becoming something new."

"Oh, yes," Ann said in a voice so eager that he was startled.

He dared a look into those green eyes, cut his finger on the fresh edge of the shovel, never missed a stroke with the file. "You sound as if you'd like that." He wiped his finger on his shirt and left a fresh stain.

"I would like that. More than anything. But you've hurt yourself." She took hold of his hand.

"Not much. I'm out of practice. At a lot of things."

She lifted the hand to her mouth, sucked at the cut, and spat the blood away as if she were drawing venom from a bite. Then she pulled a tiny lace handkerchief from her bosom and wrapped it around his finger.

"I wouldn't have had you ruin that handkerchief," he said as softly as he could manage. "Not on me."

"I've been saving it. I wouldn't have used it for any other purpose." She held the cloth tightly about his finger to stanch the bleeding.

He heard her father's spirit in her words. He watched the end of it turn purple from the pressure, letting his mind wander without purpose into the morning air. When the finger began to throb with trapped blood, he took it from her, thanked her.

"It's time I get back to work." He spoke more abruptly than he'd intended, saw her draw back again. He tried another smile, found that this one came easier. "I think the corral would be better with another side."

She laughed. "The stock does tend to wander away," she said. "What stock there is. There's just Blackie now, since the filly wandered off. I think a bear got her." She looked at him. "Father means well. But he fell ill and never was able to finish it. There are some more rails out front in the wagon, I think."

"Blackie?"

She pointed toward the barn. "In the stall at the back. You probably didn't see him last night. He's Papa's riding horse. He hasn't had much work for some time, I'm afraid."

"Well, we'll give him a little more room, anyway." He went with her to the wagon, saw the scatter of rails mixed in with leaves and shingles and trash in the wagon bed. He carried the rails back two at a time to the rear of the weed-ridden corral.

He laid out the straightest of the rails in line across the open end of the corral. Then he marked appropriate spots for supports, and began digging post holes. The girl watched. From time to time throughout the morning she went inside, apparently to help with chores. By noon, Fairchild had the posts positioned and a couple of rails in place at the east end.

"Lunch is ready," Ann called, "if you'd like to wash up."

He thought himself too dirty to eat indoors, but she insisted. So he washed himself as best he could, smoothed his hair back with wet hands, and followed her inside.

Luncheon might have been judged plain by city standards, but Ethan Fairchild found it solid and tasty. Short on meat, the Bradleys had made dumplings flavored with chicken broth. "Like faith—these dumplings—without chicken," Elgin Bradley announced, " 'the substance—of things hoped for, the evidence of—things unseen.' "

Even Marguerite Bradley laughed. "It's so kind of you to help," she said. "Mr. Bradley's been ill."

"Not at all. Perfectly fit. Never better. After lunch— intend to help—finish the fence."

"You'll help with the dishes," she said. "Now that you've shown you know how. Then it'll be time for your nap."

The gray man laughed softly. "I believe—we have dessert."

Acknowledging his leadership, his wife opened the oven, and brought out a cobbler. Ann brought the pot of coffee warmed from breakfast.

To rest a little while after his meal, Fairchild looked over the grounds. Elgin Bradley followed, leaning on his cane and apologizing for chores never done. The barn had never been fitted with doors, and inside it had no loft floor. Stacks of shingles, boards, posts, and kegs of nails lay in scattered evidence of Bradley's good intentions. Much that he had begun stood unfinished. Whatever had been finished needed repair.

Bradley announced that he must go back in to his bed. "I've mended the record," he told Ethan.

Ethan's thoughts were elsewhere. "Have you?"

"I have. In my book, you've come back to life."

He turned away and went tapping his cane back toward the inn. Ethan followed him out of the barn, nodded to himself at last, and smiled. Then he stripped off his shirt and went back to work on the corral fence.

16

For a full day while the train rolled westward behind Hagewold's mules, Manasseh Thorne had toyed with the idea of taking the Lander Cut-off. For once, even Sugarhouse and Milt Ames were in favor of something that moved the train along, though Thorne couldn't say he liked their reason.

"Silver," Sugarhouse had said, rolling the word around his lips as if it were a fine cigar. "Silver, those mule drivers said, all you can dig or gather. That's reason enough to chance a little bit of a thirsty crossing."

"Caleb, those folks were just repeating the wild stories they've heard," Thorne pointed out. "They haven't any more seen this Caldwell's Spring than we have."

"Virginia City, they're calling it now," Milt Ames said. "And it's no wild story. There's riches to be had there, and we ought to get our share."

"We might, if we were going that way. But this Caldwell-Virginia place is down the California Trail from Fort Hall, clear past the Forty-Mile Desert. And we're bound for Oregon." Thorne stroked his beard. "You've signed a compact saying so."

Joe Coates horned in. "Didn't know about no silver when we signed." He looked at the others for support. "Things change."

"Your agreement doesn't. It says you're going to Oregon."

Caleb Sugarhouse drew himself up. "I'm a freeborn American, by God," he said. "Comes to that, I guess I'll go where I damned well please."

Thorne saw that things were beginning to run the wrong way. "Or where our wives will let us go, Caleb," he said. The others laughed, and even Sugarhouse couldn't help smiling. "Listen," Thorne said quickly, "we don't have to settle this today. It's a long way yet to Fort Hall. The question's about the cutoff. Let me read the guidebook and think about it. Then we'll see."

In the end, Thorne had looked hard at the massive snowcapped barrier of the Wind River Mountains and his nerve had failed him. He chose the easier route, skirting the southern foot of the mountains, crossing the Divide along the gentle slopes of South Pass, then leaving the main trail by way of the shorter and safer Sublette Cutoff.

A few had grumbled, but Thorne carried his point. Looking back on it now, he smiled as he trudged beside his creaking wagon. From the time they'd filled their water barrels near South Pass, they'd marched five long, waterless days and sixty weary miles across the high desert. Thorne knew he wasn't the only one to feel a tremendous relief when the valley of the Green River opened before them, its wide stream bordered with cottonwood and willow bright and alive in the gray waste of sage.

"We did right," he muttered.

"What's that?" Martha turned to peer at him from under the brim of her sunbonnet. "Did you say something, Man?"

"We did right. If Lander's route has more desert to cross than this, we made the right choice."

She smiled complacently. "*You* did right, you mean. I never doubted it." She glanced back to see if anyone else was within earshot. "That Caleb Sugarhouse would've taken us barefoot over hot coals to get to some silver mine the faster."

"Caleb's not so bad, Martha," Thorne said. "There's something on his side of the argument."

But he was troubled, all the same. He felt the deeper-running current of dissent which threatened his authority. He'd counted the little knot of men gathered in the lee of Caleb Sugarhouse's wagon of a morning, had seen it grow larger as more of the train went to their side.

Side! he said to himself. If it's come to *sides*, then we're in a terrible tussle with the devil. He knew it no longer mattered what they had so comfortably agreed to months ago. Then they hadn't heard about the silver strike, hadn't smelled the bait, hadn't lusted after the bright temptress Greed. Now Sugarhouse and some others danced around her fire like naked, sweating savages.

"Man?"

He'd been thinking his way into a speech, toying the phrases into sentences and paragraphs. He shook himself out of it and smiled at Martha. She was looking ahead, toward the green oasis of trees that stretched across their path.

"Yes?"

"Is there a bridge? Or will we have to float the wagons across again?"

"Neither. According to Hempstead, there's a ferry here." He switched his whip at the lagging near ox. "Hup, there! No, we'll just pay our toll and let somebody else do all the work. Stuart's up ahead, seeing to it."

" 'Stuart,' " Martha scoffed. "When are you going to start calling him by his Christian name, Man? Seeing he's your son by law, now?"

"Um." Thorne rubbed his beard. That question made him uneasy. He had to admit, though, that Stuart had backed his authority as loyally as a real son could have. "Funny thing," he murmured. "He's been a real help. A month ago, I wouldn't have bet a bushel of donkey droppings on him ever making a dependable man. Especially after the way he—"

"Manasseh Thorne!" Martha interrupted, scandalized.

She looked quickly around again. "Don't you ever utter such a thought again! Why, if Jessica heard you, she'd never forgive you." Then Martha began to laugh. "Donkey droppings, indeed!"

Thorne laughed, too. He was glad he hadn't finished his rash statement about Stuart's having left Fairchild behind. "Might be I'll take the horse and ride ahead," he said. "Just to see how *David's* doing at the ferry."

In the brief stretch between desert and riverbank, the trail ruts gave way to something like a road. Wide, paved with white gravel from the river's edge, beaten down hard by shod hooves, it led between tall spreading cottonwoods to a couple of log houses and a ramshackle log pier floored with rough-cut planks. David Stuart rode up the middle of the road, almost able to imagine he was back in Ohio, and drew rein before a sign that said Blis's Fery. He smiled at the sign for a moment, pleased to think there was somebody in the world whose spelling was worse than his, then stood down from the sorrel and went into the building he took for the office.

A frail young woman sat behind the counter, her faded calico dress unbuttoned and folded back so she could nurse a baby. She looked up at Stuart as he came in, then shook her head.

"Mrs. Bliss?" he said.

"Ferry's closed," she said.

Stuart looked around the room. The walls were bare. The top of the counter was bare. Three chairs stood in disarray along one wall.

"That's a fine, healthy-looking baby, ma'am. Boy or girl?"

"Boy."

"About the ferry, ma'am, I've got eighteen wagons not an hour behind me coming to cross."

"Ferry's closed."

"We intend to pay."

"You'd have to, but the ferry's closed."

"We've come sixty miles and more from South Pass, from water. We can't go back. We have to cross."

The woman shrugged and shifted the baby to her other side. "You can have water," she said, "but the ferry's—"

"Closed," Stuart said. "Is there anybody else around?"

"My ma and sister and Auntie Jan. They's on the other side. Men's gone."

Apparently tired from such a long speech, she crooned to the baby and bounced it gently. Stuart let out his breath. Heavy steps sounded on the porch outside. He heard the door open behind him.

"When'll they be back?"

"Ask the Lord."

"I beg your pardon?"

"Might be the Lord knows when. I don't. Don't nobody else, either. Been gone pretty nigh two months."

"Two months! Where've they gone?"

"Down to that place where the silver is. Said they's coming back with all the silver them mules can carry." She looked up at Stuart. "That's a lot of silver, ain't it? Be worth more'n a thousand dollars, I'll bet."

Manasseh Thorne strode directly past Stuart to stand solidly in front of the counter. "We need to cross the river," he said with brisk efficiency. "Who runs the ferry here? Where's the man in charge?"

The woman said, "Ferry's closed." She pulled the infant away from her breast, draped it over her shoulder, and began to pat it on the back.

Stuart stood by without speaking. He didn't even have the urge to laugh as Thorne went through the whole thing with her. Finally, the wagonmaster stood back and stroked his beard.

"Pray tell me, madam," he asked heavily, "just why you trouble yourself to sit here in this office?"

The baby burped. "Have to," the woman said. "Somebody needs to be here so's folks will know the ferry's closed."

*   *   *

Stuart didn't wait to hear Thorne's response. He turned, left the office, walked along the beaten white road to the pier. It was more solid than it had looked from a distance. Heavy timbers laid across the log stringers formed a solid platform. To one side, a tripod of heavy logs with their ends sunk into the ground supported a thick rope. Shading his eyes, Stuart could follow the rope out to where it dipped into the river. The river ran deep and powerful, its current throwing a wide curve in the ferry rope, holding it taut on the surface.

On the far side, the ferry bumped lazily against the wooden dock as occasional waves lapped at its sides. It was no more than a rectangular raft of logs, like many Stuart had seen. The rope ran to a sturdy post at one side of the raft, then rose from there to another tripod on the bank.

Stuart heard the cabin's door close. Thorne clumped down onto the pier to stand beside him.

"God help us," Thorne said. "How wide do you calculate that river is?"

"Hundred yards," Stuart said. He thought it was probably farther.

"Wagons coming," Thorne said.

Stuart turned. The lead wagon of the train had come waddling down past the log office. Lije Holden drew it up at the edge of the pier. Others clustered up behind it, men and women starting forward toward the riverbank. Thorne looked at the river.

"We can caulk the wagons with pitch," he said without much conviction. "Float across the way we did at—"

He didn't finish. Stuart knew why. *The way we did at the Big Blue, where Sam Kenny drowned.* He wasn't used to hearing uncertainty in Manasseh Thorne's voice. He studied his new father-in-law from the corner of an eye. He hadn't noticed so much gray in Thorne's beard, nor the vee of wrinkles above his eyes.

"We can do something else," Stuart said. Thorne glanced at him, but then Caleb Sugarhouse's big voice boomed out.

"What's wrong?" Caleb Sugarhouse wanted to know. "Don't look like we'll any of us be going anywhere until they bring the ferry back to this side. Where's the agent?"

"Where you'd like to be," Thorne said. "The men have all gone off on a wild-goose chase and left their women. Ferry's closed."

"Closed?" Douglas Stuart asked, frowning in his beard.

"Goose chase?" Sugarhouse laughed. "You mean the goose that laid the silver egg?"

"Caleb," Thorne said, "I've asked you not to talk about that foolishness."

"Hell," Sugarhouse said. "There's not a man in this train that hasn't heard about the silver strike. What do you mean, the ferry's closed?"

"Never heard of anybody closing a whole river before," Lije Holden said mildly. "What do you figure to do?"

"Can we ford? I thought it was too deep to ford." Other voices joined in as the news spread back down the way.

Stuart raised his voice to be heard over the talk. "Mr. Thorne was just telling me we're going to open the ferry. I'm going across on the tow rope and untie that raft."

"Shouldn't there be a little boat somewhere?"

"There it is, right over there," Douglas Stuart said. "Bottom's nearly out of it."

"Caleb, Uncle Douglas, suppose you get an ox team hitched onto this end so you can pull it back to this side." As Stuart talked, he unbuckled his gunbelt and handed the Navy Colt to Thorne. Jessica came up to take his hat and boots and coat.

"Be careful, Davy," she murmured. "Please be careful."

"Figure on Stuart to be careful of his skin." The voice was so soft Stuart barely heard it. He couldn't tell who had spoken. He was certain it wasn't Caleb's rumbling baritone. "Ask Ethan Fairchild."

"Nothing to worry about, Jess." He didn't know if she'd

heard or not. He wasn't sure he'd heard it himself.

"I keep thinking about Mr. Kenny—" Then she stopped, looked to see whether Barbara Kenny had heard her.

"Let's tie those boots together. I'll need them on the other side."

He hung the boots around his neck, then reached up to grasp the tow rope. Hand over hand, he swung along it until his weight carried it and him down into the water.

The current wasn't as bad as he'd expected, but the water was numbingly cold. He pulled himself along the rope, thinking finally to duck underneath to the upstream side so that the current pressed him against it rather than trying to pull him off. He had to stop once along the way to rest, and his teeth were chattering uncontrollably by the time he hauled himself up onto the splintery timbers of the raft. For a minute or more, he lay there panting before he rose to wave to those on the other shore. Faintly, he heard their cheer drift across to him. He grinned to himself as he went to see to the raft, wondering if his unknown detractor had cheered along with the rest.

The raft was tied off to the west pilings. Not quite as bare as he'd thought, it had low sturdy side rails. Rope burns and the marks of chains showed where other travelers had secured their wagons. Three heavy coils of tow rope stood like buildings on the bank.

Stuart could see Sugarhouse standing with his team on the eastern shore. He hurriedly pulled on his boots, then waved his arms in signal and set about untying the smaller docking ropes. Sugarhouse's arm rose and fell rhythmically, cracking a whip whose sound came to Stuart only as the big man was raising his arm for the next lash.

The rope on Stuart's side was dry and hardened in its coils. The rope by which he had crossed was sodden and heavy. A moment or two passed before the ferry began to move. Stuart stood behind the heavy piling and began to feed the dry rope as it rasped around the wood in its half twist.

As soon as it was out from shore, the ferry caught the current broadside and began to drift south against its ropes. Stuart could only imagine the strain it must be putting on Sugarhouse's oxen. He knew very well the strain it put on him to hold his own trailing rope.

When the heavy raft was just past midstream, a pigtailed girl of fourteen or so came down to the dock to tell Stuart that the ferry was closed. He thanked her for the information. She watched him gravely.

"You don't want to do that," she told him.

"You can take it up with the wagonmaster in just a little while," Stuart said without looking at her.

"No, what I mean is, it usually takes three men to hold that rope."

He believed her. "How about one man and a girl?"

"You mean me?"

He nodded.

"I'll go ask my ma." She came up close to look at him. "What I mean is, you's want to get back farther from them pilings."

"Why's that?" he asked, not much interested.

"'Cause if you don't, you know what? That rope'll directly catch you against the post and wrap you right on round. My pa, once, he broke three ribs that way. Uncle George said he's got God's chosen luck 'cause it didn't take his hand off plumb at the shoulder."

Stuart began to back away from the piling. After he caught his breath, he looked at the girl again. "I thank you," he said.

She smiled, showing a gap between her front teeth. "Are you married yet?" she asked.

"Yes."

"Oh!" the girl said. Then she turned and ran back up the slope toward another sagging cabin. Shortly, she came back with two older, heavier women whom Stuart took to be twins. "Me and my momma and Auntie Jan's going to help you," she announced.

Stuart said, "I thank you."

One of the twins said, "This ferry's closed."

Stuart nodded without looking back, but he felt the help when the heavy women took hold of the rope and dug in with their heels.

"Surprised they got it that far with this rotten rope," the second woman said.

"Rotten rope?"

"It ain't all that rotten."

"You know it is, Jan! Them worthless men of ours was just fixing to lay in new rope, when they up and took off on us. And they wouldn't have put in a new rope less this one was ruint."

Stuart stared into the swift waters and swore to himself.

" 'Course, it don't matter much."

"Why's that?"

"They ain't none of them here to haul the ferry back this way."

Stuart craned his neck around to look at her, then stared back across the river. He saw Thorne waving his arms to signal that the ferry was docked on the eastern bank. He took a couple more twists of the dry rope round the piling and watched without means of warning them while they drove the first of the wagons onto the deck of the ferry. They had chosen Barbara Kenny's wagon to make the first crossing.

Stuart looked again at the women beside them, then at the girl. "Is there a team?" he asked the girl.

"Sort of. There's them broke-down critters my pa and them left in the corral."

One of the heavy women pointed toward the cabin. "Behind there," she said.

"What are they?"

"Oxes," the girl said. She smiled at Stuart again. "You sure you're married already?"

"Mandy Jean, you behave."

"How many?"

"Six that'll pull like three."

Stuart went up the slope with the girl following him,

found the corral, looked at the lean oxen. "Don't you feed them?"

"Some. Ain't got much fodder."

He went into the corral and began yoking the beasts to a dry and brittle-looking drawpole. They were too tired and poor to offer him much resistance. When he had them hitched, he led them back downslope to the end of the rope. They recognized it and slowed their pace in anticipation. He got them turned and backed into position and fastened the rope eye to the drawpole. The team stood wearily, heads hanging. He had no fear of a runaway.

Manasseh Thorne was waving his hat as if he'd done it a time or so before Stuart noticed. There was nothing for it. If the oxen had enough life left to pull the ferry over here, then he could use Mrs. Kenny's team for the next pull. And he could send back a new rope on the dry haul.

He flipped the hitches of rope off the piling, leaving the rope to drag against the upstream side, and took his place beside the team. Standing side by side with folded arms, the two women watched. Mandy Jean tagged eagerly at his heels.

"Hup!" he cried. He didn't have a whip to crack. The oxen lifted their heads and leaned into the harness without taking a step. "Ho! You sons of oxen! Move!"

They leaned harder, took a ragged stagger forward, stopped again.

"Here, mister." Mandy Jean offered him a long leafy willow switch. "Just sort of tickle them. You hit them hard enough to break the skin, all their insides might just run out."

"I thank you."

"You *certain* sure you're married?"

He took the switch, flicked it across the backs of the nigh oxen. "Ho!" he told them. They flinched, leaned into the heavy yokes, pulled harder. The off-side animals twitched their ears at the sound of the switch. Stuart saw the scars of the whip on their backs and wondered how many times they had pulled the sodden ferry across to the western side. "One more time! Then you can rest. Ho!"

The team dug in with splayed hooves, leaned west, and pulled, moving like six snails up the slope and onto the hard-packed gravel of the approach. The front pair had just gotten onto the level ground above the bank when the whole team suddenly staggered forward with a rush. The lead ox snorted and went to its knees as the others piled into it.

Above their noise, Stuart heard a deep, vibrating *twang!* like a breaking fiddle-string. The women let out a scream. Stuart turned to see the raft swinging downstream like bait cast into the current without a weight, trailing a broken end of rope from its far side. The wagon on board swayed, heeling over as the waves took the raft from a new direction. Faintly, Stuart heard a woman's scream and the bellowing of frightened oxen.

"Ho!" he shouted to his team, lashing hard with the willow branch now. It was no good. A fresh team of twelve couldn't pull the ferry in before it smashed against the bank fifty yards downstream.

Stuart didn't take time to think. It didn't occur to him that he'd once before had to make a decision in an instant and act on it. He wasn't aware, even, that he'd made a decision, only that a set trigger had tripped somewhere deep inside his soul.

"Keep them moving, Mandy Jean," he said. "Keep them pulling hard." Then he ran, angling downstream past the gravel margin of the road and the edge of the pier. He heard the switch lash hard against flesh before he reached the bare dirt of the long bank.

"You'll have to pay for that raft!" one of the women was shouting at him, but his thoughts were on the wagon and its human cargo. He leaned into his full stride, running on the balls of his feet, sloping downhill, moving faster than he'd ever moved in his life. Willows lashed across his face and chest. His foot caught in a tangle of grass. He fell headlong before he had time to stumble, skinning his palms, tearing the knees out of his jeans, rolled twice, and came up again running.

River reeds at the water's edge kept him from seeing the ferry raft, but he had a good idea where it would be. He ran thirty yards past that point before he stumbled through the willows to the water.

The raft had hung fire in an eddy twenty yards from the bank. Stuart couldn't imagine the rotten western rope was holding its burden against the current. It wouldn't last. Barbara Kenny was clinging to the driver's seat as the heavy wagon lurched against the chains holding it. On the raft's pitching deck, Fred Harris scrambled among the staggering oxen, trying to quiet their panicky struggles.

Stuart dived headlong into the river, remembering only when he was in the air to hope it was deep enough. He cut into the cold green water with a heart-stopping shock, tumbled in the current as his heavy boots tried to pull him down, kicked viciously and desperately until he got clear of them and could get back to the surface. Sucking in a great gasp of air, he struck out with long, swift strokes toward the raft.

"Harris!" he yelled or gulped or gasped. But it was too much to swim and shout. He swam. Halfway to the raft, he cried out again. Harris turned, looking down at Stuart like a man half-blinded. Barbara Kenny was not screaming now but seemed frozen to the wagon seat.

"Harris! The rope. Throw the deck rope!"

Fred Harris came out of his frozen trance, grasped the docking rope in stiff fingers, hurled the coil far out upstream. Stuart caught just the end of it as it shot past, wrapped a turn round his arm, and dug in for shore. He was still half in the water, throwing a frantic hitch around the trunk of a cottonwood that leaned over the river, when the western towline snapped at the raft. The docking rope sprang out rigid as a bar of iron. Stuart planted a foot against the trunk and heaved, holding his breath while the rope creaked and quivered at the very edge of breaking strain.

It held. The docking rope held until the raft cleared the current and slid into quiet water and drifted against the bank. Stuart was there to meet it. He found a second rope and tied the raft off at the southern end.

Fred Harris had finally coaxed Barbara Kenny off the wagon seat. He tried to carry her, but she wouldn't have it.

"I can walk," she said, but her eyes were not fixed on him or Stuart or anything particular. She allowed Harris to help her onto dry ground. Holding her tightly against his side, the doctor said, "Thank God for you, Stuart! There's not another man in the world would have plunged into hell to pluck us out."

Dazed and wet, bleeding where the rope had cut his hands, shivering from cold and from a realization of what he'd done, Stuart raised his head and croaked something back to Harris. He wasn't sure what he'd wanted to say. His thoughts were whirling the way the river had whirled the raft around, but he managed to grab hold of one thought and hang on.

I had another chance! He grinned foolishly at Harris and tried to stand. The doctor caught him before he fell. He wished Ethan could see him. *Lord save us, Ethan, I had another chance. And this time, I did it right!*

17

On his fifth morning at Bradley's Oak, Ethan Fairchild rose in the dawn and strode to the cold pool behind the beaver dam. Pulling off his shirt, he splashed in the icy water as he drank in the new day.

Each evening, he'd made plans to leave at the next sunrise. Each morning, he'd found some reason to stay.

First, he hadn't quite finished his repairs, then the chestnut horse seemed a touch lame, or he needed to work another day to earn supplies for the trail. Each day, the elder Bradleys treated him more like a son, though he caught Marguerite Bradley studying him with a speculative eye once or twice, and Ann treated him more like—

Like what? he asked himself. What did she treat him like? And how did he treat her?

His mind wasn't free of hatred, might never be. He wasn't done with the punishing thoughts of Jess, sleeping now in Stuart's wagon, in Stuart's arms. But every day of hard labor helped him sweat out his anger, unravel his tangled purpose.

Straightening from the pool, he reached for his shirt. Below the dam, a racoon was washing something in the stream, darting an occasional suspicious look at Fairchild before returning to its work. Fairchild laughed.

The ugly sound of it startled him. Too much thinking, he told himself. He needed some of Mrs. Bradley's flapjacks, and maybe two or three eggs. Then he would get after the weeds in the garden.

Halfway back to the inn, he met Ann Bradley coming to meet him. When she came to him, he said, "You're quite a tracker."

She took his hand. "Forrest taught me." He started to ask who Forrest was, but she said, "I guess where you come from, girls learn prettier things. Do they play the piano and sing and chat and declaim in public?"

He looked down at her. "Where I come from," he said gravely, "there aren't any girls like you."

"Oh." She looked away.

"No. Let me see your eyes. That's good. There's not another girl like you, not anywhere."

She smile a little. Afraid. Uncertain. Tender. "Is that good?"

"It is."

"And you're glad I'm as I am?"

"I am." He smiled at the echo.

"You said we might get Blackie some exercise. We could go for a ride before breakfast."

"Fine idea," Fairchild said. "I'm not hungry, anyway."

The chestnut, stale from lack of exercise, seemed glad to get into the open again. It snapped at Fairchild only once while he was saddling it, barely drawing blood. On the trail, it pranced and pawed while the placid Blackie plodded steadily along, Ann Bradley straddling the cracked saddle like a boy.

"Your horse is so spirited, Ethan," Ann said.

"Isn't he?" Fairchild smiled at her. "Which way would you like to go?"

"I like to go west!"

She kicked Blackie into a trot, westward a couple of miles along the wagon trail. Then she led Fairchild south into the foothills, along a narrow trail which he first thought she was blazing as she went. But he soon saw she knew exactly where she was going; otherwise, she would have lost the trail a dozen times. Finally, they came out into a grassy bowl rimmed with tall pines.

Alone, Fairchild might have followed the trail past without noticing the log dugout at the far edge of the clearing. Whoever lived there had not put out a sign inviting company, had instead gone out of his way to prevent the trail from coming right to his door.

The girl turned her horse toward the shack and Fairchild followed. They had not gone twenty steps before a spare, leathery man appeared from the brush as softly as smoke. He was clean-shaved, but grizzled hair hung in two long braids below his wolfskin cap. He was dressed all in buckskin, and he held a long Plains rifle. He did not exactly point the rifle at them, nor did he exactly move it away in a neutral direction.

"Mr. Elam!" Ann cried. "You startled me."

"Ann?" Elam stared up at her. "Annie, it's you, girl!"

"It is." She dismounted, laughing, and ran to him. "I've

brought my friend, Ethan Fairchild. Ethan, Mr. Elam's our only near neighbor and our dearest friend."

"Ethan, is it?" The old man shifted the rifle to his left hand. "Forrest Elam, and proud to meet you. 'Twas you I was watching whilst you rode up the trail. Didn't rightly notice Ann. She wasn't carrying so many guns. And that horse of yours has a mean eye about it."

"Sorry," Fairchild said. "We weren't trying to sneak up on you. Ann hadn't told me we were going visiting."

The old man's laugh was like the call of a crow. "Ain't nobody much ever sneaked up on this old he-coon," he said. "Light yourself down, son, and visit a spell. Good company's always welcome."

"He used to be a mountain man, a free trapper," Ann explained as they rode home. "We lived down at the Oak for a year before we even knew he was there. Then one day he came down and brought us a haunch of venison and said he reckoned we could stay. He and Father play chess sometimes."

"I'd like to see that," Fairchild said. If half Forrest Elam's stories were true, he'd lived enough excitement for Thorne's whole wagon train.

"I always like talking to him. He's been so many places." She looked at him hopefully. "Ethan, did you have some special work to do today?"

"Nothing special. Why?"

"Well, I thought maybe, after breakfast we might . . ."

"Yes?"

"You might look at Father's old wagon. Maybe you could fix it."

"That eyesore under the tree, you mean?" He laughed. "I might get it rolling well enough to move it round behind the barn. You could stack firewood in it."

Hurt showed in her eyes. "No!" she said. "Don't joke about it!"

He saw the hurt, tried to think what he'd said. "It's only a wagon."

"I depend on it." She rode in silence for a minute, her eyes fixed on the trail. Finally, she said, "It gives me hope. Whenever I see it there, pointed west, I think maybe someday Father will be well enough to go on." She turned toward him, and he saw the tears in her eyes. "Ethan, can't you work on it? Please?"

"Well, I haven't really looked at it."

"But you'll try? I'll help you if you try!"

Looking at the hope in her face, Fairchild decided a man who wouldn't try wouldn't be worth much. "We'll see," he said. "After breakfast."

The corpse of the family wagon wasn't quite as bad as Fairchild expected. The axles and undercarriage looked sound, but bed and sideboards and draw bar were cracked and rotted. More important, years of thaws and freezes had sunk the iron rims of the wheels deep into the soft soil. Fairchild could grease the hubs, but the buried spokes were most likely rotted out. He was digging out one of the wheels to see when Ann Bradley came around the porch and stood looking at the wagon as though she'd never seen it before.

"Come sit on the tongue," Fairchild said. "We can talk while I dig."

She put her hands to her face for a moment, then lowered them. With dragging steps, she came to him. The old wood groaned and crackled when she sat.

"It won't do."

"What?" He had knelt to brush away the dirt around one of the spokes. "Better than I expected. Maybe being buried helped."

"I'd never really looked at it," Ann said. She wiped at her eyes and smiled brightly. "It won't do. Even if Father was well, or if you wanted to take me—take *it*—on west, the wagon just wouldn't—" She waved a hand vaguely.

Her lower lip trembled, and she finished with a quick breath, "Wouldn't do."

He felt as if he'd stepped on a ground bird's nest and crushed the eggs. "It's a stout wagon," he assured her. "But no, it wouldn't take the trail, not as it is. It needs some—" He hesitated. What the wagon needed was to be broken up for firewood. "It needs some fixing."

She nodded, her face turned away. Fairchild put a work-roughened hand on her shoulder.

"There's not much that hard work can't fix," he said. "With some help, I might fix it."

"Could you?"

For the returning hope in her voice, he could do a lot. "I guess I might," he said. "There's lumber in the barn, plenty of leather for strengthening. We can fix up the bed and running gear pretty easy, if you're not particular about looks." Then he felt the cold touch of reality. "I don't know about the spokes and rims. I'm not much of a hand at blacksmithing. Still," he added quickly, "if we could get it into the barn, we might have a chance."

"Then let's try!" Springing up, she climbed into the wagon bed and began scooping out the litter of leaves and trash that had filled it over the years.

"Listen," he began, intending to warn her about the rotten planks. A board cracked sharply, and then there was a confused moment of snapping lumber and ripping cloth and Ann's startled yelp as she dropped through the collapsed flooring in a swirl of skirts and petticoats.

"Ann!" Fairchild started to swing up into the bed, then realized it wouldn't help to have him land on top of her. Instead, he dropped to his knees and peered underneath the wagon. "Ann, are you all right?"

"I'm all right," Ann quavered back. "I'm fine, but my arm's bleeding a little."

Fairchild had already looked. Half standing with her head and shoulders above the wagon bed and one foot on the ground, Ann hopped awkwardly. The ruins of her skirts and petticoats, caught and tangled in the splintered boards, held her suspended and helpless as a fly in a spider's web. Fairchild suddenly had a much keener idea of the shapes of her limbs than his imagination had provided him before. His imagination had not done her justice.

"Ethan."

"Let me see that arm."

"It's only a scratch. Ethan, be careful."

Ignoring her protests and one kick from her free foot, he set about untangling her from the debris of the wagon. He had to tear the stout muslin petticoats, which made her struggle the harder.

"Wait, Ann, I've almost— Ouch! Listen, I've got a horse a lot like you. Here, just one more second."

As he stretched to get at a vagrant strand of skirt, it ripped free suddenly. There was a moment of tearing and crackling. Fairchild grabbed at Ann as she fell free, overbalanced, and went down among a blizzard of skirts and leaves and dust and bare kicking legs. Ann landed on his stomach hard enough to mash the wind out of him.

He caught her in a bear hug, pinning her arms. She burrowed her face against his chest and her shoulders shook. It took him a moment to realize she was laughing, and then he laughed, too, holding her, neither of them able to speak. Finally, she raised her face to his.

"Ethan," she said.

She didn't finish. Fairchild was never sure which of them moved first, but then he was kissing her, pressing her slender body tightly to him and feeling her lips, innocent and uncertain and hungry, shaping themselves to his.

"Ethan," she breathed when they slipped apart.

"Yes, Ann?"

"This morning at the pool, when you took your shirt off."

He craned his neck to look at her. "Yes?"

"I watched you. I saw you." Her cheeks flushed a little, but her eyes were all childlike honesty. "And then when I fell through the wagon bed."

"Yes."

"You saw me." She licked her lips. "Does that mean—does it mean we love each other?"

"Love?"

"Because I know I love you. But I don't know if you do. Love me."

Dear God, he thought, what have I done here? "But Ann." He felt her name on his lips, used it again just to hear it. "Ann, you've lived alone here so long. There's a world of young men you haven't met. You can't know yet if I'm the one."

"There's not another young man like you, not anywhere."

He heard the echo of his words and smiled.

"Do you, then?"

He waited too long, finally nodded. It wasn't good enough, but it was the best he could manage. She moved against him and lifted her face to his and kissed him. After a minute he pulled back. He looked as far as he could see into the depths of those green eyes.

"Yes," he said plainly. "Yes. God knows. I love you."

"My *lands* sakes alive! What *are* you children doing?"

Marguerite Bradley's voice, more vigorous than Fairchild had ever heard it before, startled him. He sat up, cracking his head solidly on one of the crossbraces. Ann stifled a giggle.

"You two come out of there, right this minute! Can you get out?"

Together they crawled out into the sunlight. Ann Bradley was dirty, her clothes torn, her hair leaf-strewn, her lips trembling on the edge of scandalous laughter, her legs bare and white in the dappled sunlight. Fairchild didn't look notably better. He scrambled to his feet and helped Ann up.

"Ma'am, I'm sorry. I shouldn't have let her get up there."

"It was an accident, Mama," Ann interrupted, joy bubbling in her voice. "I fell. Ethan was just helping me."

"Well, I should just about say he was!"

"I cut my arm."

"What?" Mrs. Bradley pointed toward the inn. "Come inside, dear, and let's see to your arm and get you in some decent clothing. "As for you, Ethan Fairchild."

"Yes, ma'am." He was in for it and figured he deserved it.

"As for you," she said after the girl had gone inside, "you're a good man."

He didn't feel like a very good man, and he didn't know what to say. "I didn't mean her harm."

"It's just that Ann's grown up here, away from the world, away from men," she said finally. "Ethan, she's a fine, strong, decent girl."

"Finest, most decent."

"But she hasn't the experience to understand about a lot of things."

"Ma'am, I give you my word, I'd never willingly hurt your Ann. Nor take advantage of her innocence."

She looked at him for a long moment, something in her eyes he didn't understand. Then she smiled. "Thank you, Ethan," she said. "That's all I wanted to know." She turned away, then looked back at him. "You'd better get back to work on that foolish wagon. When she's changed, I'll send Ann out to help you."

The repairs on the wagon went better than Fairchild had imagined they could. By the end of the third day, he'd managed to put bed and tailboards and draw pole into a condition that wasn't actually dangerous. The spokes and rims needed the expert attention of a wheelwright, but they might last long enough to reach one if they didn't have to bear much of a load. He'd greased the hubs and axles, and had sorted through the moldering pile of harness to find what was usable. He didn't want even to think about finding a team. Not yet.

He was washing up at the trough when the buffalo

hunters rode in. He smelled them before he saw them, the first big wagon loaded with stinking green hides and drawn by a powerful eight-mule hitch. Dressed in buckskin and homespun, there were four mounted men and two drivers. At the rear of their procession a second wagon held the hunters' gear and goods. Fairchild approached cautiously, his hand near the Colt, but Elgin Bradley was already tapping his way to greet them.

"Welcome—gentlemen. At your—service."

At the head of his group, a huge red-bearded man waved his hat. Dismounting heavily, he plodded toward the porch while his men waited in their creaking saddles.

"Redwood Waller," he announced, extending a great hairy hand to his host. "Me and these varmints ain't but about half civilized. But we're middling successful businessmen and powerful tired of our own cooking. Will you have us?"

Bradley shook hands, his entire body rocking from the force of the buffalo hunter's greeting. "We'd be pleased to have you stay."

"Gracious, yes," Marguerite Bradley said. "Just let me add another cup of water to the stew."

"That would be mighty fine, ma'am." Waller turned to Fairchild. "And you, friend?"

Fairchild gave his name, lived through the experience of shaking Waller's hand, went from horse to horse greeting the other hunters. Most were gruffly silent. None smelled much different from the goods in their wagon.

Bradley said, "It'll be a while—before supper. You gentlemen—are welcome to—come in and play some— whist." He hesitated, then said, "Or—you might enjoy— a—bath—down at the—pool."

"Bath?" the first wagon driver yelled. "Hell, Red—"

Waller said, "Hush, Gawk." Then he laughed. "Fact is, Mr. Bradley, ain't none of us gentlemen been privileged to a bath for nigh two months. We'll be pleased to accept your kind invitation."

"Ah, then. My—daughter will provide you with—towels and a—lump of our own—homemade soap."

"Be glad to have her scrub my back, too," Gawkins muttered to no one special. Fairchild walked close to the wagon, held his eye, shook his head slowly.

"Hell," Gawkins said amiably. "Red told you we ain't fit company for decent folk. I take your point. I'll keep my mouth shut and my eyes off her."

Fairchild grinned. "You can look," he said. The men rode by, collected their towels, and went whooping down the trail toward the beaver dam.

Fairchild put his arm around Ann's shoulders. "Here's your chance," he whispered. "Lots of other men you can see without their shirts, be sure of your choice."

She swatted him with an extra towel. "No need," she said. "I've chosen."

He was kissing the top of her head when he saw the evening sun glint for a second on something shiny atop the ridge to the east. Then it was gone, leaving Fairchild staring. Had it been polished metal? Glass?

"Ethan? What's wrong?"

"Nothing. You go on in and help with supper." He held his nose and grinned at her. "I believe I'll move their hide wagon over to the other side of the barn."

He brought the wagon round easily, studying the far hill. He saw the smooth white trunks of aspens, the quick lift of a deer's head. Nothing else, no more reflections. Satisfied, he unhitched the mules and turned them into the corral.

At supper, it became clear that the smell of their trade had cleaved so tightly to the buffalo hunters' skins that soap couldn't entirely remove it. It didn't seem to hurt their appetite. After the meal, they went out to tend their animals. Two of the men kindled a fire out in the open yard. Then Gawkins took a jug from the hide wagon, tipped it up for a long pull, passed it to the next man.

"Just one tonight, boys," Waller said as he set it aside, empty. "We're among proper folks. Baldy, give us a tune."

The one called Baldy sawed on a battered fiddle while the rest danced or sang. Fairchild took Ann Bradley into the kitchen and helped her wash the dishes while the elder Bradleys sat on the front porch and applauded the festivities. When the fire played out, Waller bade the Bradleys thanks for their hospitality, and his men wrapped up in their robes and slept around the embers.

When Fairchild brought them out a big enameled pot of coffee before breakfast, only Waller was awake. "I notice you're not ever very far from your gun," he said.

"Good morning to you, too." Fairchild filled the big man a cup of coffee. "I notice you keep a pistol in your coat pocket. And that every man of yours is armed one way or another."

Waller threw back his head in a shower of red hair, laughing. "You keep a gun and you got good eyes. That ought to mean you can shoot. Can you?"

"Middling."

"You're the man we need."

"For what?"

"Scout. Backwatcher. Guard."

Fairchild poured him a fresh cup. "You don't strike me as needing a nursemaid."

"Line us up against another outfit at a quarter of a mile, we'd take them down. But most of the time we've got our attention set on our work. We can't watch our back ever minute. We're hunters, not soldiers."

Ethan Fairchild frowned. "Why would you need to be?" he asked carefully. "Indians?"

Waller shook his head. "Give or take a horse or two, the Indians we've met haven't caused us any bother," he said. He sipped at his coffee, looking at Fairchild across the rim of the cup. "Others has."

"Others?"

"Last week they was eight of us. Had two kind of dumb old boys just learning their way." He paused, his face turning hard. "Left them with the wagons while us'n's strung out round a good herd. Band of cannibals cut them down right by the hide wagon. Scalped one, half skinned the nother. Didn't even take the damned hides, was too green for them."

"But it wasn't Indians?"

"We got back as they was hightailing out. I took one out of his saddle at four hundred yards, and he weren't no Indian. Wish you'd seen the rest of them give it the spur!" He laughed, then stopped. "The one I took for leader had white hair, long, flying loose. Tried for a shot at him."

"Where was this!"

"But he was moving too fast. What? Where? Back southeast, about four, five days. You know him?"

"Damned right I do."

"Then you'll be wanting to come with us."

"Breakfast!" Ann Bradley called from the kitchen window. Waller finished his coffee at a gulp.

"We'd pay you in cash money, or with a full share when we sell out at Fort Hall. You think on it."

"I'm thinking on it." Fairchild paused, stared at the window. Whitehair and his gang were off in the morning someplace, four days away, maybe less. Maybe watching from the ridge, even now. If he left, the Bradleys would be helpless as chickens cooped up for the fox.

"I can't go," he said.

Waller misunderstood. "Clipped your wings, has she? If it was a girl like that, I'd like as not let her clip mine." He frowned at Fairchild, then said, "Listen, we're headed northwest, along the drift of the herd. Be at the Bliss ferry in about a month, Fort Hall maybe a month after that. If you change your mind, come chase us down."

"I doubt it."

"Man never knows. Is that natural sausage I smell?"

A half hour after breakfast, the hunters were mounted and ready. Waller leaned down to press a bag of coins into Mrs. Bradley's hands.

"Bless you, but that's far too much."

"Not a bit of it." He turned in the saddle. "Fairchild, remember what I told you. All right, Gawkins, whip 'em up. Buffaloes is waiting."

"I doubt it," Fairchild said again, but he stood in the yard, watching, until the hunters and their wagons were out of sight to the west.

It was washing day at Bradley's Oak. Fairchild left off work on the old wagon to help Ann carry the wet towels and bedclothes back up the hill. The two of them were hanging clothes on the line when a dozen riders filed slowly up the trail, dragging unwilling packhorses behind them.

"More visitors," Ann said. "Father's book'll be full for this month."

Fairchild had been watching them since they'd turned from the main road. As they drew nearer, his eye picked up the tatters and rags of uniform they wore.

"It's the Army," he said, sliding the Colt back into its holster.

"The ones you know?"

"Not likely." He started down toward the patrol, which had drawn up in the shade of Bradley's tree. "But I'll see."

"Begging the lieutenant's pardon," one of the men at the head of the detail said as Fairchild approached, "but the Bradleys is got them a new washerwoman." Sergeant Neidercutt spat to the off side of his horse. "Tall, ugly one, too."

"But he's still got that Colt you promoted for him, Sergeant." Lieutenant Cranfill slid from the saddle and offered a hand. "Life's full of surprises, Mr. Fairchild. I thought you'd be to Green River by now or dead along the way."

"I thought you'd be back in Fort Kearny."

Cranfill gave his quick grin. "We would, if it were my

choice." He turned. "Sergeant, dismount the column. Water and rest."

Ann had come up to stand at Fairchild's side. "Welcome to Bradley's Oak," she said, looking curiously from the lieutenant to Fairchild. Cranfill sketched her a salute.

"Honored, miss." He looked at her and Fairchild with equal curiosity. "We'll not trouble you long. We're warning the settlements about a particularly nasty band of renegades."

"Whitehair?" Fairchild's arm tightened instinctively around Ann.

Cranfill nodded. "Silverhorn's the name we have," he said. "Clearly the same bunch. I wonder, miss, if I might speak with your father."

"But we're—peaceable folk here," Elgin Bradley protested, folding his hands over the blue prayerbook he'd been reading when Cranfill came in. "Surely—these people—wouldn't molest us."

"There was a little place down south of Fort Laramie," Cranfill said. "Taylor's Crossing? Heard of it?"

"Why, certainly. We've crossed there."

"You won't hear of it again. Silverhorn's bunch burned it. Doctor's office, trading post, few buildings."

"What about the people?" Fairchild asked.

"Yes," Bradley seconded. "Will they—rebuild?"

Cranfill looked at him as if he were a slow child. "There's nobody left to rebuild."

"Nobody left?"

"One survivor, wounded. That's where we got Silverhorn's name. One missing. The rest." He spread his hands. "Dead, all. We lost Silverhorn's trail days ago without ever catching sight of him. He was headed this way, then veered off. Probably following the road west like a pack of wolves."

"Or cannibals," Fairchild murmured. "Would they steal buffalo hides?"

"Silverhorn'd steal buffalo chips if there was profit in it." Cranfill rose from the dining table. "I figure you're alive and this inn standing because you don't keep a store. No supplies, very little livestock. The wolves didn't smell anything here worth the trouble, so you've been passed over."

The words touched on Bible stories from Fairchild's childhood, but he wasn't just sure how. Had the wolves smelled blood on the lintels? No, that didn't fit. But they might have smelled the stink of green hides.

Fairchild thought about the men Waller had lost, considered the good folks at Taylor's Crossing, remembered what Silverhorn had done to his own life.

"Can you use another man?" he asked Cranfill.

The lieutenant raised his eyebrows. "Glad to have you," he said. "We can't pay this time."

"Where will you be?"

"Along the trail, headed for Fort Bridger. Waiting for word."

"I'll catch up."

"Very well." Cranfill nodded to Elgin Bradley. "We'll be riding now, sir. Congratulations on your luck, and my respects to your ladies."

When the lieutenant had gone, Elgin Bradley turned troubled eyes on Fairchild. "Ethan, no!" he said. "You mustn't. Vengeance belongs—to the Lord."

"Sorry, sir." Fairchild rose. "It wasn't the Lord that son of a bitch shot down and left for dead in the mud."

He was straightening his blanket on the chestnut's back when Ann Bradley came into the barn behind him.

"Ethan. We're not finished with our wagon."

"We'll finish." He threw the saddle across the blanket. "I'll come back for you, Ann."

"You'd go without me?" He could see it in her eyes that she didn't believe he would. She came on round in front of him and looked in his eyes. "It's that girl, isn't it? That Jessica who married your friend?"

Fairchild gave the cinch a vicious yank. "My friend!"

He knew if he met her eyes he wouldn't be able to leave. "It's not about Jessica, Ann. Nor about David, damn his soul."

"It is! I thought we loved each other."

"I do. We do! But Silverhorn has to be stopped."

"You don't love me. You're too busy hating all of them."

He didn't want to think about that. "I have to go."

"Would you leave me here? I thought—" She stopped, bit her lip. "I thought you *wanted* me, at least."

Fairchild caught a breath. "I did," he said. "I do."

"Then stay. Or take me with you." Very softly, she said, "You don't have to—to marry me or anything."

"Ann." He loved her, wanted her, he told himself. What he was doing was crazy. But another part of him wanted blood, wanted Silverhorn's white scalp hanging from his belt. And that side was the stronger. Turning abruptly, he caught her by the shoulders. "Ann, I can't," he said. "But I do love you. I'll come back for you, I swear!"

He clasped her trembling form in his arms, held her tightly enough to hurt his ribs, kissed her fevered face, her eyes, her lips.

But she hung limp.

"No," she whispered. With unexpected strength, she pulled away from him. "No. Not feeling the way you feel. You'll never come back to me."

She ran back behind the wagon, away from his sight. Fairchild took two steps after her, stopped. *Stay here, you idiot*, he told himself. *Do as Bradley says. Let it go. You'll lose her if you don't*. He went to her, knelt beside her, held her. "I'll come to you," he told her, "if it's on my hands and knees. God, Ann, I do love you! But I have to go."

Behind him, the chestnut snorted and tossed its head. Fairchild turned, stared into its wild eye, remembered its plunging, slashing fight against Silverhorn's wolves. He left her slumped against the half-rotted wagon wheel. "Devil," he said, and swung into the saddle. Without looking back, he rode out in the direction the troopers had taken.

18

"You said Stuart didn't have guts."

"He's got more than I gave him credit for, that's certain."

"More than most, the way he went for that ferry. Reckon why he left Fairchild on the prairie, then?"

"If he didn't run because he was scared, maybe he ran because he'd killed him."

"That's a lie!"

The two men had spoken in low tones, their voices covered by the rush of the river around the pilings, the random noises of the oxen and wagons, the excited talk of the crowd staring across the water. They hadn't noticed Francis Buttrell behind them. More likely, Francis thought, they simply hadn't thought he was important.

Both turned, Joe Coates looking surprised and Milt Ames angry.

"Oh, it's you." Ames unclenched his fists, but his voice still held an edge. "Listen, boy, you'd better watch who you're calling a liar."

"I ain't a boy. I been doing man's work same's anybody else. And you'd better watch who you're calling a killer."

Ames started a hot answer, then bit it back. Francis had spoken loudly enough for others to hear, and heads were starting to turn their way. Will Buttrell, frowning, moved toward the group, but before he could get there, Manasseh Thorne came bustling back from the pier.

"We'll have to get another rope across," he said. "Something we can use to pull back a new towline. Joe, Milt, will you see if you can rustle up enough rope? Seems to me, we'll need close on a hundred yards."

"More, I'd judge," Coates said quickly. He took Ames's arm. "Come on, Milt. I've got a hundred feet or so in my wagon, if we can find it. And I know Caleb's got some."

"I reckon we'll get enough," Ames muttered. He shot a last look at Francis. "How'll we get it across? We already got all our heroes off on the other side."

"What's that?" Thorne demanded, but Ames followed the other man without answering.

"I'll take it," Francis said.

Thorne was frowning after Ames and Joe Coates, only half noticing Francis. "What did you say, boy?"

"I said I'll take it. I'm about as good a swimmer as anybody here, 'cepting maybe Davy, and he's on the other side already."

"Wait a minute, son." Will Buttrell said. He put his arm on Francis's shoulders. "This isn't any job for a boy."

"I ain't a boy," Francis repeated. "Anyway, who's it a job for, then? Maybe you, Mr. Thorne?"

"Look here, mister, you keep a civil tone to your elders," his father said, though he couldn't quite help smiling at the idea of Thorne swimming the river. "Else we'll see who's a boy and who's not." Pursing his lips, he looked at Thorne. "Manasseh? You're not taking this seriously?"

Thorne stroked his beard thoughtfully. "This young man's got you on one point, Will. If he's not the one, who is?"

"Not me, Will," Lije Holden's twangy voice put in. "Back in the holler where I was raised, the deepest water for twenty miles was a washtub, and we had to take turns for that on Saturday night."

Francis looked around and felt his heart hammer. Without his realizing it, he and his father and Thorne had become the center of a crowd. It seemed to him that more than half of the train members were gathered around them. His three younger brothers had worked their way to the front. Emboldened by the excitement, Orren, the second-oldest, said, "Fran's right, Pa. You always said he could swim like a fish."

"You hush, Orren," Will said. "That river's not like a pond. Besides," he added, half to himself, "Alathea would have a fit at the very idea."

"I'd thought to have Stuart come back across," Thorne said. "But he and Harris will be tied up hauling that ferry back to shore for quite a while. Or we could try swimming a horse across with the rope tied to the saddle horn, but that gives us the same problem. Who's to ride the horse?"

"And whose horse to use," Caleb Sugarhouse put in. "If young Francis gets in a jam, we can always haul him back by the rope. Can't haul the horse back if the current gets him."

Will Buttrell said, "I don't know about this."

"I won't go against your judgment, Will," Thorne said. He squinted at the sun, halfway down the western sky. "But it *would* save us a lot of time."

Francis licked his lips. He'd volunteered on impulse, mainly to prove something—he wasn't sure what—to Ames. Now, everybody was watching, even Jessica Stuart, looking pretty and flushed and worried about her Davy. He just *couldn't* back down. If he did, they would all know him for what they thought he was anyway—a boy.

"Reckon I could try the horse trick," Warner Espy was saying without too much conviction. "I've rid that old mare pretty well everyplace. She'll probably take me across that little stream."

"Warner Espy, you're flat crazy," his wife said. "You can't swim a lick and you know it."

"I don't calculate to swim. Long's I hang on to that saddle horn, or even old Molly's mane or tail, I'll be just fine."

Thorne and Will Buttrell looked at each other. Francis bit his lip. They'd all three watched Stuart fighting the river's current when he crossed on the towrope. Warner Espy was older than Thorne and fatter than anybody else on the train. If he lost his grip on the mare, they'd have another burying.

"Pa," Francis said. He couldn't add *please*, like a kid, right in front of everybody, but he knew his father heard it in his voice. Will turned his deep gaze on him, frowned, shook his head.

"Well, if it has to be," he murmured to himself. Louder, he said, "Let's try it Francis's way first. Though the Lord knows what your mother will say, boy."

What his mother said was, "Suppose that rope breaks like the other one did?"

Francis stared at her. "Rope won't be holding me. I'll be holding it." He saw then that there were things mothers didn't understand.

"We'll station half a dozen men downstream on horseback," Thorne said. "Warner's already said he'll do that, and Caleb, too. Francis can strike out for this side, and they'll throw him a rope if he needs it."

Alathea Buttrell twisted her apron in her hands. "Lord's sakes," she murmured. "Sometimes, I pretty near wish we hadn't ever thought to leave Pike County."

Francis was willing to take that for consent. "Don't worry, Ma, I'll take care," he said. He looked at the wide, deep thrust of the river and tried not to shiver. "It's just water."

"All right." Thorne put on his courtroom voice. "Ladies, could we get you to step a little way off, please? Milt, do you have the rope ready?"

Before Francis had much more time to think about it,

he was sitting on the edge of the pier, stripped to his long underwear, while men knelt around him and offered conflicting advice.

"Hold still, boy," Milt Ames said. He looped the end of a long rope over Francis's left shoulder and across his chest, tying it loosely under his right arm. "You won't lose this by accident, but you can slither out of it if anything goes wrong. Understand?"

"I understand."

"We used the smallest rope we could find, but it's going to get pretty heavy before you make the far bank." Ames put a hand on his shoulder. "If you get in trouble, wave both arms. I and Joe and Hiram Miller and some others will be on this end of the rope. We'll haul you out safe, never doubt it."

Francis nodded. He didn't like Ames. He was pretty sure Ames didn't like him any better. But he could find no hostility in the man's face or voice. As far as Francis could judge Ames meant every word. His concern was genuine. For the first time, it came to Francis that people might not be all one thing, all good or bad, friend or enemy forever. Maybe people could change.

He sighed. Being a man looked to be a more complicated proposition than he'd expected. But he was ready to change.

"I'm gonna angle upstream, toward that big tree there," he said, trying to match Ames's level tone. He didn't try to point; he knew his hand would shake. "If I've figured right, the current will carry me back down to the pier." He swallowed, then grinned at his father and Ames. "If I haven't, I guess I'll end up somewheres down around Utah."

"You sure you want to do this, Francis?" Will Buttrell asked.

"You bet."

Ames laughed and squeezed his shoulder. "That's the spirit, son. I expect we'll pull you out short of Utah, if it comes to that." He stood up and called, "Manasseh, every-thing set?"

Thorne had been standing at the very edge of the pier, hands cupped to his mouth, bellowing back and forth with Stuart on the other side.

"They're ready, Milt. Get your men on that rope." He looked at Francis, chewed for a moment at the corner of his lip, then said, "Tadpole, you can go whenever you feel like it."

"Yes, sir." Francis gripped the edge of the dock with both hands, feeling splinters dig into his palms. With all his strength, he opened his hands, forced them to push. "Guess that'd be now."

He slipped into the water like a Greek hero, so it seemed to him, wondering if a Greek hero would gasp and break out in goose-bumps when the water proved bit-ter cold. He hadn't been sure about the river's depth, but now he knew that it was over his head right off the dock. He hung on to the edge long enough to draw three breaths all the way down to his toes. Then he pushed off, digging into the water with a strong, hand-over-hand crawl toward the tree he had picked for his target. Over the splash of water in his ears, he could hear Ames and Thorne calling him good luck and Godspeed. And he heard his father's shout over everything else.

"You be careful out there, Francis."

Francis figured that was about the most useless advice he would ever get, though he appreciated the sentiment. At first the swimming was easy, the burden of the rope light as it paid out in the current and drifted downstream to form a great U shape on the surface. He had time to think about his father, about advice, about how he'd talked himself into a spot he really didn't like very much. Did that still happen, he wondered, after you got older?

Gradually, the rope became waterlogged, started to sink, formed an ever greater drag on his strokes. He began to think that it was not just impeding his progress but pulling him back toward the eastern shore. Worse, he hadn't calculated its drag when he'd picked out his tree. The current was sweeping him down faster than he'd anticipated, so that he had to crab around and angle more sharply into it. He marveled at the thought of a two-pound fish pulling a line through the water hard enough to bend a pole.

A third of the way across, he began to wish he'd let an older man or a worse fool take the rope. He rolled onto his back to rest, kicking just hard enough to hold his place while he gasped in great mouthfuls of air. His fingers and toes tingled like they'd been asleep. The rope pulled harder at him.

He raised his head, looked at his father and the men on the home shore. One of them had dug in his feet and was pulling on the rope for all he was worth. Francis Buttrell tried to yell "Listen!" but a little ripple of water struck his shoulder and splashed his mouth full at the same time.

He got choked, straightened himself up to tread water while he coughed. By that time he realized that they were trying to take the wet slack out of the line. If they took out much more slack, they'd have him back on shore. He put his hands beside his mouth and shouted, "Stop that!"

His father waved to him. The man on the rope began paying it out. Only slightly rested, Francis turned again to the west and began to swim in careful, measured strokes toward that shore. *It's panic kills you in the water*, he told himself, not recognizing he was repeating something his father had drummed into him when he was six. *Man who—doesn't panic—can swim—anywhere!*

Hearing in his mind the ragged cadence of his thoughts, he giggled. Sounded like that old man. Where was it? Bradley's Oak. Ann Bradley. He thought about Ann Bradley. Green eyes. He would rest a minute, think about her eyes. He couldn't remember why he was flailing his arms so hard, why he'd been kicking. He could feel his palms slapping the water, feel his arms too heavy to lift. It didn't matter. He would just think and drift and let the current take him where it would.

"Hell," Francis Buttrell said, and all but twisted his head around to be sure his ma hadn't heard him. He dived under the water, rolling in the current, letting the shock of the river's cold power in his face and the shock of fear that jolted through his body wake him up. He kicked hard a couple of times, holding himself under, then porpoised back to the surface, shaking his head to clear the water from his eyes.

"Hell," he whispered to himself. "Blamed near went to Utah that time."

He waved an arm to show those on shore he was all right, then dug in hard for the west bank. He tried a side-stroke, then a dog paddle, but those were no better than treading water. There was nothing for it but to swim with a strong overhand pull and a steady kick. He was close now, less than thirty yards from shore, but he'd lost his tree, lost the pier, lost everything. It didn't matter. Once he got to the bank, he could figure out where he was.

Dig—breathe—kick. Fight the rope. One stroke closer. Then another. He didn't want to look up. He heard a roaring in his ears, worried about it, realized as his head cleared water again that someone was shouting at him from the west bank.

He shook his head again, gasping hard, trying to focus on the willows. Stuart. Davy Stuart was trotting along the bank, leaping and stumbling over roots and hummocks of grass, keeping pace with him in the current.

"Francis! You all right?"

He tried to nod his head, got water up his nose.

"Need me to come in and help?"

Francis shook his head hard enough to make water fly from his hair. He needed help and he knew it, but quivering there on the edge of manhood, he was ready to die before he accepted any.

Stuart honored his wishes, but he threw out a rope when young Buttrell was still twenty feet from the shore. Francis did not consider that an insult to his manhood. He grabbed on with both hands, clinging desperately while

Stuart pulled him ashore like that two-pound fish. Then he was facedown in the deep grass of the riverbank, staring at tiny white wildflowers an inch from his eyes and breathing in the warm, welcome, earthy smells of crushed leaves and oxen and damp sand.

"Quite a swim, my young Leander."

He recognized Dr. Harris's voice. "I'm Francis," he said.

"My error." The hands touching his back, lifting up on his hips, brushing his forehead to pull back an eyelid, must have belonged to the doctor, too. "You lie there and get your breath, Francis. Stuart and I will take care of everything."

Francis shook his head. "I'll help," he said. He tried to roll over, but the hands held him down.

"No such thing. You'll lie here until your breathing is normal and your pulse is back to something less than two hundred a minute. I'll send Miss Mandy Jean down with a blanket for you."

It didn't seemed worthwhile arguing. "Who?" Francis asked, but the doctor was already gone.

He woke up without realizing he'd been asleep. This time he did roll over, sitting up to blink. The river still ran deep and soft beside him. Upstream a ways, he could see Stuart and Harris on the ferry landing. The raft was gone. Francis lunged up to his knees and saw it on the other shore, paying out a thick, heavy line that ran smoothly down into the water. The towrope, he realized. A lot of it had already gone out, drawn toward the east bank by the rope he had carried.

"You been asleep."

He jumped. A girl, all elbows and bare feet and long skinny legs, sat on the sand, her arms around her knees, watching him. She held a blanket in her lap.

"Hello. I'm Mandy Jean. Who're you?"

"I'm Francis."

He felt his wet underwear clinging to him. Mandy Jean had noticed it, too. He started to cover himself, decided that would be even worse, turned away from her. He hadn't thought the problem through before he'd launched himself into the river, leaving his pants on the distant shore.

"Listen," he said. "Could I have that blanket?"

The girl smiled, showing a gap between two front teeth. "Why?" she asked, standing up. "It ain't cold."

The girl wasn't very tall. To Francis she seemed underfed, big-eyed. But she wasn't as thin and bony as he'd first thought, and her hair hung in pigtails. He liked her hair. "Yes it is," he said and grabbed for the blanket. She giggled, hanging on, and they had a brief tug-of-war before he got possession of it and wrapped it kilt-style around his hips.

"Come on," he said, assuming authority as he got to his feet. "Let's see if Davy and them needs my help."

"Help?" Fred Harris hardly glanced around. "Yes. Yoke Mrs. Kenny's oxen up with the others. We'll use both teams to bring the ferry back across."

"All right."

Feeling silly in his blanket, he found the Kenny wagon. As he began to unhitch the team, Mandy Jean stepped in to help.

"Are you married yet?"

"No. My pa says I'm too young yet to get married."

"Well, how old are you?"

He considered it a question unworthy of a man. "Older'n you."

"Bet you're not. I bet you're just big for your age."

"I'm going on eighteen."

"I heard that story before. I'm going on eighteen, too. But I've only gone as far as fifteen."

"I'm sixteen." He noticed that she was pretty in her way. Limited, untutored, but pretty. He liked being older than she. "Might' near seventeen. I'll be seventeen in October."

Mandy Jean sniffed. "Lot your pa knows, then," she said. "My sister Betsy Sue's already married and got a baby, and she's not much more'n seventeen herself. Where you going to put these oxes?"

"In front of the others on the towrope. It'll make the next crossing faster. Come on."

He started to lead the placid animals up the slope, stepping gingerly in his bare feet. Stuart had been smarter. He'd brought along boots. And his pants. But then, Stuart hadn't been swimming and hauling a ton of rope.

"It'll make that old raft go so fast it's like to boil the water!" Mandy Jean said. She eyed him critically. "Francis. That's a girl's name. And you look like a girl in that skirt."

"Can't help it," he mumbled. "Watch that front off ox. He'll step on your foot. Jean sounds like a boy's name."

She hadn't thought of that. "Let's us trade, then."

"Trade what? Here, help with this yoke. Don't you never feed these oxen?"

"Names. We'll trade names. Where'd you come from, Gene?"

He grinned as he yoked the last of the oxen into place on the draw bar. "Ohio, Frances," he said. "Pike County. You know where that is?"

She shook her head solemnly. "Long way off, I guess. You all going down to hunt silver in these big old wagons?"

"Nah." Francis shrugged. "Pa says there's nothing to this silver story. We're going plumb to Oregon, looking for good farmland. Pa says he'll know the right place when we come to it." He squared his shoulders and stood a little taller. "I'm gonna homestead my own claim there, have a farm of my own."

"I guess it'll be on a river since you like to swim so much."

"Why'd you think I like to swim?"

" 'Cause I guess you'd otherwise have come across in that little canoe."

"What little canoe!"

"One my aunt went over there in. She keeps it in the back storeroom once she gets over there."

Francis Buttrell had never hit a girl, but it seemed to him that God would let it go by in a case like this one. "Well, God . . . bless all you Blisses!" he said. Then he turned away.

"I like you. You talk 'most as nice as that Davy and lots younger." Mandy Jean lowered her eyes and smiled. "My pa used to keep some old clothes up around the barn. Might be there's a pair of pants there. I could help you look."

"All right." Francis looked at her hair, then reached out and touched it. It was soft as cornsilk. He'd let it slip his mind that he was in love for life with an older girl back at Bradley's Oak. "I like you, too, Mandy Jean."

Mandy Jean took his hand and led him up the bank. "You sure you're not married?" she asked.

With two teams to draw the rope, Stuart and Harris brought the next wagon across faster than the first and offered no excitement at all to those who expected disaster. After that, they had Lije Holden to help and still another team. Fred Harris worked with the new rope and the oxen until the teams on the eastern side had drawn the empty ferry back across. Then he made a trip to the little grove of trees where Mrs. Kenny's wagon stood in the shade.

"Barbara," he said.

She put her head out the back and smiled at him. "Is no one with you?"

"No. I've just come to see whether you're all right." He was thinking of the fright she'd had when the ferry rope broke.

"Come in and see, then. I'm just hanging out my wet things."

He hesitated, then drew back the flap. Barbara, wrapped in a blanket, was hanging dress and underthings on a line strung between two of the wagon hoops.

"I thought you were going to change into something dry," Harris said.

"I thought you might come back," she said, and let the blanket slide from her shoulders.

He had not seen her in the light before. "My God," he whispered.

"Do you like me?"

"You're lovely," he said. He withdrew his head from the flap to be certain that no one was near. Then he looked again.

"Do you really think so?" She leaned to him, kissed him. "Would you come inside?"

"What? No!" He looked round himself again. "People will be watching. I can't stay here while you're dressing."

"Would you look again, then?"

He looked.

She kissed him. "I like you to look."

"I must go. Get dressed. Someone else might come along."

"But when can we? When will there be a time?"

"Soon," he told her hoarsely. "Very soon."

He tore himself away, pretended to check the rigging of her wagon, turned back toward the river, trying to remember why he cared what people thought. There, not thirty yards away, Francis Buttrell was walking hand in hand with the ferry girl. Had they been watching him? Were they smiling at him even now? Would they tell others what they had seen? He remembered why he cared what people thought.

He forced himself to wave at the young people. They didn't even see him. Well, he told himself, I'll be damned for my worries. The puppies are just as lost in each other as Barbara and I. He dallied for a moment with the idea of going back to the wagon. Then he strode downhill to the dock filled with hope and anticipation and a certain pride.

The last ferryload of animals and their keepers came across just before dark. Campfires were burning on the level ground above the western landing slope. After supper, a crowd gathered about the Thorne fire to sing.

"A celebration for the hero," Jessica murmured to Stuart, patting his hand.

"Not me," Stuart protested. "Francis is the real hero for today." He glanced around. "Where is he, anyway? I didn't see him at supper."

"Jess," Barbara Kenny called. "Come and sing. We need a soprano."

Jess blew him a kiss and went across to the fire where Long Tom Lee was readying his fiddle. Stuart leaned against the wheel of the wagon, happy and relaxed, at peace with himself for the first time he could remember since Ethan's death.

"It went well today." Manasseh Thorne's quiet rumble might have come straight from Stuart's thoughts. "Not a wagon lost, not a soul hurt."

"We had good luck."

"Good luck and good men," Thorne said. He waved a hand as Stuart started to speak. "No, don't go modest on me. Buttrell did a fine job, and so did Doc Harris, for a Southerner. But it was you who were the leader."

Stuart shrugged, not sure how to answer. He finally settled for the courtesy his mother had taught him.

"Thank you."

"Don't mention it. Just worry about helping me keep this train moving, getting it where we planned."

Stuart heard concern in the older man's voice. He didn't understand. "I know we lost a day here at the ferry. But we'll make it up."

"It won't be rivers that keep us from it." Thorne looked

back over his shoulder. "But the people have heard of the silver strike now. Some of the men are already talking about turning down to Virginia City. Nobody's up on a platform hollering yet, but they're talking."

"Nobody's said anything to me. Nothing straight-out, I mean."

"Because they think you're with me in holding to our original plan."

"Well, they're right," Stuart said. "I *am* with you. No matter what."

Thorne put a heavy hand on Stuart's shoulder. "That's what I wanted to know." Then he turned his face back east and stared for a time at the colors of night on the surface of the water.

A while after midnight Fred Harris lay in his wagon staring out the open flap at the stars. He was tired enough to sleep but sleep had not come to him. A form appeared at his tailgate, came between him and the stars. A woman's voice whispered to him. "Is the doctor in?"

"Are you ill?" It was all he had time to say before she slipped over the tailgate as softly as a fox and knelt beside him. He put out his hand and knew at once that she was wearing nothing but her robe.

"Yes," she told him.

He sat up, concerned. "What's wrong? How are you ill?"

"It's hard to say." She nestled herself against him. "I ache. I'm lightheaded. I have a bit of fever." She put her hand on his face. "It may be catching."

"It is," he said. "I have it, too." He held her close and forgot about the stars.

"Is there a treatment? Have I come too late?"

"No," he told her. "I know a specific remedy for our condition." He undid the rear wagon flaps and pulled them together. "You've come just in time."

19

Ann Bradley got hold of a wheel spoke and pulled herself up to stand beside the wagon. Clinging to it, she drew her body along it until she was at the front wheel. She saw Ethan Fairchild stand in the stirrup, swing himself into the saddle, and ride away after the troopers at a dead gallop.

"I do love you," he'd said. *"I do love you. I'll come back for you."*

The tears lay cold on her cheeks, her passion spent, her spirit in ruins. Then she decided. She lifted her skirts and ran into the back of the inn. In her room, she gathered clothing, underthings, only enough to fill a saddlebag. Then she drew on a pair of sturdy boots. She looked around her, but there was nothing else she could take, nothing of the memories that clung to the place where she'd grown up. For a moment, she almost cried again, but there wasn't time.

I'll have to tell them, she thought. She hated the idea, but she knew she couldn't go without doing that at least. She came into the kitchen, her few belongings held before her like an offering.

"Ann," her mother said, then stopped and pressed her hands together. "Ann, dear, I've fixed you some cold chicken. You'd better eat it tonight. And there's some of the jerky, and some hard bread, and of course you'll need a canteen."

"Mother," Ann said. She saw Blackie's saddlebags, the left one bulging with packets of food.

Marguerite Bradley went on as though Ann hadn't spoken. "And your Bible. It'll be your family Bible one day.

You wouldn't want to leave without it." She frowned at Ann. "Yes, that dress is a good choice. And what else do you have? All right. I've sent your father for some of his old clothes. They won't be ladylike, but they'll cover you."

"Oh, Mother." Ann dropped her things to the floor and flew to her mother's arms, crying. After a moment, she whispered, "Thank you."

"I think these—will do." Elgin Bradley had come into the room, bent over his cane. He carried a pair of brown trousers and two shirts. "Mother, are you—sure this is—wise?"

"Of course it's not wise," Mrs. Bradley said. "We've talked that all out." She patted Ann's hair. "But it's inevitable."

"Yes," Ann whispered. Drawing a deep breath, she straightened away from her mother. She put out a hand to touch her father's arm. "I'll always love you both. But Ethan's my life!"

To her surprise, her mother and father smiled at each other, a smile of such perfect understanding that Ann was stunned.

"You were—right, Mother," Bradley said. "She's just—as you were."

Marguerite Bradley patted his shoulder. "And I've never regretted a minute of it," she said. "Not even now." She cleared her throat. "Ann," she said briskly. "You get Blackie saddled. We'll finish putting up your things. Tell your young man, when you find him, that he has our blessings."

Grace stood beside a slender white aspen along the crest of the ridge above Bradley's Oak, watching Silverhorn peer through his brass-tubed telescope. Abruptly, he snapped the instrument shut and turned to her.

"Damned girl's run off," he said. "You go round the

far side of the ridge yonder. Come back alongst the road after a mile or so and run her down."

"What for, Thoman? She can't do us any harm if she's not there."

Silverhorn shoved the telescope into his possible bag. "What's got into you, whore?" he asked irritably. "Didn't used to be you'd question and whine and find fault with everything I say." He fixed her with his one-eyed glare. "Might be I'll find me a better woman, leave you for the wolves."

Grace met his gaze without yielding. "Ain't no woman better'n me, Thoman," she said. "Not at the things I'm good at. And if'n there was one, she'd never have dealings with such as you."

"Shut up," Silverhorn told her. "Talking ain't one of the things you're good at. Nor thinking, nor telling me my business. You find that girl and stop her running loose to spread news. I and the rest'll ride in from the east after a time. We'll first let them troopers get out of hearing distance."

Grace didn't say anything. Silverhorn frowned a little, studying her. She held her face flat, expressionless, looking down toward the trail ruts more than half a mile away. The girl in the blue dress had disappeared behind the trees.

"Why me?"

Silverhorn looked surprised. "You haven't bloodied that knife of yours since poor Jonas departed from amongst us," he said. "I figured you'd jump on her like a wolf on a rabbit."

Grace turned her dark eyes on Silverhorn. She could remember when he'd been a wolf, running wild and free, feeding where he chose, leaving the rest. Now he was different. Something had changed him. Maybe it was losing the eye, or maybe he was just becoming more what he'd always been. Lately, he reminded her of a rattlesnake all coiled into itself. An old rattler, she thought, getting ready to shed his skin, not able to see clearly but striking at any warmth of life he came across.

"You've got Indian blood in you," she said.

"Not as much as you."

"No. Not near enough."

He frowned. "Enough for what?"

"To make you a man."

He blinked, not understanding. She could see him tumble the words around in his mind, sniffing and nuzzling at them like a wolf trying to get at a terrapin. Finally, he decided to laugh.

"Better man than a half-breeded slut deserves," he said. His laugh didn't go deep, and she knew he wasn't finished thinking about her. "Maybe I'll go after the girl, try her out, see if she's worth bringing along." He considered that, then laughed again. "No, it needs a bitch for a bitch. Sic her!"

Grace turned her horse sharply enough to cut his mouth with the bit and started off northwest.

"You, Grace," Silverhorn called.

She reined the horse around toward him. He looked like a wolf now, a grizzled old pack leader with one crafty eye. He jerked his head toward the hollow where his men waited.

"Any of those coyotes sassed me like you have, I'd kill him before his tongue stopped wagging. You know I would."

She grinned at him. "You going to kill me, Tom?" she asked, and felt the skin prickle along her backbone. She lounged back in the saddle, rucking her skirt up past her knees. "You going to kill Grace, after all them good times I give you?"

"What I'm saying is, don't ever talk back to me where anybody can hear. Else I'll take a stirrup leather to you, and throw you to Willard when I'm done."

Be the last woman you treat that way, she said in her mind. But she knew better than to say that aloud. Instead, she chuckled. "Willard ain't so bad," she said. "There's lots worse than Willard."

"Red whore. I told you to ride."

She rode, angling off to the northwest until she found a draw. Then she slipped out of sight under the ridge and down into the low, thick trees and brush. Letting her horse pick his way, she kept him headed mostly west. Minutes later they came into a clearing through which they could have made better time.

Grace was in no great hurry. She could still smell the dust from the cavalry patrol, and her mind was straying. She allowed herself to imagine a new life, a life of streets and houses, of children playing, of people she could turn her back on without fear of being shot down. She was sure there must be places like that, places these soft-skinned settler women came from.

Sure, she thought. *And what would you do there? Whore for them that wasn't too particular? Let the ones that hated Indian blood pay to slap you around? Wash shirts for the Army at Fort Laramie?*

She'd seen town dogs that had gone to the wild. She'd never heard of a wolf becoming a town dog.

For all her thinking, she was careful to keep the ridge between herself and Silverhorn's position on the hill. She hated the thought of him, holding her captured in the brass tube of his telescope. Did the telescope catch a person's soul, the way the Pawnee said a camera did? She'd never seen a camera. She wondered if she'd ever had a soul. If she did, had Silverhorn caught it? Or had she given it to him?

She kept to the woods longer than necessary so she would be certain to be ahead of the girl. When she came out onto the trail, she was a quarter of a mile west of her quarry, who had slowed to a walk. The girl saw her and slid the black horse south, off into the woods as softly and quickly as a doe that's got wind of a hunter. Grace walked her horse across the trail and into the woods. After a time she tied the horse and went on foot.

She was lying on her belly at the western rim of a little clearing when Ann Bradley entered it. Grace stood. The black horse snorted and shied. The girl was more than a girl, Grace saw now. A young woman in her first bloom, she put a hand to her mouth in a girllike way.

"Oh," she said, then smiled. "You startled me. I was afraid you were a robber."

"I am." Grace leveled her short pocket pistol at the woman. "Stand down. Off the horse. Now."

Young, she saw. Black hair. Eyes green as a catamount's, but not catamount's eyes; hers were wide, startled, frightened. Deer's eyes. But green. She wore a pale blue dress, simple, wide-skirted enough to let her ride astride. Thoman had made a mistake, not coming himself.

"Stand still," Grace told her. "Keep hold of that horse till I get the reins. All right. Now strip off your dress."

Staring at her, the girl did not move. "What?" she asked.

"Do it! I don't want to mess that pretty dress up more than needful."

"What? Who are you?"

Grace raised the pistol, cocking the hammer as it came level with the girl's eyes.

"Sweetie, I'm the one what's going to shoot you if you don't do like I say. Move!"

"No, wait! I'll do it. All right."

Grace moved in close as the younger woman fumbled with the round pearl buttons. The buttons were small and slippery and there were a lot of them. Unbuttoning them went slowly, partly because her hands were trembling, partly because she couldn't look away from Grace's face, nor from the revolver.

She finally got to the last buttons and straightened, holding the dress in front of her with one hand while she put the other out toward Grace.

"Listen, if you want clothes, you're welcome to some better ones in my saddlebags. Or maybe you want money? I've got a little money. Is that what you want?"

"Sweetie, we don't have time for what I want." Grace waggled the barrel of the pistol. "Too bad. Let the dress fall. That's good, right there where you're standing." The woman looked at her plainly, grinning. "That's nice. Let's see how you look without that shirtwaist."

Before the girl could understand what she meant to do, Grace caught the thin garment by its front and yanked. The muslin tore, came away in her hand. Ann Bradley gave a horrified gasp and tried to cover herself with her hands.

"Please!"

Her face was almost purple with shame. Grace laughed. You'd think nobody had ever seen her that way before, she thought. But maybe nobody had.

"Sweetie, I know some old boys back up the way would roll in the dirt and howl to see what I'm seeing. Them's mighty pretty pantalettes, with the blue ruffles and all. Bet your gentleman friend set some store by those."

Ann Bradley gulped, seeming on the edge of tears. But then she raised her head a little and said, "He never did." She bit her lip and stopped. "It wasn't like that."

"Never is," Grace said. She frowned at the pantalettes. "Wouldn't fit me. Too bad. Maybe if you'd been a little more obliging, he wouldn't've rid off and left you. Step back."

Instead of obeying, Ann Bradley put her hands to her face and started to cry. "He didn't!" Her words were muffled, but Grace heard their defiant tone. "He didn't leave me. He means to come back for me. He does!"

She raised her head suddenly, dropping her hands away from her face. She clenched her fists and stared at Grace.

"I'm not afraid of you, whoever you are. Go ahead, kill me, if that's what you mean to do. I'm not afraid!"

Grace looked at her, annoyed. Of course she was afraid. But she was hell-bent not to show it. Hell of a thing, to let some half-growed girl go traipsing out that way. What were her kinfolks thinking? And that man of hers, that scrawny gent on the outlaw chestnut? Why wasn't he tumbling her in his blanket instead of leaving her out on the prairie, helpless as a lamb amongst the wolves?

Grace frowned, sighting down the barrel of the revolver. *Helpless as a baby*. She lowered the gun. Then she took off her buckskin dress, picked up the blue one, smelled it, and put it on. She had difficulty buttoning it across her full body. "It's good you're not afraid," she told the girl. Then she lifted her revolver and fired two shots a little apart.

When she led the black horse back to the Bradley's Oak Inn, Grace was wearing a blue dress whose hem struck her a hand below her knees. It was tighter across her breasts and hips than it should have been. She'd had to leave some of the buttons undone to keep it from tearing, but she thought it suited her. And clean. Hardly a spot or a stain on it anyplace.

She saw horses untended at the water trough but heard no shooting. Inside the inn, the old man and woman she'd seen through the telescope were tied back to a post which rose to the ridge pole. The old woman began to cry afresh when she saw Grace's clothes.

The two Pawnee laughed when they saw her new outfit. One of them said, "We heard you shoot. We see you stripped her and took all the booty. Where's her scalp?"

"Never mind the scalp," Silverhorn roared. "Where's her horse?"

Grace flapped the short skirt at him and sat at the dinner table. "Outside," she said. "At the watering trough. Got the saddle and saddlebags and all."

Silverhorn nodded. "Horse-killing red whore. Goddamned good thing for you that you brought this one back." He chuckled. "How was the girl?"

"Pretty thing. You'd've liked her, Thoman. Maybe next time, you'll heed me when I tell you to go see for yourself."

"Red whore! I warned you about sassing me!"

Silverhorn drew back his hand to hit her. Grace didn't flinch, didn't move, didn't react by even the blink of an eye. She looked at him and he lowered the hand and turned away.

"All right, then. You others go tie up them horses before we find ourselves afoot here! We'll do the burning later. Them soldiers'd see the smoke a year away."

"Why?"

"Why what?" He came close enough that she could smell him.

"Why burn? What's here for us anyway?"

Silverhorn laughed. "Not much. One old muzzle-loader rifle and one shotgun. One keg of powder," he said. "Little bit of money but not enough to fret over. These people ain't industrious so's you'd notice it."

"Nor are we—thieves," Elgin Bradley said.

Silverhorn laughed. "Food, too. Food and tobacco. And some more clothes. If'n you fancy that dress so much, there's more where it came from." He waved a hand at her. "Get to filling us a tow sack apiece out of that pantry. You can look for pretties later."

"Where's Willard?"

"Oh, Willard, he's down to the barn whetting his skinning knife." He jerked his head toward the old couple. "Asked Kills Running to show him how. Thinks he can do a better job on them that's got loose skin."

Angry voices came from someplace outside. Grace cocked her head. "Sounds like Farley and Longdon are squabbling over that black horse," she said. She stepped to the door and looked out. "And there's two other horses running loose for the Army to see."

"Goddamn Farley West," Silverhorn growled. "Wish that buffalo hunter had shot him instead of our ribbon clerk." He went out the door like a bear.

Grace walked over to the post, where the Bradleys were tied. She drew her revolver, put it to the woman's head. "Willard's going to skin you, else."

"My poor dear daughter," the old woman cried.

Grace glanced back toward the door, then leaned over to whisper in her ear. Marguerite Bradley was smiling when Grace shot her through the temples.

Immediately, Grace stepped around to Elgin Bradley. In his watery eyes was no submission, no blame.

"It's a lie," he said. "Wasn't it?"

Grace shook her head.

"Good lie. Sent her on easy."

"No lie."

He looked into her eyes. "Young woman, in my bedroom, under a rock . . ."

"What?"

"Books. Save the books."

"Are they worth anything?"

"Everything. Please take them. Now, I fain would—take that journey with—Mrs. Bradley, if you'd be so kind. Thank—"

Grace rested her left hand on his rope-bound hands, put the muzzle under his chin, and pulled the trigger. She heard the others running. She put away the gun and went into the pantry and began filling a flour sack with tinned goods.

"Damned half-breed bitch!" Willard shouted. "Them was mine to skin."

Silverhorn came through the front door, saw Willard headed for the pantry with his knife out, and clubbed him down to his knees. "You can skin what you catch, but you keep your mouth off the woman. She needs cussing I'll cuss her."

Grace came out of the pantry and dropped the sack of grub next to Willard. "You can still skin 'em," she said, grinning at him. "It'll be easier now. They won't squirm so much."

"Next time, I'll skin you!"

Silverhorn said, "Willard, you get on out there and set fire to the barn."

"There's a wagon in there, old as Granny but near fixed up enough to use," Willard told him.

"Use for what? We ain't about to set up housekeeping."

"Hell," Willard said. "Yesterday you was hot to follow them damned buff hunters and take their hides. Hell, you even wanted their own skins for what they done to that pet storekeeper of yourn."

"Nothing's different. But them hunters's got a wagon. We'll use it. Team, too. You got a lucifer match?"

Willard nodded. "Yes, I've got a match!"

"Burn the barn."

Grace shoved a bag of airtight tins at Silverhorn. "You said we ought to wait till them troopers was good gone."

"True. So I did. Hold off, Willard."

Willard smiled. "My pappy always told me never to burn a house that's got a hot stove in it. There's food cooked and ready."

"You don't know who your pappy was. But it's a good thought about the food." His depth perception off a bit, Silverhorn sat heavily at the table.

Grace saw that he expected her to put food on the table like a serving woman. She had *Get it yourself* on her face before she changed her mind. A time would come for her. The right time. She believed that. She didn't know when and she didn't know what it would bring. But she had learned patience at the mission school in Kansas, or maybe she'd always had it. A time would come, and she would do what it asked of her.

Humming a tune she'd learned at the mission, she went to the stove, brought back biscuits from the warming ledge, a skillet of meat, a bowl of leftovers made into hash. Longdon and Farley West had come back in, Farley blotting at the blood that trickled from his nose. The two Pawnee followed, glanced at the dead bodies, and went out again to the porch. She watched the others a moment before she brought a few forks and laid them on the table. Only Silverhorn bothered to use one.

Grace saw they would snatch and tear at the food until

the last scrap was gone. She was not in the mood to contend with them. Still humming, she went back to the pantry and opened a jar of preserved peaches for herself. She ate the peaches carefully, using her fork, patting her lips with a linen napkin she'd found there while she listened to Silverhorn.

"Them buff hunters will have slid back off up north hoping to cut the trail of a big herd." His growl rose above the others, the lead wolf snarling down the pack. "We don't have to be in a hog-killing hurry to catch up to them. About the time they've got a wagonful of hides, we'll take that burden off their hands."

"Them buffalo guns is the problem," Willard said. "They's mighty prime shots. Kilt your ribbon clerk at near a quarter mile."

Silverhorn smiled. "Now you see why it's good we brung him along," he said. "Didn't a one of you think that was a good idea. But if it hadn't been for him, that hunter might have shot somebody important, maybe even you, Willard."

He's got so he talks too much, Grace thought. *Didn't used to explain so much, back when he was a wolf. Talks as much as an old woman.*

"What'll we do with a load of stinking hides?" Longdon demanded. "Seems like a power of trouble to me. They's easier pickings. Like here."

"Here ain't nothing," Silverhorn said. "They's a place at Fort Hall that'll pay good money for hides."

"Army'll pay good money for *us* at Fort Hall," Willard said. "Wouldn't it be better to let them cash in them skins and then we come along and knock them in the head for the cash money?"

"It's wasteful, that's why." Silverhorn sounded shocked. "They get around Fort Hall, where there's supplies and liquor and women and whatnot, why there's no telling how much of our money they might spend before we could get at them. Else the covey of them might split off in six different directions. Easier, more certain if we move in about the time they finish skinning out the last of their buffs."

"They'll have them Dragoons to shepherd them, though."

"Could be." The white-haired man grabbed up the last biscuit, put all of it in his mouth, and gave it two or three chews before he swallowed it. "Not their practice to nursemaid anybody unless it's a wagon train in some kind of need. No, I figure we'll find them buffalo boys off to their lonesome somewheres to the northwest."

Hell, Grace thought, *he talks as much as an old* man.

"What about that other bastard rode out trailing the Dragoons?" Farley West put in suddenly. "He was carrying a sight of artillery was all. Looked like a fighting man."

"What man was that?" Silverhorn wanted to know.

Grace came to stand in the doorway from the pantry. "You know him, Tom," she said. "You've seen him before. You ought to remember how he sat his horse. He's a ghost."

Silverhorn stood up from the table and turned to her. "Where the hell'd I have seen him before and how would you know?"

"You saw me kill him and a black horse, that one day by the Platte," Grace said. Then she laughed again. "Might be he was with that Dragoon patrol that did the Whitleys and Plum. That chestnut he was riding today was there, certain. Might be he's following you, Tom."

Silverhorn swung a hand at her as if to sweep such foolishness away. "Following you, more likely," he said. He didn't sound happy about it. "You say you're the one killed him."

"I don't like this ghost talk," Willard said. "What I think is that we oughtn't try to walk barefoot amid a nest of snakes long as we got a trail around them."

Grace laughed. Silverhorn turned his eye on her, glared a moment, then began to laugh himself. "I guess your pappy always said that, did he?" he asked Willard.

"May've. I don't know who my pappy was."

20

Ethan Fairchild pushed his horse too long. The chestnut had grown lazy, had eaten too much during their stay at Bradley's Oak. It was heavily lathered by the time Fairchild thought to rest. In the quietness of the lonely woods, the horse's breathing seemed to echo, but the man did not hear it.

He heard instead the breathless words of a green-eyed girl. *You'd go without me?* He studied the trail as far ahead as he could see. Of course he had gone without her. What he was about to do was dangerous. It would have been irresponsible of him to bring the girl along. He knew that.

Yet he could not thrust her out of his mind, could not keep his ears free of her voice. *Would you leave me here?* That question was an easy one to answer. What better place could he have left her than with her parents at a gentle roadside inn? He had done the right thing. He knew that.

It was time for Fairchild to make up his mind about his direction. Cranfill's Dragoons would stick to the trail. The way Fairchild had it figured, Silverhorn—*hell of a name!*—would do the same. That would be as good a place to start as any. With luck, he might be in on the kill if Cranfill caught up to Silverhorn's wolves, though he doubted the Army could catch Silverhorn. At the least, he could visit with Healy and Dutch and the other troopers again. He'd ridden enough with them that he considered them friends.

I thought we loved each other. That was a harder part. Hell, it had been little more than a month since he had sworn an oath that he loved Jessica Thorne. And here for the last few days, he had been in love with a different girl entirely. But hell, wasn't there good enough reason for that?

There was. Jessica had betrayed him, had married the man who abandoned him to die. He might hate her for that, but he didn't think he would. He hated Stuart for it. What he could never do again was love her.

I thought we loved each other. He had said those very words about Jessica. Now he had to hear them echo in the tones of Ann Bradley's voice; he wasn't sure how he was going to outdistance the desperate look in her eyes.

He forced his mind back to business. If the Dragoons couldn't pick up Silverhorn's trail, he had a good offer from the buffalo hunters. He would go with them. After all, Waller had invited him, had wanted him to go along.

I thought you wanted me, Ann Bradley had said. *You don't have to marry me or anything.* She had loved him that much.

He put his horse back up to a trot for a half mile or more, caring less about killing the horse than about the ghosts echoing in his thoughts. The motion and fresh air drove them out, but he didn't think they'd gone far.

You'll never come back to me.

Half an hour after dark, he rode into the Army's bivouac. A couple of the troopers recognized him and cheered sarcastically.

"Hey, it's the Dead One come to save us."

"Still got those scalps, mankiller?"

"Hey, Healy, come look! Your infidel's come back."

Standing at the head of the line of picketed horses, Cranfill greeted him with a curt nod, then went back to smoking his pipe and staring into tomorrow. Fairchild dismounted from the chestnut, picketed it on the line, and began unsaddling.

"See you're still riding that dark devil." Healy had

come up beside him, staying well clear of the chestnut. "Soul's as black as his hooves. I'd hoped you'd've skinned it out for boots by now."

Fairchild grinned at him. "We're old friends, Devil and I," he said. He made the mistake of patting the horse and jerked back his hand in time to save his fingers. "And I still remember how the Army feeds and waters and curries."

"Well, get on with it, then!" Healy said in a fair imitation of Sergeant Neidercutt. "Join us at the fire when you're done, less'n the shoulder straps want you. We'll put you by a cup of coffee."

"Thanks, Healy. I'd admire a cup of your creosote when I'm done."

"Sure, now, that'll be government coffee to you, civilian," Healy said, laughing. Then he sobered. "Oh, you'll be wanting to know about Hill. He died along the way to Fort Laramie, despite the ambulance and all."

"Hill," Fairchild said, then remembered the trooper who'd been wounded in the fight with Silverhorn's men. "Sorry to hear it, Healy. That's another item for Silverhorn's account."

Healy nodded grimly. "A long tally," he agreed. "And it's a bitter reckoning he'll have when his time comes. Government coffee's about cooked."

Fairchild finished with the chestnut, falling back into the routine more easily than he would have expected. Leaving the animal with a nosebag full of Elgin Bradley's oats, he started toward the troopers' squad fire. Neidercutt must have been watching, because the little sergeant intercepted him before he'd gotten halfway.

"The lieutenant's compliments," Neidercutt said, and spat accurately at a lizard right at the edge of the firelight. "Will Mr. Fairchild do us the signal honor of joining us at the headquarters fire?"

"Still planning to shoot me if I say no, Sergeant?" Fairchild asked.

"No, sir. That would upset my lieutenant. According to him, you're our honored guest this time."

"And not somebody to be dragged along by the scruff of the neck? In that case, I'll be honored, too."

"Honored to have you. I see you're still carrying Jenkins's pistol."

Fairchild nodded. "Better shot with it than I used to be, too. I've been practicing. It's a fine piece."

"If you go on looking for this Silverhorn's bunch, you'll need the practice." Neidercutt lowered his voice. "Wouldn't say it out loud, but I'm just as pleased to have you along. We got four or five green men with us, replacing them that was hurt and killed. Don't know about them. If it comes down to that, I've seen you fight." He spat toward the darkness. "This way. Lieutenant's waiting."

Cranfill was, with a cup of coffee in one hand and his order book in the other. He held out the book to Fairchild.

"Sign at the bottom of the page. Then you can have some coffee."

Fairchild took the book and pencil, scribbled his name where Cranfill indicated. "What did I do?" he asked, handing back the book. "Enlist?"

"God forbid. You've signed on as a civilian scout, at no pay. Sergeant, a cup for our new scout, if you please. This way, if you get killed it's your own fault."

"Been killed once already, but it didn't take," Fairchild said. "There're precious few that'll care if it happens again."

"Is that a fact—begging the lieutenant's pardon?" Neidercutt said, squinting at him across the fire. "The way you and that little filly looked at one another back at the Oak, I expect she'd care. I expect she'll be right put out with you if you get killed."

I thought we loved each other.

"Sorry, Sergeant. You're right. I couldn't ask for more," Fairchild said. Neidercutt *was* right. It was time he stopped that particular kind of feeling sorry for himself.

"I spoke before I thought about it. Now, what's your plan for catching this Silverhorn?"

He was lying between his blankets before the voice behind him came close enough to call to him again. *You'd go without me? I thought we loved each other.*

It seemed to him that he had just fallen into a fitful sleep when a rider came into the Army camp with the approval of their sentry and without much regard for those sleeping. Fairchild was too far away to hear the conversation between the messenger and the lieutenant; but he lay awake a good while longer, head pillowed on his saddle, looking up at the broad white trail of stars that arched over him and listening to the voice of Ann Bradley in his head.

"I'll do it, sir," Neidercutt said.

Cranfill shook his head. He reached for his pipe, then took his hand away. His mouth tasted sour enough already. The duty waiting in front of him wasn't going to make it any better, nor help the sickness that crawled in his gut.

"My job, Sergeant," he murmured. His mouth twisted into a wry grimace. "Privileges of rank."

Before he could yield to the temptation to let it wait until morning, he walked swiftly across the uneven ground. His men lay sleeping around the embers of their squad fire, one of them snoring regularly. Healy, Boyce, a rumpled empty place for Dutch Schmidt who was out on sentry, two of the new men.

"There's Fairchild, sir."

Neidercutt was at his elbow, his dark face looking as miserable as Cranfill felt. Cranfill looked down at the sleeping man, wondered again if he was really what he claimed to be, found that he didn't much care after all. A lot of men on the frontier hid some part of their past. Whatever Fairchild might be hiding, dead man or refugee from a wagon train, he didn't deserve what he was about to hear.

"Fairchild." The lieutenant knelt beside him. He slept in a surprising depth of exhaustion. Cranfill put a hand on his shoulder. "Ethan."

Fairchild stirred. "Yes. What?" He looked at Cranfill, then at the sergeant's dark shadow behind him. He sat up, brushing long fair hair back from his face. "Morning already?" he asked.

Cranfill came close to believing that Fairchild was who he claimed to be. He'd heard someplace that the time to get a man's true name was just as he woke. "Mr. Fairchild, I've got something to tell you. Come over to the fire, please."

"Sure." Fairchild threw back his blanket, pulled on his boots, scrambled to his feet with his gunbelt in his hand. "What is it, news about Silverhorn?"

"Yes." Cranfill turned to his sergeant. "Neidercutt, wake the men and get them ready to move. Breakfast bacon in the saddle and coffee later. This way, Fairchild."

Fairchild came into the firelight, blinking. Cranfill reached for the coffeepot, poured them each a cup of the thick black leftover coffee, tried to think of some other way to put things off.

You worked hard for this, he reminded himself. *This is what you worked for. Officer commanding detachment, Second Dragoons.*

"What's happened, Lieutenant?"

"Fairchild, I have bad news for you, and I don't see any way but to tell you straight-out."

"Bad news?" He acknowledged it with the air of a man who didn't believe there could be any news worse than he'd already heard. "What is it?"

"I took it you had fallen in pretty close with the folks back at Bradley's Oak."

Fairchild paused, the cup halfway to his lips. His eyes, blue and startled, pinned Cranfill. "What's the news?"

"Raid. On Bradley's Oak, probably right after we left. They burnt the buildings to the ground."

"Buildings." Fairchild blinked, frowned. He dashed the stale coffee aside and took a step toward the lieutenant. He had not put it together. "Never mind the damned buildings! What about the Bradleys? What about Ann?"

"The word I got." Cranfill found he couldn't finish. He took a sip of his own scalding coffee, swallowed it, said, "Word I got was no survivors."

Fairchild shook his head. "No." he said. "No, that's not right. It's safe there. That's why I left her, so she'd be safe!"

"They found traces in the ashes of the inn. Bones and other things."

"No."

"Couldn't tell for sure how many people. They found two at least. Probably all three."

Fairchild cleared his throat. "But they weren't sure?" His fingers bit hard into Cranfill's arm. "Ann Bradley. They didn't find her?"

Cranfill flinched, fought the urge to twist away. He covered Fairchild's clenched fist with his other hand, gripped it. "They don't know who they found." He said it as gently as he could. "Two, maybe three. Even if it's only two, there's the storeroom, the barn. Roof fell in on the barn. They couldn't tell what was in there."

"But they didn't find *Ann*. Not for sure. She could be all right. She could have got away. Couldn't she?"

Cranfill said, "I judged it was that way between the two of you." He hesitated. "Look, you'd better swallow the whole dose at once. Everything about this looks like Silverhorn's work. His bunch doesn't much leave survivors. Not even the young women, after they've—"

Cranfill stopped, bit his lip until he tasted blood. Slowly, Fairchild's head came up. The blue eyes looked into the lieutenant's.

"After they've what?"

"Nothing. They don't leave survivors, that's all."

"After they've what?"

"After they've finished with them," Cranfill said.

Fairchild flinched as though he'd been hit. His iron grip on Cranfill's arm loosened. He sagged for a moment, so that Cranfill put out a quick hand to steady him, but then he straightened.

"I see." His voice was low and expressionless. "All right. Thank you, Lieutenant."

"Fairchild, I'm sorry."

"I appreciate your telling me."

Fairchild turned away. He picked up the coffeepot and dumped its contents by the fire. Holding it, he walked down toward the creek. Cranfill watched him kneel, rinse the pot out, fill it with fresh water. Instead of rising, he stayed on his knees, holding the pot in both hands, bowing his head over it as if it were a shrine.

Cranfill took a step toward Fairchild, then stopped. There was nothing he could say or do, not right at that moment. And he had his duties. The patrol was getting ready to move.

"God help him," he murmured and turned away, leaving Fairchild on his knees beside the creek, listening to the voices in his mind.

I do love you.

Her mouth, soft and warm against his, salty with her tears.

You don't love me. You're too busy hating all of them.

Pushing away. Running. From him. From what she saw in him.

I'll come back for you, I swear.

When Silverhorn's dead and all his bunch. After the reckoning. When there are no more white-haired wolves pack to pull down the sheep. Meanwhile, you're safe here. Safe within the fold.

You'll never come back to me.

*   *   *

"Fairchild?"

He tried to keep that other voice out of his reverie.

"Fairchild." Cranfill's hand was on his shoulder. He looked up into the lieutenant's face. "We're ready to move. Healy's got your horse saddled, your gear ready." Cranfill almost smiled. "If you ever doubt Healy likes you, think about him saddling that devil horse of yours."

"Where?" Fairchild asked.

"We're going back to the Oak. We'll try to pick up the trail from there. They can't be more than a day ahead of us."

Or behind you or off to the north or south! "I'm not going."

"What?" Cranfill straightened. "I don't understand. I assumed you'd be more interested than ever in locating Silverhorn and his men."

"I am." Fairchild looked at the coffeepot he still held between his hands. The metal was cold to the touch, beaded with moisture. He set it carefully on the bank of the creek. "But I was never much on hunting with a pack. I think I'll try it on my own."

"If you find them, they'd only kill you," the officer said. "Silverhorn's picked up more men someplace. There's close to ten of them now. You wouldn't have a chance." He cleared his throat. "Look, I know this has been a shock to you. Come along with us. In a couple of days, we'll find them."

Fairchild rose and tightened his gunbelt. "Thanks, Lieutenant, but I'm not going with you," he said. "You didn't know Silverhorn was east of you yesterday. You won't know if he's slipped past you now."

Cranfill glanced at Sergeant Neidercutt, who moved a few steps closer. "I could put you under arrest, take you back with us for your own protection."

"Could you?"

The lieutenant stared at him for a moment, then shook

his head. "No," he said. "I suppose I won't. If I'd known the young lady well, I might feel the same way myself." He put out a hand. "Good luck, Mr. Fairchild."

"Good luck, Lieutenant."

The sun raised its rosy hint at the eastern horizon. Ethan Fairchild did not notice that all signs portended a beautiful day. Striving to keep himself in hand, to block out the voices in his mind, Fairchild sliced off a couple of strips of bacon he didn't want and laid them in his frying pan. It never entered his mind that he had neither bread nor eggs. He ate the bacon half raw. Then he hauled up enough water to cool his cookware and put out his fire. When he had packed, he moved out to the west, away from Bradley's Oak, listening to a voice that only he could hear.

I never thought you'd go without me. I never thought you'd leave me here . . . to die.

He followed the trail for most of a mile. Then he angled north up through the rocks and rough brush to the top of a barren hill. There he dismounted, checked his rigging. The Dragoons had pulled out an hour or more before. Looking back, he could see their plume of fine dust in the distance. For a moment, he wondered if he'd made a mistake, but then he shrugged. What he'd told Cranfill was true, though he couldn't remember when he'd reasoned it out. The Dragoons were tied to the trail by their orders. Silverhorn was free to move.

Besides, he couldn't go back to Bradley's Oak. He couldn't.

Holding his horse to a walk, Fairchild headed straight west on the theory that the Army was failing to lead its bird. It was a gamble. But the way he saw it, he hadn't much left to lose.

He'd had time to figure that the telescope he'd seen catch the sunlight above Bradley's Oak could have been Silverhorn's. If that were true, then Whitehair would have seen the buffalo hunters and their wagon of skins. He had already made one try for those hides. Why shouldn't he be following the hunters now, trailing them like a wolf on a scent?

A predator tracking other predators. That might be the way Silverhorn saw himself. Tracking the big game, waiting his chance, killing and eating whatever he could catch in the meantime.

You'll never come back to me.

Fairchild might have been furious if he had given in to his thoughts. He might have been heartbroken. Instead, he rode with the perseverance and patience of a wolf hunter. Ethan Fairchild was the predator tracking predators who were tracking predators. He pictured the others, with their hunters' eyes in front, staring straight ahead with no thought that he was behind them. Ever wary of the territory ahead of him, Fairchild did not trace the progression of predators far enough to worry about his own back.

At mid-afternoon he stopped by a muddy creek to rest his horse and give him half a hatful of grain. Ann Bradley's voice was out in front of him now, calling, beckoning him on. I'm coming, he told her; I'm coming. Just a couple of little things to do first. To himself he said, *God help the dirty bastards when I find them.*

The slanting sunlight caught on a row of evenly spaced white rocks along the crest of a rise. Fairchild frowned. There were plenty of rocks around, but these held the eye. Surely nature hadn't laid them out in such a neat row. From what he had seen on the trail, he doubted that nature ever did things neatly. Touching the chestnut's ribs lightly with his heels, he went to look.

The rocks lay in a straight, single line running roughly from southeast to northwest. At the northwest end of the row, six extra stones formed the point of an arrow.

Fairchild leaned on his saddle horn and pondered the arrow. He knew Indians sometimes made such symbols for their own reasons, but he didn't think this was an Indian sign. But who else might have left such a marker?

Why? What did it point toward or away from? And who had been expected to find it? It led toward Waller's hunting party, or at least he figured it did. It led away from the places he'd just been: the trail, Bradley's Oak, what passed for civilization. Beyond that, none of the answers that occurred to him seemed to make any sense.

He tried another tack. Who had *not* left it? The buffalo. Silverhorn, who wouldn't lead hunters along his own trail.

For whom had it *not* been intended? It had not been intended for Fairchild. But he had found it anyway.

Dismounting, he tied the chestnut to a thick clump of sage. Then he moved carefully around the arrow, trying to read the ground the way he'd seen Cranfill's Delaware scout do. The scout could probably have found a dozen things about the arrow and whoever had left it. Fairchild found only one—the prints of a shod horse in the hard-crusted ground behind the crest. Not Indians, then.

He rubbed his chin, staring at the arrow, until his lips suddenly sketched a humorless grin. The stones weren't heavy. It hadn't taken someone more than a few minutes to gather and arrange them. It took Fairchild even less time to shift them about into an arrow pointing to the northeast. Then he freed his Devil, mounted, and rode out to the northwest, following the direction of the original marker.

21

Ann Bradley had made a crucial decision. She did not say it lightly to her mother that Ethan Fairchild was her life. Nor did she lightly set out alone to overtake him. She knew something of the dangers of the trail; she'd heard enough from travelers stopping at Bradley's Oak. But she was confident she could be with Fairchild before sundown, could take back her last harsh words. And she was confident that, in spite of all, he would not send her away.

At first Ann made the lazy horse run, but within a half mile, she realized she must pace him. This journey of the rest of her life would not be made in an afternoon. She hadn't ridden quite four miles when she saw a rider in the road ahead. She kicked the horse up to a canter for a few joyful strides, certain that Fairchild was coming back for her. Then she realized the rider was not coming toward her but standing in wait for her.

Ethan? Could you be so cruel, so selfish as to make me run all the way to you?

Her question answered itself within the next few seconds. She saw that the horse was not Fairchild's chestnut, but a compact, close-coupled paint. And the rider, even at this distance, she thought was a woman.

She slowed her pace, then reined Blackie in fully while she looked ahead.

"Silly!" she scolded herself, half aloud. "You've no reason to be afraid. Not so near home as this."

But she was afraid. She hadn't realized the loneliness of the trail, hadn't expected the sudden realization that she was on her own, that for the first time in her life there was no one to help her or make her way easier. She bit her lip, tempted for a fleeting second to turn back.

"No," she said, loudly enough to make Blackie twitch his ears in puzzlement. She wouldn't be a coward, running home the first moment she saw a stranger. She'd come to find her love, and she wouldn't turn back.

The rider was still ahead, sitting her horse motionless by the edge of the trail. Ann asked herself where the woman had come from and why she was waiting on the road.

Maybe she's hurt. Or maybe she's as frightened of me as I was of her.

That was it. But still Ann was uneasy. There had been

no one in sight only a moment before. Surely the traveler could see Ann as clearly as Ann could see her. If she meant her no mischief, why did she not come on toward her?

Ann Bradley turned her horse and slipped off the road and into the woods, choosing the south side perhaps because her home was on that same side of the road. Her plan was to keep to cover until she could work her way well past that solitary rider. She'd ridden these woods and hills for most of her life, so there was no danger of getting lost so soon.

She walked the horse a good quarter of a mile down from the road before she began to work her way back to the west. There the brush grew thicker and the going more difficult, for no one had traveled the land or tried to thin out the undergrowth.

She felt safer within the brush, but she had no view of the road and no idea where the other rider had gone. It came to her that a lone rider, particularly a woman alone, was indeed unusual and portentous. Then she made a face at herself, laughing.

Like you. A woman alone, on the trail. How unusual! You've probably scared some poor emigrant lady into conniptions, and scratched yourself and your horse to tatters in these branches, and all for nothing.

Smiling, she turned Blackie up a rock-spined knob he would rather have skirted, just so that she could see the trail. She was not able to see it clearly, even then, but she was certain no rider or wagon was on the stretch where she'd noticed her mystery woman.

She paused there, thinking. She would have preferred to see the other rider moving away to the east. But the woman could easily have moved out of sight along the trail in either direction in the time Ann had spent floundering through the brush. Laughing away her nagging uneasiness, Ann picked her way down the hill, spent a moment getting her directions straight among the trees, then urged Blackie west, angling back toward the trail.

She'd lost enough time already with her foolishness.

She was pleased to come to a clearing, to be free of the undergrowth for forty yards or so. She was a third of the way across it when a buckskinned figure stood up from the brush at the west side.

"Oh!" Ann said, reining Blackie back suddenly.

The newcomer was a woman, she saw, perhaps the one who'd been waiting in the trail. Her braided black hair might have belonged to an Indian. So might her buckskin dress, its skirt hacked off shorter than Ann thought decent, its stained and blackened leather pulled tight across generous bosom and hips. The woman was smiling, but her steady black eyes held no humor at all.

"You startled me." Ann tried to smile in return. "I was afraid you were a robber."

The woman raised a short-nosed revolver and pointed it at Ann. "I am," she said.

She sounded no more threatening than a mother speaking to an unruly child. Ann had the crazy thought that she just happened to have the pistol in her hand, that perhaps she'd forgotten she was holding it.

Pardon me, ma'am, but you seem to be pointing a gun at me, Ann could say. And the other woman would reply, *Why, gracious sakes, so I am. How careless of me.*

"Stand down. Off the horse. Now."

Ann thought of urging the horse into a run, of breaking for the safety of the trees. But she was too far out into the open and she knew it. The Indian woman had already taken three long-limbed strides into the clearing. She couldn't miss if she fired the revolver from so near. Drawing a deep breath, Ann dismounted.

"Stand still," Grace told her. "Keep hold of that horse till I get the reins. All right. Now strip off your dress."

Ann stared at her, unable to believe she'd heard correctly. "What?" she asked.

"Do it!" The throaty voice hardened. "I don't want to mess that pretty dress up more than needful."

"What?" Ann fluttered a hand helplessly. "Who are you?"

She realized it was a foolish question. It seemed to amuse the dark woman. Her full lips widened into a grin, the kind of look Ann had seen on the faces of a few of the men who'd stopped at the inn. She raised the pistol, cocking the hammer as it came level with Ann's face.

"Sweetie, I'm the one what's going to shoot you if you don't do like I say. Move!"

Ann tried to think what to say, what argument would make the woman see reason. She caught the tiny tightening of the index finger on the pistol's trigger and understood, suddenly and fully, that she was only a moment from death. Her only hope lay in doing as she was told. "No, wait! I'll do it. All right."

With unwilling fumbling fingers, she unbuttoned her dress and let it fall. The woman had come closer, her eyes showing amusement at Ann's obvious embarrassment. She watched as Ann got to the last buttons and straightened, holding the dress in front of her with one hand while she put the other out toward Grace.

"Listen, if you want clothes, you're welcome to what's in my saddlebags. Or is it money? I've got a little money. Is that what you want?"

"Sweetie, we don't have time for what I want." Grace waggled the barrel of the pistol. "Too bad. Let the dress fall. That's good, right there where you're standing." The woman looked at her plainly, grinning. "That's nice. Let's see how you look without that shirtwaist."

Before Ann could imagine her intention, the woman snaked out her left hand and caught the thin muslin chemise at the throat, ripping it away with a single strong yank. Ann gasped, too terrified even to scream. Her face burned in shame as she hunched her shoulders and crossed her arms to cover herself.

"Please!"

The woman laughed. "Sweetie, I know some old boys back up the way would roll in the dirt and howl to see what I'm seeing." Her voice seemed deeper, huskier. "Them's mighty pretty pantalettes, with the blue ruffles and all. Bet your gentleman friend set some store by those."

Ann felt her skin drawing up into goose pimples, though she was not cold in the summer afternoon. A new dread crept into her soul. She clung to the woman's last words, to what she'd said about Ethan, because it offered her a hope of clinging to her own sanity.

"He never did," she said, then bit her lip and stopped. "It wasn't like that."

"Never is," Grace said. She frowned at the pantalettes. "Wouldn't fit me. Too bad. Maybe if you'd been a little more obliging, he wouldn't've rid off and left you. Step back."

Ann stared at her. *She's going to kill me now.* The words rang in her head as she stared into the woman's black, indifferent eyes. It seemed terribly important that she use those last seconds thinking about Ethan, talking about him, trying to make this woman understand.

"He didn't!" She hadn't meant to cry, but she was crying. "He didn't leave me! He means to come back for me. He does!"

She straightened, forgetting her nakedness, clenching her hands at her sides as she faced her killer.

"I'm not afraid of you, whoever you are. Go ahead, kill me, if that's what you mean to do. I'm not afraid!"

Still she couldn't help closing her eyes as she waited for the bullet. *Oh, Ethan*, she thought, *I did love you.* When she opened her eyes, the dark woman was frowning at her, again like a mother at an unruly child.

The woman crossed her arms, pulled the supple leather dress off over her head, without letting her pistol stray for more than a moment from Ann. Then she took up Ann's smaller blue dress, smelled it, and forced it over her fuller body.

"It's good you're not afraid," she said. Then she lifted her revolver and fired two shots a little apart. One bullet went into the far trees, the other into the ground.

Ann Bradley was still trembling when the Indian woman said, "Listen, girl, I have to take your horse." She unstrapped the saddle bags and let them fall. "You can keep these."

"But if you take my horse, how will I catch up to my Ethan?"

The woman transferred the revolver to the same hand that held Blackie's reins and slapped Ann hard across the face.

"Listen, I said. You'll walk. Walk west. If you go back east, you'll die. And if I judge you right, you won't much enjoy what happens before you do."

Ann Bradley felt tears running down her cheeks. She knew of course that she would die if she went back east; her life lay to the west. But it was confusing that the woman should know.

The dark woman swung easily up onto Blackie's back and reined him around the way she'd come.

"You can do what you like with my dress," she said, looking back at Ann, "but if I's you, I'd put it on."

"Why?"

"To cover your nakedness. Though you look better bare than any woman I ever seen." She grinned. "Sorry we can't spend a little more time together. Maybe I'll see you again."

"No, I mean why have you done this?"

But the woman was gone. She crossed the clearing, dipped under the hill, and came back up on her paint horse a moment later, riding toward Ann who was just pulling the well-used leather dress over her head. *She's changed her mind!* Ann thought, all her fear flooding back. *Now she means to kill me.*

But the woman only grinned at her.

"Keep on west, you hear? Don't go back and don't dawdle."

Without a backward glance, she pushed her paint northeast out of the clearing and back toward the trail, trailing Blackie behind her.

Ann Bradley began to tremble. She wanted to tear the loose-fitting, greasy dress off her body and burn it. She wanted to sit down and shake and cry and scream. In a better moment she might have sat down and laughed at her situation.

But there hung in the air around her the force of the dark-eyed woman's warning. Suddenly grateful to have the dress, to have her life, Ann forced herself forward to the west, away from the clearing and into the blessed shelter of the forest.

She never knew how long she stumbled blindly through the brush and trees, but the sky was growing dark when she came to herself. Through the branches, she could see the western clouds painted in red and orange and gold. She had to find a safe shelter for the night.

For an instant, she feared the threat of wild animals, but then she laughed bitterly at herself. *People are the worst animals*, she thought. *I must fear my own kind more than wolves or bears.*

Looking around her, she saw things she knew, the shape of a hill, the way two trees grew together in an arch. And she knew where to go. Taking her direction carefully while there was still enough light, she turned to the south and lengthened her stride until she was almost running.

Wild, crazy, anchoritic, dangerous, and indeed always armed—Forrest Elam was nothing to Ann Bradley but a gruff old man as lonely as she. She smelled his fire before she made the last turn in the trail leading to his cabin, and she saw the thin column of smoke rising from his chimney as she came in sight of his cabin. Elam would have a fire, even on a summer evening, to warm his bones as he would have said. Ann hurried across the clearing and called to him, remembering even in her distress to be careful about surprising him.

He didn't answer. Thinking he might have become deaf

with time, she called his name again and pounded at the rough wood of his door. He *had* to be home. She couldn't stand it if he wasn't. A heavy shutter covered the front window even then in the warm weather. She knocked more loudly.

At last she started around the cabin to see whether the old man might be out back at the stump where she had seen him cut firewood and split kindling. A heavy voice said, "Girl."

She stopped as suddenly as if she'd heard the shrill warning of a rattlesnake. Forrest Elam took shape and form as he emerged from the shadows of the trees off to the west side of the house. He held his long flintlock rifle.

"Mr. Elam!"

"Ann. Back again already." He frowned and looked off into the shadows. "Where's your young man?"

That was too much for Ann. She tried to choke out an answer, but her voice didn't obey her. The sudden realization that her danger was over, that she was alive, safe, with a friend, unnerved her far more than any danger could have done.

"Mr. Elam!" She couldn't tell if she was laughing or crying, but whichever it was, she couldn't stop. "Oh, Mr. Elam. Oh, God."

Quick as a mountain cat for all his years, he caught her before she could fall. "Great Godkins!" said the old man. "I hadn't a thought of scaring you, Annie. I'm a foolish old he-coon. When I heard you crashing through them trees like a wounded elk, I hadn't any way to know it was you."

Ann Bradley listened to his words, poetry to her, and put her arms around his neck, pressing her face against his shoulder like a frightened child. Awkwardly, he embraced her; then, when he had peered again into the woods all around, he led her into his little cabin.

Inside, he bolted the door, peered out a crack at his shuttered window. "Are people after you?"

She wasn't a child, frightened or not. She stood erect,

forced her trembling to stop, forced herself to speak. "No. I don't think so, anyway," she said. "But there're people out there, bad people."

She caught her breath suddenly, remembering what the woman had said. "Don't go east! That means back home." She caught Elam's arm. "Mother and Father! They're alone there!"

Her voice was rising toward a scream. She felt Elam's hands on her arms, shaking her gently.

"Easy, girl. Gentle down a spell. Before this old hoss can do much, you got to tell me what's happened." He looked at her for a moment, then seemed to change the subject completely. "I can't help notice your dress. Never seen you wear a buckskin like that."

She shook her head.

"Be good for the journey." He laughed. "You take it off some Injun woman?"

She smiled. "In a way."

"Maybe you better tell me about it."

She drew a breath, nodded, let him lead her to a rough bench by the table. She smelled a stew simmering in a cast-iron pot above the fire in his small hearth. She realized how hungry she was, but what she had to tell was more important. Stumbling over the words, clinging to his scarred hand when her voice threatened to fail her, she told about Ethan, about following him, about the strange and threatening woman in the forest.

"Great Godkins." It was the first thing he had said. He rubbed his chin, then stood and went to peer out the crack in the shutters again. "Nothing for it right now," he said, squinting at her. "Best thing is for you to eat a bite of vittles and get some rest."

"But my parents! We have to warn them!"

"You leave that to me, missy. Won't do no good out there in the pitch-black dark. And you've got to keep your strength if we're going after this Ethan feller."

"Oh, yes," she said, not understanding his last words. "I'm going after him. I love him."

"Great Godkins," Elam muttered. He dished out stew onto a tin plate and set it before her. "He love you?"

She nodded brightly. "He does. He'd never have left without me but to kill that wolf."

"But to what?" Forrest Elam had been tall, was now slumped in his back and hips; had been broad and strong, was now drawn in at the shoulders and slack of arm. His long flowing hair had once been black, was now thinning to gray and white. But the warm coal of former bright fire still burned in his dark eyes. With the warmth of those eyes he watched her, measured her words, gauged the breadth of her soul.

"He left to find and kill the man who ruined his life."

"I see. Not knowing him better, I value his valor. Not knowing him, I value his good taste in choosing you. Not knowing him, I question his judgment in leaving you to right some old wrong! If his life was ruint before he met you, it ought to've come plumb square by now."

She felt the tears again, gave way to them for a moment. "I have to find him."

"And he has to find that bad man that ruined his life, did you say? What if that bad man kills him?"

"It's my greatest fear." She looked around the neat little room, chose a seat. "It's why I must find him. I must keep him alive."

"Ah. If only we could do that for those we love."

It struck a jangling chord in her that Forrest Elam might ever have loved anyone. She studied the mystery in his dark eyes.

"And would you kill his enemies to keep him alive?"

She had not thought of that, had never contemplated violence. Still, as soon as she heard the old man's question, she answered, "Yes," with no hesitation at all.

"And if there were too many of them to kill?"

"I'd stand and fight and die by his side." She surprised herself and knew at the same time that she should not have been surprised. Ethan Fairchild was her life. Of course she would stand and fight and die by his side. And she understood better now what that meant.

"Then you've found the man I promised you would come. I hope he'll live to learn that you're his new life and his former life needs no avenging. I hope you'll live to find him and bear his children. I hope I'll live to meet him again, this man worthy of your love! Will you have some more stew?"

She realized she'd cleaned her plate while she was talking. "Please." As she ate with him, she realized how hungry she might yet become along the way.

Afterward, Elam brewed a pot of coffee. She noticed he had not asked her what her parents thought of her decision. She wondered again at his wisdom, his window into her soul, his uncanny knowledge of things she had not needed to tell him. He made her feel stupid by comparison, yet gave her courage to try her own wings.

"The lady you loved," she dared, "was she fair?"

"Aye!" he replied, as quickly as if he'd been with her in her thoughts. "Fair as spring. Pale-eyed as an eagle. Hair like honey flaxed on a loom to strands of gold." He paused, thoughtful or embarrassed, to stare into the fire. He took up a long-stemmed Indian pipe, lit it with a splinter from the fire, rested his eyes for a moment on Ann Bradley, or as she thought, on his memories of that woman long lost.

"It was how I came to be as I am." He puffed at the pipe, waiting for her reply or for his own inclination to continue or to remember his thought. "She loved me and said so. Else I'd never have come to life. We calculated to be married in the spring when I came down to rendezvous. I can see her now standing at her door where I left her, smiling after me, waving, vowing her love aloud.

"Godkins. Well, I went my way. I trapped my share and came again with aplenty of prime beaver plews. But when I came again to her door, she was there no more."

Ann Bradley thought he had been over it so many times in his mind that he had made a kind of crude poem of his sorrow. "What happened to her?"

"There'd been a raid. Even her house was gone. Only the door stood silent in its frame. The rest was ashes. I found a boy who'd lived through it. The Blackfoot had fallen on them and killed them all. They'd thought the boy dead as well.

"I nursed him until he was strong enough to come along with me. We found them, the very ones who'd done the killing. The boy knew their leader by sight. I killed him, killed them all. Took his feathers, burned his lodge, shot his ponies."

He bit the stem off his pipe, stared at the pieces, fell silent. She did not know what to say.

"It was what you had to do," she said at last. But she was not satisfied with the story. It had no happy ending. The young woman was dead.

Again, he seemed to know her thoughts. "Was all I knew to do," he said. "But it didn't bring her back. It didn't bring the peace I'd wanted. And the boy . . ."

"I think I hear it in your voice you'd come to love the orphan boy. What happened to him?"

Forrest Elam turned his face away. "Killed." He rubbed his long chin. "Killed in the fight. Seems to me that Blackfoot devil won. He'd kilt all I ever cared about in this life. I splattered myself wet with his blood, but there's nary enough blood in all the world to wash out what's happened."

She saw into his soul for that brief moment, looked through the little window he'd opened to her, knew his pain and sorrow and loneliness. Had it been a wind, it would have swept her away.

He finished his coffee, gave her a smile she'd seldom seen on his face. "I tell you so's you'll know it when you meet it."

"You're very kind."

"No such. But you're tired out, and that's a fact. You'll be missing your rest in the morning if you don't turn in." He pointed to a bed in the corner. "There's you a warm spot. Could be the last you'll find for a spell." Rising, he

took down a double-bore shotgun from pegs above the
fireplace and stood it beside the bed. "Anything bothers
you, ear back these hammers and let fly."

"But that's your bed."

"A fox must have its den and a bird its nest, but a
mountain man can sleep wherever he lays his head. You
have your rest."

He rose and gathered his coat and long gun and started
outside. She went to the door, tried again to stop him.

"Mr. Elam, I can't take your bed. Please."

He shook his head. "Old badger like me doesn't sleep
much, missy." He stroked his chin, looking off to the east.
Ann followed his eyes, saw a dim, wavering orange glow
low along the skyline. "Might be I'll take a little ride,
loosen up my old bones. You'll be safe here, but don't
forget what I said about the shotgun."

"Thank you."

He turned back to her, put out a trembling hand but did
not quite touch her face. "I'll take you where you must
go, if I can," he said. "In the morning, we'll start. But
now you must rest and I must be sure no evil's following
you."

22

Ethan Fairchild rode all af-
ternoon with one eye to the ground hoping to cut a trail.
By sunset, he had found no sign of other civilized life.
He had counted on the arrow he'd found to point him to
something; instead, he was alone under a clear vault of
sky with no company except the lasting echoes of Ann
Bradley's voice.

Even on those first dark nights after he'd been left by

the train, he had been within sight of a well-used trail.
Later, he'd been with the Dragoons, or back on the well-
traveled route west. But this evening was different. He
found himself in a land where no other man might ever
have trod. If any had, they had not left tracks.

But none of those things meant that he could count on
remaining alone throughout the night. He found a narrow
ribbon of water in a draw, watered his horse and filled his
canteens, and picketed the chestnut to graze in the grassy
bottoms. Then he made his own cold camp on the crest
of a ridge from which he had the best view. He wrapped
himself in his blanket with his back to a single gnarled
juniper and dozed a while.

When he woke to find his legs and back cramped, a
full moon had risen. Far in the western distance, moonlight glinted on snowcapped peaks, the Wind Rivers, he
guessed, if he remembered his map correctly. Perhaps a
half mile off to the west, a wolf saluted it with a long,
mournful howl. Fairchild remembered how alone he was
in the world of nature. The wolf sounded lonely, too. The
man wondered whether the wolf knew he was there, even
though he had built no fire, made no noise. It didn't seem
likely. He stood, stretched himself, found a strip of jerky
and bit off a chew.

The wolf howled again. Fairchild smiled at his imagination that the animal sounded closer. A second wolf
howled somewhere to the east. A deeper voice barked and
gave a short howl to the south and east of Fairchild's
camp. From the hollow behind him, he chestnut nickered
twice. Fairchild felt the hair rising on the back of his neck.
Not quite as alone as he would have preferred, he checked
his revolver.

Wolves wouldn't attack people, he remembered from
the guidebook Thorne was always quoting. Nor would
they approach a fire. Under ordinary circumstances, the
book had said. Fairchild shivered as a fresh chorus of
howls rose, seemingly all around him. He wondered if his
circumstances were ordinary.

He broke a dead limb off the tree, broke it again across his knee, threw it on the ground in front of him. Then he found another, broke it, placed it on his pile. He opened his horn to pour a tablespoon of powder on the wood.

Other wolves had answered the first few. Fairchild told himself that the pack had no reason to be interested in him. Surely, other prey was handy. Probably they were not even aware of him. If he'd had a fire, they would never have come so close. He would never have known they existed. He found another limb, made himself break it into smaller pieces. The cries of wolves were sounding more frequently, moving closer to him. His horse was nickering constantly. He made himself a promise never to go through another night without a fire.

Then he realized what other prey the wolves were smelling. Stepping carefully, he went down into the hollow. The chestnut was standing stiff-legged, its good eye showing white all around the pupil. It didn't even offer to bite when he slipped on the bridle and released the picket rope. When he patted the animal's neck, he found its short coat cold with sweat.

"Don't like it either, Devil?" he asked, mostly to hear his own voice. He was answered by a howl that seemed so near he wished he'd held his tongue. The horse tried to rear and kick, but Fairchild led it to the top of the hill. With some difficulty, he tied the reins to the tree.

"If we die," he told the horse, "we die together."

The devil horse didn't seem much comforted. It set its front feet and hauled backward until Fairchild feared the tree might snap. Then Devil gave up, snorted once in disgust, and stood trembling.

Fairchild leaned his rifle against the tree, made certain of his powder and bullets, found his matches. The wolves were much closer by then. Once or twice he heard their heavy feet in the loose rock of the slope. The horse snorted again. The man spoke to him.

Two or three wolves had come close enough for the man and horse to hear them growl. At the edge of the moonlight, Fairchild saw dark shapes darting, turning, twisting ever nearer. He struck a match, nurtured it, dropped it onto the gunpowder. The powder flashed but did not catch any of the leaves or twigs.

"Damn," Fairchild mumbled. He knelt by the wood, went through his pockets, found a piece of paper, struck another precious match. The paper flamed at a corner. He held it with that corner down and tried to kindle the driest of the twigs. If he noticed that the paper was a dollar bill, he did not care.

He could hear the wolves' feet by then, the sounds of their paws like those of big hounds bounding inside a dog run. But these wild dogs were not bounded. They would grow bolder, come nearer, make a run at the horse. Nearly spent, the paper burned his hand. Then the twigs caught and burned in a tiny flame. He put a few larger ones on top.

The chestnut squealed, lashed out with its hind feet. One hoof hit something with a furry thump. A wolf yelped, the sound turning into a barking snarl very close at hand.

Fairchild brought his revolver to bear on the shape and fired. His aim had not been deadly, but the effect was better than a clean kill. The wolf limped away, howling its pain and fury. For a moment the others were quiet and none came close. But the fear wore off much too quickly. After a minute they moved in again, growling, wary but quick, cunning and determined. He waited until he had a good shot at one a few feet on the other side of his tiny fire, then squeezed the trigger carefully.

The animal went down without a cry, dropped as if the bullet had snipped its connection to the essence of life. The sound of the shot and the bright flash of burning powder sent the rest of the pack in short retreat. But the fallen wolf's companions learned nothing from its death. They came back in their age-old pattern of surrounding and harassing their victims.

Fairchild tried to keep his eye on the horse, to be certain

that they did not get close enough to nip at it again. The horse was wild in its frenzy, not to run but to fight. The battle rage was on it. Fairchild had thought to make a run for it, but now he didn't trust the chestnut to flee.

He began to count his loads. If the gun did not misfire, he would have four more shots before he was forced to reload. But if he pushed it that far, he might not have time to reload. He touched the rifle to be sure of its readiness, then remembered the pepperbox in his saddlebag. Sidling along, keeping his back covered by the fire and the frantic chestnut, he retrieved it and felt better. Six more shots, though he doubted one of the small-caliber rounds would stop a wolf.

He saw another wolf dare the firelight, aimed well, shot it in the shoulder. Turning back toward the horse and the relative safety of the tree, he saw another set of glowing yellow eyes moving up in its shadow. He aimed between those glowing eyes, fired again. He couldn't tell if he hit anything. The horse leaped two feet off the ground in its terror of the wolf or of the powder flare that had licked at its belly. Off to the man's left, a bolder wolf was moving in on his flank. He spun that way, lifted the pepperbox, and fired without aiming. The dark wolf twisted away and vanished as if the night had swallowed it.

Fairchild had lost count of unfired chambers. *How many wolves would be in a pack?* He didn't know. If the guidebook had said, he hadn't read that part. *How many had he shot?* He didn't know that, either.

Keeping his back to the tree, he returned his attention to the horse, fired at once upon the nearest growling shape, knocked it down without killing it. The result was better than the rest; this one went down with a broken back, scrabbling with its front paws and howling out its misery until one of the chestnut's flailing hooves smashed its head.

The horse swung his hindquarters away from the dead wolf, pressing Fairchild into the tree. The man shouted at the chestnut, banged at it with the barrel of his revolver, but the horse was too frenzied to notice. Fighting to get his arm free, Fairchild fired at a wolf on his left.

To his surprise, the little fire was blazing gamely against the night and the half ring of wolves. They had thinned out, too, whether with bullets or fear. Because they hesitated now farther out from the fire, he put away his revolvers, and took up the rifle. He wanted to kill every last one of them and spent the first two chambers of his rifle cylinder trying. But the night was black beyond the firelit circle and his aim uncertain. He had to save his powder and caps and bullets, for there was neither store nor well-stocked wagon at hand to supply him.

He patted the horse, gentled it down, tried to see the wolves out away from the fire. They had moved back, slowed their darting, grown sullen and quiet. He built up the fire. If they feared nothing else in the world, the wolves respected fire. He intended to keep it going even if he had to burn his saddle and coat and the tree behind him. He had to keep himself and the horse alive until morning.

He broke off another limb, tore a couple of twigs loose and tossed them on his dwindling fire. The juniper crackled and snapped with sap, putting out a thin, aromatic smoke. Fairchild didn't think he'd ever seen wood burn so fast. Unwilling to put down his rifle, he laid the long limb across the flames and hoped he'd have time to arrange it later. A couple of the wolves were on their bellies crawling in toward him like Indians. He bent over, filled his hand without looking, threw a fist-sized rock at the nearest one.

It occurred to him that others might be sneaking toward him from the other side of his tree. He was right. He shouted at them. They melted back like gray shadows in a black sea. The horse screamed again, kicked out savagely without hitting anything at all.

Fairchild went around the tree to stay clear of those rear hooves and fired at the nearest black shadow on the other side of the horse. Then he whirled back to the protection of the fire. It was time to reload, but the wolves were not playing by any rules which acknowledged his need.

He set the rifle aside and pulled out his revolver. With the hammer down on the last chamber he'd fired, he stared into the front of the cylinder. Empty holes, all. Four in the pepperbox, if he'd counted right. He pulled the Colt's hammer to half cock, found his powder, looked out past the fire for members of the pack. They were moving in slowly. He shouted a curse at them, made suggestions about their parentage. Then, revolving the cylinder as slowly as he could manage, he poured a little powder down each chamber, worried more about overfilling and leaving no room for the lead balls. There was no time for patches or grease. He put a ball into each chamber as forcefully as he could with his thumb.

The horse screamed. With one hand, he put his rifle under the horse's belly, cocked the hammer, looked, fired. At close hand a wolf let out a howl that made the hair stand on the man's neck. But the shot drove all the dark shadows back for a moment. Fairchild seated the bullets in his pistol and put it back in his belt. Then, still watching the shadows, he drew his other gun.

The last limb had burned in two; the fire was very small. With his free hand, he put the two ends of the limb on the faint flames. He reached over his head and found some small branches, pulled them free, put them on the fire. It took new life. In the rising heat he could smell the wolves again. He heard them moving about, working into positions to attack. He chose his target, aimed well, winged a big lobo no more than ten feet on the other side of the fire. Then he reloaded that gun by better firelight. It was time for more wood. Or hair or hat or saddle blanket.

He broke off yet another small limb, fed it to the voracious fire. The wolves had moved back out of the firelight. For a moment he dared to think they might be gone. Then he heard them moving, heard their footfalls like the tolling of a bell, like cattle milling in a lot.

In the east the sky had changed colors to give a distant hint of the rising sun. Fairchild took some comfort in that. But he couldn't convince himself that these wolves would be daunted by the sun. In this remote world where only he and they existed, they would appear to have little to fear.

But he was wrong. The wolves were bound in the eternal tradition of their kind as surely by the morning light as by the bright moon. He did not have to kill another, but was able to keep them back with his fire. Half an hour before dawn, the last distant shadow faded into the grass. Neither the man nor the horse cared to have breakfast in that realm. Still, the man told himself, I know they aren't here. I don't know they aren't out there waiting for us.

He warmed a few crusts of bread over his fire and fed the horse a half hat of grain. Willful and stubborn to the end, the little fire proved as difficult to quench as it had been to build. With it safely out, Fairchild surveyed the battlefield.

Four wolves lay dead in the trampled grass. He didn't know how many more he'd wounded, nor how many had slunk away to die elsewhere. For himself, his bruised ribs ached with each breath and one trouser leg was shredded, apparently by teeth, though he couldn't remember when in the confused melee that had happened. The horse had a pair of deep slashes on a hind leg where a wolf had gone for the hamstring, but nothing that would keep him from traveling. With a sense of having gotten off lightly, Fairchild mounted and moved on north, walking to ease the chestnut's leg, but stopping only once before noon.

It was then, when the sun was pretty much straight overhead, he came across the first of the big, unmistakable tracks of buffalo. He moved on slowly, studying the ground until the tracks were so thick as to be indistinguishable. A large herd was moving west.

Fairchild dismounted and led the horse while he walked the ground for a time, looking for the hoofprints of shod horses. He found them, finally, parallel to the main swarm and most of a hundred yards north of it. Running along in their midst was a line of tracks laid by wheels carrying a heavy wagon. He could have shouted.

Instead he found a little stream of water, fed his horse the last of the grain since the buffalo had pretty well grazed down the area as they went, and made himself rest a few minutes. Then he set out, keeping the horse between the lines of wagon tracks, making the best time he dared. After all, he was pretty much out of food and a little low on powder. He was willing to push pretty hard to catch up to Redwood Waller and his hunters.

The tracks might have been a day old or two days. Fairchild was not eager to spend another night alone entertaining the wolves. But the pack was his best hope that the trail was not very old. The wolves were probably dogging the herd, lying up by day and coming in by night to pick the young or old or frail off the fringes. It was just possible that the presence of the hunters and their fires had kept the wolves far enough away from the herd to take an interest in Fairchild and his horse.

Once or twice during the afternoon, he rode off the wagon trail and down into the incredible wallow of buffalo tracks, hoping to find some evidence that they were not far ahead of him. Late in the evening he began to notice that the droppings of horses, mules, and buffalo alike were fresher. He laughed at the thought that he had ridden a thousand miles into the frontier to seek his fortune, only to wind up studying buffalo spoor.

It struck him he had no means of identifying the tracks he was following so relentlessly. They could belong to Waller and his hunters, but equally well to Silverhorn and his raiders. The unspoiled wagon tracks suggested the hunters. He hoped so. Anxious as he might be to find Silverhorn, he needed a fresh stock of powder and ball before he tackled an armed gang.

He looked to the percussion caps and loads for each of his guns so as to be ready for whoever or whatever lay ahead of him. Then he urged the horse on. The fact that he had not found the ashes of campfires along the trail gave Fairchild further hope that the hunters were only hours away.

He kept moving, no longer stopping to study spoor or tracks, but pushing the horse relentlessly along the new trail. The sun was sinking just as relentlessly. Fairchild began looking for likely campsites. There was no wood on the low, rolling swells of land. For a fire, he would have to rely on buffalo chips. He didn't see anything that made him want to stop.

Just at dusk, he heard from somewhere up the trail the faint strains of a fiddle playing a lively reel. *Baldy!* After another thirty yards, he could smell their camp. They would never take anyone by surprise unless they were downwind in a gale. Not wanting to take the hunters by surprise, Fairchild made plenty of noise riding into their camp.

Redwood Waller watched him come, stood to meet him beside the fire. The others hailed him. "Well, now, Fairchild!" Waller said. "I take it you're here to join us."

Fairchild stood down from the saddle, shook hands. "If the offer's still good."

"Offer's gooder'n it was before. We'd admire to have you, sure enough. They's human wolves trailing us."

Fairchild thought of Silverhorn, of his close to ten men. He tried not to think further, but his imagination showed him the ashes of Bradley's Oak, the barn with its collapsed roof, the bones—bones and other things, as Cranfill had put it—that searchers had found there.

"You've seen them?"

"No. Stronger'n that. I've felt them. Cup of coffee?"

"Appreciate it. Might be wise to keep your eye out as well as your feeler."

"What?" The big man handed Fairchild a tin cup steaming at the surface of its thick black contents.

"Hell. I just rode right up on you here. What's to keep the wolves from coming in here to drink your coffee?"

Waller boomed a deep laugh. "Hear that, boys? Old Fairchild like to have bushwhacked us cold!"

The other hunters joined in the laughter. Fairchild waited, puzzled.

"Maybe you could share the joke with me?"

Waller smiled deep in his bristling beard. "If'n you'd made a little less noise, we'd be odd-manning each other for your belongings right now. They's been a gun on you for some time."

"Gun?"

"You can count gooder'n that, Ethan. Don't you notice they's a couple, three of my boys missing? They're spread out there in the woods, on the watch. I don't expect you saw young Eye-Shot."

"Didn't even smell him."

"He signaled us you was coming, maybe five, six minutes ago. I knew way back then it must be you."

"How would you have guessed that?"

"No guess. He'd've shot the eye out'n anybody he didn't know. You'd be about the only one he'd know that could find us off out here."

"That's mighty comforting. Almost as comforting as stepping across a prairie rattler."

"I figure it'd ought to help you sleep easier tonight, knowing those boys is out there."

Fairchild nodded, finished his coffee. "You want to tell me a little more about the job?"

"Why, sure," Waller said. "All you got to do is take the place of a couple of my lookout boys during the day-time when looking out is easier work."

"Two of them?"

"The rest of us'll need to be busy at our trade. We caught up to the herd today. You've come at a good time."

"Have you got any powder to spare?"

"Powder's our business. Bullets could be a problem, but we've got plenty of bar lead, if'n you have a bullet

mold for them guns of yours. Pay'll be a share of the
hides. Suit you?"

"Seems more than fair."

"Is more than fair. But we'd rather stay alive to give
you a share than to see the damned wolves steal them."

Gawkins looked up from his seat beside the fire, scowling at Fairchild. "How're we so sure he ain't one of the
lobos hisself?" he asked.

Waller took a step toward his hunter. "Be polite,
Gawk."

"Hell, Red, all of us have always spoke our minds
around here," Gawkins said. "All we know about him's
he was already at the Bradley's Oak when we got there."

"Gawk, be good."

"And was still there when we left." Gawkins stood,
brushing off the seat of his trousers with his hands. "Thing
is, he was so tight with that little swatch of gingham at
the Oak, I didn't figure anything could part him from her.
If he was so stuck on her, why ain't he still there keeping
her warm of a night?"

"Gawkins," Fairchild said, in a tone that made Waller
whirl to stare at him.

You'd leave me here? I thought we loved each other.
Fairchild barreled into the lanky hunter, head down, legs
and fists driving. Gawkins, astonished, tried to grapple
with him, but the power of the charge sent them both
tumbling into the fire. Gawkins screeched, and the two
rolled clear in a shower of sparks. Fairchild came up on
top, slamming blows blindly at Gawkins, at his face,
throat, arms, chest, whatever he could reach.

With a roar, Gawkins arched up, drove a knee into Fairchild's back, bucked him free. Fairchild hit his head without knowing it and scrambled around on all fours for
another driving charge, pounding at the other man until
Gawkins again was able to thrust him away.

In the break this time, Gawkins staggered back against
the wagon, snatched at his belt, came out with a long,
keen skinning knife. He held it low in front of him, his

eyes on Fairchild. His expression was less of anger than of surprise and fear.

"Stay back! I'll gut you, if'n you don't."

Fairchild never thought of the revolver at his belt. He saw the knife, but it didn't matter to him. The only thing that mattered was getting to Gawkins, pounding in his face, breaking his bones, wiping out the words in his dirty, lying brain. Fairchild set his feet for another rush, started forward.

Something smashed across his neck and shoulders like a thunderbolt. He went down hard into momentary blackness. There was dirt in his mouth and the taste of blood. When he tried to rise, people were holding him down, and he heard the boom of Waller's voice above the buzzing in his head.

"Hold him, now! You, Baldy, get his guns. We ain't having no killing in this camp, less'n I do it!" Fairchild heard the clear, cold snap of a rifle being cocked. "Gawk, you stand still and put by that knife, or you'll never skin another buff."

The men holding Fairchild heaved him to his feet. He shook his head and peered blearily around. Waller stood like the tree he was named after, a Sharps buffalo gun held like a twig in his big hands. Gawkins was pressing back against the wagon, his arms held high.

"It weren't me, Red!" Gawkins protested. "You saw him. I wouldn't never have pulled ary knife, excepting he was bent on tearing my head off! You saw it!"

"Sure did," Waller rumbled. He looked toward Fairchild. "Gawk needs his head punched ever' now and again, Ethan, but he didn't say anything to kill him over."

"Damned if he didn't," Fairchild panted.

"I know he spoke rough about your girl, but that's just his way of—"

"She's dead."

Waller's voice died. "What?" he asked in a different tone.

"She's dead."

"Dead!"

Fairchild tried to shake free, but couldn't. "It was Silverhorn's bunch. Same bunch chasing you. Raided the Oak the day after I left. Killed everybody. Killed Ann." He drew a ragged breath. "Goddamn them all, they killed Ann!"

"Great Lord of mercy," Waller breathed.

"And, goddamn *me*, I wasn't there. I wasn't there to stop them."

"Great Lord of mercy." Waller waved a hand at the three holding Fairchild. "It's over. Turn him loose."

They did, shamefaced, mumbling sympathetic noises, patting him clumsily on back and shoulders. Gawkins leaned against the wagon for a moment, his eyes and mouth wide. Still holding the knife, he walked over to stand before Fairchild.

"Ain't no wonder you come at me," he said solemnly. "Been me, I'd've did just the same." He flipped the knife around, offered the handle to Fairchild. "Can't take the words back, but if you're minded to cut out my tongue, here's the tool for it."

Fairchild looked at him for a moment, looked at the knife. He shook his head. "Appreciate the offer, Gawk. Reckon I'd rather have another cup of your coffee instead."

23

- -

Fred Harris waited until most of the members of his train were taking their noon rest before he sought out Manasseh Thorne who stood watching the oxen. The wagonmaster had just lit his pipe to enjoy a bowl before the afternoon's trek.

"Dr. Harris," Thorne greeted him with no special warmth. "Not coming to report a sickness, I hope. We're behind schedule now. Can't afford any more problems."

Harris laughed. "Actually, the news isn't quite that bad. I've been wanting to talk to you about myself and Barbara Kenny."

Thorne stroked his beard. "I noticed you made your lunch with her again today," he said.

"I've asked her to marry me."

"So soon?"

"I've been thinking about it for some time," Harris said, surprised by the question. "A man has to live fast in a fast land. It seems uncivilized at times, but life is short and time rolls by twice as fast out here."

"I had reference to the widow." Thorne tapped his pipe, brought out a match and relit it. "It's hardly more than three months since she lost her husband."

Harris looked at the spent match where it fell. *Thorne doesn't like me*, he realized. He wondered why. "Life goes by as quickly for a woman as for a man out here," he said. "Maybe more quickly. Either of us might have been killed at the ferry."

Looking away across the seemingly limitless high desert, Thorne kept the pipe going, pulled as well at his own thoughts, but said nothing.

"We'd thought you might perform the ceremony," Harris said.

"I'll think on it."

Fred Harris had more to say, but he held back, unwilling to risk Barbara Kenny's honor any further in an apparently ill-advised conversation. "Don't trouble yourself," he said at last. "Good day, sir." He turned away. Immediately, his eyes found Barbara Kenny standing at the tailgate of her wagon.

He went across to help her load up her cooking things. His own wagon was ready but for rehitching the team. He smiled at her, but her expression was a pressing question.

"He was no more unpleasant than is his nature," he answered her.

"Which was adequate, I'm sure." She lifted the gate and fastened it.

Harris mulled it over. "Yes. But my disappointment lies more in what he did *not* say, although what he said had the effect he wished."

"And what effect was that?"

"To bring the conversation to an end."

Barbara Kenny laughed. She had been right when she guessed that Thorne's speech was adequate to his purpose, and she also thought she could guess more of that purpose than Fred was admitting. But she did not intend to try. The wagonmaster's motives didn't matter to her. The man who would be her husband had gone to Thorne to tell him their plans and explain that they would be keeping company, had tried to tell him as a courtesy, had tried to tell him so that he would not be surprised by gossip. But it no longer mattered. She did not care at all what Thorne thought.

Neither, she realized, did she care what anyone else on the train thought. Lena Ames and Mrs. Coates and anyone else who was interested could make her the subject of their gossip; it would make no difference. She had lost one man she loved along this trail. She would not waste a moment loving Fred Harris.

For some reason, Fred cared what the others thought. She hated it for his sake. These were not her people, after all. They had not been her first husband's people, either. Oddly enough they were not even Fred Harris's people. Why did he care?

"My dear," she said. "We have each other, you and I. We aren't alone in this big land. If the people on this train begrudge us that, then they simply forfeit their share in our happiness."

"I suppose." Harris chewed at his lip nervously, staring off to the west far down the road.

She followed his gaze to an approaching wagon. As it came closer she saw that it was headed for the spot where they'd stopped for nooning. A big wagon, it was heavy enough to need a twelve-mule team. The driver sat tall and spare and a bit ragged in the seat, turning his head constantly from side to side. *Like a live scarecrow*, she thought. Next to him on the seat, a round little man rocked with the sway of the wagon as if he were a leather ball tethered to an upright double-barreled shotgun which alone kept him anchored to the seat. Along the side of the wagon ran the owner's sign: Westrow's.

Barbara Kenny knew some Westrows in Ohio, but none of them stood much over five feet in height. It appeared that the wagon's driver was a good foot taller. Still, Barbara wondered. She left her wagon and went along the trail.

Harris called "Barbara?" after her.

"Come on." She gestured toward the other wagons. "These aren't our people. Let's go meet some strangers."

She was among the first in the group that gathered near the wagon when it rolled to a stop. When the scarecrow stepped down from the high seat, she asked him her question.

"No, ma'am," he replied. His voice was full and deep and resonant out of a thin and bony chest. "No, I am not acquainted with any Ohio Westrows. I know no other Westrows but those who own this line."

"Aren't you Mr. Westrow?"

"Oh, now I see." The driver laughed softly. "Oral, leave that gun and help me with the water barrels. No, ma'am. I am not myself a member of the Westrow family. I am merely employed by them."

"I beg your pardon."

"It's a large line. Mr. Westrow doesn't drive anymore."

"It was silly of me."

Fred Harris said, "What was?"

She turned to look at him. "My question."

"I don't believe you could ask a silly question."

"Sweet of you, but quite in error."

Caleb Sugarhouse had begun talking with the guard. "Where you out of?" he asked bluntly.

Barbara saw the round little man look up at Sugarhouse, judge him in some fashion, and turn back to the mules. "Fort Hall, most lately. Away yonder in Oregon City's where we hail from."

"Hear that's a lively little town. Caleb Sugarhouse."

Barbara watched him put out his square, strong hand and wondered whether the round man would take it. She looked at Sugarhouse and wondered whether she would take it. He was one of those who were not her people.

"Oral Tibbs." The guard let go the harness with one hand, shook with Sugarhouse, went back to work.

"Guess the folks in Fort Hall's heard all about the silver strike down in Nevady."

"I expect they have." Tibbs laughed in a shrill whinny. "Seems most of them's headed down that way already. Them and everybody else that ain't tied to a post."

Sugarhouse laughed. "You boys must be making good money hauling freight, else you'd be down there digging out some of that silver for yourselves." He turned and followed Tibbs, who had unhitched his team and was leading them two at a time to the water barrel. "Tell me the truth, now. Have they really struck silver as big as folks say?"

"I can only tell you what folks say. It's big talk just now."

"Is it true, then, that they're taking out a thousand dollars in ore every day?"

"I can't tell you what's true. I can only tell you what people say. But I've heard them say they're taking lots more out of the ground every day. Some say it's more like that amount every hour."

"You don't believe it?"

"If I believed it, I might be down there digging myself."

"Might be? Why, hell, from what I've heard, you'd be a rich man inside a week!"

"I'll wait until it's proved to me," Tibbs said. "Then I'll consider it."

"Proved to you? Why, by that time the whole thing could be over."

Oral Tibbs looked over his glasses at Sugarhouse. "I'm afraid it would be over before *I* got there, no matter what."

"You that slow?"

Tibbs whinnied. "I'm that unlucky."

Sugarhouse turned to the other men from the train. "Well, you boys hear that? There's silver, all right. Silver waiting to be dug out of the ground!"

"In Virginia City?"

"Down that way. Not far from it."

"How far's it from here?"

Sugarhouse took a well-handled piece of paper out of his coat pocket, unfolded it several times, knelt, and laid it out on the ground.

To Barbara Kenny he looked like a frog crouched over the tattered map. Like flies waiting to be gobbled up, Coates and Milt Ames and Warner Espy huddled around him. Even Lije Holden and Douglas Stuart came over to look. All of them spoke animatedly as they calculated the distance, projected the time it would take, tried to imagine how much silver they could mine in one working day.

"My God," Sugarhouse surmised, "a man wouldn't have to spend the rest of his life digging. Think about it. Once we get there, we won't need more'n a week—say a month at the outside—to dig our fortune. You, Ames, I know you've been worrying about getting on to Oregon."

"I'm wanting to get on to Oregon, too," Hiram Miller said. "Still, if it wouldn't take long, I might not mind making a fortune first."

"Well, then, this deal's just made for you!" Sugarhouse insisted. "Look here, now, at the map. See. We drop off the main trail at the Hudspeth Cutoff to go to Virginia City."

"I see."

"Then from Virginia City we cut right back up this way, see?"

"And that's Oregon?"

"Right up that same way. Hell. You might say this's the back door to Oregon!"

"If a man came through it with a wagonload of silver, they might roll out the carpet and call it the front door to Oregon!"

"There's the truth."

"Beats farming all hollow, that's for sure."

"I don't know as I hold with that," Lije Holden observed in his twangy voice. "Man on his own land, with his family, and nobody that can put him off, he's got more than any wagon full of silver."

"It's a far piece down there," Hiram Miller said. "And I've heard tell there's desert drier than hell's pavement along the Humboldt. And suppose a man didn't find that much silver?"

"If we didn't find any silver!" Sugarhouse laughed. "Oh, ye of little faith."

Barbara Kenny turned to Harris and drew him aside. "Do you believe there's really so big a strike in Virginia City?" she asked breathlessly.

He nodded. "I expect there's a fire somewhere under all that smoke."

"Have you thought about it, then? Have you considered going that way?"

Harris laughed. "A bird's nest on the ground, lined with silver," he mused. "If there were enough so that a man didn't have to claw and kill the ones next to him to get at it, it's an opportunity that may not come again in a lifetime."

She thought about it, listened to Sugarhouse kindling his own fire with the twigs of anxious men desperate for some glory. "So you'd go, if it weren't for me?" she asked Harris.

"I?" His eyes opened a bit wider in contemplation.

"It's a fair question," she insisted.

"Then it's a fair question for you. Would you like to go?"

"If I were a man . . ." she mused, paused, let it go.

"If you were a man," said he, "I wouldn't ask you."

Sugarhouse was saying, "Yes, I know we all agreed to the terms of the trip."

"I pledged my word," Lije Holden said. "Besides, there's plenty of land to be had in Oregon, rich or not."

"But we didn't know then there'd be a silver strike! All right, you planned to go to trail's end and buy some land and farm it."

"It's all I know."

Sugarhouse snorted. "Then this is the time to learn something new! Look, man, the iron's white-hot in the coals! We've got to strike. We've got a chance to mold our futures, a chance to be rich!

After that, if you still want to farm, then you can buy *all* of Oregon and plant it in turnips!"

"I don't know anything else."

Sugarhouse shook his head. "Are you such an old dog you can't learn?"

Douglas Stuart had been listening, contributing little. Now he asked his question. "Why does it matter to you, Caleb, whether we go with you? I've not made up my mind. But I have to wonder. Would there not be all the more silver for you if you went alone?"

Sugarhouse threw up his hands. "A man tries to share a boundless fortune with his friends and they question his motives. I give it up!"

Barbara Kenny led Harris a few feet farther away. "He needs them for the same reason Thorne needs them," she said. "Doesn't he? It takes a certain number of wagons and people and guns to maintain a defense in this lonely land."

"It does. Or to haul wagons up and down hills, or to repair ferries."

They looked at each other and smiled, Barbara slipping her hand into his. Then Harris said, "You're right, of course. I'm so weak, so bent by every wind. I hadn't thought of that."

"You!" she cried. He was the strongest man she knew.

"Yes. I was thinking only of us. Of what money could mean to us when I begin my new practice."

It came to her that she was being selfish in her fears. "It was my husband's dream," she said at last.

"What!"

"He'd heard of the strike. We came on this journey for no other reason."

"I didn't know." He said it as if he did not want to know even then.

"It cost him his life."

She saw Sugarhouse folding his map. Across the way Manasseh Thorne was coming through the oxen, coming toward the gathering. She noticed for the first time that another knot of men had congregated around the scarecrow wagon driver. They merged with Sugarhouse's group.

"I *am* thinking of going myself," the scarecrow was saying as they drew him along. "It's a great temptation. But I have a wife and family to feed. I'm leery of quitting my job."

"But you know the trails, man. You could lead us there, probably save us some time getting there."

Sugarhouse smelled fresh blood. "You thinking of doing the bold thing?"

The scarecrow shuffled his feet, seemed uncomfortable in the crowd. "I'm thinking," he said.

"These boys is right. We could use you. And you could use us. We can all be rich as Westrow!"

Manasseh Thorne walked into the gathering, looked at each man in turn. "Gentlemen, since all of you seem so intent upon saving time, I will remind you that we should have been hitched and on the road this past quarter hour."

"We're talking about the future," Sugarhouse answered.

"We all agreed on this trip together. We're all moving toward the future we planned."

"Now we're talking about the future that's come up since we left home."

"Playing with words is not your longest suit, Caleb."

"Well, it's yours! That's what you lawyers do. Play with words to dazzle the rest of us honest folk."

"Are you making this a question of honesty?"

Barbara Kenny did not care. These were not her people. But Thorne fascinated her. He was older than Sugarhouse and stout in the way that older men took on weight, whereas Sugarhouse was simply stout, stronger in the way that nature made him, meaner in the way he would say the world had made him. Would Thorne dare to test him in physical combat? He spoke as if he would! She was afraid for him.

He did not seem afraid. "Let me be plain, then. You signed an agreement to carry this trip through to the end. I signed that same agreement. It is a legal and binding document."

"This is a free country!"

"It is. And you were free to sign a contract with the members of this train. No one coerced you."

"That's as may be. But any man's got the right to change his mind in a free country."

Warner Espy had a second thought. "Wasn't there an article in our agreement about changing our minds at some unforeseen point?"

Thorne regarded him with respect. "Yes." He said it as if some honesty deeper than good judgment drove him. "We did plan for the unforeseen in that very way."

Throwing his nose up as if to sniff the air, Sugarhouse demanded, "What way?"

Thorne cleared his throat, pitching his voice for the courtroom. "You'll recall, gentleman, and ladies," he added with a bow toward Barbara and Helen Coates, who had just come up, "we patterned our party on the suggestions of Captain Marcy, whose idea it was that we draw up an obligation. 'Wherein each one should bind himself to abide in all cases by the orders and decisions of the captain.' "

"We was crazy if we signed a thing like that."

"This is a free country!"

Thorne interrupted because they were getting away from the topic. "I won't judge your sanity, nor infringe upon your freedom as citizens. I'll merely remind you of the obligation we took on. We agreed to watch and guard our own as well as each other's stock, because the welfare of our expedition depends upon each wagon, and each wagon depends upon the whole. In short, we agreed not to leave you by the wayside if you lost your oxen."

"We did agree to that!" Joe Coates exclaimed. "I remember that part."

"In the same document, we agreed the captain should be sustained in all his decisions."

Barbara Kenny saw one of the men produce a folded paper from his pocket and hand it to Sugarhouse. "There's more to that article!" Sugarhouse bellowed. Raising his finger in the air, he read from the document of agreement: "Let's see. Here it is. 'in all his decisions *unless he commit some manifest outrage, when a majority of the company can always remove him, and put a more competent man in his place.*' "

Will Buttrell stepped up in Sugarhouse's face. "And what outrage do you suggest Judge Thorne has committed?"

This *will* be a fight, Mrs. Kenny thought. Those two stout, gruff men will fight it out to determine *my* future. *Oh, these are not my people!*

Sugarhouse could not put a name to it. Finally he said, "It's a outrage him trying to force us on to Oregon now that we're panting to go to Virginia City."

Barbara Kenny smiled. Ahead even of Thorne, she saw the weakness in the agreement. It had left the word *outrage* most general and undefined. But maybe that was how it should be. A vote of the people could declare any act of their leader an outrage and wrest leadership from him.

Looking then at Caleb Sugarhouse, she saw that he coveted the power of that position. In that moment, she realized that all his spite along the way accrued to his envy. Now he wanted to turn the party toward Virginia City. But from the first and more than anything else he had wanted to command.

Judge Thorne intervened again. "My reference was to the amendment for the privilege of the minority."

"What? Say that over."

"For the purpose, I believe, of allowing any family within the party to settle along the way if it chose, we added—it's at the end, if you're looking for it, Mr. Sugarhouse—a section stating that the wishes of the majority should not be binding upon a minority."

"What wishes?"

"Lawyer talk."

The judge said, "I disagreed at the time. During the course of our journey, however, I've come round to the opinion that it was a wise provision, indeed."

"*Damned* lawyer talk!"

"What the hell good is a vote if the majority don't rule? Didn't you say something there about the minority winning?"

Buttrell said, "I remember the provision, Caleb. Seems to me you took the other side of things when we drew it up."

"Well, I don't take that side now! It's a hell of a note when the few rules the most!"

"It doesn't mean that, Caleb," Thorne said with exaggerated patience. "It means any difference of opinion may be brought to a vote, but that the prevailing side cannot then force the smaller group to go with them."

"*God*damned lawyer talk!"

Caleb Sugarhouse was silent a moment, thinking that out. "So, if the most of us in this train was to vote to make me commander—"

"Assuming that."

"—and I was to say we take a little detour down to Virginia City *on our way* to Oregon—"

"Assuming that you should."

"—why then the other few of you wouldn't have to go along with us?"

"That's correct. It's also correct that, should those of your persuasion be the few, we couldn't force you to continue with us."

"Damn sure couldn't."

Judge Thorne was done with the discussion. "Gentlemen, the road beckons. I notice some of you cartologists have been studying your maps. You will have noticed that the road to Virginia City forks off just above Soda Springs. That gives you a day or two to consider, longer if we stand around here much more. Today, I hope to make the Bear River and solve our water problems. I'll be ringing the bell in ten minutes."

Barbara Kenny studied the judge, studied his words. *He never meant to fight Sugarhouse with his fists*, she thought. *He fought and won with words. I dislike him with very good cause. But among this group, if I must choose, I'll vote to go with him.*

24

Thoman Silverhorn waited out away from the fire half an hour before daylight. After a few minutes, Willard came to stand beside him.

"I want you to get a good early start this morning."

"Where to?"

"I want you close up on them buff hunters so's you can see their outriders. Keep to the draws as best you can.

I don't want them to see you. Don't want them to know we're tracking after them."

"Why press them, then? Why'nt we just wait until it's time to hit them?"

"You ain't hearing. I don't want you to press them. I'll bring the others on along real slow, so as not to give them no warning. I want you to see who they got on watch."

"I don't know their riders, don't know none of them."

"They's only two of them you need to know."

"I told you that's two more than I'd know."

"Don't tell me. Put your hand over your mouth and attend to me. This one of them riders, he ain't so big, ain't so small."

"I see him already."

"I told you to keep that forehoof over your smart mouth. The way you'll know him is he'll be riding a big sorrel with a blaze face and he'll have a hawk feather in his hat. Now. You see him in your head?"

Willard nodded.

"Don't shoot him."

Willard nodded again. "Can I knife him, then?"

Silverhorn scowled at him. "No, dammit! Do you see him and they're nobody else in sight, you talk to him."

"Talk?"

"It's what you're best at. He's my man in their camp. He's the one's been laying out them arrows pointing toward their camp."

"Well, he's doing a goldamned poor job. That last one took us plumb nearly to the Black Hills, and would have if Kills Running hadn't've cut their trail."

"Shut up. You can ask him about that."

"He won't shoot me?"

"No damned great loss if he did, but I've took special pains to tell him not to shoot anybody without he's give him a chance to say my name. You remember my name, don't you?"

"I'll have my hand on my gun before I say your name.

Everybody in the goldamned country's got a bounty out on you."

Silverhorn nodded. "It's gratifying to be recognized. Just don't never get the idea of trying to collect it yourself."

Willard grinned. "You said I'd need to know two of their riders. What's the other one look like?"

"Fair-haired. Tallish. Was riding a chestnut horse with white mane and tail you can see a mile away. Guns hung all over hisself and that horse. He's been dogging me like a bad tooth, and I'm tiring of it. You see him, kill him."

"I'll make a point of it. You want his scalp?"

Silverhorn pulled a gold coin out of his pocket. "I'll give you this for it."

"Keep it warm for me. I'll claim it before dark."

Ethan Fairchild rolled out of his blankets an hour before dawn to build up the fire. Uncertain whether he had heard the distant howl of a wolf or had dreamed it, he knew there would be no getting back to sleep. He tried a cup of lukewarm coffee from the pot. Heat would not have helped it. It was thick, bitter as quinine, old as rock. He emptied the grounds with the last of the black soupy liquid and filled the pot with fresh water.

Redwood Waller had been up before him and came back into the camp quietly as the shadow of a red bear slipping along the prairie. "What the hell've you done with my coffee?" he demanded.

"Good morning to you, too. That coffee was mostly grounds. It must have been in the pot a month."

"Takes a month to cure proper."

The word *cure* reminded Fairchild of the hides moldering on the wagons. It was a fitting word to apply to the buffalo hunters' coffee.

"This new'll be ready in a minute."

"It'll be ready about next Tuesday if I can keep you

racoons from turning the pot over and losing all the virtue out of it."

Fairchild saw the water beginning to boil, put in a handful of coffee, and stirred. Then he put the lid in place and let the fire do its work. "You ready to try a cup?"

"First-day green-grounds coffee? Rather drink water." He went to the wagon, pulled a jug from the jumble of goods, and took a good pull. "Thank the Lord it ain't come to that yet, though."

Fairchild shuddered, wiped the dark scum out of his cup, and filled it with bubbling coffee. "What's my duty?"

Waller jammed the cork back in his jug. "After breakfast, we'll be following the herd. You'll ride ahead of us looking for anything else that moves or looks interested in us."

"For the herd?"

Waller leaned back and bellowed a laugh. "Sure, for the herd. And look sharp!" He laughed again. "Little thing like forty thousand buffer, they're liable to slip plumb past you."

"Scout and guard, then?"

"That's right. I'll fry us up some grub. You get your breakfast, then take Eye-Shot's place while he eats. When we move, just follow the herd, if you can find their trail! They're maybe half a day ahead, moving slow."

"What if I spook them?"

"They're blamed hard to spook. If you do, they'll stampede sometimes, maybe right over you. But they won't usual even worry after we start shooting. You'll see." Waller had half a dozen slabs of bacon sizzling in a big skillet. He turned them, spilled grease, ignored the flash of flame. "Too stupid, maybe, to be afraid."

Fairchild saw Eye-Shot moving toward them through the trees. "How'd they last so long, being that stupid?"

"They're tough, strong, fast, mean. And there's God's own bounty of them. But it's my opinion they won't last long, not with all the damned people filling up the country and taking advantage of the buffs' stupidity."

Like us, Fairchild thought, but he didn't say it. Waller had turned to a young man with the front of his hat pinned up with a thorn.

"Eye-Shot, squat by the fire and I'll fry some hardtack to wrap around your bacon. You remember Fairchild. He's with us now."

Eye-Shot nodded to Fairchild. "Didn't know there was no hardtack left."

"Little green at the edges. You'll need the mold to flavor Fairchild's new coffee."

"New coffee? New *today?*"

"Sorry about that."

Fairchild took up his rifle and headed off the direction Eye-Shot had come from. Fifty feet out from the camp he crossed a set of wolf tracks. His skin moved and the hair stood on the back of his neck, but he kept going.

His job was keeping the human wolves off the hunters. His hope was to catch sight of those human wolves. When he did, his new job would be over. His real business lay with those raiders. *If I knew a quicker way to find them*, he told himself, *I'd be doing it.*

The morning was cool and his watch was uneventful. He saw nothing but a couple of antelope standing like statues against the eastern skyline. He didn't think of shooting, however. It seemed more his place to keep watch than to let every creature in earshot know where he and the hunters were.

After half an hour he went back to camp, spoke to the others, saddled his horse. Thirty yards off to the west Eye-Shot appeared along a slope and stood waiting for him.

"Glad to have you with us," the young hunter said. "Mighty glad. Can you use that rifle?"

"I can dig a hole with it when I don't have a shovel."

Eye-Shot smiled and caressed the stock of his own Sharps. "Good enough," he said. He chuckled. "Reason I'm glad is for the coffee. That stuff Red brews would make good wolf poison. See you."

He turned and angled back up the slope as quickly as

he had come. Fairchild took the other direction. *Like riding point and flank for the train*, he thought. *And look how that turned out.*

With the early sun behind him, he had an easy view of the monotonous country around. His eye was drawn to the rampart of mountains rising to the west, but he kept his attention closer to home. Waller's suggestion that he *felt* Silverhorn's gang lingered in his mind. The raiders could come from any direction. They might even be out ahead of the hunters lying in wait for them.

He stayed close enough to the buffalo trail to smell its lode of dung. Obviously, he was getting closer. He took the high path where the buffalo had trampled a narrow creek into foul-smelling slush, then angled upslope toward open land. Even then, he was amazed when he topped the rise and found the herd stretched out before him.

"Lord save us!"

After that one involuntary whisper, Fairchild held his breath in awe and fear. The closest ones were less than thirty yards away, huge, shambling, shaggy, smelly beasts, all head and shoulders and massive humped neck. Their hindquarters looked slender as a deer's. He couldn't see the far side of the herd through the haze of dust they raised in their slow, constant plod to the northwest. As far as he could tell, the buffalo paid him no mind at all. They were as indifferent to his presence as the silent mountains.

The chestnut horse was trembling. Fairchild turned it slowly and drifted out of sight below the hill. Hearing no thunder of hooves behind him, he rode back along the swath of their trail to meet the hunters. The creaking of wagons and gear told him they were down along the creek. He saw that Gawkins was not among them, probably riding rear guard somewhere to the east.

Eye-Shot Barker met him on horseback. "Found them already?"

Fairchild nodded.

"How many'd you count?"

"Count? I couldn't even see all of them at once."

"Don't matter. They's that many it's the herd."

"I expect. Want me to keep an eye on them?"

Barker laughed. "Where'll they go? You might ask Red where he wants you. Ask nice; he's mean when he ain't had his coffee."

Fairchild worked his way down to the lead wagon and found Redwood Waller. "Herd's up ahead."

"You told Eye-Shot?"

"He said you'd have a place for me."

Waller stood in his saddle, looked around. "I'm nervous some about them cannibals. I can smell them."

Fairchild doubted that. The smell of the hide wagons wasn't gamy or rank, but live and fresh and penetrating to the bone.

"But you haven't seen them?"

"Smelling don't mean they're close by. Means they're going to be. Seeing them is your job."

"How far out you want me to ride?"

"How you think best. The thing is, you don't want to act the same two days in a row or one morning and that afternoon. Else they'll be laying for you."

"You really think they're that close?"

"I wouldn't fall over in a faint if I learnt they's watching us two right now."

Fairchild felt his skin crawl, felt his hair rise. Human wolves were as stealthy and clever as the howling kind. He had pictured himself dogging Silverhorn, but now the white-haired son of a bitch was tracking him, if not watching him already. Fairchild intended to kill him, and he would if he lived. It came to him that he'd have a better chance to live if he used his eyes to the sides and behind as well as to the front.

"I don't see Gawkins. Is he on watch?"

"Gawk's sweeping around the herd to the south."

"I'll take the north."

Waller wet a finger and held it up. "Wind's in the west," he said. "Stay downwind of the buffer, whatever you do. Man-smell will spook 'em right enough. Sure, go north. Get the lay of the land and smoke out anybody hiding."

Fairchild backtracked to the previous night's camp, then went east another quarter mile to be certain no one was trailing. Rabbits and crows were busy in the knee-high grass, but Fairchild kept his attention as far out to the fringes as he could. It came to him that he hadn't seen the dumps of refuse, discarded possessions, dead and rotting animal carcasses, that littered the broad trail the Thorne wagons had taken. *We could keep the country clean*, he thought, *if we made a law that people couldn't leave the trail*.

He stayed near the creek until he found another covered draw by which to ride north. After half a mile, he cut back west. That was when he heard the first shot. It startled him, even though he had been expecting it; the hunters were at work. The shooting went on at fairly even intervals as he rode the higher land skirting the area.

Half an hour later he came back into the plain where he'd seen the buffalo. The herd had drifted a few hundred yards at the most. A puff of smoke on the far rim showed him where one of the shooters had set up, resting his heavy rifle on a rod with a cradle for the barrel. Through the wavering pall of dust, he could see here and there a buffalo on its side. The others treated its fall no more seriously than if it were taking a nap. He didn't see any movement among those on the ground, no cripples. *Professionals*, he reminded himself.

Fairchild had done his share of hunting, stalking, waiting, hoping, perhaps getting one quick shot at a startled deer. But he couldn't equate that with this calculated slaughter of the unaware. He hoped he would not be caught grazing when Silverhorn's wolves started shooting.

He turned his horse west, hearing each distant shot boom and echo like a sounding cannon working to bring the drowned to the surface. If he could hear it that clearly, anyone within a couple of miles would hear it, too. Cautiously, he strayed to the north, always scanning the distant ridges and skyline.

At mid-morning he saw movement on a lightly wooded knoll off to the northeast. He froze. There had been no glint on glass or metal, no bright show of color, no sound. He judged the knoll to be a half mile off. He might have seen an antelope or a bear, even a solitary old bull buffalo. Or it might have been, as he'd first thought, a horse with mixed colors.

In case someone had a glass on him, Fairchild turned away and kept riding. As soon as he was out of sight of the knoll, he turned straight north to come at it from a higher vantage. He was pretty certain the movement had meant nothing, but pretty certain wasn't enough. He picked his way to the high ground that ran down toward the knoll, waited, watched. Leaving the unwilling chestnut, he darted across the ridge and the backslope until he was close to the knoll. Seeing and hearing nothing but birds which should have been quiet if anyone were near, he walked down to it.

The knoll turned out to be clear for ten or twelve yards across the top, rocky enough to show no prints. Finally, he found what he was looking for. The hoofprint lay where dirt had silted into a shallow basin. One print left by a shod horse. It was very fresh.

Fairchild had the thought that a wiser man wouldn't have left his horse and come on foot to the middle of a wilderness. Not knowing if that other rider was looking at him down a rifle barrel, he made no sharp moves but returned to the Devil as briskly as he could walk without running. It nickered at him before he could see it. *No luck like fool's luck*, he thought, and the chestnut tossed its head in seeming agreement.

It took him several minutes of casting about to find the trail left by the other horse. It had been walking steadily toward the eastern end of the ridge. Not wanting to follow the trail right into the muzzle of a rifle, Fairchild circled back, then made his way slowly along the northern slope.

Finally he tied his Devil to a clump of sage, knowing anyone who tried to steal the horse would get the treatment he deserved, and walked through the brush to that point where the ridge began sloping back toward the plain.

The other horse nickered at him the moment he stepped out of the brush. Hobbled on the north side of the ridge, the gray horse had his ears pricked, his wild eyes fixed on Fairchild. The first bullet ripped through the brush close by his shoulder. He hit the ground, crawled backward, rolled away to one side. He expected more bullets to come seeking him, but the other man was not wasteful with his powder.

Slinking back, Fairchild managed another look at the clearing. A gaunt man with a scraggly beard was loosing the hobbles on the gray, glancing around furtively, stepping up into the saddle. He still held his revolver.

Just as the rider whirled his horse, Fairchild stood, swinging up the Colt rifle. It was in his mind to order the man to stop, but the rider saw him, clawed the gray back around, and fired wildly. He was bringing the pistol down for another try when Fairchild's bullet tumbled him off his horse.

Fairchild whistled, but the gray horse wasn't having any; thoroughly spooked, it tore along the ridge and back out into the plain until Fairchild lost it. Shrugging, he walked across to the fallen rider, hoping to find some sign of what he'd been up to.

The man crabbed around like a crippled wolf, scrabbling for the fallen pistol. Fairchild took a quick step and kicked it away, then thrust the rifle's muzzle down until it almost touched the wounded man's face.

"Shoot, goldamn you," the man wheezed. "You've done for me. Get it over!"

Fairchild bent, grabbed the man by the shirt, tore a small golden stickpin from the lapel. "You took this from Elgin Bradley," he said. "Sometime in the last couple of weeks."

The other hocked up a mouthful of blood and spat it at Fairchild's boots. "Didn't—ask his name," he gasped.

"I want to know about the girl."

"Goldamn." The oath came out rumbling, blood-frothed.

"What're you going to do about it? Kill me?" Hard hit and bleeding heavily, the man found his thought amusing. He tried to laugh but it came out "Hell."

"Not kill you." Fairchild kicked him in the ribs, felt the cartilage give. The man's voice went to a bubbling scream. "Not right off. Where's the girl?"

White-faced, the man spat, fought for breath. "Wasn't me!" he said.

"Wasn't you what?" When the man failed to answer, Fairchild aimed at the same spot, felt bones yield before his toe. "I'll keep you alive long enough to break every bone you've got. Now. What did you do with the girl?"

Curled in agony, the man coughed for a long time. Just when Fairchild thought he'd pressed him too hard, he gasped out, "Wasn't me. Grace. Silverhorn give her—to Grace." His tortured face twisted into a snarl. "Wish it had—been me. Known she was yours, I'd skinned her."

Fairchild kicked him hard enough to lift him off the ground, drew back his foot again.

"Wait! I never seen her! Goldamned squaw said she done it. Worse. I never—"

"You didn't see her dead?"

Fresh blood welled in the man's mouth, overflowed down his cheek. He shook his head. Looking up at Fairchild, he said, "Finish me."

"Where's Silverhorn now?"

"Fin—"

"I'll finish you." Fairchild put the muzzle of his rifle in the man's face. "If you tell me where to find Silverhorn. He sent you out here to die. Tell me where to find him and I'll even the score for you."

The man arched his spine like a poisoned dog. He seemed to be trying to speak, to gasp out some last word, but all that came was a flood of bright arterial blood. He stretched out shaking hands toward Fairchild, shuddered all over his body, then dropped back stiffly into the bloody grass.

Fairchild walked the area beyond the body. From the sloping ridge he could see a greener spot not far below. The plusher foliage surrounded a spring. A young woman's voice flowed from the spring murmuring *I never thought you'd go without me.* "No, nor leave you to die," Fairchild said. "God knows it should have been me instead!"

And then his thoughts turned on him to drive him down on his knees with the suggestion that David Stuart might no more have intended to leave him to die.

Fairchild crawled to the spring and drank like a man dying of thirst. As he raised his head, wiping his mouth with the back of his hand, he saw a few yards off a row of white stones laid out in the shape of an arrow.

"Hell," he said.

He heard a horse running toward him, lifted his rifle, saw the gray stop at its rider's body. Fairchild spoke softly to the horse, caught him up, and tied the body across his saddle. Then he led him back to Devil, and set off toward the distant camp. *Had this man laid out the arrow or found it there by the spring?* A voice whispered in the breeze around his ears.

You'll never come back to me. "I will when I die. It won't be long."

Waller had told him not to be predictable, and he was beginning to think that good advice. He took a different route back to camp. When he realized that they had quit shooting, he figured it must be nearly noon. Then he saw that the buffalo were moving.

The movement had barely begun at the fringes when the entire herd surged into motion like dark lightning that set off its own rumble of thunder. Fairchild spurred the chestnut hard north, trying to draw clear of their path, hauling at the reins to drag along the gray and its bloody cargo. The ground shook under the pounding hooves, and a roll of dust hid everything except himself and the straining Devil until they crossed a ridge into light and open air.

When the thunder died to a distant murmur, Fairchild rode to camp. Leaving the two horses around a bend in the draw, he strode in. Gawkins had a fresh fire going and a pot of beans bubbling. "Sit yourself, Dusty," he hailed Fairchild. "Get yourself a plate. You look like them buffs stampeded right over you."

"Feel like I breathed most of their dust." Fairchild stretched. "Guess I'll wait a bit before I eat."

"Wait too long and there won't be nothing. But I got a mess of buffer tongue roasting. Be done shortly."

Redwood Waller came up on foot, carrying two long rifles. He took a cup of today's coffee and drank it off without complaint. Then he turned to Fairchild. "You see anything this morning?"

Fairchild said, "I've got something to report."

Waller followed him down to the horses, looked at the body slung across its horse. "Something to report! Is that what you call it?"

"Found him up by a spring in the hills. He's one of those that's dogging you."

Waller pursed his lips. "He tell you that?"

"He did."

"This one won't dog nobody no more," he said.

Fairchild was surprised that a man's death should disturb Waller who had slaughtered hundreds of buffalo. "There's plenty of others. I found a row of rocks made into an arrow pointing right to this camp."

"He make it?"

"I don't know. But if he didn't make it, he knew where to look for it."

Waller's face went dark. "Who'd be spying for him?"

Fairchild shook his head. "You'd know better than I. But Silverhorn can't be too far back. What if we go for them now, wipe them out before they come for us?"

Waller shook his head. "We don't know where they are or how many," he said. "And we've got a damned Judas at our backs. Better we wait and look sharp."

"How about me riding back to scout them?"

"Can't afford to lose you. I figure you couldn't help but lay into them by your lonesome." Waller lifted the dead man's head by his hair, looked at his face. "Never seen him. We'll let the others have a look before we bury him."

None of the others admitted to knowing him. Fairchild offered to dig the grave.

"Let the dead bury the dead?" Waller said, and laughed more than Fairchild thought that deserved. "No, Baldy and Saul'll do the burying for what's in his mouth and his pockets. I want you to do like I said."

"How's that?"

"Wait. Ride wide and cover us while we're skinning out today's kill and pegging down the hides." Waller looked more solemn than Fairchild had ever seen him. "And look sharp," he said. "Damned sharp."

25

Douglas Stuart had said little during the arguments over the train's route, but he'd turned the matter deeply in his mind. And, as Thorne had said sarcastically a few days before, he'd studied his map, penciling in lines for new roads where there had been none. One of the routes he'd learned of from Oral Tibbs ran from Soda Springs across to the City of Rocks in the edge of Nevada. It was another cutoff, especially if a person wanted to go to Virginia City.

Tramping beside his wagon at an ox's pace toward the

sunset, he thought about it. Sugarhouse had demanded a meeting of the company that evening. Stuart suspected he planned to call for some kind of vote, a showdown over leadership of the train. He was sure Sugarhouse had too few votes to overturn Thorne as leader, let alone to swing the party toward Virginia City. Which wouldn't matter, since no one could coerce the minority. Because he was Davy's uncle, the men assumed he was with Thorne. In fact, Douglas Stuart had gradually thought himself over toward the Sugarhouse side.

He gave one of his rare smiles. Sugarhouse would be surprised, no less than Thorne, that mild, conservative Douglas Stuart would run after a silver boom. Certainly, Davy had been surprised when Stuart carefully broached the matter to him.

"You, Uncle Douglas? You're the last one I could imagine digging for silver."

"I've no thought of digging, lad. In a rough and sinful mining camp, the services of a master gunsmith will be beyond price. I'd meant to let them bring the silver to me."

"I hadn't thought of that."

"Nor had I, until lately." He paused, then said, "If you were still minded to be my apprentice, you could try your hand at the mines, with a respectable job if that failed."

Davy had thought that over. "I don't know," he said. "I have responsibilities now. There's Jessica to think of."

"Aye. And Virginia City will be no place for a young lady. You'd have to leave Jessica behind."

"I'll think it over."

Up ahead the wagons were swinging out to the right into a ground where they would camp for the night and the next night as well. The steaming alkali waters of Soda Springs were undrinkable, but the women of the train had planned for weeks upon washing clothes there. Keeping his own counsel, Stuart attended to his stock and ate a silent supper.

He was equally silent when Manasseh Thorne called

everyone together after the meal, and while Thorne and Sugarhouse flogged their way through the whole matter again. Only when everyone seemed as sick of hearing the arguments as the speakers were of presenting them did Douglas Stuart rise and ask to be recognized.

Manasseh Thorne stared as though he'd never seen him before. "Douglas?" he said. "Have you a word for us?"

"Aye, so I have." Stuart wasn't used to speaking in public. It brought out his Scots burr more strongly than usual, but he made the best of it. "It's my idea there's no need to part our ways sae soon. The freighters mentioned a route called the Hudspeth Cutoff, from here across to City of Rocks. Should we follow it, we could save time and miles."

"But we'd miss Fort Hall."

"Aye, so we would. But those who wish to go to Nevada would be closer, and those who favor the high trail to Oregon would not be far off it; and we'd all have that much longer together to weigh the matter."

Perhaps because each group thought him to be on its side, or perhaps because no one had ever heard him say so much in one week, the members applauded Stuart. He felt his cheeks get hot, and he glanced from side to side to see that they really approved and weren't merely making fun of him.

Although his face did not seem to agree with his own words, Sugarhouse said, "Makes sense." Men of both parties looked at each other, shrugged, nodded their agreement. At last Manasseh Thorne spoke up.

"As wagonmaster, I'm properly in charge of picking our route. But even I can find no reason to argue with what Douglas says." That brought a laugh, and Thorne smiled. "We'll have our vote, if you're ready."

A cheer interrupted him, one that seemed split about evenly among those on either side. Thorne waited until it died down, thinking it a good sign that they could agree to cheer.

"But I must point out that we have little information

on this Hudspeth Cutoff. It's certainly the shorter route, but it wouldn't be the first cutoff that was a harder passage than the long way." He gestured to the west, toward the frowning ridges beyond the river. "That's what we must cross."

"Looks pretty rough," Hiram Miller said doubtfully.

"No worse than California Hill."

"I remind you also that if we bypass Fort Hall, we may some of us run short of supplies."

"Aw, hell," Joe Coates said. "He's trying to talk us out of it again."

"No, listen," Will Buttrell protested. "He's right about the supplies."

"He's trying to scare us off."

The discussion spread, threatened to drown Thorne out. He raised his hands.

"Joe and you others, I'm not trying to change your minds. Nor am I opposing Douglas. It's my duty as wagonmaster to interject practical considerations. We run risks any way we choose to go. Let's understand those risks before we vote."

The contending voices weren't stilled. After a moment, Caleb Sugarhouse's boom rode above everything else.

"No, listen," the big man said. "Manasseh's right. Best we think it through."

In the startled silence, Thorne beckoned to Sugarhouse. "Caleb, you have the floor."

"Well, I ain't the hand you are at orating," Sugarhouse said, but he stepped up beside Thorne. "Let's try it this way. Anybody specially short on supplies?"

Husbands looked at wives. Families consulted. "We lost some things at the river crossing," Caroline Espy said. "Corn meal and flour, mostly. We'll need more pretty soon. Those kids eat like a tribe of locusts."

"Warner ain't no slouch, hisself," somebody said.

Barbara Kenny raised her hand. "I have more than I need, since there's only me. I can share with you."

Both Espys looked surprised. "Why, thank you, Miz Kenny," Warner said. "Right neighborly."

"I do have an ox that's not looking well," Barbara added. "I'd meant to buy another at Fort Hall."

Manasseh Thorne said, "We still have—how many, David?—several in the common herd."

"Eight or nine, I think."

"There. If needs be, you can draw upon them." Thorne looked around. "Anyone else?"

"I thought these weren't your people," Fred Harris murmured, leaning closer to Barbara.

"They aren't," she whispered back. "But the train's stronger if we stay together."

He watched her eyes. "And maybe by the time we reach the end of the cutoff, you'll have made up your own mind?"

She nodded quickly and turned back toward Thorne.

Sugarhouse was making a joke, saying he'd "found more trading posts along the way than the guidebook gave us leave to expect." He laughed. "More than I had money to buy at, anyways." Then they laughed with him. "So I figure chances are that Fort Hall wouldn't be the only place we could find supplies."

"That's the truth."

"Let's vote."

Wagonmaster Thorne said, "We've no motion to vote on." He looked at Sugarhouse, offered him the chance to make the motion. Sugarhouse didn't trust him.

In the interim, Will Buttrell said, "I move we keep the train together, until we get to the City of Rocks, anyhow, by taking this Hudspeth Cutoff."

Almost as many applauded as had clapped for Stuart. Douglas Stuart wished that he'd had the wit to phrase his comment as a motion, but he didn't worry about it. Whoever got the credit, he'd helped in keeping the group together. Since he might likely take the silver trail himself, he did not want the bad feelings to start any sooner than needful. And he feared his decision would mean parting with Davy.

David Stuart hadn't said much himself. He was caught, as it seemed to him. He knew now that his uncle was leaning toward the silver fields. He himself hadn't rejected the idea entirely. Left to his own choosing, he would cheerfully have followed the lure of riches.

But he was no longer left to himself. *You'd have to leave Jessica behind.* Once before, he'd had to leave someone behind. Though the circumstances were different, the decision still haunted him.

Then, there was Manasseh Thorne. He felt a debt to Thorne, for being Jess's father, for agreeing to the wedding, for his actions since. *Hell,* he reminded himself, *Thorne's given me a position of trust. I can't go against him now. A wolf's more faithful than that.*

He put his arm around Jess and looked into her eyes. He couldn't read her thoughts on the matter. But the others were voting. "What're we doing?" he asked her.

"Voting to stay together."

He raised his hand. Almost everyone did.

"At least until we get to City of Rocks. Weren't you listening?"

Stuart shook his head. "Sorry."

An hour later they climbed into their wagon, got ready for bed. Jessica said, "Davy?"

"Yes." He was getting undressed while he looked out the wagon flap to see how the camp was faring.

"You do think it's safer, staying together?"

"Sure. There's safety in—"

"A bundle of sticks!"

"Yes." He laughed at her mimick of her father's voice. He tried it himself. "One stick is easily broken."

"But numbers are tough!"

He laughed again. "I love you," he told her.

"No!" she whispered. "Surely not!"

"Want proof?"

"Constantly. But you do want to go to Virginia City, don't you?"

"Me?" He looked back toward her. "No. Why?"

"I've seen something in your eyes."

"Dust."

"Davy."

"There may not be any silver." She started to interrupt, but he added, "Even if there really is silver, and I really did go there to find it, where would I dig?"

"Seems like there really is. What do you mean where would you dig? In the ground!"

"Do you own any ground in Virginia City? Or anywhere in Nevada?"

"As much as I do in Oregon."

"If there was any land unclaimed, it had claim markers all over it ten minutes after somebody said the word *silver*."

"Even so."

He heard a tone of disappointment in her voice. Turning, he looked at her. "Do you *want* me to go? I'd be away for God knows how long."

"*What?*" She sat up suddenly, heedless of the blanket slipping away. "Away? From me? What are you talking about?"

Stuart blinked, distracted. "Nonsense, Jess," he said. "I'm talking nonsense." He could believe that she'd thought of going. It excited him to think so, but it called to mind all the good reasons for not going. "You don't think I'd take you to a place like that."

"You don't think you could leave me behind!"

For a moment, they glared at each other. Then Jessica started to laugh. "Well," she said cheerfully. "We don't have to worry about that anymore!"

She was right, Stuart thought half ruefully. He had talked himself out of the whole idea. "I didn't know you'd ever given it a thought," he said.

"Are you crazy?" She laughed. "I'd given it two or

three thoughts. But now I can set it aside as foolishness. I don't own any dirt in Nevada!" She held out her arms. "Don't sit and stare like a booby. Come over here. Let's see some of that proof."

Two mornings later the Thorne train turned onto the slightly fainter ruts of Hudspeth's Cutoff. David Stuart left at first light to scout the trail ahead, came back in time for a quick breakfast and a report to Thorne, and led the wagons out of the camp before the sun had topped the western mountains.

He didn't mind changing trails and plans. Since he would never see the trail to Fort Hall, he could easily believe they'd chosen a better route with a better view. The trail ran for a time along the curve of the Bear River, then began to climb the west side of the valley. Before long, the way grew steep. At the crest of the first climb, Stuart reined in to look back toward the train.

There the wind was colder. He buttoned his coat to the chin. The wagons had stopped just at the foot of the grade. He could make out men going back to a wagon that had fallen out of line.

"Shoot."

Stuart looked at his watch. They hadn't been on the road a full hour. He couldn't count the times Thorne had warned them. *Check your wagons over at night*, he'd told them. Warm axle bearings might turn without complaint in the evening, then lock up completely in the early cold of morning if they needed grease. Stuart scanned the country ahead, shrugged, then rode back to see what was holding up the train.

A knot of men had gathered at Barbara Kenny's wagon. Stuart figured he could guess why she hadn't checked her wagon the evening before. He also figured he would be a poor one to throw stones. But the problem wasn't with the wagon, nor with the widow Kenny. The nigh off ox of her team was down on its knees, its head hanging limply.

"Joe, can you get Doc Harris?" Stuart said. "Got a patient for him. Oh, hello, Fred. Can you look at this ox?"

"It's the one she said." Harris dismounted from the nondescript gelding he rode. "I've been out on flanker. Can somebody get my bag?"

Harris knelt beside the beast and went over it with those big hands of his. From horseback twenty feet away, Stuart thought the ox was dead, but Harris called for help to lift the animal's head. "We'll have to get him out of the yoke," he said.

Standing in the shade of Stuart and his horse, Sugarhouse whispered up to the rider. "Didn't need a damned doctor to tell us that!" He laughed. "I expect Thorne'll have a service and read over the ox and look to us to give him Christian burial."

In spite of himself, Stuart smiled. "Well, maybe not so bad as that," he said mildly.

"Hell!" Sugarhouse said. "We're about to lose another day because of that fool woman trying to manage a wagon alone. Shouldn't never have allowed it."

Stuart started to ask when they had lost a day on Barbara Kenny's account. Perhaps the big rough man was blaming her for the runaway ferry. At the last second, he held his tongue. He didn't want an argument, particularly not with Sugarhouse. The train was peaceful, at least until they reached the City of Rocks. With a noncommittal grunt, Stuart got off his horse and went over to help with the ox.

The ox was not dead. Its sides heaved in short, shallow drafts. Its blackened tongue hung out and its nostrils looked unusually dry.

"Fever?" Stuart asked.

Harris glanced at him hard enough to chasten him but quickly enough to keep the rest from noticing. "Let's back the wagon away and give him a chance to catch his breath."

Stuart and five or six others put their backs to the wagon while Barbara coaxed the oxen backward. "Is he going to be all right, then?" she asked.

Harris shook his head. "Oh, no. He's pulled his last mile."

"You didn't answer me about the fever," Stuart murmured.

Harris looked around quickly, saw that most of the men were going off about their business. "No need to get people worrying about that again. Anyway, I don't think so." Harris frowned. "It looks like the alkali poisoning."

"I'll tell Mr. Thorne."

"Tell him it wasn't Mrs. Kenny's fault."

Stuart met Thorne coming back from his lead wagon, lighting his pipe. "I understand someone didn't check her livestock before we started," Thorne said between puffs.

"The doctor says it's alkali poisoning. I think maybe the ox was just used up. Want me to cut one out of the herd?"

Thorne had another try at lighting the pipe. "Of course. Her husband paid his part, and I promised her we'd make one available." He stroked his beard. "I'll grant I didn't expect it quite so soon."

"She did mention it."

"What?"

"She told us about the ox when we were voting."

Thorne drew at his pipe. "So she did. How many are left in the common herd?"

"I'll get you a count when I bring the ox."

Stuart went halfway back along the train to the little herd of livestock. It was Francis Buttrell's turn to haze them along. Stuart counted only six. One of those belonged to Milt Ames, who was resting it and using train stock in its place, strictly against the wagonmaster's policy.

"Morning, Fran," Stuart said. "Mrs. Kenny's going to need one of the herd. Can you catch up the best one and bring him up to her wagon?"

"I can. But I'm supposed to stay here."

That was true. Stuart decided he was getting too accustomed to delegating work to others. "You're a good man," he said, and rode among the oxen. They parted lazily before him. It came to him to wonder whether it wasn't a better idea after all to rotate them so as to keep them all in fair shape.

One turned from him and lumbered away as if to refuse service. Stuart immediately chose him, cut off his clumsy retreat, and drove him up to Barbara Kenny's wagon. Ames helped him wrestle the unruly animal into the yoke and hitch it to the drawbar. Barbara Kenny was standing beside Harris who still knelt by her fallen ox.

"Well?"

"I can't tell you if he'll get up again. If we leave him, he may get stronger. There's a chance he'd survive."

Caleb Sugarhouse had come up to survey the situation. "Might as well shoot him," was his opinion. "But then Thorne'll want to butcher him for the meat, and we'll be out another couple of hours." He snorted like an angry boar. "If we'd took mules to start with, we'd be most of the way to Virginia City. But no, you people knew best when you chose these oxen."

"Give me a few minutes," Harris said. "Maybe I can get him up."

"If you leave him on his own, he wouldn't last long among the wolves," Stuart said. He had been thinking about it, thinking about Ethan Fairchild and what might have happened to his body.

"Hell, it'd save us hitching up a team to drag him, if he'd just get up and walk over there as far as them bushes."

Harris said, "If I get him up, it won't be for you to shoot."

Sugarhouse put a heavy hand on the doctor's shoulder. "If I take a notion to shoot him, I'll shoot him, being you don't carry a gun to finish off your mistakes."

Harris got to his feet. He was taller than Stuart had ever

noticed. Stronger. But Harris had forgotten the rest of them. His eyes took in nothing but Sugarhouse.

"I want you to understand something, Sugarhouse."

"Whoa-ho!" Sugarhouse said. He grinned at the doctor. "What've we got here?"

"You, sir, are a common bully. I have given you every opportunity to display yourself as a gentleman. You have taken every opportunity to demonstrate that you are not. To the point of this moment, I warn you that this ox belongs to Mrs. Kenny. Lay your hand to it without her leave, and you'll answer to me."

"To you?"

Sugarhouse blinked, apparently unable to find anywhere to put a load of language of that sort. Stuart was equally unbelieving. But he saw the big man's face redden as he realized that Harris was insulting him, that men were staring.

Barbara Kenny saw the same thing, faster than Stuart. "Just a moment," she said.

Sugarhouse didn't even glance at her. Harris said, "Please, Barbara. This has nothing to do with you."

"Nothing to do with me? It's my blessed ox!"

But Stuart saw that Harris was right. The doctor's anger had nothing to do with the ailing animal; it stemmed from something in Sugarhouse's rough joking. And Sugarhouse was about to express his own frustration and impatience and general bad temper by pounding Harris into beefsteak. Sugarhouse took a half step, his big fists raised. Feeling like an idiot, Stuart stepped between the two men.

"Caleb," he said.

It stopped Sugarhouse. Stuart had never used his Christian name before. He blinked, turned his head, looked at Stuart.

"Fred," Stuart said, "let it be."

"A gentleman does not tamper with a lady's stock without her leave," Harris said, but it was all right. Stuart saw Caleb Sugarhouse's eyes clear. He could almost read the big man's thoughts.

What the hell do I care about Kenny's sick ox? If I make a fight of this thing, I'll lose ground with some that haven't decided whether they're with me or not. He backed away a step, relaxed his fists.

"By God, sir, I wouldn't tamper with another person's stock! I only meant I'd do it for you since you haven't no gun."

"That's quite different."

Manasseh Thorne had come up behind them. "Gentlemen," he said, "are we falling out over a draft animal?"

Sugarhouse shook his head, shrugged his shoulders, held his hands open.

Harris said, "I've fallen out with him, all right."

Thorne frowned in surprise. "You'd get crossways over an ox?"

"Over a woman's property," Harris insisted. Then he stopped. A more familiar expression came across his face. He blushed.

Sugarhouse smiled. "Manasseh," he said, his voice smooth as honey spilling from the hive. "We've had us a misunderstanding here, and it's of my making for sure."

Thorne stared at him. Stuart almost laughed.

"In my desire to be of service to Miz Kenny, I've misspoke myself and give Dr. Harris the idea that I would bring harm to her stock. I offer my apology to them both."

For a moment, all stared openmouthed, unspeaking. Then Thorne said, "Harris? That all right with you?"

Harris hesitated until Barbara Kenny grasped his arm.

"Thank you, Mr. Sugarhouse," she said. "I accept your apology." She gave Harris a little shake. "We're ready to forget the entire matter."

Thorne said, "Fine. Now let's get our ox into the ditch!"

Stuart laughed first. Not that it was all that funny, but if Thorne had ever intentionally made a joke, Stuart couldn't remember it.

"Get the ox *in* the ditch!" Sugarhouse said, suddenly understanding. "Ah-ha-ha!"

Then the others began to join in. After a moment everyone within earshot was laughing.

Even Harris smiled. "Give me a minute," he said. He filled his hat from the water barrel, then threw the water in the ox's face. The ox rolled its eyes, flared its nostrils, shook its head. Harris took it by the horns and twisted its head as sharply as he could. The animal drew in its tongue and gave a deep bleat of protest. When it tried to get up, Hiram Miller joined Harris at tugging on its horns. Sugarhouse grabbed its tail and twisted. On their third try, the ox got its back feet on the ground, heaved up its rump, and stood unsteadily.

The group cheered. Harris brought it another hatful of water, let it drink. Then, while Sugarhouse twisted its tail, Harris hazed it back to join the other free-running oxen.

"It'll keep up or it won't," he said to Sugarhouse's question. "At least it's got a chance."

"Dr. Harris," Thorne said with deep gravity, "if you have completed your medical efforts, may I now get my dad-blamed wagon train moving again?"

With equal gravity, Fred Harris swept off his hat and bowed. "Judge Thorne," he said, "you may."

Before they found a spot level enough to make camp for the evening, they had spent a couple of hours double-teaming the wagons up a steep, rocky trail through a cut that made the stoutest of them wonder why anybody had ever followed Hudspeth across his cutoff.

Sugarhouse spent the day counting up in his mind who was with him and who was against. Ames and Joe Coates and a couple more were ready to start for the silver fields. Hiram Miller was leaning that way, egged on by his wife. Douglas Stuart seemed interested.

Thorne, of course, had his ears laid back and his heels dug in, hell-bent to go to Oregon. Davy Stuart and his new wife would go along, if only for peace in the family.

Lije and Sarah Holden had made it clear land was more important to them than silver.

The others, so far as Sugarhouse could see, were undecided. The Buttrells had enough young'uns to dig up half the mountains in Nevada, but they were worried about the desert crossing. The Lees, Doc Harris and the Kenny woman, and all the others might still be persuaded either way.

Somewhere below those thoughts he could put into words, Caleb Sugarhouse began to worry. It was one thing to envy Thorne's leadership of the train, and part of that same thing to wart half the members into mutiny. But the closer he came to the role of leadership, the more Sugarhouse felt the depths of gray and unspoken dreads. Tonight his uneasiness took the form of a molten lump of ore that stuck in his stomach, put him off his feed at supper, and kept him awake long past midnight.

26

"Blue Eye," Thoman Silverhorn said, "I've been thinking."

The Pawnee nodded. "That is well," he said gravely. "There is much for Silverhorn to think on. It is better to get wisdom than gold."

Silverhorn scowled. From the wreckage of Bradley's Oak, Blue Eye had salvaged a gray frock coat of Elgin Bradley's and a tall beaver hat. Between the clothing and the tags of Bible talk he'd picked up from the missionary who'd taught him English as a boy, he reminded Silverhorn of a hawk-faced circuit preacher.

"I'd rather have the gold."

"The idols of the heathen are silver and gold."

"Listen," Silverhorn began, then got hold of himself. He could never tell about the Pawnee. White men were easy to read. Men like Longdon or Farley West or even Willard, with his big mouth and his small ideas, never fooled him for a second. Indians were different, and Silverhorn's own mixture of Indian blood seemed to give him no help. He was never quite sure they weren't laughing at him.

"Listen," he said again. "I want you to ride out ahead."

A gleam of interest showed in Blue Eye's face. "Willard rides out ahead."

"That's why. Willard don't know to put on his hat when it rains. He should have got hisself back here before now. You go see what's become of him. Don't get close enough for them hunters to see you, just for you to see them."

"And when I see what's become of him?"

Silverhorn had been thinking about it most of the day. "Bring Willard back here," he said. "Oh. If that man with all the guns is out away from them hunters, kill him. If you see anybody else, stay away from them."

"I do not speak if your man comes out away from them hunters?"

"You know about him?" Silverhorn stared hard with his one eye. "You know which one he is?"

Blue Eye nodded.

"You know more than you need to."

"Wisdom resteth in the heart of him that hath understanding. You spoke to Willard of a scalp. Of a gold piece for a scalp."

"You got too good of ears. Gets you tangled up in other folks' business."

"The workman is worthy of his hire."

"You bring back the gun-man's scalp and we'll talk about the coin."

"The words of a wise man's mouth are gracious, but—"

"God*damn* it!" Silverhorn cried. "All right, you thieving heathen! The coin for the scalp. Just you be good and damned sure it's the right scalp. I ain't paying for just any old piece of hair."

Blue Eye nodded. "Happy is the man that findeth wisdom. I go."

Blue Eye rode away at the canter he always used when he set the pace. He had no trouble following Willard's trail, even when it disappeared from the mass of prints on the main buffalo swath and ascended a rocky slope. The Indian rode up the hill where there were no visible tracks, knowing the trail had to reappear, having a pretty good idea where that would be.

When the trail did not reappear, Blue Eye paused, looking at the ground and working out a new appreciation for Willard. He had not believed Willard capable of laying a trail so difficult to follow. The tracks turned up again finally, Blue Eye never having doubted that they would. After that, he paid more attention, studied the tricks Willard had used to cover his trail.

He took for granted the way the white man had kept the ridge between him and that area where the buffalo hunters had most likely been working. When the trail suddenly crossed the ridge and dropped down across a flat spot where a rider would be clearly visible for several hundred yards, Blue Eye reined up to puzzle over it. Dismounting, he removed his beaver hat and lay in the short grass at the crest, studying the grassy meadow and lower ridge.

A faint pall of thin dust hung like smoke in the air beyond that second ridge. Buffalo. Buffalo without number, like the sands of the sea. Blue Eye had never seen the sea, but he knew the buffalo had been on the plain, had run away in haste. The hunters would be busy now with their skinning.

Still on his belly, he slid over the crest and slithered down through the low cover to the clearing. Willard had kept his horse to the rocks so as to leave no tracks. But in the middle of the clearing lay one clear hoofmark, a shod horse. Willard's horse. Blue Eye could not be certain what Willard had intended. Had he been drawing a rider up to meet him, or had he become careless? White men often got distracted by small things of no importance. The one who had left his bootprints beside the print of Willard's horse had not been careful.

When he was certain which way Willard had gone, he crawled back over the ridge to his horse and paralleled the trail to the lower reaches of the ridge. He was looking for the man who made tracks on foot, but he smelled the soft mosses and damp ground of a spring. He saw the stone arrow before he saw the spring. The arrow pointed straight at him.

Unsettled, he dismounted, tied his horse, and crept up to a bastion of rock that jutted suddenly from the face of the ridge. He wanted a different view of the spring with its arrow pointing not toward the buffalo hunters but toward Blue Eye. They did not like him, that arrow, that spring. It was a bad sign. No men or buffalo lay behind him in the direction the arrow pointed. No. It was aimed at him, and at One-Eye Silverhorn. He did not like it. It made him smell blood where there was no blood.

He lay in a bed of soft grass and studied the spring with its ominous arrow. Many signs and tracks lay around the spring, but he did not wish to examine them. He slipped away down the eastern side of the ridge where the arrow might not be able to follow him. The smell of blood became stronger, not a spirit-smell, a real scent that warned him death lay ahead. Had a wounded buffalo found this place to die? He didn't think so.

Blue Eye was close before he saw it. The darkened red mass on the grass and ground startled him, drew him back to the reality of real and strong danger. He knew the footprints of Willard as well as he knew his own. And he saw among them the prints of that other man. He read the scene immediately. Willard had fallen and died in that spot. The arrow had not been meant for him but for Willard. Blue Eye studied the bootprints of a second man, the hoofprints which had led him to that spot, the milling tracks of Willard's horse.

When the tracks left that place they fell in beside the tracks of the other man's horse. The one who killed Willard had taken him west and south on his own horse. Had it been the man with many guns? He couldn't tell. It could have been any of their outriders. It might even have been the man Silverhorn trusted in their camp. But if he saw the tracks again, man or horse, he would know them.

Because the sun was coursing low in the sky, Blue Eye turned and loped along beneath the ridge for fifty yards before he crawled again to the top. He spent several minutes watching the country. At last he saw a rider looping out from the distant trees of that far ridge. The rider was not the man of many guns. Nor was he the man of Silverhorn's trusting.

Blue Eye went back to his horse and rode a bit north of east in order to put himself well out of sight and range of the rider. After a mile, he turned back south to the trail of the buffalo. Then he rode straight to Silverhorn.

Silverhorn was not pleased. "Who killed him?"

Blue Eye shrugged.

"Hell," he said. "Now I'm short a man and you've probably left them a trail right to me."

Blue Eye said nothing. The One-Eye should know better. His words were as the crackling of thorns under a pot. Blue Eye had left no trail for the hunters to follow. But he also had brought no fair scalp, would get no gold coin.

"Well, get over there and eat. You're going to need it before long."

Thoman Silverhorn was uneasy. Grace could see it in the set of his shoulders, in the brooding frown that hung on his brow. More, she could guess the reason. Willard's loss and the report Blue Eye had brought worried him, especially the part about the arrow. There was something worrisome about the arrow, something personal.

Grace had planned to slip away up the gully where they'd made camp while the sky was before dark. She wanted to read farther in the book the old man had told her about before he died. The old man had said it was worth a lot. Though she hadn't read a book since her child days at St. Mary's Mission, she was remembering how. But she decided she'd better stay around camp for now. She didn't want Silverhorn to know about the book.

"Grace."

She'd taken another book, too, one the old man had seemed to set great store by. It was small and blue, with a white man's cross worked in gold on the cover. She hadn't had time to read it, had seen only that it opened easily to certain places and was filled with tiny print.

"Grace! Damn you, woman, pay attention!"

Grace hadn't realized Silverhorn was speaking to her. He so seldom used her name that it sounded strange from his mouth. She turned toward him, suspicious. He smiled broadly and beckoned to her.

"Grace. Get yourself over here, woman. I got a job for you."

She waited long enough for him to notice, then grinned. "All right, Tom." Rising, she shook down the folds of the dirty blue dress, careful to give West and Longdon a look at her legs. "Just any little thing you want!"

"How about me, Grace, when you're finished with Thoman?" Farley West wanted to know.

"Maybe with your horse. He smells better," she said, and grinned when West cursed her.

Silverhorn watched, scowling. "Whore," he muttered. "Come over here, away from all them long ears."

She followed him down the winding course of the gully for twenty yards or so. When he stopped, she put her arms around him and nestled close.

"This what you want, Thoman?"

"Not that." He pushed her away, scowling. "I want you to kill a man."

Grace turned her head to look along the gully. She could see the faint glow of the fire where Longdon and West and the two Pawnee tore at the meat which was their supper.

"Which one? West is the one needs killing. Rafe's all right. If you want the Pawnees killed, you'd better do it."

"Not them. That one you say you killed before."

"Fair—" Grace bit her lip. She'd almost made a mistake. The leather-backed book had told her about the man. Like an Indian name, maybe. "Fair-hair with many guns."

Silverhorn nodded.

"About time you were minded to ask me. You should have sent me first."

"I'm sending you now. I want him out of my way."

"Be night soon."

Silverhorn laughed. "You do your best hunting in the night," he said. "Blue Eye'll tell you where they are. If you get there before it's total dark, might be you can pick him out, get right up to him, cut his throat in his blankets."

Grace grinned at him. "Just his throat, Thoman?"

"Hell, I know what you'd rather do in his blankets! But you cut his throat and bring me his scalp."

"What're you giving for his scalp?"

Silverhorn swore. "Isn't they no one about this camp that don't hear my every word that's spoke?"

The woman said, "You talk too much. Everyone hears."

"Red whore. You talk too much!" He stared at her as if he had not decided whether to kill her or let her live. "So's you remember to get in there and get your job done, I'm going to burn them about daybreak. You're still in there wasting time, you'll burn with them."

"You'd miss me, Tom," she said. "You'd be awful cold and lonely without your Grace."

"You'll die thinking that one day. Get moving."

Grace checked her weapons, rolled her blanket and strapped it behind the saddle, and tore a piece of meat off the remaining rabbit at the fire. She ate slowly, talking to Blue Eye about the camp. Kills Running came to offer

advice on getting into camp and avoiding the arrow. Both
Pawnee were concerned about the arrow.

"It may be a sign our time here has passed," Kills Running said in Pawnee. "It may be we should return to our
people along the Muddy River."

"I have no people," Blue Eye said flatly. "Whoever
findeth me shall slay me."

"Whore," Silverhorn said. He loomed up over her, fists
planted on his hips, the firelight playing on his scarred
face. "I meant for you to go now, not tomorrow."

"Just getting ready, Thoman."

Grace finished her last bite of rabbit, wished for a linen
napkin, wiped her hands on the skirts of her blue dress.
She slipped out the long Arkansas knife and whetted its
blade on the sole of her boot.

"Well, get yourself along, before I slap you there!"

She watched him draw back his hand. Dodging the
blow would have been easy. She even knew that he expected her to dodge. But he had called her by name, had
given her the most important job he had. She grinned at
him, said nothing.

Silverhorn swore. His hand cracked across her cheek.
She took the blow, rocked sideways with it, came back
up straight with the knife in her hand. She stopped just
as the point touched him below the chin.

Silverhorn froze, sucking in his breath. "Red—" he began.

She pressed the point upward. A thin line of blood ran
down the blade toward her hand. Silverhorn shut his
mouth and stood taller.

"Don't call me that, Tom. Not ever again. My name is
Grace."

Rising, she drew back, keeping the knife out level before her as she backed to her horse. Once in the saddle,
she wiped the blade on her dress and slid it into its sheath.
No one had said a word. Grace drew out her rifle, laid it
across her lap pointing pretty much at Silverhorn.

"You'll get your scalp," she said. "A special scalp. I'll see to it. And you can keep your gold."

She rode out of camp without looking back, daring him to shoot, but listening carefully for the sound of a rifle hammer locking back.

She rode the buffalo trail, watching for the signs Blue Eye had described, finding the tracks that led up into the hills. At the rising hump of the first ridge, she turned west to save time. She understood the circuitous route the tracks would take. She also understood where the hunters would be and how she wanted to come at them.

She stopped when she recognized the ridge where Blue Eye had found the spring and the arrow. Leaving her horse in the shelter of a cut, she slipped into the same vantage he had used. Then she waited for the moon to rise. While she waited, she noted the lay of the land, wished for light to read her book, listened to the sounds of night birds calling, rodents running, wolves howling, one horse walking.

The horse was a hundred yards away, maybe farther. She did not move or take alarm but waited as quietly as a darker part of the rock outcrop. The rider passed in the flat valley below her. *Not even trying to stay out of sight*, she thought. When he was twenty-five yards below her, she whistled like a nighthawk.

The rider stopped his horse in his tracks, looked toward her tree, waited. Even in the starlight, she could see the hawk's plume in his hat. She whistled again.

He said, "I can't whistle, not even that bad." He held his rifle so that it covered the rocks. "Come out or I'll start shooting."

"Please," she said. "I'm not but a poor woman what's lost her path." Leaving her rifle, she stood and walked out into the early moonlight, her hands hidden by the folds of her dress.

The horseman lifted his rifle and held it pointed at her as she approached. She came right up to his horse, raised her left hand to pat its neck. The man held his rifle steady.

"I don't know you," he said. "Nor didn't expect no pretty woman to just stroll up and say howdy. What are you doing out here in the middle of this wild country at night?"

"I was looking for you."

"Who sent you?"

She looked up at him and grinned. "Thoman," she said.

The rider leaned toward her, frowned, blinked. "Aw, hell," he said, lifting the rifle barrel away from her. "Why'n't you just say so?"

She drove her right hand upward. The needle-sharp point of her knife caught him below the chin, just where she'd tickled Thoman. She felt resistance, felt it give, felt the double-edged blade plunge in until the hilt thumped against his chin.

He made no cry, just a gasp of surprise and a flopping twitch as she pulled the knife free. She took his rifle. She set it down, rubbed the anxious horse's neck, gentled him down. When she had wiped the knife on the rider's leg, she put it away.

Then she took up the Sharps and led the horse past the spring and over the ridge to the thicket where she had left her own horse. Cutting a strip of rawhide, she tied the rider's feet to his stirrups. After that she tied his hands to the saddle in front of him. Riding her own horse, she led the other back down to the buffalo trail, headed him back east. When she was confident he would continue as he was going, she looped the reins to the rider's wrists and whacked the horse across the rump with her hat. The horse took off along the road at a trot.

"Here he is, Thoman," she said quietly. "You can take the scalp yourself and earn the coin."

She stood down, found a couple of rocks, and threw them after the uncertain horse. It hadn't offered to turn back. She left the road, looping off to the south. *Now for a word with the other one*, she said to herself.

She rode until she figured she was south of any guard the hunters might put out. Then she turned west. For an hour she rode at a walk, keeping her horse in the soft dirt as much as she could. By morning light, a child would be able to follow her trail, but that wouldn't matter. What mattered was silence in the dark.

Finally, she hid her horse again, found good vantage on a brushy knob, and waited. For two hours she sat in timeless Indian patience. No rider came. No one tried to come up behind her. She might have been the only human on the world below the moon.

Grace knew there would be another guard. Of course, he might have gone looking for the missing one. Maybe they had expected him to report back and had gone out looking for him. She didn't think so. Maybe they didn't have any other riders out. She didn't believe that, either.

Half an hour later, she saw him. She had no more than a glimpse of his movement through the trees, but she knew it was the one she'd been expecting. He was north of her, riding below the skyline of a hill, staying out of the moonlight. She smiled. This one was clever. He had been worth the wait.

He didn't appear where she'd expected to see him again. Did he somehow know she was there watching? Had he gotten past her to flank her or come up behind her? She didn't like to think about that. For several minutes she studied the slope opposite. It rose to a steep, flat nose of broken rock topped with scrubby head-high trees. The rider had stopped, had taken a stand in the grove.

She grinned to think that he might be watching for her, might even have known near enough where she was to wait her out. It was possible, but she did not think so. Perhaps he was draining his bladder, having a smoke, watching as she was watching. He was worth the wait.

Grace moved, slipping down the hill as softly as a sigh in the dark. At the very bottom of the slope, hidden in the last shadow, she looked for a long time across to the shadows. Finally, she saw the horse, but not its rider.

Had he left the horse to walk on foot as she? Was he

waiting in the thicket to ambush her? If the man had left the little grove, she would surely have seen him. If he waited for her, she was right where he would expect to see her.

She slipped back up the slope and then bore west until she came to a dark gully connecting the two stands of trees. Because it was possible that the rider had done the same thing on his side, she drew her knife and went down on her belly to slide through the rocky cut. As she had supposed, no one was there.

At the other end of the gully she rose to her knees beside a tree, making no extra shadow, making no noise, watching from a new angle. The horse had not moved. It was standing three-legged and head down, apparently asleep. She grinned, moved to the next tree, heard the man. For several moments she did not move. The sound had come from the ground much nearer her than the horse.

She kept her eyes shut until her pupils were as large as they could ever be, then opened them slowly to catch every slant of moonlight. The man was in his blankets, sitting at the base of a tree, either asleep or keeping the best watch she'd ever seen a white man keep. As she eased nearer, the moonlight fell on the light-colored hair below his tipped-down hat.

He was the one. Fair-hair. Fair-Child. She had killed him once before, him and his horse. The horse had stayed dead, but the man had come back to life. Knife ready, she moved silently to the opposite side of his tree, poised herself, stopped frozen at the noise the man made. Grace grinned when she realized he was snoring.

27

Ann Bradley was in the saddle when the first sunlight touched her back. She rode eagerly but without the blind haste with which she had begun her journey. Forrest Elam led the way, slouched loosely in his saddle, his knees drawn up by stirrups that seemed far too short for him. Ann followed the old leathern man at a pace he assured her would save the horses while they covered as many as twenty miles in a day.

"It'll take a day or three to break these fat and lazy crib-fed horses to the saddle and the trail," he'd said. "I know you'd like to be in Fort Hall tomorrow, but truth is, we won't get there at all less'n we go easy here at the beginning."

She thought he was more worried about her strength to take the trail, and she was determined to hold up to any pace he could set. If he worried about her, he didn't show it. He hadn't looked back to check on her progress a single time that she had noticed. But then his ears would have told him that her horse was following along.

No sooner had she thought it than the old man turned easily in his saddle to look back at her. She smiled brightly at him. He nodded to her and watched her horse for a few steps. Then he bent his attention back to the trail.

They had eaten at four and put out the fire in Elam's hearth. Then, before Ann thought it light enough for man or beast to see, they had ridden out to the west on their way to find Ethan Fairchild. If he could be found.

"Should we go back?" she'd asked at breakfast. "I'm worried about Father and Mother. The way that terrible woman talked, she might have robbed them next!"

Forrest Elam was shaving together a mixture of tobacco and oak bark to pack his Indian pipe. "Child, you got to choose," he said. "I'll take you wheresomever you want to go, be it back to the Oak or on to find your true love. But you've got to say which it is."

"But can't I do both?"

He shook his head gently. "There's no going both ways along a trail, child. We can go back, but we might never catch up to him then. That boy's tracks gets fainter every minute. Of course, you can always go home after you've found him. But you got to decide now which way your stick floats."

"Then I'm going after Ethan. There's nothing else I can do."

Soon, the sun rose high enough to paint the farther hillside and highlight it with late-blooming blue larkspur running up tall stalks. As they came up out of that shallow valley and slowed against the upslope, Ann noticed that the blossoms were bluer and more delicate than they had seemed from a distance. It would on any other occasion have disturbed her to see those which the horses had trodden, but on that day she did not think of it. Her decision behind her, she thought instead of her journey, wondered where it would lead her and whether in time.

Before long, she felt a nagging worry. "Mr. Elam?" she called to the old man's back. "Are you sure we're going the right way?"

Elam craned his head around like a wrinkled tortoise. He wasn't quite laughing, but the lines on his face had deepened in repressed amusement. "Figure this child has lost his path already, girl?" he asked.

"Of course not! I mean, I can see we're on the trail, but how do you know this is the way Ethan went?"

Forrest Elam rubbed his chin. "Come on," he said. "Ride up here beside me for a spell, Annie. There's things you need to notice in case I don't last forever."

She urged her horse on a little faster, rode level with

Elam's long-shanked sorrel. The mountain man pointed to the ground a little to the side of the main trail.

"See them tracks?"

She stared at the ground, saw a set of hoofprints, nodded.

"That's him. We cut young Ethan's trail about half a mile back, been following it since. He crossed here."

"Ethan did! How can you tell?"

Elam pursed his lips. "That's a right good point," he said. "Never gave that a thought. His horse crossed here, that ugly-souled chestnut. Can't say who was riding him. Might have been my old aunt Tillie, though she was a mite heavy. The weight's about right for your young man."

She laughed. "How can you tell it was his horse?"

"Seen his tracks before. Still the same as they was."

She thought he was teasing her. "When would you have seen his tracks!" Then she remembered. "You saw Devil's tracks when we rode up to your cabin."

"He snapped at me. I'd notice his tracks anyways, but that set them in my mind."

She laughed again. "You're just trying to cheer me up," she accused. "I'll bet you couldn't tell those tracks from Blue's if they lay side by side."

"Being as he's my horse, I'd know Blue's in the dark." He looked at her, saw the laughter. "I guess it is funny."

"No! I only meant I can't think how."

He reined up. "Get down and stand by him. Look at his tracks. He drags his nigh hind foot. Look. His left front shoe's a bit off, narrow at the heel."

She looked, didn't believe he could tell tracks apart, knelt and put her hand across the print to measure it at the heel. The left shoe left a print a fraction narrower than the right. She rose, put a hand on the saddle horn, looked down again. "You can see that from the saddle?" she asked.

"Clear as print." He turned his horse and set off following the single cold trail across the creek and then along the other bank.

When she caught up to him, she said, "You have a splendid eye. What is it you see in these tracks to make you think they're Ethan's?"

"Each shoe has the tiny letters *E.F.* engraved just at the front."

"What! His initials? The Devil wasn't even his horse. Besides, you couldn't possibly see that from the saddle." She looked earnestly at the older man, saw the etched lines at the edges of his eyes, and knew that he was teasing her. She looked back to the trail. "Oh, of course," she said. "Now I see them. Clear as print."

"You'll forgive an old boar, hoorawing the greenhorn," he said. "Look, now. To start with, they're government shoes."

"That makes a difference?"

"Next, that devil horse has a cast to one eye. Cocks his head a smidgen when he walks, like he's going sideways. See how that one hoof falls out of line."

"I'd never have noticed something like that."

The creases in his face deepened into a near-smile. "We learned it fast in the old days, us'uns as didn't go under." He rubbed his long chin, remembering. "You'd school yourself to know those prints if'n that horse belonged to a Piegan looking to lift your hair."

She believed it.

At noon Elam checked both of the horses over carefully. He laid out a circle of stones and put a small amount of wood on top of some leaves and twigs he had set afire with surprising ease. Wanting to help as much as possible, she dipped water from the creek to boil a pot of coffee. Though she had never developed an adult taste for it, she knew that Elam liked coffee, and she figured she would need it, too.

He watched her prepare the coffee without a word as to the proportions of her mixture; and when it was ready, he drank it. "Good coffee," he said. He gave her a strip of jerky from his own bag, bit off a bite for himself.

She thanked him on both counts.

"You don't need to eat it all right now," he told her. "That strip'll keep you busy till supper if you let it."

"I see." She was glad to know she didn't have to get it chewed and swallowed right then. She put the rest of the strip in her coat pocket.

"Tell me again about the woman who took your dress," Elam said suddenly. "Indian woman, you thought she was?"

"Part Indian, at least." Ann Bradley blushed at being reminded of the dress. When she thought of the Indian woman, she shuddered even in the warmth of midday. "Her eyes were almost black, and she had black hair in braids."

"Highwaywoman with a gun, uhm?"

"I thought she would kill me," Ann said simply, remembering the dark eyes and expressionless face.

"Reckon why she didn't?"

Ann heard the question, but couldn't quite believe Elam had asked it so casually. "Pardon?"

"Why didn't she? Seems as if it was her intention from the start. Yet she left you your coat and your money."

"It wouldn't have been much."

"That's not to the purpose. Much or little, it was there for her. It's a puzzle, right enough. You don't think something scared her off?"

"No."

"Nor that she was bluffing you, didn't really mean to shoot?"

Remembering, Ann shivered. "No. I don't think that. But all she took was my dress."

"You'd be dead if she'd wanted you so. No, it was vanity," Elam mused.

"Vanity?"

"She wanted to wear your pretty dress. And she never used the gun."

"Oh yes, she did. She discharged it twice. Into the ground."

"Aha. Why did she do that? Why waste the powder to fire her gun into the ground? First vanity. Then deceit."

"Deceit?"

"She thought someone would hear it."

"Oh. I see. But there was no one else to hear it."

Elam lifted his eyes from her face to look back in the direction they'd come. He sighed.

"What is it?"

"Nothing. Nothing now." His face held a sadness she had never seen but always expected to see in it. "You said your Ethan's gone off to kill a man."

Ann Bradley nodded.

"He give that man a name?"

"He did, once. A strange name." She frowned, then gave a half-laugh. "I'm afraid I don't remember. I was upset."

"What kind of man?"

"A bad man."

"So you said last night." Forrest Elam laughed. It seemed to do him good. The sadness lifted from his face. He laughed again. "I'm pleased he hadn't thought to kill a preacher. They's laws against killing good men."

"But you meant what kind of man. Ethan called him the man with white hair."

"White hair?" Elam's gray eyes seemed suddenly sharper on her face. "Old man? A white-haired old man?"

"Not old, I think. Middle-aged maybe."

"Ha. Middle-aged if he was to live to be a hundred." The older mountain man smiled. "Albino?"

"What?"

"You think he was born with white hair, pale eyes?"

"I don't know. I don't think so. Ethan says he was dark. Part Indian maybe."

"Waugh," the mountain man said. He turned to stare at the farthest ridge off to the north and west. "Well, we'd better get after them." He finished his coffee, offered her another cup, and poured the rest of the pot on the fire.

"Do you know who he is, the man with white hair?"

"Maybe." He pursed his lips, thought about it. "That name you don't remember. How was it strange?"

Ann closed her eyes. "I remember it wasn't like a name at all but more like two regular words run together. There was metal in it, iron or tin."

"Silver?"

She stared at him. "That's right," she said. "How did you know?"

"Heard a name like that once. Belonged to a man with white hair. Best we be riding, missy. Ain't getting no closer to your young man, us palavering here."

When she saw that he would say no more, she rinsed out the coffeepot at the creek, threw back the rinse water, turned to the horses. Elam had already loaded his gear and climbed into his saddle. She stowed the coffeepot, then followed him out onto the broad westward trail again.

They rode steadily in spite of Elam's caution about the fat horses. Here in the open prairie, the wildflowers were golden, blowing low on the rolling swells of grassland, blooming after every shower, all but glowing under the midday sun. The wind blew steadily from the west, warm and dry. Field larks rose from beneath the horses' hooves to sail stiff-winged for a few yards before settling again.

Ann saw it all and loved it, riding west as she'd always dreamed, while Forrest Elam tracked Ethan through the jumbled tracks of the Dragoon camp, away from the main trail, off to the north alone. She never saw him bend his neck to look down, but every time she looked down, she saw the trail someone had left riding alone to the north. The only thing left for her to hope was that the rider had been Ethan Fairchild.

Anxious as she was to overtake Ethan, she did not complain when Elam finally came to a spring he considered right for a camp. Ann was tired, thirsty, sore from riding such an unaccustomed distance. But she was still determined, game for dealing with whatever might come between her and Ethan.

But her guide was tired, too, as she could tell in the sad slump of his posture. He was no more accustomed to riding than she and no more accustomed to camping out. It came to her that they were a poor pair to make such a journey.

Elam was busy with the horses. He unsaddled them, rubbed them down a bit, and picketed them. Then he made his circle of rocks and built a fire. "I'll make the coffee," he said. It was the first time he'd spoken since noon.

Ann found the packet of jerky, unwrapped it, and put it near the meager fire. With no real idea how long their supplies would need to last, she was hesitant to open anything else. Elam came back to the fire, put the pot on to boil, looked across at her.

"We'll eat the bread before it goes bad. They's some dried apricots here, too. I wonder if you'd mind gathering us up some more firewood."

Ann brought in a few armloads of dead wood that she figured would burn well. She wasn't sure whether he really wanted the wood, since he made such small fires, or wanted to keep her busy. Just before dark she heard a distant wolf. After that, she brought in a couple more loads of wood. They ate their supper. Then he grained the horses, talked to them, checked them over.

Ann Bradley stood beside him watching. "You said you might have an idea about the man with white hair."

"Waugh." For a second, he seemed to be debating with himself. Then he said, "I been studying on it. There was a Kansas man I heard of had white hair while he was still young. 'Course, that was a good ten years ago. Silverhorn, they called him."

"That's it," Ann said. "The name Ethan used. Silverhorn."

"I had it Silverhair in my mind. Watch out for him, they said, he's a bad one. Ran with the worst cutthroats in the country, led them like as not. Kept him an Indian woman, just a slip of a girl, she was then, I guess. They said she was twice as dangerous as him."

"Indian woman?"

"Part Indian, it could've been."

"You don't mean the woman that took my clothes?"

"Can't say. Don't know. Doubt it. Silverhorn's woman's supposed to've been mean enough to kill you with a look."

"She came close to that."

"Come down to it, though, she didn't hurt you even a mite. Gentle with you as if you's a baby in swaddling clothes. Don't sound like anything I ever heard about Silverhorn's woman."

Ann Bradley mused over it. "That's why you asked about her at noon."

"It was."

"You thought she fired the gun for someone to hear."

Elam did not answer but began checking the saddles, fiddling with the gear.

"You aren't telling me who you think she hoped to deceive because you don't want me to believe that she was Silverhorn's woman. Why?"

She didn't expect him to answer. He didn't. She stared into the coals of the small fire and thought about the Indian woman firing her gun. Laying another piece of her firewood across the coals, she watched smoke rise from it as it began to catch. *The woman had told her to keep riding west. Why would she have said such a thing?*

"Oh!" She'd seen what the old man must be thinking. "Mr. Elam, you think they were at the inn! Do you think the woman fired the gun for their benefit?"

"If that were true," Elam said slowly, "it would've been the luckiest day of your life."

"And the unluckiest for my parents!" Ignoring protesting muscles, Ann leaped to her feet. "We have to go back! What if they doubled back and went to the inn?"

"Child, you've chose."

"But I didn't know!"

"Ann, girl, whatever's happened at the inn has happened," Elam said. "It's over and done with. There's nothing you nor I nor any but the Almighty can do about it." He stared into the fire. "You're not needed there. But your young man's took out west after the man with white hair. Might be, Ethan'll need a smidgen of help before he's done."

"Yes," Ann said. "I suppose you're right." She looked at herself, at him. A young woman, too helpless even to escape from one of her own sex who might have killed her. A half-crazy old man living with memories of a frontier half a century old. "What could we do to help Ethan?"

Elam laughed aloud, a high cackle, and slapped the stock of his long percussion rifle. "Child, old Grizzly-Killer and me's got a shot or two left in us yet. And might be we can do a little something with you."

He rose and went to his saddlebags, returning with a leather pouch and a smaller version of his powder horn, each with its own leather thong. She slung the horn across one shoulder and put the pouch on the other, adjusting them at her side.

"Powder, ball, bullets, and bullet mold. Now you look like a mountain woman," he said. "And a right pert one, at that. I might find it in me to envy your Ethan."

She blushed. "But it's all on the surface. I don't know how to use any of this."

"Reach into that possible bag. Bring out what you find."

By the firelight she examined the revolver Elam had given her.

"It's an old Colt forty-niner," he said. "Pocket pistol, they called them. Never had much truck with it myself, but it's about a size for a young lady. That's the loading lever you're fiddling with."

She looked at him helplessly. "I've never held a gun in my hands before. Not even Father's old shotgun." She shrugged. "The Oak has always been so peaceful."

She saw him wince, didn't know why. "They don't educate young'uns hardly a'tall these days," he growled.

"Well, it ain't likely to be peaceful along this trail, not by a long chalk. It's time you learned."

She looked at his grim, sharp-featured face, then at the pistol in her hands. It was something like the one the Indian woman had pointed at her. Ann remembered staring into that black muzzle, closing her eyes, waiting to die. She hadn't doubted the woman could kill her, didn't doubt it now.

But could Ann do the same thing? Could she point that small revolver at another human being and pull back the hammer? She knew that much about it. But squeeze the trigger? Could she really kill someone, even to save her own life, or Elam's, or Ethan's?

The night before, she'd earnestly told Elam she would die for Ethan, would kill for him. Now, suddenly, cradling the heavy, ugly pistol in her hands and remembering the Indian woman's dark, emotionless eyes, she began to understand what those words meant.

"All right," she said. She folded her hand around the walnut butt of the pistol, knowing that act meant as much a loss of innocence as anything she'd ever do with Ethan. "I want to learn. Show me how."

28

Ethan Fairchild checked in at the hunters' fire at two in the morning, refused a cup of coffee, and went right back out, though he was off duty. They thought that he wanted to get away from the hide wagon; he let them think so. That was part of his motive, but he also wanted some time of his own. From the first, he'd liked the hunters in spite of their rough ways. But now that he was convinced one of them was a traitor, everything had changed. Now he saw sinister meanings everywhere—behind Gawkins's wild mood swings, in the furtive comings and goings of Eye-Shot Barker, among the oddities and jokes and casual speech of the others.

He rode back out toward the perimeter, deciding to lend a hand on guard duty for a while before bedding down away from the others. Waller and Gawkins were taking the last shift riding guard. Eye-Shot had gone out on the same sweep Fairchild had ridden earlier and hadn't yet returned, so there might be four riders out for a short time.

Avoiding the bright moonlight, Fairchild covered the area south of the camp for half an hour or so. Finally, when he had seen no other riders, he entered a grove of scrubby trees on the shadowed crown of a hill. He unsaddled and picketed his horse, then found a place to unroll his blankets. After that he walked a short tour inside his fortress of trees, listening as much as watching to be sure that no one was in the area. Ever since he'd crossed paths with Silverhorn's rider, he'd wondered when the rest would come or whether they would come at all since they'd lost that man.

Of course they would come. But they wouldn't come at night. If he figured them right, they'd come when the mules were already hitched to the hide wagon to save them the trouble. Hell, they'd probably come at mealtime! Whenever it was, he'd need his rest, because he intended to be ready to kill them.

He slept hard and heavy. An hour before dawn he dreamed he was in the barn at Bradley's Oak. He'd been working on the wagon, getting it ready to take Ann with him to Oregon. Ann had brought him out a drink of water. She was wearing the blue dress he'd admired, and she wouldn't give him the water until he'd kissed her.

The kiss waked him. It was real. *She* was real, palpable, alive! He tried to put his arms around her but she was too quick for him. When she dodged back away from him he had just enough moonlight to make out the pattern of Ann's blue dress.

"Ann?"

"Grace."

The woman wore Ann Bradley's blue dress but she was not Ann. He could have killed her for being someone else. Then he remembered where he was, remembered the name Silverhorn's man had spoken before he died. With a speed born of sudden fear, Fairchild reached for his revolver. The holster was empty. He lifted his fist.

The woman said, "Don't move around." To emphasize her words, something nicked Fairchild sharply under the chin.

He quit struggling. "Where'd you get that dress?" he said.

"You're the fair one. Fair-child. Funny name for a white man."

"Who are you?"

"Heap warrior. About to count coup. On you."

"What the hell for?" He thought her crazy. If she'd run with Silverhorn, she was certainly crazy, certainly a killer as well. He slid a hand toward the pepperbox pistol under his saddle.

Grace's knife bit deeper. "Easy." He saw the flash of her grin in the darkness. Then a shaft of moonlight fell on her face and he knew her.

"You were with Silverhorn," he said. "You jumped your horse over me when I was down and half-dead in the gully."

"Killed you once then," she said. Her free hand moved under his blanket, yanked at his belt. "Could've killed you just now. Still can, if you don't hold still."

Fairchild stared into her face. She was the one who'd killed his horse and left him to die, cut him off from the wagons and his entire life. And she was wearing Ann's dress!

"You killed Ann!"

"That snip of a gal I shucked out of this dress? No such. She's alive as you, last I saw of her. Here, finish stripping off them pants."

"What!"

"You want this knife through the top of your skull? Move!"

Fairchild considered it, then began to wriggle out of his trousers. "This's your idea of counting coup?"

She laughed. "Beats lifting scalps," she said. "They's no use to anybody. Now the shirt."

"What the hell tribe are you from!"

She pressed the knife, brought bright warm blood, focused his attention. He started to unbutton his shirt. A horse came up at the edge of the woods, stopped.

"Fairchild!" the rider called. "That you in there?"

Fairchild ignored it. Waller's voice offered some hope of rescue, but he was not about to give the Indian woman any reason to test his palate with her knife.

"Fairchild, I can't find Eye-Shot nowhere! You seen him?"

As if there were no other soul in the valley with them, the woman said, "Get up." She rose as she said it, keeping the pressure of the knife at his throat.

He got up, felt his pants slipping, grabbed at them. He could hear heavy steps as Waller came in on foot. The woman pressed herself against him and kissed him on the mouth again without ever moving the knife. He was still holding his pants and holding his breath when Redwood Waller cursed the chestnut horse and blundered into the open beneath Fairchild's tree.

"Fairchild?" The big man stopped, stared at Fairchild's state of dress, at the woman. "What the hell is this?"

Grace took a step back, produced a pistol in her left hand, and wiped a trickle of blood off her knife. "I'm Grace," she said.

Waller gaped at her. "Who?"

Grace said, "I come to help you. I've done it. I guess I'll be riding."

"Help us what!" Waller said. He looked at the revolver in her hand as if she were a trained animal with a toy. "What is this, Fairchild?"

"She's counting coup."

The woman laughed. "Maybe another time," she said. She had not taken her eyes off Waller. "You the boss here?"

Waller nodded, still trying to figure it out. "I am."

"I like you. I'll ride out now, or I'll stay and work for you. You're going to need me."

"I'll need somebody to nail the lid on my coffin, too," Waller said, "but I ain't ready just yet."

"You don't think I can help you?" Grace asked, offended. "I've done killed his spy out'n your midst and sent him back."

"Whose spy?"

"Thoman's. Silverhorn's. The white-haired one's been dogging you."

"The hell you say."

"The hell she says," Fairchild told him. "I've seen her with him."

Waller reached for his pistol, looked at the gun in Grace's hand, stopped. "The bastard sent you in here to kill us in our sleep?" he growled.

Grace grinned at Waller. "He did. Had I obeyed, you'd be dead," she said. "You still can be if you're set on it."

"You said you killed one of my men."

"One of Silverhorn's men."

Waller looked at Fairchild as if he were the judge in some strange contest. "She mean Eye-Shot?"

Fairchild said, "I want to know where the girl is if she's alive."

The pistol barrel flicked his way. "Shut up," Grace said. "Me and the big man's talking. Young fellow, medium-sized, funny hat with a hawk's feather in it."

"Eye-Shot! You murdering red cutthroat."

"He was waiting to shoot you in the back when Tom came down on you."

"It's all a damned lie."

"Think about it, Red," Fairchild said. "Why would she lie about that? She could've had us both dead right here."

"Don't look like she wanted you dead."

Fairchild cinched his pants. "I wish you'd put that knife away," he said to Grace. "The gun, too, if you would."

"When the boss, here, tells me to ride or stay."

"I can't exactly do that kind of choosing looking down the barrel of that big gun."

Grace holstered the revolver but kept the knife in a position to throw it easily.

Fairchild said, "I want to know where you got that dress."

"Why? You want one like it?"

"I'm not fooling around. You took it from a woman at Bradley's Oak. That right?"

Grace said, "I traded for it."

"At Bradley's Oak?"

"Yes."

Fairchild's face went dark, his eyes bloodshot. He made a fist, took a step toward her. "You killed that poor girl for her dress?"

"I already told you different. I was sent to kill her. I let her live, just like you."

"The hell you did! They said there were no survivors!"

"They weren't there." Her hand flashed suddenly in an upward arc. The heavy knife split the three-foot distance between the men and quivered in the trunk of the juniper. "I could have killed her as easy as that. I chose not."

Waller pulled his pistol and pointed it at the woman's face. Fairchild stepped against her, held her gun hand.

"Where is she?"

"How in hell should I know?"

He put his other hand to her throat. "Tell me, or you'll never draw another breath." Fairchild had begun to tremble. He tightened his grip on the woman's throat.

"Aw hell, Ethan, she could be telling you true," Waller said. "Seems like to me I smell smoke. You had a fire in here?"

"Give me your gun! I'm going to kill her."

"I could have killed the girl," Grace said. "I let her go.

I could have killed you three times now, not counting the one I really did. I let you go."

"Where is she?"

"If you don't let go my neck, I will kill you now." With her unseen free hand she pushed the muzzle of a stubby Colt's pocket revolver under his ribs. "I'm not fooling around."

Fairchild moved back far enough to look down at the gun, heard the woman cock the hammer, took his hands away from her throat. "I asked you nice, by God, where the girl is."

"I don't know that, *by God*. I took her clothes and let her live. I fired my gun so the others would think I'd kill her, and I took that black horse so's Thoman wouldn't kill me."

"She's still alive? You promise me she's alive?"

Grace grinned at him. "So, she's the reason you don't want me to count coup on you. Last I saw of her, she was alive as you and me, and pretty near naked as Eve. If she's died by now, it's none of my doing."

Fairchild flexed his hands. The revolver no longer frightened him. "I ought to kill you anyway," he said.

Grace laughed. She let the muzzle of the revolver rock up toward his face as she lowered the hammer. Then she spun it on her finger until the muzzle pointed at her own belly. She thrust it at him butt first.

"Go ahead, if you're minded. But I don't think you're the sort to kill me for helping her." Her teeth gleamed in the moonlight. "Nor even for taking advantage of your virtue."

He took the pistol, pressed its muzzle against her body while he thought about Ann Bradley.

"Hell," he said, and lowered the hammer softly. He reached across and lifted the heavier gun from her holster. She opened her mouth to speak to him. "Yes, I know," he told her. "You could still kill me. But you're not in the mood." He half believed it.

She grinned at him, then turned her attention back to Waller. "Do you want me to kill him?"

"What?" Waller asked.

"I'd kill him for you. I'll kill anybody you say."

Waller was amazed. "Why, then kill yourself!" He took her wrist, twisted it until she spun with her back against him. Then he put away his gun and drew her other arm behind her so that he could grip both wrists in his big left hand.

The woman turned her head back toward him, her eyes half closed. "You're strong. Strongest man I've ever met."

"Strong enough to break your neck, you damned heathen wench."

She showed him her teeth, threw her head back against his face, and laughed. "Maybe." She left the word hanging in his ear like a dare.

"Where's your horse?"

"Turn me loose. I'll go get him."

"Hell. Fairchild, get me a rope or a chain or something to tie this bobcat up."

"If Ann left right after I did, where is she? Why didn't she catch up? Even afoot, she might have done that."

"We can sort that out when you've brought me a set of manacles. Don't you smell smoke? You don't suppose those fools have let the campfire get out of hand?"

Waller dragged the woman toward his horse. Half in a daze, Fairchild gathered up his guns and gear. Then he saddled Devil. Then he heard the first shots.

For a moment he stood holding the horse, listening, trying to imagine who would be shooting so early in the morning, trying to tell where the shots came from.

Waller was shouting at him. "Fairchild! Come on, Fairchild. I smell smoke!" He had tied the woman's hands behind her. He shoved her against a tree, looped the rest of the rope around her a couple of times and tied it off on the other side.

Fairchild and Waller hit their saddles at the same moment, drew out their rifles, and rode hard in the direction of the smoke which now billowed west in a great cloud. The shooting had all but stopped. They made the half mile back to camp at a gallop, in time to see two riders at the edge of a wall of smoke firing into what had been the hunters' camp. Flowing white hair fell over one of the riders' shoulders and down his back. Fairchild gave the Devil its head, aimed his rifle, and fired at the white hair.

Immediately, the big man whirled his horse and shot at them. It was still dark enough to see the flame in the midst of the white powder smoke. Fairchild fired at the smoke. Even as he drove his horse off to the side, Silverhorn fired again.

Waller let out a grunt as if someone had knocked the breath out of him. More bullets came past Fairchild as he turned to see Waller let go his reins and topple off the far side of his horse.

"Red!" Fairchild reined Devil back hard, fighting the chestnut's wild battle-lust. The horse wanted to charge right into the middle of Silverhorn's bunch. Finally, it squealed, stumbled, and fell. Fairchild stepped out of the saddle going down, just as two more bullets whoomed above him. He came up on one knee and fired at the riders. One of them reeled in the saddle, leaned far off to the rear like a man tossed by a rough bronc, then clung as his horse disappeared behind the smoke.

Silverhorn fired once more at Fairchild, then wheeled his horse and followed the wounded man. Fairchild emptied the rest of his cylinder into the smoke. The Devil had trotted away from him toward the smoking camp. Fairchild whistled after the headstrong animal. Then he ran back to Waller's horse. It had stopped, its reins dragging the ground next to Waller. The big hunter lay in a tumble as motionless as a dead man.

Fairchild put down his rifle and knelt beside Waller. The hunter was breathing, but there was a spreading patch of red at the back of his coat. Fairchild knew without thinking that the bullet had passed through. When he turned Waller over, the big man rolled his eyes and took Ethan by the throat.

"You white-haired son of a bitch," he said.

Fairchild grabbed him by the wrists, wrestled the heavy hands off his neck. "It's Ethan," he said. "Be easy." Then he saw the cut on the side of Waller's head. A great blue bruise was already rising around it in a lump. The hunter had fallen on a rock. "It's all right. You fell on your head."

"Damn good thing," Waller said. His eyes began to clear. He tried to sit up. "Did you rout them?"

"Yes. Don't get up. Let's see where you're hit." Fairchild heard a horse coming from the south. He reached for his rifle, remembered that it was empty, took up his revolver, and brought it to bear on the woman riding down on him.

She showed him her palms, then rode up close before she dismounted and went to her knees beside Waller. Fairchild saw that she was wearing her weapons again and might have used them if she chose. Instead she opened Waller's shirt to examine his wound.

Waller said, "How is it?"

"He hit you hard enough," she said. "I told you you'd need me."

Fairchild looked at Waller's chest. The bullet had struck him between his left nipple and shoulder joint. There was plenty of blood, but no squirting or pulsing of it from the wound.

The woman put her ear to his chest. "Breathe."

"I'm breathing. And it damned well hurts."

"Do it without talking. Breathe hard."

Waller inhaled, grimaced, let the air out.

"Good," Grace said. "Missed your lung. You'd been ten yards closer, he'd've hit lung or heart."

"God of mercy," Waller said. "That hurts."

"Good," the woman said again. "Bullet bites are my long suit. Sit up."

Waller pushed himself up with his right arm, took a

hard breath and tried to smile. He looked at the woman's belt. "What you ain't going to do with this bullet bite is fish around for it with that damned Arkansas toothpick."

"The bullet went through," Fairchild said.

Grace said, "Good. Thoman always uses enough powder to make his bullet sing."

Waller said, "God of mercy." He did not like to talk of internal organs and the speed of bullets. "What's happened to my men?"

Fairchild said, "I don't know yet."

"Well, go find out! And them hides. If they've burnt, I'll set fire to that white-haired son." He winced at the effort and held his breath.

"Your men are dead," Grace said. "Less'n they got real fast horses."

Waller kept a hand to his wound and cursed in a whisper.

"He going to be all right?"

"I'll fix him."

Fairchild wasn't sure. "Sure you want me to go, Red? You all right alone with her?"

Waller nodded. "I'd break her neck," he gasped.

"Not today." Grace looked up at Fairchild. "You won't find nobody alive, won't find no skins."

"If you hurt him, I'll cut your heart out with your own knife."

She grinned at him. "If I take his scalp, I'll leave it for you."

"Damn you."

Waller said, "Go on. I've got to know."

Fairchild climbed on Waller's horse and rode slowly up to the camp, looking for riders. He caught up the Devil and led him in tow. When he stopped, the chestnut horse slid in close and bit him on the left calf. He clubbed the Devil across the bridge of his nose with a revolver barrel, climbed down, tied the horses.

Off to the east the land was blackened. Sheets of smoke rose from the remnants of grass already burned to its roots. Off to the east beyond the ruined camp, a great wall of flame lay under a boiling roll of smoke half a mile from north to south. Fairchild felt the strong west wind at his back driving the fire away from him.

Then a lull in the wind allowed a backblast of heat that struck him head-on. He twisted, turned to run, tripped and fell. As he scrambled up again, the wind picked up to drive the heat and thinning smoke away from the camp.

"God," Fairchild whispered. It was a prayer. His stomach knotted, heaved. It had not been the scorching leftover heat that hurt him but a smell he'd never encountered before. No one had ever even tried to describe to him the stench of burning human flesh, and now no one needed to.

He got to his feet, found his hat, then ventured back toward the area which had been the hunters' camp. He saw a rifle with its stock still burning. The coffeepot sat on the coals, sooted over, burned black, but intact. A wisp of steam escaped its mouth. One or two blankets were strewn smoldering about the site. Last, he saw the bodies. Two men had been caught, had died there. Their smoking black bodies lay where the wagons had been.

One wagon was gone. The rest of the hunters were gone. Fairchild tried to imagine the battle. The men would have smelled smoke on the wind. They'd had time to escape, but two had tried to save the wagonload of hides. He couldn't tell which two.

The rest would have run to the east. Silverhorn would have expected them to do that. He would have had the body of his men waiting to pot them as they ran from the fire. Those who ran had probably died first, before Silverhorn's men came in to get the wagon and kill the remaining two. At least those poor wretches must have been dead before the fire got to them. He hoped so. Looking at the putrid smoke steaming from their bodies, he joined Waller in the thought that he would set fire to Silverhorn if only he could.

He decided in that moment that he would track Silverhorn down if it took him the rest of his life and half of eternity. When he had walked the perimeter of the camp as closely as he could down to the south, he walked it back to the north. There he found the fresh body of a man he didn't know. This one had not been in the fire though he lay now in the charred grass, his face and clothes covered with soot from his fall. This would be the man he had shot half an hour earlier.

Ethan Fairchild stared at the body in disgust. He wanted to hang the body on a fence as a warning to others of his kind. He caught a waft of smell on a sidedraft of breeze from the campsite and wanted to cut this man into pieces and scatter him for the buzzards and coyotes.

Instead, he went back to the horses, got on Devil, and led Waller's horse back across the plain. Grace had moved the hunter down into a shaded draw. How she had done it, Fairchild couldn't imagine. Waller was naked to the waist except for a blue-gingham bandage wrapped neatly across his chest and shoulder and tied off in a knot. The woman's skirt was six inches shorter.

Waller looked up at him, waiting for the report. Fairchild said, "Two dead where the wagon was. The rest are gone. Hide wagon's gone."

"Maybe the others got the wagon clear. We've got to go find them, help them."

Fairchild shook his head. "I don't think so." To Grace he said, "Tell him."

The woman did not grin. "Thoman would have been waiting for them, there." She pointed east beyond the camp. "They would have waited until your men had the wagon hitched and ready to go before they killed them."

Waller looked at the woman a long moment. "And you're one of them," he said at last.

"Not now. Now I'm one of you."

Waller made a growling sound. "If you were so damned anxious to help us, why didn't you say nothing about the fire and attack in time for us to stop it?"

"You couldn't have stopped it."

"We'd've made a damn good try."

"You made your try. Here you are."

"If we'd got here sooner—"

"You'd be dead."

29

- -

The Hudspeth Cutoff would have been a difficult passage for a strong man on a good horse. It was a thoroughly miserable trek for women and children and tall wagons and oxen. On the third day, Manasseh Thorne's worst fears took tangible shape in a wall of low, hard, rolling gray clouds that flung over the mountain crests to give the train two hours' warning.

Then, much too early in the year, it began to snow. At first, no one believed it except Manasseh Thorne who had predicted back in June that snow would overtake them before they got through the mountains.

Will Buttrell had held his quiet peace about Thorne's prediction, never fully believing it but never denying that it was possible. He had spent his life keeping himself and his family and his animals in the middle of belief, behavior, and the road. Thus, when the snow began, he wasn't surprised. But he couldn't help worrying, all the same.

"Will, it's not even the first of September," Alathea Buttrell said. "It can't be snowing yet!"

Will Buttrell smiled gently and waved his hand through the flakes that were coming down thicker and faster with each passing minute. "Reckon this is something else, then. But whatever it is, it surely favors snow."

"William Buttrell, it's nothing to laugh about!" Alathea stole a look back at the three boys, who were dancing, laughing, trying to catch snowflakes on their tongues.

"You boys get right in that wagon and get your coats on. You'll catch your death, frolicking around like that."

"Aw, Ma."

"Michael and Homer, bring your mother her shawl," Will added. "Be quick about it. Orren, you find Francis's coat and take it back to him."

"Oh, boy!"

Francis was out on horseback, riding drag for the train. Orren, fourteen years old, had lately been hinting he was about as much grown as Francis, could take some of the same responsibilities. It gave Will Buttrell a strange pang to hear it, pride mingled with a touch of sadness to think the boys were growing up so fast.

"Will?" Alathea said in a quieter voice. "We'll be all right, won't we? It can't keep snowing. Not this early."

He could tell what she was thinking, indeed, what everyone on the train had been thinking since the heavy-bellied snow clouds had first rolled in.

Donner!

There had been other parties lost on the trail, caught by the snows, wiped out by disease, or decimated by Indians. But no other tale conjured up fear and dread like the memory of the Donner disaster, back in the very early days of the trail.

"We're not following the same route they did," Will said without thinking.

"Who?"

"Oh." He caught himself up. "Sorry, I was just thinking." He smiled at his wife. "We're pretty high up in this pass. It can snow here about anytime it wants to. It'll clear off in a day or so."

He knew what answer Manasseh Thorne would have for that. *It'll cost us a day. And we're still a long way from Oregon.*

Will Buttrell turned up his collar and kept his team moving. From the next wagon behind him, he heard Caleb Sugarhouse complaining about the sudden cold wind and the damnable snow and Manasseh Thorne, whom Sugarhouse clearly but for reasons unspecified held responsible.

At noon, they did not take time to circle the wagons or unyoke the teams or gather to visit. Each family cooked as best they could and ate inside their wagons. When he and Alathea and the children had eaten, Will turned the boys out to play with the Miller twins.

"I believe I'll get a little exercise, too," he said. "Maybe walk back along the train to hear the gossip."

Alathea smiled at him. He was going back to see that Francis was all right, and he knew he hadn't fooled her at all.

"Have a nice walk," she said. "I'm going up to the Miller wagon. Maybe Becky and I can get a few stitches done on that quilt."

Will walked down the line of wagons speaking to each family in turn to see whether anyone was cold or needed any help he could give.

Sugarhouse said, "Yes, you surely can help. Alls you got to do is make up your mind to come along with the most of us down to Virginia City."

"I'm thinking on it."

"That's right. You don't like to be rushed and you don't like to decide until you're sure you've thought it through."

Buttrell smiled. Sugarhouse was a pretty good mimic; he'd given Will back his own words closely enough. "I couldn't have put it better." To Mrs. Sugarhouse he said, "You staying warm, Sue?"

"Surely am. But I'm glad there's no danger of snow on the trail down to Nevada. I wouldn't have a peaceful moment the rest of the trip, just worrying about those passes ahead."

"The thing for you to remember," Sugarhouse added, "is you ought to decide now, before it's too late."

"I'll decide."

Buttrell touched his hat and walked on. Near the Kenny wagon, Doc Harris and Barbara Kenny were trying to make a couple of decent-sized snowballs to throw at each other. Because the snow was as yet so thin and dry, they were throwing handfuls of white powder.

"Fred, Mrs. Kenny," he said. "Everything all right?"

"Fine, Will."

They waited in a respectful truce until he was passing between them. Then they threw their clouds of snow at him from both directions. He took long enough to scoop up a couple of handfuls to throw back at them, then retreated, laughing with them.

His son Francis came past on horseback, bundled in his winter coat, headed for the home wagon.

"Fran. We saved you a bite of lunch."

"Thanks, Pa," Francis said impersonally. "Gotta hurry, though. They need me back on station."

He went on without stopping. *So the rest won't think him still a boy*, Buttrell thought. He could remember when he'd behaved about the same. And he could remember a time when he'd been about as heartbroken over a pretty young thing as Francis was about his ferry girl. *Had my own father to blame, too.*

Will Buttrell was not certain he'd done the right thing when he refused to bring her along with them to Oregon. Francis had come pretty close to staying there.

If he'd been a year older, he would have. A year from now he may go back. I don't think so. But it does make me feel like those in the old country that arranged their children's marriages.

When he saw Stuart's sorrel tied to the brake on his wagon, he knew that David Stuart had come in for lunch with his wife. He wondered who was out riding watch. Stuart and Jessica seemed to be doing well enough. *Much better than I ever expected.* Will had seen the way Jessica looked at Ethan Fairchild before his death. He wouldn't have been surprised if she'd married Ethan. Then a day or two after Ethan was gone, she'd fallen in with Stuart and married him at the first opportunity.

Will Buttrell didn't need anyone to draw him a picture why that might have been. But it certainly seemed that somebody would have to draw Stuart a picture. Of course, anybody who would draw him such a picture ought to be shot. And he probably would be!

David Stuart had really taken hold, just like Will's son. Stuart took on any job suggested to him. He'd been a hero at the Green River Ferry crossing. He had negotiated a silly race with a mule-drawn train and hoodwinked them into taking the worser nooning place. The young man had a free mind, as well; he'd insisted on going back to look for young Fairchild's body, and Will had heard the account of that expedition from Francis.

There were still a few who either hinted or said straight-out, though not to Stuart's face, that he had killed Ethan. Will Buttrell hadn't made up his mind on that count. He knew the young bucks went off alone that day to rattle their horns over Jessica Thorne. That would have been Stuart's idea. Buttrell wouldn't have done such a thing even in his youth but he found it difficult to fault Stuart.

His own guess at the time had been that Stuart, being the stronger, had killed Fairchild without intending to. Today, he was not so certain. He had come to depend on and to trust Stuart until he could almost believe the story of marauders killing Ethan.

With Francis accounted for, Will finished his walk, rounded Warner Espy's wagon at the end of the column, and strode back toward the front of the train.

"Oh, Will," Martha Thorne said. "Man just went back for a word with you. You must have passed by on the other side of the wagons."

"Anything wrong?"

She gave a rueful chuckle. "I think he just wanted to be away from me and my questions about how long the snow would last." She looked up at the heavy clouds. "What do you think?"

"I'd bet on Manasseh's answer. He was always the best at judging what the weather would be."

Martha thought that funny. "And you were always the most diplomatic one."

She turned to put away her luncheon things and Buttrell went on back toward his wagon. Halfway there he met Thorne coming back. "Judge," he said.

"Will."

"What does your map show on up the way?"

"It isn't much help."

"David scout us up a pretty good spot to spend the night?"

Manasseh Thorne looked even more somber than usual. "I worry more that we'll stop for a night or a nooning and find ourselves there next spring."

Will looked at the low sky. "Looks like the snow is thinning out."

"You think so? Already? May be."

The snow stopped by suppertime. Stuart had found a place wide and flat enough for the wagons to circle. It seemed to Will that most people were in better spirits for the afternoon's experience. He spoke to Warner Espy when they were turning their oxen into the wagon corral for the night.

"Just a freak," Espy said, laughing. "Nobody'll ever believe we had three inches of snow in August!"

When Alathea woke him the next morning, Will looked out the wagon flap to see a good foot of snow on the ground. The sky was a clear, cold blue with not a trace of cloud nor a breath of breeze. The white covering sparkled and shone in the slanting morning sunlight as brightly as if everyone had lit his lantern at the same time.

Alathea said, "Do you remember that Barnes boy that nearly went blind from staying out half a day playing in the snow?"

He thought about it, nodded. It had been at the edge of his mind when she said it. "I was just thinking of it."

"Isn't that amazing?"

"Snow blindness?"

"No. That we were thinking the same thing."

When she looked, he was laughing. "We've always thought the same," he said, "except when you made those last two of ours boys."

"Silly. You wouldn't trade for either of them."

"One girl wouldn't have hurt anything."

"Maybe this next one, then."

"What?" When he looked, she was laughing at him. He put on his boots and coat and hat, then climbed out to check on the livestock.

Manasseh Thorne met him at the corral and stood beside him with his hands thrust in his coat pockets. "If you were in charge of this group today, Will, what would you do?"

Will thought about it. "Can't remember I've ever been in charge of much of anything," he said.

"Even so."

"Then I believe I'd spare our oxen trying to pull in the snow and our having to stare at the road," he said. "I'd declare it a day for the men to hunt."

"Hunt what?"

"Meat. If anything's out today, we ought to see its tracks. If nothing's out, the hike'd keep everybody busy and take up any mischievous energy. I think I'd send them out in bunches, though, so nobody would get lost or froze."

"That'll keep the men busy. What about the rest of them?"

"Good day for the women and young'uns to mend, read, gather firewood." He paused, then added, "Pray."

Thorne snorted. "Especially that last."

In return for a lot of tramping through the snow and the burning of a lot of good powder, the hunt netted four deer and one mountain sheep. Lije Holden had dropped the sheep from a rocky ledge into a snowbank at a range the others of his party swore was nothing less than three hundred yards.

"Wasn't all that much shooting," Holden insisted. "And, till I got hungry, I never thought much of a man that'd shoot sheep."

Caleb Sugarhouse had returned in an unusually quiet mood. His party had not seen any game, but they'd crossed the trail of a bear whose prints were larger than Sugarhouse's boot.

"Ain't no animal in the world got feet that big," Milt Ames laughed. "Sure wisht you'd brought him in, Caleb."

"You're welcome to go out and get him," Sugarhouse said. "The boys and me, we decided we were as near to a bear as we needed to be. Manasseh, what say we double the guard on the livestock tonight? Could be he might decide to do a little hunting of his own."

The women and boys of the train had cleared off a pretty good-sized site in the middle of the wagons and stacked in enough brush and firewood to build a big bed of coals. Buttrell and Hiram Miller tended to roasting part of the day's bag over the coals, and the group ate well without wasting.

"It's cold enough so the rest of the meat will keep tonight," Will said. "If there's any left after that, we can salt it down tomorrow night."

"Which is a damn good thing," Milt Ames told Will. "Else we might have starved right here in this shortcut."

Caleb Sugarhouse said, "We may yet sit right here and starve if Judge Thorne has his way."

Ames said, "If Thorne has *his* way! Hell. We wouldn't none of us be here if it weren't for you wanting to go off course chasing after silver, now would we?"

"Truth be told, it's rightly my fault," Douglas Stuart said. " 'Twas I who suggested we all stick together through this cutoff."

Tom Lee said, "It's easy enough for him to say that since he believes that God chose him to suggest this cutoff way back before he finished the fence around Eden!" They laughed.

"Gentlemen," Will said, "we may as well blame God

for the snow, too, as to blame ourselves for being in it. This might be a pretty good time to oil our harness."

On the second morning, Will woke to find the air still chilly, but the sun promising to melt the remaining snow. By noon, the wagons could move out of the pass. For a time the going was muddy. The oxen toiled, the wagons slid, the drivers cursed them both. But the weather definitely had cleared. Two days later they crossed the toll bridge at Marsh Creek, found bridge and buildings deserted except for one stray dog.

"Gone for the silver," Manasseh Thorne said.

David Stuart said, "They didn't leave anybody but this fellow to tell us the bridge is closed." He bent, scratched the dog's ears. It licked his hand. "Looks like I got a dog out of the deal, anyway," he said. "Come on, boy."

"Another mouth to feed."

"I'll risk it. Worse comes to worst, we can eat him."

In the late evening of the eleventh day, the train pulled into the City of Rocks. Caleb Sugarhouse had been right in guessing a trading post might be nearby, and its owner had resisted the call of the silver fields. Even before they thought about supper fires, the women flocked there. They had to buy carefully, but they had to buy. The extra days in the pass had caused them to use up valuable supplies.

When the men had unyoked and corralled the oxen and found wood for fires, they too went into the store to replenish their own supplies of tobacco, bits of broken harness, and the like. Will Buttrell bought a bag of peppermints with the idea that he'd please the boys with a pocketful apiece and his wife with the bag. In the back of his mind was the memory of what fine medicine peppermint had been for his stomach on an occasion or two.

None of them spoke to each other as much as usual. Buttrell knew they all were thinking of the showdown bound to come now that they'd reached the end of the cutoff. After the evening meal, Manasseh Thorne stood by a central fire, cleared his throat, and announced a train council meeting.

"We've come to a parting of the ways," he said. The idea seemed to slow his speech, and for a moment he stood gazing at the distant dark horizon.

"Some of you have already decided to take the lower trail with Caleb and seek your fortune. I've given that idea more than a little thought while staring at the rumps of oxen for the past hundred miles or so."

A few in the group laughed. They sensed a different mood in the man they had chosen to lead them to Oregon. But no one spoke. They sat numbly or wandered about restlessly or stared at the smoke rising from their pipes.

Thorne went on. "I've come to a few conclusions, though in this moment I do not speak for anyone else. Caleb, you've always been a good neighbor. You've helped more than one family in this group, helped them raise barns, even helped them bring in crops when the weather threatened. This evening it is clear to me that I can in no wise blame any of you who shall choose the lower trail. I ask only that you not blame me for going on to Oregon."

They might have applauded in a different place, on a different evening, to remarks on a different subject. Instead, they sat soberly. Even Caleb Sugarhouse chose not to comment.

"Very well, then. We've come this far together as friends, and we'll in God's grace go our separate ways as friends. We have come through a great deal together, not the least of which lay along Hudspeth's Cutoff."

More of them laughed. Thorne smiled.

"At our last council meeting, we agreed to decide on this evening which way each would go. I have nothing more to say than I've said. Caleb, do you want to make any final remarks before we vote?"

On the other side of the fire, Caleb Sugarhouse stood

and looked around at those behind him and to the sides. "I guess I ought to thank you, Judge, for coming this far with us. I guess all of you know I'd be glad for every last one of you to come on down to Virginia City with me." He offered Thorne his hand. "You, too, Manasseh."

"Let's vote," Thorne said. "Those for Virginia City, stand with Caleb. Those for Oregon, come with me."

Will Buttrell was the first to join Thorne. For him, Sugarhouse's last remark had been the deciding factor. At last the situation came mountain-air clear to him. Caleb Sugarhouse had nursed a festering sore from the day they first chose Judge Thorne to lead them. Now Caleb had made that clear. Even if the judge decided to go to the silver field, Caleb would be the new leader.

Will hadn't changed his expression, hadn't considered sharing his thought with the group, didn't expect Alathea to be surprised at his decision. She had probably known all along what he had just then realized. He might spend the rest of his life wondering about that silver, but he would not follow Caleb Sugarhouse.

David and Jessica Stuart came next, hand in hand. Barbara Kenny and Fred Harris came from opposite sides of the group, but stood together behind Thorne. Lije Holden unfolded himself slowly and sauntered over. Long Tom Lee, whom everyone had expected to join Sugarhouse, hesitated a moment, then walked over to Thorne's group. Douglas Stuart, whom everyone had counted in Thorne's party, hesitated not at all before joining Sugarhouse.

As the sides divided, Will Buttrell saw Francis standing in the firelight in the dwindling pool of undecided. Something caught in his throat. Francis had been acting the part of a man, figured he was a man. It was plain now that he meant to make his own decision. And if he decided on the silver fields, there was precious little Will or Alathea could do to stop him.

Leaving the Thorne group, Will walked over to him. "Son," he began, saw the closed, stubborn expression on the boy's face, paused to think what to say next.

"I'd wanted to talk to you, Francis." David Stuart had come up without either Buttrell noticing him. They turned toward him.

"What about?"

"We're going to be pretty shorthanded, what with seven wagons and one of them Mrs. Kenny's," Stuart said. "I was hoping you'd see your way clear to come with us. We could surely use another good man."

Francis Buttrell stared at him for a moment, then looked back at his father. Will put a hand on his shoulder.

"Just what I'd meant to say."

Francis looked at them a second longer, and then he smiled. "Sure, Davy," he said. "If you put it that way."

30

Forrest Elam smiled to himself at the thought that he could still see better in the dark than any other human he'd ever met. He'd gotten his traps together and gotten Ann Bradley awake and fed and ready to take the trail in time for the two of them to ride before daylight.

"I'm sorry to be so slow, Mr. Elam," she said.

"I'm sorry to be so sudden, but we got to ride long hours if we aim to overtake your young man before he overtakes his destiny."

For his own part, Elam had never put much stock in the idea of changing other men's destinies. But he'd given his word to help the girl. Naturally enough, she wanted Fairchild alive. Elam figured she wouldn't find him in that state unless they got to him before he tackled Silverhorn.

In the way of the mountain men, Elam had always been willing to allow destiny its free hand, but dragging his heels would be tampering with destiny as surely as rushing. And he was just about ready to tamper with destiny. He'd visited Bradley's Oak the night Ann had come to his cabin, had seen it while the fires were still burning over the ruins of the buildings. He hadn't been able to tell her. Not yet, not until they knew more about Fairchild.

"Hup," he told his horse as he urged the animal up a new slope.

Ann's horse was laboring more than his, but that couldn't be helped. *Better to drive a good horse into the ground than keep it sound and bury a good man.* Not that he could be certain Ethan Fairchild was a good man. He was the man Ann had set her cap for, and that would have to be good enough.

Late in the day they rode into a shallow draw with a trickle of muddy water along the bottom. Elam had started up the far slope before he thought to pause. Water hadn't been all that plentiful, and here was a good supply. Given more leisure, he would have unsaddled and spent the night. He looked back at Ann.

"Good spot for a camp," he said. "How are you feeling, girl?"

Ann laughed. "Terrible. But we're racing with destiny, and we've two hours of daylight left."

"Great Godkins! All right, we'll water and rest the horses and ourselves. Then we'll camp where the night finds us."

He saw the stone arrow before he got down. Dismounting, he knelt beside it, running his hand softly over the rocks and the ground around them. The stones had been moved. Someone had first arranged them to point northwest. Maybe a day later, another hand had shifted them, and had done a middling job of hiding the original indentations they'd made. Now the arrow pointed northeast.

"But what does it mean?"

Ann was standing a few steps back, frowning at the arrow. Elam rocked back on his haunches and rubbed his chin.

"Blessed if I know, Ann, 'cepting there's been considerable sneaking around. You tend them horses and fill our canteens, whilst I see if can I cut some sign."

There was sign aplenty, once Elam cast around the spot. Some unknown horse had come and gone from the spot first, its tracks almost hidden by time and other trails. Ethan's Devil had headed out northeast, all right, up to the first rocky ledge. Then its tracks disappeared. Elam made a wider sweep and found them down the slope, now headed as much west as north, the way the arrow was laid out to point in the first place. Later still, a sizable party had passed that way, paused, gone off to the northeast.

"It don't make a lick of sense," Elam muttered.

"What don't—doesn't?" Ann asked. He realized that, under the guise of laying out camp, she'd been watching him anxiously. "Can you tell? Have we lost Ethan's trail?"

Elam snorted. "Girl, this old man could track a butterfly through a buffalo herd, just by sniffing the powder off'n its wings. One time on the Yellowstone . . ." He stopped, frowning. "Thing is, he's not the one laid out this arrow. But he sure enough shifted it to point off yonderways instead of the way he went."

Ann looked blank. Elam didn't blame her. Nobody would have left Fairchild a sign to follow, so the arrow was meant for somebody else. Fairchild had done his best to mislead that somebody. But what did the arrow point toward, and who had made it? Standing and looking into the distance, Forrest Elam wondered what other elements were at play in this game.

"Ain't nothing to worry about," he told Ann. "We know which way your young man went, and that's the mainest thing." He stretched himself on the soft grassy bank of the creek and closed his eyes. "Ann, you set them critters loose to graze and ease your joints a spell. We'll just ask your Ethan what he was up to, soon's we catch him."

The sun was still well up when they set out again. Elam ignored the false trail Fairchild had laid and cut straight to the northwest.

"Mr. Elam?" Ann pointed. "Didn't Devil's tracks go off that way?"

Elam chuckled. "Good eye, girl. But let's see if we don't cut his sign again just over this rise."

They found it just about where the old man expected and followed it in just about the way he himself would have taken. "Knows what he's doing," he called back to the girl. "Smarter'n most, your young man."

They made a dry camp not long after sundown in the shelter of a rocky outcrop that thrust like a single fang out of the smoothly rolling grassland. Elam built up a tiny fire of buffalo chips back against the rock face. Sitting by the fire after supper, smoking his new pipe, Elam thought for a time of the boy who had gone with him so many years earlier to find the Indian raiders, the boy who had died helping him slay his dragon.

For a long time, he hadn't been able to let his mind rest on the boy. But now by the fire, in the presence of Ann Bradley, he was able to think without sorrowing. It did not escape him that he might this time find himself in the position of the boy, dying to slay his companion's dragon. Dying would not be so bad. Failing to help the girl would be much worse.

The following morning he was down in his back and hips. The old rheumatism had caught up to him. Ann saw him as he was crippling his way out of his blankets.

"Are you all right, Mr. Elam?"

She was tending the fire, moving slowly, hitching in her steps now and then as though every joint hurt. Probably they did, he thought, but she was bent on not showing it.

"Certain sure," he said. He moved next to the fire to warm his bones, staying near it until he thought his clothing would burn. After that he walked around the area while the girl made some of her weak coffee.

The thought of getting back in the saddle was a somber one, but he did not flinch from it. After all, if an old leather man was saddlesore, a poor tender young girl must be awfully uncomfortable. Hell. If she could do it without a word of complaint, he could do it singing.

He sliced off a couple of chunks of bacon and put them in the pan. Ann Bradley had gone off out of sight to tend to some business of her own. When she came back, she asked, "What's that you're humming?"

Elam hadn't realized he'd been humming. "Man knows he's off tune when they ask him what he's singing," he said. "Old song. Learned it from the Crows. Teach it to you sometime, but first we'd best get this salt pork ate. We ought already to be in the saddle."

"We can eat riding."

Elam stopped their trek twice during that day, once at eleven o'clock and again around three. "I know all this riding's hard on you," he told Ann. "Not easy on me, either, nor on the horses. They're the ones that matter. Tomorrow we'll make up for it."

"How far behind do you figure we are?"

"Hard to say how fast he may've been moving. I don't figure he's gained so much on us."

"But if he's still two days ahead of us, how will we ever catch up to him?"

"Got to stop sometime. Likely we'll catch him up then."

Close to dark, Elam held up his hand, stopped their progress. Ahead, vultures circled and dived to land and rose heavy and slow from something on the ground.

"Wait here for me," he said.

"What is it?"

"I don't know. Wait here, and have that lady's Colt of yours ready."

Then he rode on through the brush toward the ugly, heavy smell coming from the top of a hill. Someone had built a fire, partly with green wood. He could smell that along with the death. It wasn't human death because that was a smell different from all others.

When he found the wolves, he admired Fairchild for the fight he and his horse had put up and won. He faulted the younger man for camping there and for building a tenderfoot's fire. When he was certain that Fairchild had ridden out alive, he went back to the girl and led her around the area.

"Is he in there, then?" she asked. She stopped her horse, turned him toward the site of the fire.

"No. But he's been there. He left a passel of wolves dead around his fire."

"Do you think he's all right?"

"Him and that demon horse got out of there alive."

"Do you think we're getting closer?"

"Can't say. Let's make an extra half hour tonight. In the morning we'll be closer."

Before full dark, though, they came upon the wide, desolate backwash of the buffalo herd's trail. Fairchild's tracks disappeared into that trampled chaos and not even Forrest Elam's most careful examination could sort out the tangle.

"Best we make camp here," he said. "We'll wait till sunup, then see if them tracks don't sort themselves out."

Ann agreed without enthusiasm.

"We'll find him," Elam insisted. He knew she was near exhaustion. "Ain't never lost anybody yet, not permanent, that is. Why, I remember back once on the Tongue River, I lost a set of tracks for three days and then found them again on solid rock."

Pitching his voice low and slow, he yarned her to sleep. But he himself sat long into the night, watching the stars wheel past and hoping he'd told her true.

In the end, they could do nothing but assume Fairchild had followed the herd. Elam kept Ann to the main trail while he sallied off left and right. They'd been riding most of the morning when he finally found the unmistakable print of the Devil's shoe on a flat bench. He rode back to Ann hoorawing like a greenhorn at his first rendezvous, and the two of them hurried on with renewed hope.

In the early afternoon, they found the site of a large

camp. "Maybe as many as eight or ten. Six sure," Elam said. "But no wagon."

Ann said, "The wagon tracks come in. Oh, and look, here they are again leaving."

"Let's take just another minute. Look here now. You can find every other track in camp on top of the wagon tracks. But this one here's the Devil's track. Hard to understand that the others didn't wipe it out. The wagon come through here first of all, but it didn't stop. All the others come later."

"Who? When?"

"Fairchild first, maybe with the wagon. The ones that made this camp after him."

"But who would they be?"

He didn't like the possibilities for that. "Army, maybe."

"No, he was with them earlier. Besides, these aren't the marks of government shoes."

Elam wished he had never given the girl an idea how to read tracks. "Could be just about anybody."

Her eyes were level on his. "Could it?"

"No. I'll tell you true. The chances is better than even this camp was laid by them he was looking for."

"Behind him? Tracking him!"

"Don't think they was. Looks like they was here a couple of days at least. Not like they was chasing somebody."

"Why would they have stayed? What were they waiting for?"

"For the buffalo hunters to finish up'd be my guess."

"And Ethan?"

"Can't say. You said Ethan knew the buffalo hunters?"

"We all did. Mr. Waller invited him to come be their guard. I heard part of it."

"Waugh." That made all of it fit together better than he had expected. What he didn't like was that the outlaw camp was over a day old.

"Let's ride," Ann said, reining Blue out ahead. "We have to hurry."

"No," Elam said. "What we have to do is take it slow

and cautious. This Silverhorn and his bunch, they could be between us and Ethan now. We can't go riding up onto them by mistake, not if you want to live to see your young man again."

"Oh!" Ann put her hand to her mouth, then to the butt of the pistol Elam had given her. "Oh, I didn't think of that."

"Then it's a mortal good thing I did." Drawing out his long rifle, Elam laid it across his saddle. "I'll lead. You watch our backs and shoot at anything that moves except'n me."

Just when it was too dark to tell much about it, the smell of death stopped Forrest Elam again. They found the wide swath of burned and blackened prairie where the buffalo hunters had camped. Even after the fire, Forrest Elam could smell the hides which had been there and the scent of human death which was the only smell he liked less.

"Are we too late?" Ann asked.

Elam turned, quickly motioning her to silence. "We wait," he whispered. "Back behind that hill, quiet as two mice hiding from an owl. Whatever's there, we'll find in the morning."

What they found in the morning was six graves together and another off away from them.

"One side wiped the other out," Elam said.

"Which?"

"Silverhorn wouldn't have buried the dead."

"Then where is he? Where's Ethan?"

"Godkins, girl, that's the question." Elam rubbed his chin and pondered. "Must have been Silverhorn set the fire. Could be the hunters had beat them off, moved their wagon while their camp was burning around them and then come back to bury the killed." He shook his head. "Don't seem likely. And where's everybody at?"

"Mr. Elam? How about the tracks?"

"Tracks. Why, I was just settling in to look at them. Don't you worry."

Ann was quiet while he sorted through the jumbled trails that led in and out of the camp. He worried about her, stealing glances at her white, set face, but there was little he could do. She was tougher than she'd looked, that was sure, but she had a lot of sorrow coming. He hoped Fairchild's death wouldn't be a part of it.

"What is it?" she asked. "What have you found?"

"I'm looking at the tracks of them that buried the dead, as I judge."

"Is that a shovel?"

He had hoped she wouldn't see it. "What's left of one."

"I have to know."

Elam didn't like the idea of digging up the dead. On the other hand, the wrong thing about showing her the tracks was that he didn't have any way to know who had been riding the horses. This wouldn't be the first time he'd been fooled about that. But he had to keep the girl level. "You'll recognize this set. It belongs to Fairchild's Devil."

"Then he isn't dead! Thank you!"

Elam too figured that Fairchild was alive. The best reason to believe it was the horse's temper. Very few men would choose to ride the chestnut unless the alternative was being dragged behind it.

The Devil had moved out first when the burying was done, moving at a gallop. Two other horses had followed more slowly. Strangely, one of those horses had been in the outlaw camp.

"Best as we know, Ethan headed out west, going hard," Elam said at last.

"Then that's the way we'll go."

They passed below the field strewn with huge buffalo carcasses, now blackened from the fire. Vultures and ravens fought with the coyotes and wolves over the leavings. All of that was too familiar to Elam to interest him. On the other side of the creek Fairchild's tracks and those of his distant followers fell in with the wagon tracks.

Ann Bradley read it, too. "Is Ethan protecting the wagon or chasing it?" she asked.

"Chasing it. See that track and these? His horse is moving twice as fast as those pulling the wagon. If he'd been with the wagon, he'd have run right into the back of it."

"Oh. Then you think Silverhorn has the wagon and Ethan's following him?"

"Seems likely."

"Ethan may already have caught them!"

She said it with a sort of joy mingled with pride, then fell silent. Perhaps, Elam thought, it had occurred to her how badly outnumbered he would be if he did overtake the outlaws.

31

Ethan Fairchild finished covering over the last grave. He'd acquired considerable experience in that line since his first days with the Dragoons, and he couldn't say he'd enjoyed it much. Still, he was the logical one for the job. Grace wasn't interested. Waller was in no shape to bury his hunters, and they couldn't be left for the animals and elements.

He'd found a shovel with most of its handle intact in the ruins of the supply wagon and gone to work. He couldn't say he'd put the men six feet under, but he had given them decent covering, and he could leave it to Redwood Waller and the woman to put up markers. Thrusting the shovel into the ground a last time, he mopped the sweat from his face and shoulders and went for his shirt.

"I'm obliged, Ethan," Waller said huskily.

The hunter was sitting up, some of the color back in his face. The makeshift bandage on his chest and back was bloody, but the blood was drying to rusty red. Maybe Grace did know something about doctoring, after all.

"It's nothing," Fairchild said.

Grace. The woman knelt at Waller's side, the torn blue dress hiked up until it showed her bare thighs. She held a canteen to Waller's mouth, then dabbed his lips with another rag from the dress.

"Thanks, you soulless she-devil," Waller said.

Grace grinned at him. "It's nothing. Told you, I'll do whatever you say."

The big hunter opened his mouth.

"Don't," Fairchild warned. "We need her. Somebody's got to look after you."

"Look after me, hell! We're going spang after that white-headed bastard and skin him out for moccasins!" He braced himself on Grace's shoulder, tried to rise. "Take more than one bullet to finish me. Aaah!"

The woman eased him down again as gently as if he were a sick cat. "Don't try to get frolicsome," she told him. "You break that wound open, and Fairhair here will be digging a great big grave. Real shame, too."

"Can he ride?" Fairchild asked.

"Hell, yes, I can ride!" Waller growled.

Grace nodded. "Got to," she said. "Nothing here to make a travois with. Be all right if he takes it slow." She studied Fairchild for a moment. "You're minded to go on ahead, take on Tom and them."

It wasn't a question, but Fairchild nodded anyway.

"They're making for Bliss's Ferry, figuring to sell the hides to Fort Hall. You know the way?"

"The wagon'll leave tracks."

"I'll tend Redwood. Nothing will harm him that don't kill me first."

Fairchild had mixed feelings about that, but he settled for another nod. Come down to it, he figured Grace would be pretty hard to kill.

"Ethan!" Waller protested. "You ain't figuring to leave me alone with this bitch wolf?"

"Not much choice, Red, unless you want to let Silverhorn off." He grinned at Waller. "Besides, she likes you."

"I like you," Grace agreed.

"That's what I'm damned well afraid of!"

Fairchild caught Devil and made to mount, but Waller called him back. Expecting another plea not to be abandoned to Grace's mercy, Fairchild led the horse along. It bit him on the calf.

"Listen, Ethan, afore you go," Waller said.

"Yes?"

"Well, it ain't fitting to leave the boys this way. Maybe you could say some words over them?" Waller grimaced. "I would, but I don't know as my own credit's extra good where it counts."

Fairchild started to speak of wasted time, of Silverhorn getting away, of his need to be on the trail. He stopped with the words unspoken, remembering. Thorne had always been in a terrible hurry, but never so much that he couldn't take time to do what was right. Lieutenant Cranfill, with the strain of command, and wounded men to nurse, and Silverhorn's bunch one jump ahead, had stopped to read over poor Jimmy Jenkins; and his troopers thought the more of him for it. And he knew beyond doubt what Elgin Bradley would have done. Fairchild saw it suddenly as a link among those dissimilar men, common ground, one of the things that set their kind apart from Silverhorn and his wolves.

"I'm not much of a hand," he said.

"Wait," Grace said. She went to her pony, fumbled in the saddlebags, returned holding a small blue book in both hands. "Here," she said. "There are things in here."

Fairchild stared at the book. Opening the cover, he saw inside three neat lines in faded blue ink. *To Elgin Bradley, on the birth date of his daughter Ann Elizabeth, June 8, 1841.* The signature was illegible. He looked up at Grace.

"Damn you."

"He give it to me," she said. "It and his nother book, where I learnt your name."

"Ethan," Waller reminded him, "I need her alive." But it wasn't necessary. Fairchild couldn't name the emotion he felt toward the woman, but at the moment, it had nothing to do with killing. Turning away, he walked stiffly to the graves, Devil pacing stiff-legged behind. The book opened easily to the passage Fairchild wanted.

" 'I am the resurrection and the life,' " he began.

Fairchild rode out with his revolving rifle across his lap and Waller's heavy Sharps slung to his saddle. As if sensing a fight to come, the chestnut behaved like someone's pet lamb, responsive to every touch of its rider's knees. Fairchild picked up the wagon tracks where they emerged from the creek and fell in to follow. Silverhorn's wolves had a few hours' start, but Fairchild intended to catch them before he slept.

He rode hard for half an hour, slacked off to let the Devil rest, and went on, keeping the tracks in sight. He didn't even think of stopping at noon. Devil apparently felt the same, holding to a steady, untiring pace until the chestnut's flanks were bathed in sweat. The wagon was taking the smoothest, clearest path and that made the going easier.

Soon the country grew rougher, steep rocky hills with stunted pines fighting the thin soil on their tops. The wagon had gone more slowly, the driver having had to pick his way between rocks and fallen trees. Valleys and ridges cropped up more often, but the wagon had found ways to get through. Fairchild found himself stopping at every creek or pool to let the chestnut drink.

Maybe Silverhorn's driver knows the country, Fairchild thought, *or maybe he has a good map. I haven't had a map since I got lost off the train.* He was pretty certain of one thing after a few hours trailing the wagon. It was headed west. It might tack north or south when it had to, but it always came back on its real course.

In the early afternoon, he came to the top of a sharp ridge, saw where the wagon had crossed on a slant and sought the smooth way down into a stand of pines. He dismounted in the shelter of a nest of tumbled rocks. Devil had gotten over his fit of good behavior. Fairchild dodged a hasty kick, snubbed the horse down hard, and tried to think. He was losing valuable time following the serpentine path the wagon had taken.

Silverhorn. How would the renegade deal with a little problem like a man dogging his trail to kill him? Maybe he would leave a sharpshooter hanging back in ambush. Or maybe he'd lost enough men at that trick.

The wolves would never believe a pursuer had taken time to bury the dead. They would have expected him sooner, might even have begun to think he wasn't coming at all.

At the next detour in the wagon tracks, Fairchild held due west. That course took him sharply up a slope strewn with angular boulders and spotted here and there with straggling pines. From the crest of the ridge he could see nothing but a series of parallel ridges rising to the west. The wagon must have found a better route.

If he went on west, he might lose track of the wagon entirely, or he might make up some of the time he had lost. *Fort Hall*, he thought. *If I lose them, I'll find them again at Fort Hall*. He rode down the slope into the next valley, holding west as best he could and watching for the wagon tracks.

Within a quarter of an hour he cut the trail coming back from the north. He kept to the direct path west. When he came to the top of the last of the hogback ridges he saw a line of broken brush in the valley below. He figured it would be the wagon's trail. After studying the terrain and looking for any signs of an ambush, he rode down to the trail, saw the wagon tracks, and continued straight up the next ridge. The bullet droned past his face just before he heard the rifle report.

Fairchild had time to locate a white puff of powder smoke, no more than a hundred yards to the north and atop the ridge. Then the Devil broke into a dead gallop toward the sound. The horse's cavalry-charge technique had worked pretty well at Lodgepole Creek, but Fairchild had a different plan for this new situation.

By main strength, he hauled the chestnut's head around, forcing his Devil uphill at an angle to take him away from the bushwhacker. Another bullet came roaring by, passed behind him as he leaned forward onto the horse's neck. Fairchild leaned to his left, hiding as much of his body as he could behind the Devil. When they were just at the top of the ridge, a third bullet struck the pommel of his saddle with a solid thunk. Fairchild let out a cry, rocked back, slid off the horse on the left side. He hit hard enough to knock the breath out of him, but held to both rifle and reins.

The chestnut horse screamed as the reins jerked its head sideways. For three mad seconds, it danced and whirled in a real contest with the man. Then Fairchild got control of it, tied off the reins and checked over his Colt rifle. Cradling the Colt, he crawled through the low brush and rocks until he found a couple of steer-sized boulders with a tree growing between them. There he took his stand and waited to see whether the bushwhacker would come to confirm his kill.

The wait stretched into minutes, a quarter of an hour. Then he understood. The shooter was waiting for his prey to bleed to death. Fairchild lay quiet, watched the ravines and ridges to the east and west.

For all his alertness, he almost missed the man. Something at the corner of his eye changed color, moved, was gone. He turned his head slowly, saw nothing, saw movement, saw a man materialize like smoke from the rocks along the western edge of the ridge. He was dark-skinned, an Indian perhaps, and he moved with a silent flowing grace that made him seem a part of the hill. Fairchild waited until he could see the man's curiously light eyes and the pattern of his shirt. Then he cocked his rifle and started to rise.

At the click of the Colt's hammer, the Indian whirled

and fired. The bullet went wide no more than a couple of inches.

The Indian had already thrown down his rifle and brought out a revolver when Fairchild's bullet slammed him back among the rocks out of sight. From the brush where the man had disappeared, Fairchild heard a quick fluttering, like the drumming of a partridge, then silence. Remembering his own trick, he cocked the Colt again and came fast across the open space, ready to shoot.

He didn't need a second shot. The Indian lay on his back, his eyes wide. Blood fanned out behind him on the ground. Fairchild took his rifle and his box of linen cartridges, looked down at him for a moment, then left him where he lay. There was no time for a burial.

He found the Indian's horse waiting like a trained dog at the spot where the first shot had been fired. The ambusher had waited for a pursuer to come along following the wagon tracks. Fairchild was alive because he'd come across the trail from the wrong direction. A heavy gunbelt with two Navy Colts in its holsters lay across the saddle. Fairchild took the Indian's horse in tow, carrying the extra weapons and his saddlebags. Then he went on west, following his wolves.

If the men with the wagon were closed enough to hear the shots, Fairchild would catch up to them within an hour or so. If not, he still might come up to them before dark. All he needed was the blind luck to dodge any further bullets and to cut the wagon tracks farther down the way. He would have preferred to know how many men Silverhorn had with him. On the other hand, he would have preferred to be sitting by a warm hearth with Ann Bradley, drinking a glass of buttermilk.

Ann! Are you really alive? And where in God's name are you?

He shook his head. No time for that. If he wanted to see Ann again—and he wanted that more than anything he'd ever imagined—he would have to keep his mind on the job at hand.

Slipping up for a look over the next ridge, he saw neither wagon passage nor any nearby cover for an ambusher. With hope in the blind luck he would have to have, Fairchild rode directly downslope, across the short valley floor and up the next rise. He varied his speed and direction to make as poor a target as he could manage. His luck held.

At the far rim he saw clearer country as the ridges played out into gentler hills covered with gray sagebrush. Across the low hills, he saw a frail cloud of dust moving away from him. His luck was blooming.

He struck the wagon tracks strung out toward the farthest hill where the dust had disappeared. Beside the tracks lay a pile of rocks and brushwood, a confusing sign of human passage. Had they started to build a fire? A cabin? Then he saw the remains of a wagon wheel, its iron rim missing, its spokes splintered.

A wagon wheel had finally broken down. They had stopped long enough to pile logs under the axle and install Waller's extra wheel. The hub was still warm. Fairchild felt that he'd not only called down a rain of good luck on himself but had set her evil sister loose on his enemies.

He rode hard for half an hour, then left the clear trail and drifted off to the south at an angle which would take him to a bluff from which he could expect a better view. There he crept to the edge and lay on his belly to look across the broader valley. The wagon rolled along on what was now an obvious and well-traveled road. Waller's mules were pulling it at a fast walk. A half-dozen tied horses trailed the wagon, but Fairchild counted only two riders. If there were any flankers, he didn't see them. In the middle distance, a broad swath of green bisected the valley.

Bliss's Ferry, Fairchild thought. *If there's a ferry, there has to be a river.*

Below him, the rim fell away in a sheer drop of forty feet or more. To reach the valley floor, he would have to backtrack. He calculated the time it would take the wagon to reach the shelter of the trees along the riverbank. Then he looked at the rimrock that curved off to his left. He could never get to the river before the wagon crossed, but he still had a chance.

Keeping back from that rim, he rode at a canter to the highest point he could find. He got down, tied his horses well, and took his rifles up to the scattered boulders on the very edge. Guessing the wagon at a quarter mile away, he clicked up the ramp sight on the Sharps, rested the long barrel on the boulder, and centered the bead on the white cover of the wagon. The amount he should lead his target was pretty much of a guess, so he drew back the hammer, made his guess, and squeezed the trigger.

The big rifle boomed a cloud of white smoke. Recoil, more like a mule's push than a mule's kick, shoved Fairchild back and half around. For what seemed a long time, nothing else happened. Then a fountain of dirt rose into the air twenty yards ahead of the wagon.

"You want to watch that old rifle," Waller had warned him before he'd left the camp. "Accuracy's not what it should be. It'll shoot as much as an inch high and an inch to the left at two hundred yards."

Laughing, Fairchild hauled down on the trigger guard and slid a fresh linen cartridge into the rifle's breech. By the time he'd capped the nipple and settled the sights on the valley again, the wagon had stopped. He could see the riders casting about frantically, trying to find where the shot had come from. Fairchild looked for the white-haired man, didn't see him, sighted instead on the nearer of the riders, a man on a gray horse. Remembering to hold a little lower this time, he fired.

He should have missed the twisting target, but his luck was still good. The man reined up his horse at just the wrong moment. Blood burst from the gray's neck just forward of the shoulder. It broke down in its withers and fell, throwing the rider hard. The man hobbled to his feet, limping, and his fellow outrider raced to pick him up before Fairchild could load again.

Fairchild had the shot, but passed it up. The wagon had turned almost broadside to him. For a moment, he saw a tall, white-maned figure poised on the wagon's seat, staring back toward him. Then the white-haired man grabbed the whip and lashed the mules furiously toward the river.

Fairchild's bullet slammed into the packed hides in the wagon. He knew his chances of hitting Silverhorn from that angle were slim, but he didn't mind. At least the big outlaw would know Fairchild meant to kill him. That accomplished, Fairchild estimated the rapidly increasing range and dropped a shot ahead of the galloping mules. Silverhorn was slinging the heavy wagon from side to side, causing it to sway precariously as he tried to make it a poorer target. Carrying double, the roan gradually overtook and passed the wagon, its riders not even looking back.

Ignoring the men, Fairchild kept up a steady fire at the wagon and team. He was down to three cartridges and had just about given up hope when one of the eight mules suddenly collapsed in the traces. Another tripped over its fallen mate and went down, and suddenly the smoothly running team disintegrated into a screaming, kicking, plunging tangle of desperate animals. The wagon slued sideways, went up on two wheels, then slammed down upright with a crash that carried all the way to Fairchild's ears.

Silverhorn was down before it stopped moving, slashing at the snarled harness with a long knife, trying to cut the fallen mule free. Fairchild used his last three rounds going for the outlaw, but the mules were in the way. He did succeed in downing the nigh leader with his last shot, driving the survivors into an even greater panic. Then he gathered up his guns and raced back to the horses. This was the best he could hope for. If he could find a way down to the valley in time, he would have the silver wolf in a trap.

"Run!" he told the chestnut horse, and the Devil heard

and ran, dragging along the dead man's unwilling mount.

But the luck that Fairchild had ridden so far finally broke down. He had to double back all the way to the main trail to get down to the valley floor. By that time, the wagon was nowhere in sight. Along the trail to the river, he passed the dead horse, two dead mules, a third that kicked and thrashed with a broken hind leg. He paused to put it out of its misery and to scan the treeline ahead. On the ground near the mules, he found the remains of another smashed wagon wheel and deep gouges where the wagon had been dragged off anyway.

"Well, hell," he muttered, but he wasn't completely displeased. Even if they succeeded in crossing the river ahead of him, Silverhorn's wolves weren't going to be moving fast.

Half an hour before sunset he came down the paved slope to the Green River ferry. The raft rested against the far shore, rolling idly with the waves from the current. He waited a few minutes, saw no signs of life on either bank. At the near shore he saw the deep wagon tracks running right down to the edge where it must have gone onto the raft. They had beaten him to the spot where it would have been easiest to stop them.

He sat there a moment in his saddle staring at the wagon tracks, thinking. Silverhorn knew Fairchild had not been there, had not crossed ahead of him. So, what would they do about him? And how was he to cross the river and get at them, knowing they might be laying for him on the far side? He had not entirely settled the matter in his mind when he saw the white puff of a rifle from the far bank. An old saying about a bullet with a man's name on it flashed through his mind as he whirled the Devil hard to the side. The horse reared and threw its head back. Fairchild, thinking about the bullet, tried to dodge, but something hit him in the face. He slid backward out of his saddle into the swift cold water.

32

Seven wagons moved north along the California Trail, trudging at the pace of oxen, well closed-up and without stragglers. Behind the last wagon, two young boys on horseback herded three loose oxen, a milk cow, and eight horses.

Will Buttrell was driving third behind Barbara Kenny's wagon, holding his team near enough the tailboard to take more dust than he normally would have. *Driving close*, he decided, *because the few of us left together have to close ranks*. He spent a moment more in reverie, then shook his head.

"Be stopping soon for nooning," he said to his wife. "What do we have for lunch?"

"We still have a ham from your deer," Alathea said. "We'd better eat whatever part we want today. I'll fix it with that wild mustard Sarah Holden found." She looked at him. "And I want you to quit your moping."

"I'm not moping."

"I didn't ask you to deny it; I asked you to quit it. If you're worried about the judge holding his mettle, quit that, too. He'll hold."

"I wasn't."

"Besides, we've still got seven wagons, and the young Holdens with us, and David Stuart, bless him. I'm perfectly confident that you and he could face down a band of Indians by yourselves, if it came to that."

Will Buttrell looked at his wife. Her eyes were still red from secret crying over her parting from Becky Miller. Of all those eleven wagons that had gone with Sugarhouse, the Millers were the biggest loss to the Buttrell family. The Miller twins had been just of an age to play with Michael and Homer, and Will had shared many a discussion on hunting and farming and politics with Hiram. But Alathea and bouncy, laughing Becky Miller had been special friends, and Buttrell knew his wife was feeling the hurt more than the rest of them.

"What are you looking at, Will Buttrell?" she demanded. She turned her head, brushed at her eyes with the back of a dimpled hand. "Dust is uncommon bad today."

Will kept looking as he marveled at the luck of his choice in marrying her, marveled at the luck of his choice in making this trip and keeping to their original destination. "I thank you," he said.

"For what?"

"For being my wife."

He felt her stare on his cheek for a time before she returned her attention to the trail or the tailgate of the widow Kenny's wagon. Will Buttrell was happy in his world. His wife helped convince him he'd made all the right choices. He couldn't take credit for them, but he could be grateful. And he was.

"Will!" David Stuart was riding along the line of wagons, coming in from his position on the point. He reined up beside the Buttrells. "Company coming. Judge Thorne's going to be stopping the train."

"Oh!" Alathea Buttrell said. "That's nice. Who?" She saw Stuart's grim expression and stopped.

Stuart answered the question anyway. "Horsemen, six or seven of them. All men." He hesitated, then said, "I don't much like their looks. Judge says be ready for trouble."

"What kind of trouble?" Will asked.

"Any kind. Get the kids inside. And it might be best to have your rifle handy."

"Orren and Michael are back with the livestock," Alathea said anxiously. "And Francis is riding drag."

"I know. I'll get Lije Holden to keep the boys company with the stock. He's our best shot."

Buttrell had another question, but Stuart had already spurred past. Judge Thorne was drawing his wagon to a halt. Barbara Kenny slowed to a stop in front of Buttrell, pulling her wagon a little way off to the right. Will slanted his to the left. Behind him, Fred Harris was easing an old Colt revolving cylinder shotgun out of its case and onto his lap.

Will turned his attention to the north. He could see the riders approaching now, without haste, perhaps without plan. No, he decided, they did have a plan, for they'd swung from a column into a wide line abreast that blocked the trail.

"Will," Alathea asked, "do you think they're bandits?"

"Don't know." Buttrell loosened his revolver in its holster. He reached behind him for his muzzle-loading rifle, wishing he'd followed the recommendation in Marcy's guidebook and gotten a revolving Colt. "But we'll be finding out what they are in about three minutes."

He watched the oncoming line of horsemen. Beside him, Alathea neatly laid out a dozen bullets and the extra powder horn. He hoped Francis was riding too far back to become involved in any fray. But of course they would all be involved. He couldn't hope to control Francis's destiny much longer, in life or in death.

Only in marriage, he thought, then shook his head. It wasn't a good time to wander into old reveries.

He laid the revolver between himself and his wife on the wagon seat and held the rifle ready. Should there be no need for arms, he could apologize later for bristling. Ahead of him the widow Kenny was draping her shawl over some shiny object in her lap.

Out to the southeast a horse was coming as fast as Stuart's. Will did not have to look to know it was Francis. He kept his eye on the approaching men. He counted seven. If there was a hymnal among them, he did not see it.

"Hello the wagons," one of them said as they verged onto the road a few yards ahead of Thorne's oxen.

"Good day, gentlemen," Thorne returned their greeting. He remained on the seat. Buttrell couldn't see Martha anywhere, guessed she must be back in the wagon.

"Good day for traveling." The one in the center was doing all the talking, figured to be the group's leader. He was a close-eyed little man with an unkempt gray-shot beard and a bare mane of dark hair mingling toward gray. "Where y'all headed?"

Judge Thorne said, "West."

"Oregon, then. Don't seem to be very many of you."

Behind the Buttrell wagon, Fred Harris had stepped down to stand between the noses of his team and Buttrell's tailgate. He held the heavy shotgun with its hammer cocked back like a growling dog's ear. "We're more than you," he said in a voice that made the hair on Will's neck stand against his collar.

The leader looked at Harris, measured him by some unfathomable gauge, turned back to Thorne. "Don't want to keep you. But we're a little short of supplies."

Will didn't doubt that. The men were trailing only one packhorse and its burden looked light. *Has it come down to this, then, that we'd fight and kill and die over a few pounds of food?* It seemed to him a terrible thing, yet he cocked his rifle and eased the muzzle more carefully toward the men. A few days earlier he had killed a buck at fifty yards in the snow. He had no doubt that he could kill a man at fifty feet in good weather, and he didn't have time to wonder whether he would. His Alathea was just beside him on the seat. *By God, I'll kill you every one before I'll let you harm her.*

David Stuart reined in his sorrel between Thorne's team and the men. "Gentlemen," he said.

Will Buttrell thought, *I couldn't have put it better myself.* It came to him that Stuart had killed two of the deer on their hunt in the snowy pass. He noticed that two of the riders were wearing parts of Army uniforms. He noticed too that all of them had their hands on or very near their weapons.

"I'm Bobby Gates," the little man said. "I won't hold you up by introducing my companions. We too are in a bit of hurry. We're overdue at Virginia City." The other men laughed. "Thing is, we'd admire to have one of your wagon and teams and a load of food."

"Easiest thing in the world," Stuart said amicably. "I'll sell you my wagon for a thousand dollars. Gold."

For a moment the leader did not reply but stared at the wagon scout. Finally, he laughed.

Bobby Gates took off his hat and held it out toward one of the others. "Boys," he said, "I want you to take up a collection amongst yourselves and give this man his money. In gold. If you don't find it in gold, maybe we can give it to him in lead."

Harris stepped clear of the wagon and shouldered his shotgun. Will Buttrell aimed his rifle, heard Francis cock his heavy Colt Dragoon somewhere behind. Guns and harness rattled on both sides. A falling feather would have tipped the scales into a face-to-face shootout.

David Stuart said, "Hang easy. We may not need to kill these men." Beside his horse the stray spotted dog whined.

Bobby Gates hung fire, his hand on the rifle across his lap, his eyes fixed on the revolver already level in Stuart's hand. "We're easy!"

Stuart rode a couple of steps closer. "We're a religious group," he told Gates.

"What's your religion? Guns?"

"We're cannibals."

Gates blinked. "What?"

"We haven't had anything to eat but deer and turkey since we left the last settlement."

"Eat?"

"We're willing to make you a trade. Give you a buck deer for that big fat fellow in the back."

"Trade!" The little man didn't know whether to laugh

or not. He started to, changed his mind, glared at Stuart. "What are you, loco?"

"Just hungry. How about it?"

"Hell."

"Long Tom. Cut loose that buck hanging on my wagon."

Tom Lee said, "You sure?"

Gates said, "No deal."

"Cut it loose."

Lee went back to Stuart's wagon in half a dozen long strides. Drawing out a long hunting knife, he cut the deer loose and let it fall.

The big man in Gates's group said, "Let's fight, Bob!" He looked uneasily at Stuart. "I'm not letting them damn cannibals eat me!"

"Maybe one of the others," Stuart said. "Sounds like he'd be pretty tough."

"I'm hungry," said Fred Harris who had moved forward to stand between Gates and Barbara Kenny. "I know a recipe'll take the toughness out of him. My recipe and a slow fire."

"Not fighting, not trading," Gates shouted. "You're damn crazy. All of you!"

"We'll leave you the venison," Judge Thorne said. "My riders'll watch until you've claimed it and gone. But you fire one shot, and we'll kill you every one. Now back off the road."

With that, he cracked his whip sharply enough to frighten his own oxen. His lead wagon shoved forward past Stuart. Tom Lee and Harris got back on their wagon seats, still with guns in hand, and moved out with the rest.

As they passed him, Alathea Buttrell shook her head at Davy Stuart. To her husband she said, "He ought to be ashamed of himself."

Will nodded. "Damn sure should. That venison was close to spoiled yesterday evening."

Alathea laughed. "Well, then," she said, "I don't know

a single self-respecting cannibal that'd've wanted to eat it anyway!"

Two days without incident brought the train to the junction of the Raft River with the Snake. There the trails joined again. The northern trail ran up to Fort Hall, and the route to Oregon stretched west in a hard-beaten, rutted line across the open prairie from the ford. Thorne called a halt and a day of rest in the grassy meadows where the rivers ran together.

Dealing with a smaller group, Thorne seemed more at ease, less inclined to bluster and bellow orders. To Stuart, it seemed the whole party was closer, had gotten to know each other better, had taken on a new shoulder-to-shoulder determination to complete their trip.

"We're going to make it, aren't we?" Jessica asked him that night by the communal campfire. "We're really going to Oregon, and a new home and a new life."

Stuart glanced around. She'd spoken softly enough so that no one else heard. He answered in the same tones.

"Sure we are. Together. Did you ever doubt it?"

He'd laughed as he said it, but the expression in her blue eyes was sober. "Once or twice," she whispered. Then, before he could do more than wonder if she was thinking of Ethan, she rested her hand on his arm and smiled. "But I'll never doubt us again. I promise."

"Folks!"

Long Tom Lee's voice startled everybody. He spoke so seldom and so much to the point that the others turned as one to see what was on his mind. He had wagged a heavy wooden keg into their midst and plunked it down.

Will Buttrell said, "My Lord, Tom, I wouldn't set that powder quite so close to the fire."

Lee scooped out a handful of the black powder and tossed it into the flames. Stuart reached for Jessica and Will Buttrell flinched backward, but nothing remarkable happened.

"Snow got in the powder stores unbeknownst," Lee said.

"What?"

"Didn't none of us think to shut that wagon flap tight. Snow got in and set on them keg lids and filled the bed three, four inches deep around them. Then it melted. Had they been bulbs, they'd be about due to sprout out."

Manasseh Thorne was on his feet. "Do you mean all our powder is contaminated?"

"I mean it got wet."

"All of it?"

"Best as I can tell. They's maybe some good in the middle of every barrel. I wouldn't know."

"Thing is," Lije Holden put in, "it'd be chancy to have to trust it while looking down the barrel at a grizzly bear or a Army-deserting silver hunter."

They laughed. Then they fell into a deeper silence. "Fort Boise's up ahead," Will Buttrell said into the quiet. "Can't we stock up there?"

Thorne shook his head. "It's nigh onto two hundred miles to Boise," he said. "Worse, the guidebook says the fort's been abandoned. There's nothing we can depend on for supplies until away out past Farewell Bend."

"What's closer?"

Judge Thorne opened his map, found his glasses, and studied their position by firelight.

"We're right here," he said as much to himself as to anyone else. "Fort Hall's forty miles or so east, but we have to ford the Raft to get there. It'd take us three or four days, as many to get back where we are now."

"Lose a week," Holden said. "Maybe get caught in another snow. I don't much care for snow, truth to tell."

David Stuart said, "I could take two or three good horses and make it to Fort Hall in two days. If you'll head west at a modest pace, I ought to catch you before long."

Jessica said, "I don't think you ought to go alone."

"We're through the worst of the Indian country," Stuart said. "I don't think there's anything to worry about. If we take the wagons back, we'll all lose a week and be no farther along."

"Couldn't we go on?" Barbara Kenny began, then paused as if she weren't sure how her idea would be received. When everybody looked her way, she finished, "Couldn't we go on without powder till we get where they have some?"

Holden shook his head. "Not meaning to be contentious, Miz Kenny, but I believe you and Stuart both have the wrong of it," he said. "Book says there's Bannocks in this neighborhood, and I hear tell they can be as cantankerous as any."

"I agree," Fred Harris put in. "What if we meet another gang like the one today and have to use powder?"

The judge had thought it through. "All right. I'm sending you back, David, but not alone. You'll take three horses and another man on horseback."

"I can make better time alone."

"I will not put you or anyone else out alone in this wild land." Thorne smiled suddenly. "And I *am* still the wagonmaster, even if we're a handful. Choose a man to accompany you or I will choose for you."

Fred Harris cleared his throat. "I'll go, Judge, if it suits you. Mrs. Kenny and I would like to ride back and be married at the fort."

"Oh, how nice!" Alathea Buttrell said. She and the other women, all except Jessica, gathered around Barbara Kenny.

Manasseh Thorne looked at his wife, read her eyes. "Well, if you won't hold David up," he said. "Each of you can trail an extra horse."

"I can ride," Barbara Kenny said. "They won't be holding back for me. I can change horses without touching the ground."

"Very well."

Jessica had stayed with Stuart, staring at him with wide eyes. "Davy, please. I don't feel right about this. There's something about it." She shrugged helplessly. "I can't explain it. But I wish you wouldn't go."

Stuart touched her cheek. "You mustn't doubt," he said quietly. "Remember? And I'm leaving this old spotted dog here to watch after you."

"I remember. But I'm afraid for you, for us."

Louder, Stuart said, "Judge, if you don't think it'll endanger the train, there's one more man I'd like to have along." He looked at Francis Buttrell. "Francis, would you ride with us?"

Will Buttrell never heard his son's answer nor ever doubted what it had been. He glanced at Alathea, saw the bright tears in her eyes, and turned quickly away. At last he put an arm across his son's shoulders.

"Be careful, Francis."

Francis Buttrell smiled. "Keep your powder dry," he said.

33

Thoman Silverhorn was worried. It wasn't a feeling he was accustomed to, and he didn't like it. He'd had a clear easy shot at the two men coming at him through the smoke. He'd held steady on the one Grace had called a ghost, the fair-haired man with the guns. And he'd shot the wrong man!

"Goddamn you, Thoman," Farley West complained, "this was supposed to be easy!"

West pulled up alongside Silverhorn, his gray matching strides with the big black horse Silverhorn had gotten at Bradley's Oak. Ahead of them, Blue Eye drove the hide wagon over the uneven ground while Kills Running scouted ahead for the softest route.

"Goddamn *you!* It *was* easy," Silverhorn growled at West. He rode uneasily in the saddle, looking back over his shoulder from time to time. "You're alive and hearty and sitting there cackling like granny's speckled hen, ain't you? We got the hides that we went for, don't we?"

"I guess so."

"And we're on our way to sell them, split the money, have us a spree, ain't we?"

"But they've damn-nabbed near kilt us all off," West said. "There's just you and me and them two savages left. And I'm the one to tell you, I don't trust no heathen Indian!"

"Well, how many ways did you want to split the money?"

"Oh, I see!"

"Pay attention now," Silverhorn told him. "It ain't them Pawnees you have to worry about, it's me." He pushed himself up in the saddle and glared along their backtrail again. "I'm shut of listening to you beller. You relieve Blue Eye on the wagon box. Send him back to ride with me."

"But Thoman, them hides stink worse than a skunk's nest."

"You say one word and I'll sic Kills Running on you. He gets through, we'll have us one more hide to sell. Only it won't be no buffalo."

West stared as if to see whether Silverhorn really meant it. He didn't. The way West's back was scarred from whipping, his hide wouldn't bring a nickel anyway. But Silverhorn was close to the end of his tether, and that was no mistake. He placed a big hand on the butt of his right-hand pistol and gave West a one-eyed glare.

"You moving?" Silverhorn had his gun half out of its holster.

"Sure, Thoman." Snapping his mouth shut like a frog swallowing a fly, West spurred his horse ahead fast to catch up to the wagon.

"God*damned* no-good worthless bastard," Silverhorn

muttered as he shoved the pistol back into its holster. If and when they got the wagon close to Fort Hall, he resolved there was going to be one less way to split the hide money. West might not be worth skinning, but his big mouth and his contentious ways had surely earned him a good killing.

But not too soon. Silverhorn reined in his mount, stood in the stirrups, squinted back the way they'd come. Even West might come in handy, at least until they managed to swat that gadfly who'd been stinging them every step of their way lately.

Silverhorn had to admit to a pinch of truth in what West said, though it was a truth Silverhorn didn't want to hear from a mangy loudmouthed hunk of coyote bait. By rights, they should be riding along safe in their numbers without a living enemy in the world, nothing on their minds except a big payday at Fort Hall. Instead, they were shorthanded and watching their backtrail for the gadfly.

It bothered Silverhorn that he'd missed what he'd aimed at. He knew his one eye couldn't have crossed. All it could do was stare right down the barrel. *Hell, I can't shoot crooked with that eye!* It had to mean he'd moved the gun. Silverhorn didn't believe in ghosts. But he couldn't deny his luck had gone sour, and the souring had started when first he'd crossed paths with the Gun Man.

"Anyone following?"

Blue Eye had come up, stopped a few yards shy of Silverhorn. If he had any complaints, he kept them behind his pale dispassionate eyes. The Pawnee weren't much given to complaints. Silverhorn wished he had a dozen more of them and one less of Farley West.

"Hell, yes, there's somebody following," Silverhorn said. "Can't see him yet, but he'll come. The way we're having to tack back and forth with this wagon, he's like to catch us, too."

"The ghost man?"

"Ain't no ghosts."

"Will Grace ride with him?"

Grace. The fair-haired Gun Man had shot Rafe Longdon clean off his horse, close enough to Silverhorn that
the bullet could have hit him instead. Silverhorn had not
lost his nerve. He'd never do that, would still be fighting
and kicking and squalling while they tried to nail down
his coffin lid. He would have ridden at the Gun Man,
traded him three shots for one, put all three in his craw.
But he hadn't known where Grace was.

He paused, rubbed his chin, thought about it. "I don't
know," he said finally. "Can't tell. She sent us back Eye-
Shot dead. Maybe she made a mistake."

"It was her way of giving challenge."

"What?"

Blue Eye paused while he reconsidered the unfamiliar
English word. "Her challenge," he said. "A warrior's challenge. She rides with the ghost man against us."

Silverhorn didn't like to think so. He'd given Grace no
reason to turn against him. Hell, he'd treated the red
whore better than she deserved, and he ought to take a
lesson from that! But she'd sent him back the wrong man,
his own man, dead. And then the man she should have
killed had come riding at Silverhorn, shooting as he came.

Had the Gun Man killed Grace? Silverhorn didn't believe it for a minute. But he couldn't be sure that Grace
hadn't gone over on him. If so, she might have been drawing a bead on him while he was shooting at the Gun Man.
Or right this minute!

"Could be they caught her," Silverhorn said, glancing
back again as he and Blue Eye turned to follow the
wagon. "Could be they taken her captive."

Blue Eye shook his head once. "She rides against us,"
he said. "Surely to defy Israel is she come up."

God of misery, Silverhorn muttered to himself. Then he
reined away from the Indian. They rode steadily through
the morning, making poor time toward Fort Hall because
of their numerous detours to follow the shape of the land.
They would do better when they cut Sublette's trail at the
Green River, Silverhorn knew, but still he chafed with

impatience. He and Blue Eye had taken turns dropping
back to watch for pursuit, but none had shown up.

Had the Gun Man come through the fire and got caught
in it? If he was following their trail, he was surely as hell
taking his time. Maybe nobody was dogging them after
all.

Longdon was shooting same time as me, Silverhorn
thought. *Could've been him as hit the buffalo hunter.
Could've been I didn't miss the Gun Man at all. Sometimes the best-aimed shot'll track right through a man
without never touching bone. Kills him clean, only he
don't notice it until he looks down at the jaws of hell
opening up to welcome him home.*

Silverhorn liked that explanation. It trimmed the loose
thread he'd thought was dangling and it brought back his
confidence in his marksmanship. But he didn't stop looking over his shoulder.

At the noon halt, he called Blue Eye aside. "Got a soft
job for you, Indian."

"Thy tongue deviseth mischiefs."

"Hold *thy* tongue! All's I need you to do is ease back
off over along that ridge." He pointed back to the east.
"Find you a good spot. Hide your hoss. Sit a spell and
wait. Anybody's following us, he'll come right along with
his nose to them wagon tracks in the valley."

"The ghost man?"

"Ain't no ghosts. Bring me his scalp and you'll get your
gold piece."

"If Grace rides with him?"

Silverhorn hesitated just a second. "If she *challenges*
you, kill her," he said.

"You make mock."

"Hell," Silverhorn replied. "Kill them all! Gold piece
for every scalp you bring me. If'n they don't come, you
can catch up to us at the ferry before dark."

Blue Eye nodded. "I go." He turned his horse gently
and rode back toward the ridge.

Silverhorn watched him for a moment, then snapped

across at West, "Take up some slack on them reins. Stay out of them holes, else you'll bust us down. Ain't you able to drive a team?"

"It's them hides, Tom. I can't hardly stand it. Don't you smell them?"

"Sure. Smells like money to me. You just keep close and follow. I'll take your place on that soft seat soon's we come to a place them jackasses can navigate."

"When'd that be?"

Silverhorn didn't know when that would be and he didn't bother to answer. He took over the lead, leaving Kills Running to hang back and watch their trail. The way grew easier, and Silverhorn moved to pick up their pace. He was scouting out the best way amongst the sage on some low rolling hills when he heard the crash and West's shouts behind him.

Drawing his revolver, he rode back at a gallop. Kills Running met him. "Wagon's broke!" he shouted.

"Broke?"

"Gone to its knees. A wheel."

Silverhorn swore, put away his gun, kept riding until he came to the wagon. West was off the wagon seat staring at the left rear axle hub. He took a step forward and gave the side of the wagon a kick.

"Goddamnit, I told you," Silverhorn said.

He dismounted, got down on one knee to study the damage. The hub and nut were in place. That was good luck. But the spokes had broken, the iron rim rolled off God knew where. Bending to look beneath the wagon, he saw the rest of his luck. Along with the heavy iron wagon jack, the buffalo hunters had an extra wheel lashed to the bottom of the floorboards.

"Save your boots. Go get something to put under that axle." He cursed himself for having burned the other wagon.

"Hadn't we better just leave this stinking wagon?"

"Get some wood under that axle!"

"Ain't nothing to use, Thoman. Can't the three of us

fix this wagon. Why, hell, we'd need back all them we've lost."

Silverhorn said, "Kills Running, is your skinning knife right sharp?"

The Indian drew his knife, grinned at West, ran the ball of his thumb lightly along the blade. He held up his hand to show the blood on his thumb.

"Why, hell, Thoman, you needn't be so touchy about it. I thought you was funning. I'll get down the wagon jack." West started to scramble under the wagon. "Where's Blue Eye? Can't the three of us do it alone."

"Keeping them off our ass if they's any of them left. Shut your mouth and get that jack. Kills Running, you an me'll cut some brush, look for some big rocks to prop up that axle. God*damn* me for not bringing that other wagon!"

They hitched two of the mules to the long arm of the jack and levered the wagon up, then stacked brushwood up to the axle. Silverhorn got a fresh bite with the jack and they repeated the process until the wheel hub was well clear of the ground.

"Get you a shovel, West. Dig a hole under this hub."

"A hole? What for?"

"So's we don't have to lift the damned wagon any damned farther to get the damned wheel on, that's what for. And if you ask another damned fool question, I'll damned well bury you in it when we're done."

While West scratched at the ground, Silverhorn found the wrench and removed the axle nut. Kills Running cut the extra wheel loose. As soon as they had it in place and greased and the nut tightened and the mules hitched up again, Silverhorn got on the wagon seat and whipped up the team. The wagon lurched a couple of times, then pulled off the brushwood with a scraping crash. The new wheel rolled smoothly.

"That's good, Tom," West called. "Want me to take over driving again?"

"No, I damned well don't," Silverhorn said. "You get

back and ride drag for us and keep an eye peeled. Kills Running can scout, and I'll drive. If I want something done right, I'll damned well do it myself."

Half an hour later, riders and wagon started across a broad, flat valley. Silverhorn felt better. They'd reached Sublette's trail. Blue Eye had not caught up to them as yet, but Silverhorn hadn't expected the Indian to see anyone on their trail. And he could see the trees ahead that marked the course of the Green. With that deep, wide, swift river behind them, they could forget pursuit and think what the hide money would buy. It would buy a lot, split three ways. He didn't figure West would last far past the river.

Wrapped in those pleasant thoughts, he didn't understand at first when a little tree of dirt suddenly sprouted from the sage a dozen yards in front of the lead mule. Then he heard the boom of the Sharps, flat and sudden with distance, and he did understand.

"Damnation," he muttered. "If you want something done right!" He should have been the one to wait for the Gun Man. He should have shot him, cut his throat, taken his scalp, done whatever was needful to make sure his ghost didn't rise again. *If you want something done right, don't leave no half-crazy Indian to do it!*

In the midst of his thinking, he'd hauled back on the traces to stop the wagon. Twisting his head from side to side, he looked for some sign where the shot had come from. Kills Running was riding back to meet him. West was coming up fast from behind, braying some damned foolishness as usual. Then West suddenly reined in, raised his arm to point back the way they'd come.

"He's back there."

The next .52-caliber slug arrived with the sound of an axe going into pine. West's horse screamed and pitched sideways, then slid down on its nose. West sprawled over its head, rolled, fell, lurched to his feet. Kills Running was galloping down on him like he was a warrior in trouble instead of a damned nuisance. As the Indian hauled

West up and wheeled his own horse away, Silverhorn rose in the wagon seat. He'd seen it, too, the smoke from the shot, far back along their path. He saw, and he knew the Gun Man had seen him.

"Want something done right," he muttered, turning to whip the mules into a desperate floundering gallop toward the trees. "You better damned well do it yourself! Hup, mules!"

The next bullet slammed into the packed hides, hard enough and near enough so that Silverhorn felt the impact. He bent lower, shouting at the mules and lashing with the whip. Other bullets fell at intervals, throwing up dirt ahead and to either side. One ripped through the wagon sheet and crackled over Silverhorn's head so close it hurt his ears.

"Damn-*nation!*"

Just as he'd started to think he was out of range, one of the mule team leaped in the traces, arching its back the wrong way. It went down, dragging the one behind with it, and then the whole team was fighting, kicking, braying in panic, all cohesion lost. Silverhorn felt the wagon sway, catch, start over. He stayed with it, fighting the lines, trying by sheer will to bring it down intact. It finally smashed down right way up, but he heard the splintering of broken wood.

Throwing himself off the box, he tried to cut the dead mule free, ignoring the bullets that fell like deadly hailstones around him. There were only three more shots, though one knocked down the lead mule. Another had broken a leg in the fall, and all were crazy-wild. Silverhorn became aware that Kills Running was with him, helping to quiet the frightened animals. West, on one of the extra horses, had a rifle ready, though Silverhorn knew he'd be as well off throwing rocks at the Gun Man and his Sharps.

Somehow, they got the dead and injured mules out of the way, two of the horses in makeshift harness in their place. Dragging its back wheel like a bird with a broken wing, the wagon crept on toward the river. West and Kills Running rode cover, but the Gun Man didn't appear. At last, Silverhorn let the exhausted animals drag to a stop at the brink of the river. A log raft sat at the edge of the pier.

"Hey, mister, what in tunket are you driving so hard for?" A scrawny man had come out of the ferry building to gawk at him. "Can't you see that wheel's busted?"

"You got other wheels?"

"Just them on our wagon 'crost the river. And they ain't for sale. I reckon we can send to Fort Hall for one."

"Who else is here?"

"Just my wife, Jan. Rest's on the t'other side, my pardner and his family. Ten dollars to cross, seeing the wagon stinks so much."

"Let's get ready."

West and Kills Running came up as the ferry man was securing the wagon to the raft. They rode their horses on board and dismounted, tying them to the rails.

"Ain't seen him, Tom," West said. "He likely can't figure how to get down off that bluff."

"He'll figure it out," Silverhorn said. "But damned if he'll get over this river so easy."

"Ten dollars, mister," the ferry man said. "And a dollar apiece for these other fellers. I ought to charge you for the extra horses, but I'll let it go this time."

"Kills Running will pay you. Go to the cabin and pay him off, Indian. His woman, too."

Kills Running stalked up onto the cabin's porch and threw open the door.

"Hey, wait a minute," the ferry man called. "My wife's in there." He waved hastily to the people on the far side of the river, then hurried after the Pawnee.

The big tow rope began to draw tight as the oxen on the far side pulled. The raft bumped against the dock. Inside the ferry building, a pistol boomed twice. Silverhorn heard a woman begin to scream. The scream stopped suddenly in the middle.

West said, "Too bad about the woman. We're powerful short on those."

"No time." Silverhorn raised his voice. "Hurry up, Indian. We're moving."

Kills Running ran lightly across the porch and down the bank, jumped across the few feet of open water onto the raft. West caught him with a steadying hand.

"Was she pretty?"

"Too fat. Long hair, though. Brown."

Another man met them at the pier on the west side. "Hey, what was all the commotion back on the yon side? Where'd Burt go?"

"Inside. You got a wagon here?"

"Sure, back in the barn, but it ain't for sale."

Without haste, Silverhorn drew his right-hand revolver, cocked it.

"Hey!"

"Thanks," he said, and shot the man through the head. "You two attend the rest of them. I'll tie off the ferry and see about us gettin' a new wagon wheel."

Within the hour, they had a new wheel on the hide wagon and a new team of oxen, poor and scrawny though they were, to pull it. "Ain't as fast as mules," Silverhorn said, "but they'll do us to Fort Hall." He slapped West on the shoulder. "Cheer up, there's women at Fort Hall."

"Don't see why we couldn't've saved one out, just for a while," West said sulkily. "They was two of them on this side, and that young one was middling pretty."

The crack of a rifle sounded from the near shore below them. Silverhorn grabbed his own rifle from the wagon box and hurried down toward the river, West close behind. Kills Running met them at the edge of the dock.

"Ghost man killed Blue Eye. Now ghost man's dead."

"Ain't no ghosts."

"He rode down onto riverbank. Fair hair, shining in the sun. I shot. Horse stood up and spun around. Ghost man fell off over horse's ass."

"Where is he, then? By God, I'll swim back to take that scalp."

"No scalp. Fell in the water, never come up. Horse galloped into the water, too. Never slowed, never stopped. Swam like he-coon against the current. Drifted off downstream. Ghost man's dead."

Thoman Silverhorn smiled. For the first time that day, he didn't feel the pressure of the Gun Man at his back, on his trail. "Ain't no ghosts," he said.

34

Ann Bradley was tired when she and Elam rode down in sight of the Bliss's Ferry landing at Green River. The body they'd found along the way had offered little to cheer her, except it hadn't been Ethan Fairchild's. Elam puzzled for a while over the three dead mules bloating along the trail leading to the ferry, then shrugged and pointed to Fairchild's tracks going past.

"He was alive here, anyways," the mountain man said. "And still giving them blizzards, as I read these sign."

Ann nodded. Her attitude varied between pride in Fairchild's ability to kill his enemies and fear that his prowess or luck would fail before she found him.

At the ferry landing a couple of horses stood three-legged in the shade. The raft was gone. Small on the far side of the river, a woman was just climbing out of the water onto shore. Ahead of Ann, Forrest Elam got off his horse with more difficulty than he wanted her to see; she looked away. Then she dismounted and tied both their horses while the mountain man went up to the building. She was not surprised to hear voices as Elam spoke to a man in the office.

She went down to the edge of the dock, dipped her handkerchief in the cold clear water, and washed her face. On the west side, the woman was putting a little boat in the water. Then she started back across with the tow rope tied to the skiff. She seemed to be rowing as easily as a man. Ann went up to the ferry office to see what her guide had learned.

"And when we got here," the other man was saying, "I found him back here on the floor against the wall. Grace drug him out back." Then, seeing Ann, he said, "What's this? Ain't you that little gal from Bradley's Inn?"

She hardly recognized the big red-haired buffalo hunter at first. His face was deathly pale beneath an untended beard and a liberal coating of dirt. His buckskin shirt hung open down the front, and he was wearing a good portion of her blue gingham dress around his shoulder and chest for a bandage. The material was stained with old blood.

"Mr. Waller, isn't it?" She had liked him before. Now she forgot her manners. "Where's Ethan?" was the best greeting she could manage.

Redwood Waller shook his head. "Girl, he thinks you're dead. Damned if I didn't think so, too, begging your pardon." He stared at her as if he feared she might vanish. "But you ain't, are you?"

Elam said, "Them's not the nicest hellos ever spoke. Thing is, Annie, your young man's still after the white-haired trash as shot Waller, here. Looks like they've all done crossed the river and gone. I'm about to have a look at the tracks. I was going to tell you, Waller, that Fairchild's young lady is alive and doing very well for one that's rid as far as she has."

Waller said, "I wish I could answer your question about Ethan, girl. But we haven't unraveled that yet."

But Ann Bradley was not listening. She had been staring out the window. She turned and went outside and down to the river. The woman in the boat was wearing the rest of her blue gingham dress. Ann took her little Colt's revolver out of her coat pocket and held it in wait.

Elam came up beside her on the bank, noticed the blue dress but did not comment on it. Instead he threw the woman a line and tugged her little boat up to the bank. "Looks like right hard rowing, towing that rope," he said.

The woman did not reply. She kept her hand at her waist, gripping the hilt of a knife but not drawing it from the sheath.

Ann raised the pistol in both hands, pointing it at the dark-eyed woman. "Leave the knife and belt in the boat," she said. "Then I'd like you to climb out here and strip off that dress."

"What?" Elam said.

Pleased that her hands didn't tremble, Ann drew the hammer back until it locked. "I wouldn't want to spoil it when I shoot you."

Grace let the belt fall, climbed out onto the landing. "I'd be glad to trade it back to you on account of it don't fit me too good." She began to unbutton the wet and dripping dress.

"We might talk this over inside," Elam suggested. "I'd ask you not to shoot her until you hear a little more about this."

Without turning her head, Ann flicked her eyes toward Elam, then back at Grace. "We'll see, Mr. Elam," she said. "But this is personal, quite personal." She waggled the pistol barrel at Grace. "Now take off the dress."

Grace grinned. "You've grown up to a regular little wildcat, ain't you, sweetie?"

"No. But I want the dress."

"Wait," Redwood Waller said hoarsely. He was leaning against the door frame of the ferry shack, one hand holding the bandage. "I'd want you to know Grace has come over to Ethan's side. Saved his life, most like, and surer'n hell she's saved mine."

Grace waved a hand at him. "Don't worry over it, Red. Fair's fair." She took one arm out of the dress.

Ann looked at her a moment longer over the sights of the Colt. Then she lowered the pistol slowly. "No," she said. "Leave it on. I intended an eye for an eye, but that isn't right. Besides, we didn't have a congregation before."

Grace said, "I thank you."

"Do you really know Ethan?"

"I don't know you'd call us friends. But I can guess why Fairhair likes you so. You got more grit than I'd figured you for. This dress is not quite the same condition as you give it. Might be you'd not want to trade for it back."

Ann smiled. "I've gotten good service out of yours," she admitted. "I believe I'll just let you keep that one as a gift."

She looked around at Elam. "Do you think he got across?"

Elam took her arm and led her down along the bank. "I saw that devil horse's tracks headed off down this way," he said.

Ann looked back to see the dark woman button the blue dress, then go about hitching two horses to the ferry rope. Staring across the river, she saw the big raft leave the shore and forge toward the faster water.

"Here," Elam said. He let go Ann's arm and went down on one knee for a closer look at the tracks. "Something spooked him, see? Right here. Must've been a earthquake or a cannon salute." He whirled back a step or two. "Well, would you look at that?"

Ann was looking. She saw it even as the old man told her. Ethan's horse had turned back to the west and leaped into the water. "What then?" she asked. "Where'd they go?"

Elam got to his feet with a bit less grace than a mountain goat. "Right off along there." He pointed across the water, a bit downstream. "See the tracks."

"Tracks in the water?" She laughed again. Her new hope that Ethan was alive had made her giddy, she thought.

"No," he said, "but I'll want to have a look on the other side. Let's go help them get that raft over here."

Instead, he studied the wagon tracks coming down to the landing, grunted, got in the skiff. "No," he said when she made to follow. "Best you stay here. I'll see to pulling the raft across."

She didn't understand, but she'd grown accustomed to accepting his orders and swallowing her questions. She watched him sitting tall in the tiny skiff and rowing in long, smooth strokes that made him look younger. She saw him reach the other shore, tie off the boat, and climb up to the other office.

She thought that he stayed inside longer than he should have. When he came out, she thought he was not standing as tall as before. He waved to her, then disappeared around the corner of the building. After a moment, he came back leading a team of mules that looked too frayed and tired to resist him. Beside him a barefoot girl walked timidly along carrying a baby that Ann could hear crying all the way across the water.

Redwood Waller said, "Ladies, if you will. I wisht you'd get these skittish horses aboard that ferry."

Grace took a full turn of rope around the stanchion to keep the raft from slipping downstream. Then, when the three of them had the four wild-eyed horses tethered to the ferry, she waved to Elam. Almost immediately they could feel the raft moving into the current.

Still cheerful at the prospect of seeing Ethan soon, Ann enjoyed the ride. If she had ever been on a ferry before, she did not remember it. The swift water began to carry them a little off course, but it seemed to her that the raft was a magic carpet skimming across the water, leaving no tracks. She laughed, felt the others looking at her, and blushed.

Fifteen minutes later, the ferry touched shore, shuddered, and held fast. She leaped onto the bank and helped Grace with the lines while Waller tried with his one good hand to untie the tethers. Ann could see then that the girl Elam had found was very young, no more than fourteen or fifteen. She wasn't nursing the baby, but swaying with it in an effort to quiet its fretful crying. Still, she took every step that the old man took, as if afraid to be separated from him for a moment.

Ann started up to the ferry office to thank the owners and pay them if she were able. Forrest Elam called across to her, "I'd rather you didn't go up there."

"Why?" she said, sounding like a little girl even to herself. Then she recognized the tone of his voice and became afraid. "Is it Ethan?"

Elam shook his head. "You help with the horses."

She was too frightened to listen. She broke into a run and made it into the little house before anyone could stop her. Inside, the air was close, the smell entirely new to her but entirely clear. People had died there. She tried to turn away but had to look, had to know whether it was Ethan. The body of a man lay across the desk, looking almost as if he might straighten up and welcome her. Almost. He was not Ethan.

She took two steps to the side so that she could see the rest. Two women lay sprawled on the floor. One lay with her arm extended toward the open back door. The other was sitting against the side wall as if someone had nailed her to the logs. Her blouse was open halfway to her waist. Ann Bradley took in the horror. The sitting woman had been nursing the baby not long before she died.

Then the smell overwhelmed Ann, and she had to turn back outside to draw in big breaths of fresh, clear air off the unmindful swift river. Forrest Elam came up to her with the girl at his elbow.

"I begged you not," he said. "Here, come walk along the bank with me." He put his long arm across her shoulders and guided her. The girl and the crying baby clung to his other arm. "This poor thing," he told Ann, "is Miss Mandy Jean Bliss. Them's her kin in there, and we'll see to their proper burial after a minute."

The girl began crying along with the baby. Ann

stopped, put her hand on the girl's cheek and spoke to her. "Let me carry the baby," she said.

"No!" the girl screamed. She drew away, clinging to the baby as if she'd been threatened.

Grace came along beside them. "Let me," she said. She dropped to one knee and spoke to Mandy Jean in a soft, crooning voice. Ann couldn't hear the words, but she was sure they weren't in English. After a moment the girl's eyes rolled back round to color and she looked up at Grace.

"Are you a sure enough Indian?" she asked.

"Far's I know, sweetie," Grace said. She put out her hands, palms up. "Can I hold your young'un now?"

Mandy Jean didn't scream, but she looked fearfully at Elam. The old man said, "You can let Miss Grace take the child for a spell. You have my word she'll be good to it."

The girl licked her lips, then shyly held out the scream- ing, kicking baby to Grace. Grace took it as softly as if it were made of eggshells. As Ann watched in baffled wonder, the Indian woman cradled the child in her arms, bent her head over it, began some strange, wordless song. After a few moments, its crying stopped and it batted at Grace's cheek with a pudgy hand.

"Have to find something to feed it," Grace murmured, raising her eyes to Ann's.

Ann nodded numbly. Mandy Jean sat down cross- legged and began to cry as if there were no measure to the depth of her sorrow. Elam went down on one knee beside her to comfort and reassure her, but a lifetime's habit drew his eye to a line of hoofprints in the softer dirt. Ann knelt also, put her arm around the girl's shaking shoulders. Then she saw Elam studying the prints and knew before she bent close enough to see them that they belonged to the Devil.

"Ethan," she breathed.

She spoke to the girl. "Did you see the man on this horse, Mandy Jean?"

The girl looked at her, broke into fresh tears. "They was lots of horses," she sobbed.

"This one would have come by after the others had gone."

"Big reddish horse? Yellowy mane?"

"Yes."

"They wasn't no rider on hit."

Elam nodded. "Tracks'd make me think not."

Ann stopped as tears came to her own eyes. "Then he didn't get across."

Mandy Jean looked into Ann's eyes as if she hoped to find in them an answer to her pleas. "They killed my folks!" She put her face in her hands and cried afresh.

Elam said, "I'd expect he went across in that skiff. We'll find his tracks directly. It's all right now. It's all right. Don't cry now." He might have been speaking to either or both of them, but neither could stop crying. After a moment he stood, coaxed them to their feet, and led them back toward the ferry office.

"I can't go in there," Mandy Jean said.

"I know. I'll want you all to wait with Waller and the Indian woman. I won't be long." After that he went into the shed, came out with a shovel as if he didn't know how to hold it, and went over to a little grove of trees above the river to the north.

Grace took the young women with her down to the river and dipped her sleeve in the cold water. Then she touched it to the baby's mouth until it began to suck water from the cloth. She looked up toward the office. "You got any milk?"

Mandy Jean shook her head. "No'm. I think they's a egg or two in there, but I wouldn't go back in there for nothing."

Redwood Waller said, "Why hell, miss—begging your pardon—but where would it be?"

She told him and he went away toward the building in the short, uncertain steps of an injured man. After a few moments he came back with a coffee cup in his huge hand. He gave it to Ann, then took two eggs from his coat pocket.

"Break one in that cup," Grace said. "We'll save the other one."

Ann cracked the egg, drained it into the cup, and tossed away the shell. Grace opened her dress to expose a breast, broke the egg yolk and stirred it with her finger. Then she put the yellow liquid on her nipple and offered the baby a taste.

Waller turned his back and went up the hill to watch Elam dig. Ann heard him say, "That white-haired son of a bitch's likely halfway to Fort Hall with my wagonload of hides by now!"

"I don't doubt it and I hate it. But we'd have to be as bad as him to leave these poor folks unburied."

"Why, hell! I didn't mean that. Fairchild would have run him down and finished him before now if I hadn't asked him to bury my dead compadres. I just can't help it ever now and then thinking about how this Silverhorn leaves all these bodies everywhere he goes and still gets away with honest folks' goods and livelihood. And I hadn't been shot up this way, I'd be helping you same as I'd been helping Ethan."

The women walked along the river bank while Grace fed the baby and the mountain man dragged the bodies across one by one to the graves he had dug. He had to row across to get the two from the other side. He did not call to them until the graves were closed. Then he asked the girl what she planned to do. Mandy Jean had no plan but began to cry again.

"You got a animal to ride?" Elam asked.

She shook her head. "One of them mules, maybe." Her lip trembled again and she bit it. "Them bad men, they left their mules, took some of our oxes to pull their wagon. They're maybe in the barn." She started that way, then turned back again, looking at the five graves. "Can't we do something? Seems like they ought to be something done for my folks." She started to cry. "Something *else!*"

"We never intended it no other way," Waller said. He pushed himself upright. "I'll do it this time. Grace, get your book."

"We'll follow the tracks," Elam had told Ann as they put the deserted ferry behind them. He'd saddled Mandy Jean one of the mules and turned the rest of the livestock free. "That devil went off up the trail after the wagon. Can't be sure, but it looks to me like he's making deeper tracks again."

The tracks went west along the trail, were still going west when night fell and they made a dry camp in the high desert of the Sublette Cutoff. Ann was sitting on her blanket beside the fire, watching the flames and thinking of Ethan, when Mandy Jean laid her head in Ann's lap.

"You so pretty and them green eyes," the girl said. "You married?"

Ann shook her head, wiped back unexpected tears. "Not yet," she whispered.

"Me, either, but I aim to be. Soon's as I catch up to Francis Buttrell. Him and me'll get married and raise this baby along with our own."

"Francis Buttrell? I know a Francis Buttrell."

"He come through in a wagon. He's older'n me and not married, neither. He's a pretty boy." Mandy Jean sat up, suspicion on her narrow face. "How'd you know him? You like him?"

"He came through in a wagon," Ann said. "And he's a nice boy. But I don't like him in the way you're talking about."

"Well, I like him. And he liked me. Lots." She stopped to look into Ann's eyes with new doubt. "That's enough, ain't it?"

Ann nodded. "Yes," she said, stroking the girl's long tangled hair. "Yes, that's all there is to it."

Ann lay wakeful during the night. The next morning, she went aside from the others to the place where Grace sat alone, feeding the baby with the last egg.

"Hungry little feller," Grace said. "We'll have to figure him something more."

Ann sat down beside her. "Grace," she said, "that prayer book you had yesterday. It was my father's, wasn't it?"

Grace looked at her, hesitated, looked down at the baby. She nodded. "You can have it back," she said. "Like the dress. He did give me them, the leather book, too." She raised her dark eyes to Ann's again. "No cause you should believe me."

"I believe you." Ann stopped, swallowed. "They're dead, aren't they? My parents are dead?"

"Yes."

"And the inn?"

"It's gone, too. Thoman and them burned it." She closed her dress, dandled the baby, then passed the child carefully to Ann. "I said as how I done all I could for them. But I didn't. You or that old Elam man or your Fairhair or Redwood, you know different. You'd've died to help them."

The baby squirmed in Ann's arms and waved its fists, its eyes squeezed tightly shut. Ann rocked it, not answering Grace.

"You ought to kill me," Grace said.

Holding the child tightly to her, Ann Bradley stood up. "No," she said. "But don't tell the others I know." She half smiled. "Mr. Elam wants to spare me."

By mid-morning, they found where the wagon tracks left the road. The Devil's tracks left the road right between them. Ann Bradley's heart grew light in her chest as if it had quit beating. Riding off across the country after the wagon gave her the sudden feeling that Ethan Fairchild could already be lying dead over the next hill. Of course, he could be lying dead at the bottom of the Green River for all that she could prove.

As if he knew her thoughts, Forrest Elam rode up beside her to say, "You've come too far to look back in your mind now, Annie. We've believed he got across that river, you and me. Now we need to bet on him just a little while longer."

"Little while?"

"It can't be far now." He had not more than got it out of his mouth before they heard the thin but clear reports of distant gunfire.

35

David Stuart set out for Fort Hall with Francis Buttrell, Barbara Kenny, and Fred Harris. Each led a fresh horse. They rode with all the enthusiasm of young people on a holiday from their normal duties. As the old married man of the group, Stuart felt more than one qualm about leaving Jess behind. Whether he'd admit it or not, her fearful premonitions had worried him. Despite her brave smile as they parted, he knew she hadn't forgotten her doubts.

Harris and Barbara Kenny lagged a bit behind, caught up in talk about their wedding and their plans for making a future in Oregon. Along the way northeast on the Fort Hall loop of the Oregon Trail, they could not avoid comparing the flat and open plains of the Snake to the rocky switchbacks of the Hudspeth Cutoff.

Stuart agreed. "It's amazing how much better a road and its countryside look to a man when he's not shepherding a string of wagons. This land along the river looks so good it'd give a man pause about going on to Oregon."

Young Buttrell laughed. "Hell," he said, testing that vocabulary he figured was adult, "Oregon may be more than half full by now anyways!" They laughed with him.

Stuart said, "Let's change to our spare horses and ride, then. I want to see the sights at Fort Hall."

Fort Hall turned out to be walled with a white plastered stockade visible for miles. The fort was no more than eighty feet square, but its walls stood fifteen feet high. Stuart's party rode in at the south gate where they were stopped immediately by a sentry who wanted to know their business.

Stuart said, "We're with the Thorne train, and we've come for supplies. Well, Mrs. Kenny and the doctor here would like to see the chaplain, as well."

"What kind of supplies?"

"Foodstuffs, mostly. I have a list, if you'd like to see it. And we need seven kegs of gunpowder."

The sentry nodded as if he'd expected just such an answer. "I'll ask you to wait until I hear," he said. Turning his head, he shouted, "Sergeant of the Guard, post number one."

Finally, a sergeant came up trailed by two more troopers. He listened to the sentry's report, then looked at Stuart.

"This way, all of you. Commanding officer wants to see you."

Stuart put in another word. Harris made a reasoned plea. Buttrell was working himself up to the same chore. But the more they tried to explain their situation, the less interested the sergeant seemed.

"Dismount. We'll see to your horses. Follow me."

The sergeant led them into the tall central building, his men closing in behind, suspiciously like guards. They followed him inside the two-story adobe building and along a dark hall to stairs which rose to the upper floor. In the middle of the western hall, the guard stopped, knocked at a closed door, and entered at the sound of an official voice.

The sergeant saluted. "Civilians, sir. Sentry on the gate

says they're looking for supplies. Says they wanted enough powder to blow up a mountain."

"Thanks, Sergeant." The officer stood to return the salute, then sank down behind a rickety field desk again. He was a spare, bearded, gray-haired man in the blue-piped uniform of infantry. "Mrs. Kenny, gentlemen," he said. "I'm Captain McCree."

"Captain." Stuart introduced himself and the others. "I'm riding lead scout for the Thorne train out of Ohio."

"Thorne train?" the captain said. "Are you ox-drawn, horse-drawn, or mule-drawn?"

Stuart did not take the point of his question, but the answer to it was easily enough given. "Oxen."

"Where are your wagons?"

"We took the Hudspeth Cutoff." Stuart shrugged. "Maybe a mistake in a number of ways. Part of it was we got our powder wet. The train is down at the junction of the Raft River with the Snake." He waited. When McCree didn't answer, he said, "If that satisfies your curiosity, Captain, we need to get about our business. The other wagons are waiting on us."

McCree raised a hand. "Yes, the others," he said. "Who is your wagonmaster?"

"Judge Manasseh Thorne of Pike Country, Ohio. And my father-in-law. I asked him for the privilege of coming up to Fort Hall for the supplies."

"Seems strange you'd have bypassed us in the first place and then come back this way."

"Probably is. We took a vote, decided to stay together through that cutoff to see whether folks wouldn't change their minds."

"Change their minds?" The captain steepled his hands and studied Stuart. "About what?"

"Look, is this necessary, just to get some powder?"

"Changed their minds about *what*, Mr. Stuart?"

Stuart glanced at Fred Harris, who shrugged. Drawing a deep breath, Stuart said, "More than half our party determined to go to Virginia City to seek their fortunes. The rest of us turned north for Oregon."

"So you parted at the City of Rocks?"

"We did."

"And your train is ox-drawn."

"I told you it is."

"You would be willing to swear that they were not mule-drawn?"

"I would, if there were any reason to. As it is, I've had about enough of this. Do you mean to hold us up indefinitely?"

McCree laid his hand on the desk beside the papers he'd been examining when they came in. For the first time, Stuart noticed the heavy revolver lying there. The captain rested his hand on the gun.

"As long as I see fit, Mr. Stuart. When did you discover the wet powder?"

"Day or two—wouldn't you say, Francis?—after the others went down toward Nevada."

"To your knowledge, then, those other wagons are well down that road to Nevada without any powder reserves?"

"I don't know." Stuart hadn't thought about the others. Had their powder gotten wet? It came to him that the broader a man's knowledge of distant events, the more he would have to worry about. "I suppose that might be true."

"Mr. Buttrell, can you tell me the name of the first settlement west of Fort Laramie?"

Francis Buttrell frowned. "I guess you'd mean Bradley's Oak," he said. "I don't think it was an oak, though."

McCree didn't smile. "Are you aware Bradley's Oak no longer exists? That it was burned to the ground and every inhabitant slaughtered?"

"What?" Barbara Kenny pushed forward, went to the captain's desk. "No. Not those nice old people. And the girl? What was her name?"

"Ann," Francis Buttrell said. He walked across, ignoring McCree's sudden movement, to stare out the second-floor window.

"How could that happen?" Barbara asked.

"My question was directed to Mr. Buttrell."

Francis turned. "No," he said. "We didn't know that. Listen, how about Bliss's Ferry? Is it safe?"

The captain looked startled. "Why do you ask?"

Francis Buttrell did not answer.

Stuart said, "What does it have to do with us?"

Fred Harris stepped up to take Barbara's arm. "I have the same question, sir. Your news strikes us without tact or subtlety. It was at Bradley's Oak that Mr. Stuart was married. Francis was a close friend of the Bradleys' daughter."

Buttrell turned back toward McCree. "Was it Indians, or who? I want to know what dirty sons of bitches did that!"

"I'm still wanting to know, myself. Be seated, gentlemen." McCree picked up the pistol. "Over there. I have just a couple more questions. There was a mule train that passed through Bradley's Oak a few days after your own."

"Hagewold's train," Stuart said. "Yes. They overtook us close to South Pass."

"If by chance you had learned of the massacre from the mule train, it might have occurred to you that the members of that train were responsible."

"But we didn't learn it."

"And, had you formed such a suspicion, perhaps you would have considered pursuing them and destroying them yourselves. You might have used up all your powder in the doing."

Stuart stared into the captain's eyes. He'd had no experience with madmen. He had heard stories, and he had gone with other boys up to spy on old Hermit Henry back at home. But now he sat in the office of and at the mercy of a genuine madman. He looked at Harris, hoping for some special insight, but the doctor would not take his eyes off the captain. Stuart decided to try one more application of logic before he turned to more desperate measures.

"Sir, we might still attack anybody we thought had harmed the Bradleys. But we had no reason to suspect a train of wholesome people just because their wagons were drawn by mules. Had we suspected them and wished to overtake them, we would have needed wings to do it. Our only traffic with them took place in those very few minutes they required to pass us and go on their way."

The captain's eyes changed a bit. "You didn't follow them through South Pass?"

"They didn't go by way of South Pass. They took the Lander Cutoff. Mr. Thorne decided that route was too dangerous, so we came the other way. We did not follow them."

"But you did meet their scout, Mr. Smith?"

"I met their scout, Mr. Drexel, and their wagonmaster, Mr. Hagewold. They did not have blood on their hands."

The captain smiled wanly. "Only fate on their foreheads."

"I beg your pardon."

"Mr. Stuart, until today, the Hagewold train has not been heard of since it left Mormon Ferry on the Platte."

"But we saw them after that."

"Precisely. You report that they took the Lander Cutoff. If that is so, and I am not at the moment questioning your veracity, then they never emerged."

"Never emerged? I don't understand. Maybe they turned back."

"Mr. Stuart, there has been no news of the Hagewold train since the day you saw them. They haven't passed anyplace along the trail, east or west. Nor have my patrols found any trace of them, not even along the Lander Cutoff."

"No trace? Of a single soul?" Stuart stared at him. "But Hagewold's train was bigger than ours. Two dozen wagons, at least."

"Twenty-eight. One hundred and nineteen souls."

"They couldn't just disappear. Maybe they didn't take the Lander trail after all. Either way, how could they carry enough food to feed themselves all this time?"

McCree simply looked at him.

Stuart saw in the captain's face that they would not have had enough food, that they must by now have perished. *The broader a man's knowledge!* Stuart wondered how God, knowing every human accident and folly, could possibly endure the deep sadness of all He had set in motion. Had He known that mankind's freedom of movement and thought would so often end in disaster? Teetering there on the brink of that eternal question, Stuart wished for his uncle's calm faith that everything had been foreordained ages before this world began. But McCree was speaking again, and Stuart gave it up, left infinite sadness to God.

McCree addressed the man and woman before him. "Mrs. Kenny, Mr. Harris. You are free to seek out our chaplain. His office is in the building just by the main gate." He smiled and stood, offering Harris his hand. "Please accept my best wishes for your future."

"Thank you, Captain," Harris said. "Davy, you coming?"

"I'll be along in a minute, Fred. Don't start without me."

Then the captain returned his attention to Stuart.

"How much powder have you lost?"

"Seven kegs. That is, in the wagons of us still going to Oregon."

Captain McCree began writing. "Then I will not keep you, for I imagine that Mr. Thorne and the others will be somewhat at the mercy of the elements and the human riffraff that come their way before you return." He put down his quill, dusted the page, and handed it to Stuart. "Give this to the sutler at the trading post. He will see you get the powder and anything else you need."

"Thanks, Captain. I'm sorry I got upset. I can see now why you were interested in us."

"Perfectly understandable reaction, Mr. Stuart. No offense taken." McCree had already gone back to the papers on his desk. "Good day to you, sir. And good luck."

Going down the stairs Buttrell said, "Hell a-mighty. Seems like he didn't want to know nothing but whether *we* killed those people or *Hagewold* killed those people or whether *we* killed Hagewold or whether *we* killed off the rest of our own train!"

"About the only thing he didn't accuse us of was suicide."

"What?"

"Come on, Francis. Let's get our powder and get out of this madhouse before they chain us to the wall."

"Why would they do that?"

"*Why* is a young man's word that's wasted here in the midst of older men's settees. Come on."

They were presenting their written order for the powder when a lieutenant of Dragoons came up to them. He watched them a moment before he spoke. Then he fixed his eyes on the older. "Your name Stuart?" he asked.

Stuart nodded.

"Oscar Cranfill," the officer said. He offered his hand. "This isn't official. Just like to talk to you a minute." He motioned toward the corner where a table stood beside a couple of chairs.

Stuart said, "Francis, finish up our order here." Then he sat at the table with Cranfill.

"Cap'n tells me you're with the Thorne train."

"That's true." Stuart supposed that people at forts must not have much to do if they had so much time for carrying news around. Now this one was going to question him.

"And you're the scout?"

Stuart nodded.

"Where're you out of?"

"Listen, I don't want to take up your day," Stuart said. "Ohio."

Cranfill turned to watch Francis counting the powder kegs. "Back in Ohio," he said, "you ever know an Ethan Fairchild?"

The question could not have struck Stuart harder if it had come out of a cannon. Apparently it was the work of every gossipy officer in Fort Hall to open old wounds and pour salt in them. He nodded. "I did."

"You know him well?"

"Grew up with him."

"I saw his marker couple or three months back. You know anything about that?"

"My wife put up the marker."

"Your wife?"

"Well. She wasn't then," Stuart said.

Hell, no, she was more his girl then than mine! It feels almost good to tell somebody about it. He wanted to explain to Lieutenant Cranfill that he had been Ethan's best friend and worst enemy, his greatest benefactor and his strongest detractor, the man who should have fought by his side and the one who left him to die.

Cranfill said, "Why did she put up the marker?"

"He was dead. Why does it matter to you?"

"Was he a terrific horseman that could handle the worst horse in the world?"

"Ethan? No."

"Your friend magic with a gun, regular killer?"

The question took a load off Stuart's shoulders. He laughed. "Not hardly. What're you getting at, Lieutenant?"

"Your friend a man about my height? Blond hair? More bone than muscle?"

"So you found his body. God knows I looked for it, tried to give him decent burial."

"I found him and his own marker standing right next to each other."

"What?"

"I'd'nt believe a word of it. Have no idea yet who he really was. Alls I knew was he couldn't be who he said he was. A child could see he'd just taken that name from the marker. I'll give him this, though. He was the outridingest, outshootingest son of a bitch you ever saw." Cranfill laughed. "Said he was a *farmer!* Tried to tell me he got lost off your wagon train. You never heard such a story. Claimed he was fighting you when a man with white hair and a gang with a woman in it came along and shot a black horse out from under him—"

Francis Buttrell remembered the next several minutes as what it must be like to get caught up in a whirlwind. David Stuart took him by the arm and half dragged, half carried him out into the open air. "What about the powder?" Francis wanted to know.

"I'm counting on you to get it back to the train."

"Where *you* going?"

"I'm going to see if I can get a dream out of my head."

"What?"

"I got to finish something I left undone."

"Then I'm going with you, Davy."

"Can't be."

"Going to be."

"No. I'm looking down the barrel of a chance I never expected to have again in this life."

"Chance to what?"

"I won't take time to tell you now. But I believe you'll remember that I told you about the ones that jumped Ethan and me back at the Platte."

"You know where they are? Then I'm going."

"You're going straight back to the train in a hurry."

"Davy, please."

"There's people back there counting on you."

"Counting on us both."

"If it was only me I'd take the powder to them. But I'm asking you to take it, Francis. Give me my chance!"

"All right."

Buttrell heard a few more scraps of the story from Stuart as he went outside, watched him saddle the sorrel and ride away to the east. Francis went back inside, found the newlyweds and told them to take the powder back to the train.

Then, having given his friend twenty minutes' head start, he saddled his own horse, took his and Stuart's extras in tow and rode out along that same east road.

How do you know where they are? Francis had asked him. He'd figured it was a fair question to end the whole scheme.

"I know where they would be if they came on along from where they last were seen. Cranfill knows."

"Knows what?"

Stuart had told him about the buffalo hides. *They can't bring them anywhere but Fort Hall. So it doesn't matter whether Silverhorn got the hides or the hunters kept them, they have to come this way.*

Francis Buttrell hadn't understood all he'd heard, but he understood one thing. The road to Fort Hall ran through Bliss's Ferry. If the people who'd killed Ann Bradley were headed that way, Francis surely as hell meant to see they didn't get Mandy Jean.

By keeping a fresh horse under him all the time, leading one and riding the other, Francis caught up closely enough to Stuart to keep him in sight. Stuart was pushing hard. A dozen miles out of Fort Hall, they passed an incoming emigrant train without pausing, leaving its people to wonder what the older man had done that he should flee so desperately from the younger who pursued him so relentlessly.

Buttrell made a separate camp along the river that night, getting little sleep because he didn't know how early Davy would start. Even so, he almost missed him in the half-dark before sunup. He followed for another half-day of hard riding, gradually closing the distance. Then Stuart bore hard off to the left, taking a less traveled way, and

Buttrell knew where he was. They were back on the Sublette Cutoff, riding west to east this time at a horse-killing
pace. He'd just about made up his mind to pull up beside
Stuart when the distant shooting started. Stuart left the
road immediately and rode down toward the mouth of a
rocky, brushy canyon.

When he saw his friend take up a stand on the south
side, Buttrell let go the extra horses and drove his mount
across to the north side. He tied his horse and dodged
through the brush until he found a good spot across the
gap. Stuart had begun shooting. At last he saw the men
who were shooting back. One of them had long white
hair.

Francis was carrying his father's rifle and powder, but
he had never shot at a man before. He didn't know
whether he could do it, but he knew he had to help Davy.
It was why he had come. The white-haired man whirled
his horse and rode right up the far side of the rough canyon mouth back to the south and east. But another man
came riding hard along the north bottom of the canyon,
straight at Buttrell.

The rider hadn't seen Francis. He was angling across
to get behind Stuart. As Buttrell watched, the man slid his
rifle into its boot and drew out a long-handled hatchet.
Without thinking or aiming, Francis lifted the rifle and
fired. He missed, but the rider pulled up sharply, wheeling
his horse around. Dropping the war hatchet, he grabbed
for a pistol, fired twice toward Buttrell. Francis had never
heard bullets coming his direction before. If he'd had
time, he would have been terrified. Instead, the boy who
would be a man dropped the rifle, drew out the less familiar revolver, and leaped to his feet.

He was not thinking of making himself a better target
but of getting free of the brush. He accomplished both.
He cocked the Colt, lined up the front sight in the notch
of the hammer, and fired. The man came partway out of
his saddle, dropped his pistol, then reseated himself.

Whirling his horse again, he fled back down the canyon at a headlong gallop.

Francis reached for his rifle and began to reload it. Off to the south, David Stuart was whipping his sorrel horse up the slope as if he meant to kill it. If he was gaining any ground on the white-haired man and his big black horse, Francis couldn't tell it.

36

Ethan Fairchild saw powder smoke bloom among the pilings on the opposite bank. He tried to turn the horse, to evade the bullet with his name on it, but the wild Devil threw up its head, struck him in the face, knocked him into the water.

Even at the bank, the river wasn't shallow, dredged out to its rocky floor by the strong, unceasing current. Fairchild sank until the light was an eerie green and his lungs ached under the weight of the water before the bitter cold shocked him back to consciousness. Not remembering at once where he was or why, he swam.

Close above him an enormous animal plunged into the water and whirled away, swimming hard. Fairchild moved parallel with the shore without knowing it. Then he saw the dark outline of an object floating on the surface. He came to the top beside a skiff, took hold of it, drew in great gulps of air.

Twenty feet out from the bank the Devil was swimming strongly toward the far shore. On that bank a man had emerged from the pilings. He carried a rifle, trotted along the bank, looking right at Fairchild. Fairchild moved a bit to the side so that he had the skiff between him and the man on the west side. He clung to the boat for several minutes, peeking out now and then to watch the horse's progress. It was still swimming powerfully but drifting downstream all the same.

On the other bank, the man with the rifle had been joined by two others. Fairchild recognized the white-haired man, heard the bellow of his laughter above the splashing rush of the water. Rage burned across his mind but he held still, filled with a sense of his own helplessness.

His powder was wet, the two pistols he carried useful only to pull him lower in the water. His Colt rifle had gone into the river, and Waller's Sharps was still with the Devil, certainly wet and useless even if he'd had it. There was nothing on God's earth to keep Silverhorn from making his leisurely way across the river and killing him on the spot. Nothing but the hope that they might think him dead already.

When he looked again, the three men were no longer on the dock. Fairchild clung to the skiff until his body grew numb from the cold and his fingers ached from the strain of holding on. Finally, he turned, seized the edge of the dock. On his third try, he managed to flop up onto the rough planks where he lay gasping while feeling returned to his limbs in pins-and-needles agony.

No one came for him. No one shot at him. He sat up, shivering, still confused. He looked across, saw the chestnut horse out on the west shore shaking its flaxen mane and tail.

Fairchild felt himself over for the bullet hole, found nothing except a bloody and aching lump on his forehead. Then he walked up to the ferry office, wondering vaguely why no one had come down to help him. The phrase *leaves no survivors* was just going through his mind when he saw the ferry man lying facedown on the floor near his counter. The body of a heavyset woman was nearby, surrounded by blood from a gash in her throat.

Fairchild went behind the counter, found nothing, looked in the shed off the back. It was not empty. Ap-

parently Silverhorn's wolves had not taken time to search.
A big tin of biscuits stood on a shelf. Next to it lay a
cotton sack of lead bullets. They were the wrong caliber
to do him any good, but he had bullets. Trying to swallow
a bite of dried biscuit, he walked out onto the porch of
the shack and saw the Indian's horse, standing as quietly
as a trained dog at the edge of the trees.

"Damn," he said, cursing his own stupidity and the ache
that seemed to fill his head with pain instead of thought.
In a moment, he'd dropped his own gunbelt and he had
the dead man's twin Navy Colts. *Dead man's guns*, he
thought. *Seems like the only sort I ever get.* Draping the
belt over his shoulder, he looked almost hopefully across
the river, but Silverhorn and his wolves were nowhere in
sight.

He supposed that while he was still lucky and still dripping wet he might as well try for his rifle. He found the
place where Devil had stood at the shore and whirled.
Slipping back into the cold water did not seem the brightest thing he'd ever done, but it didn't seem bright to go
after Silverhorn without the revolving rifle. At last, he
drew up his determination and slid under the water, allowing himself to sink to the bottom. On his third try, he
found the rifle and brought it back to the surface, plunked
it out on the bank.

Not waiting for anything else, he stripped the saddlebags off the Indian's horse and threw them into the skiff.
After some thought, he unsaddled the animal and turned
it free to go where it chose. Then he rowed quietly across
the river. With a revolver in one hand and the useless rifle
in the other, he slipped into the willow thicket along the
bank. They grew up the slope forty or fifty feet until they
verged into a grove of cottonwoods. There he saw the
tracks of other wagons. These could have been made by
the Thorne train, he mused. But he had not time to wonder.

He made his way from tree to tree, keeping away from
the pilings and the west ferry building. When he came to

the far edge of the line of trees, he could just make out
the shape of the Devil standing head down and forlorn
at the side of the west road. He whistled to the horse and
hoped.

The saddle and his extra powder were wet, and the
charge in the big Sharps was ruined, of course. Those
things he would sort out later. The horse was exhausted
and the man was in no shape to run a race. But he climbed
slowly into the saddle and urged the Devil away to the
west at a leisurely walk. He might not get far before dead
dark, but he didn't want to stay at the site of Silverhorn's
latest massacre.

*And I can't let the white-haired son of a whore get to
Fort Hall ahead of me.*

When it was too dark to go on, he made camp. Remembering the wolves, he saw to the fire first, glad Waller
had had the foresight to offer him a corked medicine bottle filled with sulfur matches. He gathered dry sage and
built a fire that would have made any Indian cringe and
any wolf keep his distance, choked down a couple more
of the biscuits, and turned to the problem of his gear.

He put the saddle and his boots and gear close enough
to the fire to have a chance to dry. In the morning he
would oil them if he woke early enough. First he took the
cylinders out of the Colt rifle and the Dragoon. Then he
drew the bullets out of them and the Sharps and threw
away the caps. Getting the sludgy powder out of the
chambers was harder; but, having no choice, he managed
it. When he had them cleaned and dried and recharged
from the Indian's supply of powder, he checked the Navy
revolvers. The pepperbox could wait until last.

Not entirely to his surprise, the powder was all but gone
by the time he'd charged the twenty-odd chambers and
seated their bullets. He would have to shoot well, waste
no shots. Dark thoughts of firing his last chamber led him
to wipe the damp off his knife and sharpen it.

"After that," he said aloud in the direction where the
chestnut was noisily cropping the dry prairie grass, "it'll

be up to you to bite and kick them to death." The Devil whinnied.

Fairchild was awake and moving as soon as he could see to walk. He fed the horse some soggy grain, ate the last of his biscuits, and saddled up. The niceties of currying and oiling would have to wait. He rode easily for a time, then gradually worked the horse into a road pace.

Late that afternoon, he followed the wagon tracks off the road. For a mile or so he hung back, wondering why they had left the road, expecting an ambush. At last he decided they had good reason to avoid roads fairly close to an army post. He tried to close the distance, saw that the tracks were leading down toward a canyon.

"If we can catch our fish before they get out of that barrel," he told the horse, "we'll have them for supper." Devil tossed his head agreeably, then darted his nose down to snap at Fairchild's leg. "Maybe you don't like fish."

He rode the Devil hard for more than half a mile, then slipped up to the rim of the canyon. Down in its lower reaches, the wagon was rolling along with some difficulty. One rider was strung out far enough behind to stay out of the dust. Another rode ahead, scouting. Fairchild tied the horse, took out the buffalo rifle, and sat down to make a good rest for the barrel. He set his sights on the wagon driver, expecting him to have long white hair. He didn't.

Fairchild shot anyway. The driver slumped forward, then fell backward off the seat as the team surged forward. Ethan saw before he shouldered his second rifle that Silverhorn was the lead rider. But the big man moved before Fairchild could aim, running his horse hard toward the mouth of the canyon, slinging a shot or two toward the canyon rim. The rear rider had come up fast, passed the wagon, and headed for the western end of the canyon.

Fairchild didn't care. He wanted the man with white

hair. He fired three quick shots at Silverhorn before he remembered he was low on powder. He waited for the big black horse to bring the outlaw into a clearing. Then he fired another round from his rifle. The bullet must have come close, because the white-haired man turned immediately toward him and fired at his smoke. Fairchild was not entirely surprised by how close the bullet came. But Silverhorn was moving again, presenting no target amidst the boulders and occasional trees.

Fairchild loosed the Devil and rode along the rim with the hope of cutting Silverhorn off before he could reach the mouth of the canyon. Then he heard more shots from the west.

"What the hell?" he asked Devil, getting no satisfactory answer. He could see the puffs of smoke as Silverhorn aimed west, fired, kept going. Fairchild didn't understand what he was shooting at. Then the white-haired man turned his horse and angled back up the canyon slope toward the southern rim.

The Devil swerved off to the left so sharply that he nearly unseated Fairchild. They had come to a great shoulder of rock that the rider had not even seen. He clung to the saddle for a moment, then gave his attention back to guiding the horse through the rough terrain. A moment later, he was around the worst of the rocks and headed back toward the canyon when Silverhorn's horse scrabbled over the rim and came straight for him.

When the white-haired renegade saw Fairchild, he let out an awful whoop and spurred the tired black with all he had left. Ethan used the last two chambers in his rifle, let it fall, went to his Navy Colts. Devil jerked his head down, almost tearing the reins from Fairchild's hands, and broke into his usual suicidal charge straight at Silverhorn. For once, Fairchild had no objections. He wanted to close with this man, shoot or stab or strangle him at a range where Silverhorn would have no doubt who his nemesis was. He let go the reins, took a Navy Colt in each hand.

In front of him Silverhorn was cursing, spurring, shooting at each stride. Ethan got off two good shots, felt certain that one of them touched Silverhorn, kept riding. The big white-haired man flung away his revolver, hauled out a shotgun, leveled it and fired before Fairchild could react.

The Devil caught the bulk of the charge of shot in the side of his neck. Bright blood sprayed out over the laboring horse and back into Fairchild's face. With a horrible squeal, the chestnut reared, lost its footing, went down.

It came to Fairchild that he had been there before, done those things before, lost a good horse and been sprayed with blood and failed to bring down that white-haired son of a whore. Then the rocky ground rose up to strike him across the jaw and tumble him senseless past the dying charger.

David Stuart whipped Fairchild's sorrel up the slope. The white-haired man's big black horse was stronger, however, and was carrying the outlaw away from him. Stuart saw the horse slip on the rocks at the canyon rim, go to one knee, climb back up to stride, and go on with a limp. He saw then that he was gaining on Silverhorn, coming closer with each stride, partly because the black had changed direction and was quartering across Stuart's path. But the sorrel was tired, was going soft in the withers. Stuart didn't care.

He found his revolver. The white-haired man was shooting, but not at him. For the first time Stuart saw Ethan Fairchild closing headlong on Silverhorn, exchanging shot for shot. Stuart had already fired twice before he knew it, was aiming for his third shot. He saw the big man lurch in his saddle and knew that his bullet had struck home. He fired a fourth time, saw the bullet take its toll. But the big man rode on with some kind of determination Stuart couldn't understand.

Then Silverhorn screamed something that came to Stuart as "—thing done right—goddamned well—myself!"

The outlaw threw down his revolver and pulled out a heavy shotgun. Before Stuart could get off another shot, the white-haired man let go one barrel at Ethan. It dropped Fairchild's horse little more than twenty feet short of the staggering black.

Fairchild fell and rolled. The big black's progress carried him well past before Silverhorn got him turned and came back. Horse and rider both looked finished, but Silverhorn stayed in the saddle, pointed his gun down toward the fallen rider as if he were entirely unaware of Stuart.

David Stuart came on, his horse failing, his gun wavering. But he sent another shot, saw it stagger the rider, jolt him sideways, make him shift the gun away from Fairchild to seek a new target. Close enough to see a scar across Silverhorn's face, close enough to see the bore of the shotgun lift toward him, close enough to be sure— Stuart fired his last shot. It struck Thoman Silverhorn in the forehead like a stone from a shepherd's sling. The shotgun boomed into the empty sky. Silverhorn flung up his hands and toppled sideways out of the saddle, dead before he fell.

The sorrel quivered to a stop, slumped to its knees as Stuart came out of his saddle on the run. He had come within ten feet of the tumbled bundle of bones that once had been his best friend when the bundle suddenly moved. With infinite effort, Fairchild pushed himself up with one hand. With the other, he pointed a Navy revolver at David Stuart. Stuart skidded to a halt, felt his face go pale, stared into the muzzle of Fairchild's gun.

"Ethan!"

He could see that Fairchild was stunned, still in a daze. He might have time to reach his own pistol, to save his own life.

No! It's his call. I'm the one that left him. I've often enough said I'd take what he gave me.

Hoping Jess would understand, he held himself steady. For a very long moment he waited for the shot, staring, wondering, fearing, doubting.

Then Fairchild lowered his gun, wiped at his eyes, got up to one knee. "My God, Stu, forgive me," he said. "I thought there for a minute you weren't coming back to help me!"